The Celtic Cross

T. J. Walter

First edition

Print Typeset by Electric Reads
www.electricreads.com

1. The head.

'It is my belief Watson, founded upon my experience, that the lowest and vilest alleys in London, do not present a more dreadful record of sin than does the smiling and beautiful countryside.'

Arthur Conan Doyle.
The Adventures of Sherlock Holmes (1892).

Matthew Prior had been woken by the shrill ringing of the telephone some time before six. As he reached for the receiver he thought, 'Whenever the damned thing rings before the alarm clock you can be sure it is not good news'. This was no exception. A voice at the other end of the phone said, 'Sorry to disturb your sleep, sir, but there's been a killing. The area car crew have found a head stuck on a spike over a gate.'

He responded, 'You're kidding me, is this some kind of a prank?'

'No, sir, it's for real.'

Twenty minutes later Prior found himself on the B3296 following the directions he'd been given to get to the scene.

He had spent most of his detective career in Exeter, a busy city in this, the quiet south west. But promotion to DCI had brought him to the furthermost reaches of England, to Cornwall a thinly-populated, jagged wedge of rocky terrain jutting out into the Irish Sea. Here it was mostly open country with only the occasional small town. He had been heard to boast at dinner parties that this was the first occasion that he'd worked in an area where the animals outnumbered the people. But he'd soon learned that country folk are no more law abiding than townies. The only difference was that here you had to travel further between crime scenes.

On reflection, he thought, there was one other important difference working here that was worthy of mention. The Cornish were a race apart. In most respects they didn't consider themselves to be English at all. They even had their own flag and language, although hardly anyone spoke it these days. But the flag was flown proudly around the county far more often than the Union Jack.

As often happens when driving through the dark, his mind was busy with its own thoughts. The phrase that came and stuck in his head was 'In the dead of night'. With 15 years in the job his cloak of cynicism had grown pretty thick; now he had little time for superstitious nonsense. Nevertheless, there were things that went bump in the night. Not vampires or werewolves but people who preyed on others. Under the cover of darkness all manner of nasty things happened. And Prior had a sense of foreboding about this case, cynicism or no.

Another thought occurred to him. His wife, Jeanette, had told him several times that he was too sensitive to be a murder detective; he got too involved in the victims' lives. In a sense she was right, he did try to put himself in the shoes of the victim, tried to feel what the victim might have felt in the time leading up to his or her death. That was the only way he could find the answers to some of the questions he needed to ask. The most important being, 'Who wanted this person dead and why?'

The problem was that once the case was solved, the anguish he'd discovered stayed with him. And with each case it accumulates, rather like radio activity, and was just as dangerous. He knew that without the support of his wife and children, he would by now be well on the way to alcohol dependence or the nuthouse, like so many of his colleagues.

The worst part, of course, was dealing with the bereaved. With most murders, it was amongst them that the killer was to be found. Looking for signs of guilt while trying to show concern for their loss was like walking a tightrope. Suspicion and sympathy did not make good bedfellows.

Prior's reverie was interrupted when he saw a road sign. It said simply 'Penwin 1'. He turned off the B road onto an even narrower lane. The high hedgerows on either side closed in on him. In the beams of the headlamps, it was like driving through a dark tunnel.

Suddenly a small animal dashed out in front of the car. He slammed on the brakes and sought to swerve to avoid it. But there was no room to manoeuvre and he felt rather than heard the crunch as it ran under a wheel. He cursed out loud.

The figure in the seat next to him stirred; Detective Sergeant Siobhan Williams, his partner. He'd picked her up from the pavement outside her flat in Truro and she had not spoken a word after grunting an acknowledgement of his greeting. They made a good team. After a few glasses of wine in the company of friends, she called herself the delicate foil to his broad sabre, although Prior would have said it was the other way round.

She was as sharp as a button but when she felt the situation warranted it she had a caustic tongue. Nor was she afraid to use it on Prior, regardless of the rank difference. Her comments kept him on his toes. In her early thirties and single, she was tall, slim, blonde and attractive. But her intelligence and sharp tongue did not encourage suitors and her relationships rarely lasted long.

She said, 'Don't worry, the crows will enjoy the meal as soon as it gets light, sir.'

He glanced sideways at her but couldn't make out her features in the semi-darkness. 'So, you're awake, are you?'

She seemed to think about her answer as if testing the air. 'It's difficult to sleep the way you drive.'

He sighed. 'God, I'm surrounded by critical women. I was trying not to hit the poor animal.'

'Well you didn't succeed.' She paused then added, 'I'm sure that's sexist, sir, suggesting that women do nothing but criticise.'

He gave her a glare that was wasted in the darkness.' That's another thing women do, twist my words. What with Jeanette, Owen and you, it's a constant barrage.' Jeanette was his wife and Superintendent Patricia Owen his divisional chief.

'That's definitely sexist, sir. But you know we only do it because we care.'

He opened his mouth to respond then noticed a halo of bright light ahead and closed it again. The hedgerow on the left had given way to a high dry-stone wall. As they rounded a curve he saw a patrol car with all lights blazing parked fifty yards ahead. He slowed down and drew up behind it.

Switching off the engine he got out of the car. His nose picked up the stench of rotting leaves. It had been a wet autumn, as if he needed reminding, and the fallen leaves were already decaying. In the quiet of the night, he could hear the sound of the patrol car's strobes as they clicked on and off. Their intermittent glow cast strange shadows in the treetops on either side of the lane.

Two uniforms turned to greet him. He recognised the elder of the two, Charlie Trimble, the brother of one of his team of detectives. Prior acknowledged his greeting but his eyes were already on something in front of him. A man's head had indeed been impaled on a metal spike.

Beside him Siobhan gasped. A puff of wind stirred her shoulder-length fair hair. She shivered involuntarily. 'God that is so gross. What kind of monster would do something like that?'

Prior frowned. 'Be quiet, I'm trying to think.'

He stopped five feet from the head and looked around. Rows of iron rods with sharp spikes at the top soldered to crosspieces, formed a matching pair of gates that guarded the entrance to a country estate. The human head had been rammed onto one of the spikes. On either side of the gateway, eight- foot dry-stone walls topped with razor wire stretched off into the darkness. The estate owner obviously valued his privacy.

Prior's first thought was that this was some macabre prank by medical students from the nearby training hospital. But he immediately dismissed that thought; blood had oozed from the gaping wound beneath the head and pooled on the tarmac below. This was not the head of some long-dead cadaver stolen from the morgue; this man had died not long before the head had been cut off. Prior's limited knowledge of pathology told him that the blood would have coagulated quickly on a cold night such as this.

The face was like a death mask. Its eyes stared blindly off into the distance. Its mouth gaped, caught in the stricture of a silent scream. The blood from the ragged wound where a neck had once been had pooled on the tarmac below. Prior couldn't suppress a shudder at the thought of the anguish the man must have suffered in the moments before his death. Clearly, he had seen it coming.

A frown appeared on the detective's face as he began to reconstruct. He stretched his arm above his head; it barely reached the top of the spikes. He was a full six foot tall and would have been unable to ram the head down onto its spike while standing on the ground.

Over his shoulder, he said, 'Pass me a torch, Charlie.'

Taking it, he shone the beam on the top metal cross-piece of the gate. It had a sharp edge; adhering to it were a few tiny slivers of wood. He smiled grimly, pleased with this small discovery. 'See these, Siobhan, the killer used a ladder.'

She didn't respond.

He glanced at her. 'Come on Siobhan, pull yourself together, I need your help here.'

'This just makes me want to puke, sir.'

'Then go across the road, this is a crime scene.'

She took a deep breath, holding back an angry retort. But his words were having their effect; her brain was beginning to function again. She licked her dry lips. 'Yes, sir, I'll be OK. Thank god I didn't have any breakfast.' After a moment she added, 'How did he get the thing here? I can't imagine he walked here with it tucked under his arm.'

'Unless he came from the estate. But then the ladder would have been rested on the other side of the gate. So, he had a vehicle. Now, where will he have parked?'

He shone the torch on the road beneath their feet. There was a trail of blood droplets leading to the pool on the tarmac below the head. He followed the trail to where it began ten yards away on the road, where there was another small pool of blood. He quartered his torch beam across the tarmac, looking for any signs left by a vehicle; there were none.

He looked around him. He could see nothing beyond the beams of the headlights. But the direction of his gaze mirrored his thoughts. They were five miles from Truro the nearest town, on a narrow country lane that branched off the B3192 a mile back. Half a mile further on it passed through the village of Penwin, then looped back to the B-road. It was not on the road to anywhere and carried only local traffic and there was damned little of that, especially after dark.

Siobhan frowned, her mind still on the sequence of events leading to the head being here. 'It doesn't look as if he was decapitated here. Surely there must have been a blood bath when that was done.' She wrinkled her nose at the thought.

Prior nodded. 'You're right, but let's concentrate on this scene for the moment.'

He turned to Trimble. 'Exactly what time did you find this, Charlie?'

'Five thirty-two, sir. I made a note when I called it in.'

'Was that the first time you passed here tonight?'

'No. We came past just after midnight, checked this gate to the estate and the other one in Lamb Lane. It wasn't here then.'

'How can you be so sure, you might have missed it in the dark?'

'No way sir. We checked the whole perimeter of the estate, especially the gates. The estate owner, Mr. Sinclair, complained earlier this week about an intruder, so we were paying attention.'

'An intruder, what kind of intruder, what was he doing?'

Trimble shrugged his shoulders. 'No idea sir. There was a note in the parade book; it didn't give any details. All it said was that an intruder had been spotted on the estate. I think the entry in the book was signed by Inspector Bradley.'

'And has anyone spotted this intruder since?'

'Not as far as I know; we certainly haven't seen anyone and we've been on nights all this week.'

'Tell Inspector Bradley to contact me with the details ASAP.'

That earned a nod from Trimble.

Prior moved on, 'The message we got said that you think you recognise the head. Who is he?'

'You know I live in Penwin, sir?'

'I didn't, but go on.'

'His name is John Wright, aged about twenty-five. Lived in the village and worked here on the estate.'

'Was he married, any family?'

Trimble smiled, 'The younger generation don't seem to get married these days, sir. But he lived with his girlfriend Jenna. They don't have any kids thank goodness. His parents live in Grampian up the road I think.'

'What do you know about him?'

'Nice enough lad. Not wild like some. Not the brightest of blokes but steady like.'

Prior smiled grimly. 'Not the sort of epitaph you'd put on his gravestone, is it?'

Trimble didn't respond.

Prior moved on, 'Were there any disturbance calls nearby last night?'

'No, sir, nothing on the radio.'

'What about his relationship with this Jenna, any tension there?'

'Not that I've heard, everything seemed hunky-dory.'

Prior nodded thoughtfully, 'What did he do on the estate?'

'He was a farmhand, sir. I've seen him about on his tractor when I was on days.'

'What about the estate, how big is it?'

'It's big, well over a thousand acres, mostly farmland.'

'And the workforce?'

'Not as big as you might think. The owner, Sinclair, sacked over half of them five years ago when his father died; brought in a load of new machinery.' There was a note of distaste in his voice.

Prior gave him an enquiring look. 'Couldn't have been very popular with the locals?'

'No sir. Half-a-dozen families had to move away. There are no other jobs around here except at the clay works and they're not taking on new people.'

Prior frowned. 'Do you know this Sinclair?'

Trimble nodded with a grim expression on his face. 'Cedric Sinclair his name is. But the family have had the place for donkey's years. Been called up here a couple of times. Once was for a couple of young lads fishing in the stream. Sinclair threatened to shoot them if they came back. The other was someone dumping rubbish on his land. That time Sinclair threatened me with the Assistant Chief Constable if I didn't put a stop to it. He's an arsehole, sir. Acts like lord muck; treats his workers like serfs and us no better.' He looked at Siobhan and added, 'Sorry about the French sarge.'

She smiled. 'Sounded like good old Anglo-Saxon to me, Charlie.'

Prior ignored the exchange. 'How many people actually live on the estate?'

'Not a lot. There's Sinclair and, I think, a husband and wife team that run the house; their name is Brighton. Then there's the estate manager, Thomas Callaghan, and an old cowman. He's in his seventies, been there all his life, far as I know. That's about it, the rest of the workers live in the village.'

'Has Sinclair got no family?'

'He's got a son, he's in the army. Sinclair is divorced from the lad's mother.'

Prior gave him another enquiring look. 'What else do they say about Sinclair in the village?'

'Nothing good, there's lots of gossip of course, I get it from my wife. There's an old dear lives in the village; she's been doing the cleaning up at the house for donkey's years. She's always going on about him. She reckons he only got married to produce an heir. Once his wife had done that, he kicked her out. The son stayed here as a kid; I don't think he had a choice. But he left as soon as he could. He doesn't even visit his father now, even when he's on leave. I hear that he stays with his mother; she lives in Dorset somewhere.'

'So, is the farm profitable?'

'Far as I know, very. It's a mixed farm, couple of hundred head of cattle, sheep, and cereal crops. And they've had good harvests recently. Besides the Sinclair family have old money, they're filthy rich.'

As they were talking, the headlights of a vehicle approached the scene. A moment later a white Transit van pulled up beside them. Two people got out, George Bailey and Sally Hinds, Prior's crime scene investigators. Two more pairs of eyes were immediately riveted on the head. Bailey said, 'Blimey guv. What's this, student rag week?' his broad Cockney accent so different from the soft West Country brogue of the locals.

'This is not a good time for your humour George. Get some kind of screen up here before the media vultures arrive. I don't want them snapping their damned cameras at this.'

Bailey nodded soberly. 'Yes guv. Mind you, it'd take a brave editor to put this on the front page.' He was pulling on his evidence suit as he was talking, 'There's coffee in the van if you want some.' Then, he turned to his companion, 'Get the tent out Sal, we'll have to rig something so we don't have an audience.' He grinned and added, 'Less you want to be on tele in your moon suit.' Hinds nodded without comment. In fact, she rarely spoke; she was the perfect partner for the chirpy Cockney.

Watching the interchange, Prior smiled despite himself. Bailey had been with the team for just a year. He had learned his trade in London. Then he'd married a local girl he'd met on holiday and moved to Truro. He'd brought his expertise with him as well as his humour. And his Cockney accent.

Turning back to the two uniformed constables Prior said, 'Get yourselves some coffee, we could be here for a while.'

More headlights approached, two cars in convoy. They pulled up behind the van. Four of Prior's team of detectives got out, their eyes drawn like magnets to the thing on the gate. Prior spoke to the senior among them, DS Quigley, a stocky figure in his fifties.

'Albert, mind where you tread, there's blood and gore everywhere. Let's get organised before the vultures arrive. First thing, I want more uniforms up here; these two are on nights and will want some sleep once they've made their notes.'

Quigley nodded sombrely, his eyes not leaving the head.

'I want this side of the lane sealed off so that George and Sally can do their jobs. Then I want the mobile enquiry van brought up here; we'll need somewhere to do the interviews. I think we'll put it on the estate if the owner will let us; that should keep us away from the bloody press.'

Quigley nodded again.

Prior went on to tell Quigley what was known about the victim. He added, 'Once we've done at the scene here, Siobhan and I will have a word with the estate owner, then we'll go and see the girlfriend and give her the bad news.

You get the mobile van organised and get the team to start interviewing all the people on the estate. Most of the farm workers live in the village but they'll be arriving shortly.'

Quigley nodded, again without comment. Then he turned to the three detectives with him. 'OK you lot, stop gawking. You heard the boss. Spread out along the lane. See what you can find and mind where you put your feet.'

Reluctantly they took their eyes off the head and went to do his bidding.

For the next ten minutes Prior prowled impatiently around the scene, carefully avoiding where the crime scene investigators (CSI') were working. He needed to get the enquiry started but protocol dictated that he wait for the pathologist, Professor Penhallon, who was a stickler for such matters.

Siobhan appeared at his side. 'What do you think sir?'

'I think it's going to be a long day, Siobhan.'

'Yes, sir.' She waited for him to go on.

'First question is why here and why this bizarre display?'

'That's two questions, sir.'

He gave her a glare, 'I see you're feeling better.'

She ignored the look and the comment. 'Do you think it's some kind of warning?'

Prior nodded. 'Maybe. But who's warning who about what? This is the twenty-first century AD not BC.' Then he shook his head, 'And why choose a farmhand as the victim? No, it must be personal; something to do with Wright himself.' After a moment's thought he added, 'No point in speculating at this stage. Let's move on.'

He turned to Quigley. 'Albert, I can't wait any longer, it'll be light soon and there will be people about. We'll leave you to look after things here. Siobhan and I will go and see this Sinclair. You know what needs to be done. When old Penhallon arrives tell him I'll be back shortly.'

Quigley nodded.

Prior turned back to Williams. 'Now, how do we get into this bloody place?'

She gave him a strange look. 'What about through the gates, sir? There's an intercom on the gatepost.'

'I can see that. I meant without disturbing the crime scene.' He raised his voice, 'George, we need to open the gate to go up to the house, have you finished with it?'

'Yes, guv, providing you're on foot. We're still sorting out the blood trail on the tarmac here, so I don't want a car driving over this bit. Just mind where you tread.'

Prior pressed the bell-push on the intercom device on the gatepost. There was no response; he waited a few moments and pressed it again. At the third ring there was a click and a voice said, 'Yes, who's there?'

'It's the police, Detective Chief Inspector Prior. I need to speak to Mr Sinclair.'

The voice said, 'The master doesn't receive visitors before nine, sir.'

Prior showed his irritation, 'Well he'll have to make an exception. This is an emergency and you'll have to wake him. Now, open the gate.'

There was a brief pause before the voice said, 'Yes, sir.'

There were more clicks, and then the twin gates started to open before them. The severed head moved with it, shaking from the vibration caused by the electric motor powering the gates. Prior chuckled, 'I hope the damned thing doesn't fall off, old Penhallon will have a fit if he finds it's been rolling about in the gravel.'

Williams shivered at the thought and said nothing.

Carefully looking where they trod, the two detectives moved through the gateway. They found themselves on a gravel driveway lined on both sides by trees and thick shrubbery. All the trees had bare branches and the smell of rotting vegetation here was much stronger. Their feet crunched on the gravel as they walked. After thirty yards or so they crossed a bridge over a stream. Soon after that the trees gave way to open grassland; the driveway continued up the hill.

Prior glanced at his companion. 'Oh yes, get onto force HQ, Siobhan. Get a helicopter up here as soon as it's light. We need the area searched; the body must be somewhere. And the chopper might help keep the damned press away.'

'Yes, sir, perhaps they'll send a Huey with guns and missiles; that would certainly keep them away.' She smiled as she rummaged in her shoulder bag for her mobile phone.

2. The house.

'Every cock will crow upon his own dunghill.'

13th century proverb.

As they walked up the drive, Prior's mind was busy trying to make some sense of the crime scene. Over 90% of murders were domestic and quickly solved; a jealous lover striking out in anger, a wife beater finally going too far, or simply the result of a violent argument at home or in the pub. But these were impulse killings, what the French call crimes of passion. In those cases, the killer usually collapsed in remorse, ran away, or tried to conceal evidence of their deed.

Displaying his victim's head on a gate hardly fell into that category as it drew attention to the deed. And another thing; while there was certainly passion involved here there was also a degree of planning; the killing and butchering had been done elsewhere and the head brought to the estate entrance to be displayed in this grisly fashion. The killer had even brought a ladder with him. Unless they were dealing with a maniac, there had to be a reason, not just for the killing but for the display. Yet another thing was the chosen location; that too had to be relevant.

This brought his mind back to the immediate task; hopefully the estate owner would be able to shed some light on why his gate had been chosen. And that presented a problem for Prior. Since working a rural beat he'd had several clashes with the landed gentry. Almost to a man they seemed to consider themselves above the law. On the odd occasion one fell foul of it, he invariably tried to use his influence to wriggle out of whatever he was accused of. There was no evidence so far that Sinclair had done any wrong but Prior doubted that he would submit happily to questioning by a humble police officer. When dealing with such people his instinct was to burst their bubble. But that would not get him the information he required. He would have to curb his temper and tread carefully.

As they emerged from the trees, objects became more discernible as there was the first hint of dawn on the horizon. Ahead of them was the silhouette of a large house. As they drew closer Prior was able to make out more details. It was a huge edifice built of local grey stone. The central structure was two stories high with a flat roof bordered by crenelated battlements. An empty flagpole jutted out at an angle above a grand entrance. On either side of the central structure were single storey wings. Built of the same stone they had sloping, moss-covered slate roofs. The result was an unattractive sprawl.

In front of the house, a gravel path circled an ornamental fountain. But no water spurted from the mouth of the stone fish above the cement pond. In the semi-darkness, the whole scene gave the impression of past grandeur sadly now fallen into neglect.

Prior saw Siobhan look back towards the gates. The head was not visible through the trees but a halo of light marked the spot where the police vehicles were. Reading her thoughts Prior tried to bring her mind back to the task ahead. 'The place looks a bit run down, doesn't it?'

She turned back towards the house. 'Mmm, I expect Sinclair's too tight to spend money on it.'

Rounding the fountain, they approached the entrance to the building. A broad stone staircase, flanked on either side by balustrades led up to a huge iron-studded oak door. Carved stone lions sat on each side as if guarding the entrance. Prior said, 'I hope those lions aren't rampant, Siobhan.'

She smiled indulgently. 'No sir they're dormant or at least asleep.'

'Well, keep your eye on them in case they wake up.'

This time she just rolled her eyes at him.

On the door was a large knocker in the shape of a lion's head; a slightly less ancient looking bell push was set into the doorframe to one side. Prior chose the bell push and was rewarded by the sound of chimes inside the house. He grinned. 'I think we're about to meet a real live butler.'

She pursed her lips but resisted another roll of the eyes.

There was the sound of bolts being drawn, then the massive door opened. Standing before them was a man in his forties. Despite the hour he was immaculately dressed in grey striped trousers, white shirt, carefully knotted tie, a black waistcoat and jacket. He was clean-shaven and what was left of his dark brown hair was carefully combed across his balding scalp. His face bore no expression at all. His skin was sallow, almost reptilian looking. Despite his age there were few lines on his face. Prior had the irreverent thought that if he smiled the face might crack.

In a neutral voice the man said, 'Yes, sir, are you the policeman I spoke to?'

Prior produced his warrant card and introduced himself and Williams. 'We need to speak to Mr. Sinclair. The matter is urgent.'

'Yes, sir, I have roused the master; he will be with you presently. May I ask you the nature of your business?'

Prior gave him a hard look. 'No, you may not.'

Without turning a hair the butler said, 'Please come this way, sir.'

In front of them was an impressive entrance hall. It was dominated by a huge oak staircase leading to the upper floor. Polished oak banisters led his eye upwards to the rear wall at the top of the stairs; it was panelled in oak and adorned with portraits of men on horseback wearing suits of armour; or in cavalier dress standing with one hand on a sword. It was easy to imagine, in days of yore, the lady of the house dressed in a fabulous gown making her grand entrance down the staircase to greet her guests. 'Perhaps I've watched too many period dramas on the tele,' Prior thought.

On the ground floor all the walls were also panelled in oak. In fact, there was so much oak everywhere you could have built an old ship of the line out of it. Old but expensive looking carpets covered the stone-flagged floor. The butler led them to a passage on the left of the staircase and opened a door in the panelling. With an expansive gesture he ushered them into a room. 'If you would kindly wait here, sir, madam, the master will join you shortly.' He left, gently but firmly closing the door behind him.

When they were alone Prior said, 'What did I tell you, a real live butler? I half expected him to ask for my business card. I could just see him presenting it to his master on a silver platter.'

Siobhan smiled. 'I wonder if he irons Sinclair's newspaper each morning, sir.'

'That wouldn't surprise me.'

Prior looked around the room; more oak panelling on the walls with more portraits of Sinclair's ancestors. 'Grim looking lot, aren't they? Not a bit like the family snapshots we've got on our mantelpiece.'

'Mmm, eyes too close together and mouths like sword cuts. Why is it the rich never smile when they're having their portraits painted?'

'Probably bored with just sitting there; either that or they had bad teeth. Dentistry wasn't up to much in those days; did you know that Nelson lost all his teeth to decay?'

She smiled. 'Makes you wonder what Lady what's-her-name saw in him. Perhaps he had a good butt, sir?'

Prior returned her smile. 'Hamilton, Siobhan, Lady Hamilton, and you won't see any portraits of his butt.'

'Pity, sir, one of a man's best features.'

He didn't grace that with a reply. Instead he turned his attention to a mahogany display cabinet. Behind glass doors was a complete dinner service. Each piece was decorated with a hunting scene in soft shades of green and brown. He counted the settings; twenty-four. He shook his head. 'How the other half live, twenty-four settings. Jeanette panics if we have more than six for dinner.'

'Does she iron your newspaper sir?'

'You must be joking; she doesn't even iron my shirts.'

3. Cedric Sinclair

'Money can't buy happiness.'

19th century proverb.

A few minutes later the door opened with a flourish and Cedric Sinclair swept into the room. He was slightly built and below medium height. Just like his ancestors portrayed in the paintings, his eyes were set close together, his nose long and thin and his mouth a razor slash across his face. Despite his lack of height, he managed to look down his nose at the two detectives. No doubt something he'd learned at public school, Prior thought. Sinclair's face wore the arrogant expression he no doubt used on his underlings. Something else he'd no doubt learned at public school. Despite the seriousness of his mission, Prior could hardly supress a smile as another thought crossed his mind; the man probably practiced the haughty look in a mirror as he had it off to perfection.

Even though he had clearly just woken up, the landowner was dressed in a style befitting his position. He wore a burgundy-coloured, patterned, dressing-gown over pale blue silk pyjamas; on his feet were leather carpet slippers. The detective judged him to be just the far side of fifty but thought he could be out five years either way. Clearly he had been disturbed from a deep sleep after a busy night, as he was unshaven and looked hung-over. He'd hurriedly run a comb through his hair, missing a few strands that stuck out at the sides. Prior took an instant dislike to him. Nevertheless, he managed to meet his gaze with a neutral expression on his face.

The man didn't offer his hand or introduce himself. In a haughty tone that belied the words he spoke, he said, 'Please forgive me for keeping you waiting, Chief Inspector. I gather you are here on an urgent matter. Please be seated.' He spoke with the careful enunciation and clipped tone that he had no doubt learned at the same public school that taught him how to look down his nose at people and wear arrogant expressions on his face.

Out of the corner of Prior's eye he saw Siobhan stiffen. She knew him well, especially of his lack of patience with those who put their sense of their own importance above the needs of a police enquiry. She too had to suppress a smile at the thought that the next ten minutes could prove interesting.

Making certain that his face gave no hint to his thoughts, Prior said in his best 'talking-to-the-public' voice, 'Thank you, Mr. Sinclair. I apologise for disturbing you so early in the day but I felt I must inform you of our presence.' He turned to Williams and added 'This is Detective Sergeant Williams and I am Detective Chief Inspector Prior.'

Sinclair barely gave Siobhan a glance. 'And what is the reason for your presence, Chief Inspector?' He managed to sound as if he were addressing the local fishmonger.

With an effort Prior managed to keep the neutral expression on his face. 'I'll get to that in a moment, sir. But first I need to ask you a few questions. What time did you go to bed last night?'

That seemed to throw the man off balance for a moment, as Prior had hoped it would. But he quickly recovered. 'I don't see what business that is of yours, why do you ask?'

'It's a simple question, sir; one I'm required to ask in the circumstances.'

'What circumstances?' he snapped.

Prior knew this was a battle he couldn't win so said, 'Something was left on your front gate last night, sir. I need to pin down the time it was put there.'

'What are you talking about, what was left on my gate?'

'A human head, severed at the neck.'

He carefully watched Sinclair's reaction. The man opened his mouth, and then quickly closed it again. He licked his lips then finally spoke, 'That's ridiculous, this is the twenty-first century not the dark ages.'

'Ridiculous or not sir, it has happened. And I have to try to make sense of it. I'll ask you again, sir, what time did you go to bed last night?'

Sinclair licked his lips again and delicately scratched an eyebrow. 'Midnight, or there abouts.'

'And your staff, sir?'

'My staff? They weren't here, it was their night off.'

Prior couldn't resist a faint smile. He saw Siobhan stiffen as he said, 'And where do your staff go on their night orf?' parodying Sinclair's pronunciation of the last word.

Sinclair appeared not to notice, his mind busy elsewhere. 'They visit Mrs Brighton's mother; they do so every Tuesday.'

'Where does the mother live, sir?'

'Somewhere on the coast, Newquay I believe.'

'What time do they return from these visits, sir?'

A supercilious smile appeared on Sinclair's face, he was recovering from the shock. 'You would hardly expect me to monitor my staff's movements on their night off, would you Chief Inspector. They are required to be here in time to prepare my breakfast the next morning. Other than that, I've absolutely no idea what time they return. And besides, they would use the servant's gate in Lamb Lane. They would be most unlikely to see anything on my front gate.'

Prior smiled. 'Of course, sir, the servant's entrance, how silly of me.' He paused for a long moment before adding, 'Did you have any visitors last evening, sir?'

This really seemed to throw Sinclair. His finger went to his eyebrow again; Prior noticed a slight tick in the skin around his right eye. He took a long moment before answering. 'Why should you be interested in my visitors?'

'Presumably they would have left by the front gate, Mr Sinclair?'

'Had there been any visitors, Chief Inspector, I'm sure they would have reported seeing a head on the gate.' By now he was becoming aggressive; clearly there was something about his visitors that he did not want to reveal.

Prior continued to probe. 'I'm sure they would have, sir. What they are not so likely to have reported is what they didn't see. I need to pin down the time the head was put there, so if there were any visitors I will need to speak to them. Are you saying that you did have visitors last evening?' Prior noticed a thin film of sweat had appeared on Sinclair's forehead.

Now his face turned a shade of bright red. He snapped, 'I will not be subjected to an interrogation, Chief Inspector. I...'

He was interrupted by a soft knock on the door. He shouted 'Yes?'

The door opened to reveal the butler with a tray of coffee. Sinclair glared at him and said testily, 'Just put it down there Brighton. That will be all.' He waved his hand dismissively.

Prior noticed his hands for the first time. They were small and pink with long thin fingers and carefully manicured nails. Clearly, they had never been near the handle of a spade. His dislike of the man was growing by the minute.

The butler put the tray down on an occasional table and withdrew quietly.

Taking the opportunity to divert the conversation away from his visitors of the previous night, Sinclair said in a more conciliatory manner, 'Is this some prank by medical students, Chief Inspector? I can't believe something like this could happen in this day and age.'

'I assure you this was no prank, Mr Sinclair. The expression on the face suggests that he died in a state of extreme terror.' Prior had no compunction now about shocking some truth out of the man.

Siobhan intervened for the first time, clearly trying to defuse what she saw as a potentially explosive situation. 'Mr. Sinclair. Would you like some coffee?'

He turned to her. 'What? Oh yes, how rude of me. Would you oblige by pouring for us please?'

She did so and Prior waited until they were all seated again. Once they were he said, 'No, sir, this was no prank. We think the victim was one of your farm hands, John Wright?' He took a sip of coffee.

Sinclair frowned. 'Wright? Yes of course I know him. That's dreadful, who on earth would want to kill him? This is unbelievable.'

'When did you last see the lad?'

'What, see him? Well I don't quite know, a few days ago I think. I don't run the farm myself you know; I have a manager, Callaghan. He deals with the hands.'

'Do any of the hands live on the estate, sir?'

'No, just Callaghan and an old cowman. The remainder live in the village.'

'What time do they arrive for work?'

'Early. I expect they will be arriving now. But they all use the Lamb Lane gate, they won't have seen anything.' He took a gulp of his coffee. Then he added, 'Do you have any idea who might have done this dreadful thing?'

'Hardly sir, the head was only discovered an hour ago.' He took another sip of the excellent coffee. 'I understand your family have been here for some time, sir?'

Sinclair smiled, 'You could say that; since the Norman Conquest in fact.'

'Has anything like this happened before sir?'

He laughed out loud. 'No, of course not. That practice died out with the Ancient Britons didn't it?'

'As far as I know, yes but someone seems to have started it again. Have you any idea why he chose your gate?'

'Now you are being ridiculous, Chief Inspector, I'm sure it was chosen at random.'

'You wouldn't be in dispute with any of your neighbours then?'

'What are you suggesting, some ancient feud? These days disputes are settled in court. My family haven't been involved in a duel for several hundred years. Don't be ridiculous, Chief Inspector.'

Prior took a deep breath, determined not to rise to his bait but his voice had an edge as he said, 'The idea might sound ridiculous, but the fact is the head was put on your gate. My job is to find out who put it there and why he chose your gate. Hence, I am obliged to ask you these questions.'

Sinclair's hand went back to his eyebrow, confirming Prior's conviction that there was something he was hiding. He said, 'Yes of course you do, Chief Inspector. Please forgive me, this has come as something of a shock.' He paused then added, 'Please ask what questions you must.'

Prior sipped his coffee again. 'This is excellent coffee, sir, what is it?'

He answered absently, 'Jamaican Blue Mountain, I have the beans sent up from London.' After a pause he said, 'Now, your question about neighbours. There are, of course, several neighbouring farms. I have no serious dispute with any of them beyond the odd broken fence or straying cattle. In fact, we share some of the heavy farm machinery; far too expensive to keep things like harvesters for just one farm these days. I assure you we have no dispute that would cause one of them to go to these lengths.'

'What about your staff and estate workers?'

'What about them? Do you mean how do I get along with them? In most cases their families have worked for the family for generations. I treat them fairly, Chief Inspector, I can't imagine any of them having a grudge against me. Most live in the two villages, Penwin and Grampian. If you enquire you will find that my family have done a great deal for those villages over the centuries. You won't find anyone there who bears a grudge.'

This massive distortion of the truth took Prior a moment to digest. Was it an outright lie or did he really believe it to be true? Astounding as it was, Prior concluded that he did believe it, his body language suggested that to be the case. Whatever else Sinclair was, he did not come across as being an accomplished liar.

Prior moved on, 'Can you think of anyone you might have upset recently?'

He shook his head vigorously. 'No, Chief Inspector, no-one at all. The only people I've had any disagreement with are the local archaeological society. They are constantly making requests to dig on my land looking for ancient hill forts or some such nonsense. After a while their requests become somewhat tiresome. But I can't imagine some professor of archaeology sanctioning such behaviour in a fit of pique, can you?'

Prior ignored the question. 'What exactly is the nature of your dispute?'

'Hardly a dispute Chief Inspector, a disagreement. For years they have been seeking my permission to excavate my top field. They suggest it is the site of an old Celtic settlement. But I won't allow it. Mine is a working farm and having university students tramping back and forth across the land would be too much, to say nothing of the damned holes they want to dig. But this has been going on for years. In fact, it is some months since I last had any communication from them.'

Prior probed further, 'What makes them think there might be an ancient settlement on your land, sir?'

'Aerial photography Chief Inspector; small planes buzzing around frightening my cattle; but I soon put a stop to that.' He sounded quite smug.

'So, no archaeologists have actually been on your land?'

'No, and nor will they as long as I am alive.'

'What about rights of way on your land sir; are there any?'

'Yes of course. There are two footpaths that cross the land at right angles. When the gates are open during daylight hours, hikers can come and go as they please. Provided, of course, they stick to the paths and close the gates to the fields behind them. I simply won't allow people to dig on my land.'

Prior picked up the 'as long as they stick to the paths' bit. He could imagine Sinclair with a shotgun, daring anyone to pause to pick a blackberry. There was no community spirit at all in this man.

Siobhan had been busy scribbling notes throughout the interview. She looked up. 'Who made the application for the dig, sir?'

Sinclair glanced at her irritably. 'A man named Miles, if I recall correctly. He's a lecturer at Truro University.'

'Do you have an address for the man, sir?' she persisted.

Sinclair sighed tiredly, 'I'm sure we do, sergeant, you can get it from my farm manager or his secretary. But look, I'm sure they have nothing to do with this matter.'

She smiled primly, 'I'm sure you're right, sir, but, as my chief inspector said, we have to check everything.'

'Yes, of course.'

Siobhan looked at Prior. He nodded and took over the questioning again. 'What about hunting, sir, do you allow hunting on the estate?'

Sinclair laughed. 'Fox hunting, certainly not. My farm manager keeps the foxes down with a shotgun. I have no time for such frivolous pursuits. My father used to shoot a few birds for the table and I catch a few trout in the stream. But I see where your thinking is going, Chief Inspector. I have absolutely no truck with those rather silly animal rights people. Not even any contact.'

'What about business rivals?'

Another supercilious smile. 'I'm not in business. I do have some investments in the city, but my accountant looks after those.'

Prior paused for a long moment, then pounced, 'Who were your visitors last evening, Mr Sinclair?'

The man glared at the detective. 'I have already told you, Inspector, I will not have you question me about my private affairs. I shall report your persistence to your superiors. Now, if that is all, I would like to have my breakfast.'

Prior kept his expression neutral, ignoring the reduction in his rank. He turned to his companion. 'Have you any more questions, sergeant?'

She shook her head. 'No sir, I think we've covered everything.'

He turned back to Sinclair. 'Thank you, sir. We will of course have to speak to all the people who work on the estate. We have a mobile enquiry van that we use for such purposes. Have I your permission to bring it onto the estate?'

Back on safer ground, Sinclair visibly relaxed. He nodded. 'Speak to Callaghan, I'm sure there's room in the farmyard, but please use the servants' gate, not the front one. And please keep me informed of the progress of your enquiries.'

Prior nodded, 'I'm afraid no-one can use the front gate for a while, sir, whilst my forensic team do their work. And thank you for the excellent coffee, Mr. Sinclair. I'm sure we'll talk again.'

Sinclair didn't get up from his chair as the two detectives left. He sat sipping his coffee as if he'd already dismissed them from his mind. Outside the door, Brighton, the butler appeared as if by magic.

Brookes said, 'Mr Brighton, we will have to interview you and your wife later. Please make sure you are available.'

The butler nodded, 'Yes, sir, we will be here in the house all day.'

He escorted them to the front door, closing it firmly behind them without uttering another word.

4. Professor Penhallon

'Dead men tell no tales'. Or do they?

Updated 17th century proverb.

As the huge oak front door to the house closed behind them, Prior heaved a huge sigh. 'What an arsehole; I felt like picking him up by his scrawny little neck and shaking him.'

'Mmm, for a moment or two I thought you might, sir. I can see why the locals can't stand him.' She laughed and added, 'I loved your question about the staff's night orf.'

He smiled with her, 'It was wasted on him; he's such a pompous ass I don't think he even noticed.'

They lapsed into silence as they walked back down the drive. Dawn was rising, if somewhat reluctantly. The sun seemed disinclined to make an appearance as heavy clouds still blanketed the sky. Nevertheless, the birds in the trees bordering the driveway were greeting the new day.

Ahead of them, despite the arrival of dawn, halogen lights now illuminated the ac-tivity around the gates. In their brightness the severed head stood silhouetted on its spike. The sight of it brought them abruptly back to their purpose in being here.

As they walked, Prior went over in his mind the little they had learned. Apart from the head itself, the only forensic evidence at the scene seemed to be the slivers of wood on the outside iron cross-piece of the gate that may or may not have come from a ladder used to put the head on the spike. Sinclair had been no help at all. His snotty attitude was typical of the so-called upper classes when questioned by people they considered below their station. But there were a couple of things that seemed a little off. His reaction when asked what time he went to bed was one; the other when asked about his guests.

He glanced at his companion. 'Well, what do you think Siobhan?'

'I think Sinclair's an arsehole, sir, as you said.'

'That's helpful; anything else?'

'I'm wondering who his visitors were last night. Clearly he had visitors. He really looked agitated when we pressed him for their details. And you were brilliant, didn't lose your temper once.'

'Don't be bloody cheeky. But you're right about his re-action. That could just be the class thing, didn't take to be-ing pressed by mere police officers. But even if he's hiding something, I can't see him having anything to do with the head. If you're going to butcher somebody, you're hardly going to draw attention to yourself by sticking his head on your front gate, are you?'

She shook her head. 'No sir.' She paused, and then smiled as another thought crossed her mind, 'But I think the butler probably did it. Did you notice he looked like An-thony Hopkins? Perhaps he's the reincarnation of Hannibal Lecter.'

'That's very useful, Siobhan, any other observations?'

'I think it's going to rain, sir.'

'Can we be serious, sergeant?' Prior said, losing his patience.

'Being serious now, sir, I was just giving myself time to think. Sinclair seemed genuine enough apart from the issue of the guests. I didn't spot anything else in his reac-tion that was out of sync. Did you?'

He frowned, shaking his head. 'More like a feeling than anything concrete. He showed the classic signs of lying when I asked him what time he went to bed. I'm sure something was going on here last night; he'd certainly had a skinful. But whether that had anything to do with what was going on at his front gate, I don't know.'

He smiled and added, 'He actually seemed surprised that anyone would have the cheek to put something on his gate. He seems to genuinely believe that the locals think the sun shines out of his rear-end.' He paused, scratching his head. 'One thing you can guarantee, he'll be straight on the phone to the Chief Constable about our visit. Let's see what filters down from HQ on this'

Siobhan remained silent.

'But there is something else nibbling away at the back of my mind. I seem to re-member hearing somewhere that the Celts used to put the heads of their defeated ene-mies on their gates as a warning to others. Don't you think it's a bit of a coincidence that archaeologists want to dig up a Celtic settlement on his estate and someone's stuck a severed head on his gate?'

'Yes, sir. I do think it's a coincidence.

'And?'

'And nothing.'

'I've told you before; there are no coincidences in mur-der cases, don't forget what Sherlock Holmes said. I'll bet there is a connection.'

'Sherlock Holmes wasn't real, sir. Are you suggesting that this was the work of some university professor?'

'Real or not, he made a lot of sense. No, of course I'm not suggesting that but it could be some local nutter who's a history buff and is trying to make a point. You heard what Charlie said about Sinclair's popularity with the locals. We can't rule out the possibil-ity of a connection.'

They walked in silence for a few moments. Then he glanced at her, 'Well, have you any other ideas as to why the killer chose to make such a ghoulish display of his handi-work and on Sinclair's front gate?'

'If I'm honest, I haven't yet got over the shock; I haven't a clue.'

Prior frowned, 'I suppose I might be clutching at straws. Let's see what his girl-friend has to say. Who knows, it might turn out to be a domestic after all.'

She frowned at this but said nothing. But the idea that a young girl would do this to her boyfriend because he had been over the side was too bizarre for words.

They reached the gates. A tall makeshift plastic screen had been erected across the entrance to the estate, shielding the head from the view of people in the lane. Uni-formed police had cordoned off the nearside of the lane for twenty yards in either direc-tion. Even in this quiet location and so early in the morning a few people had stopped to try to catch a glimpse of what had caused all the police activity. And the press had arrived.

One or two cameras flashed as the two detectives emerged into the lane. Prior ignored them and approached his two CSIs. Now they had more light they were metic-ulously searching the tarmac, looking for any debris that might have been left by the killer or his vehicle.

Then Prior saw the green-clad figure of the county pa-thologist, Professor Thomas Penhallon standing by the es-tate wall chatting to a uniformed sergeant. Penhallon was a tiny figure of a man in his late fifties. His features were pinched and he wore a carefully-trimmed moustache. His head was virtually bald although hidden at the moment by the hood of his evidence suit. What he lacked in physical stature he more than made up for in aggression. He was renowned for his grumpy nature, especially when called out early in the morning.

Prior changed direction and approached him. Without preamble he said, 'What do you think, Professor?'

'Ah, back at last, nice of you to find the time for me'. He paused for effect and then added, 'He's dead, Matthew.'

Prior ignored the jibe. 'I'd say that's a shrewd observation Professor. Anything else you can tell me?'

'I'm a pathologist not a magician. The only thing I can tell you at this stage is that whoever cut his head off is no surgeon. I wouldn't trust him to carve the Sunday roast.'

'Well that narrows the field a bit. Any ideas on the time of death?'

'It was a cold night last night. That will have speeded up coagulation. But it's very difficult to tell how advanced rigor mortis is from just a head. And with no organs to ex-amine and no stomach contents, I'd only be guessing at a time of death.'

'I suppose there's no chance of even a guess at cause of death?'

Penhallon gave him a glare. 'This is not some idiotic quiz show, Matthew. I don't guess, I estimate. I've had a close look at the head. There is a contusion on the back of it, but I doubt that killed him. Blunt instrument trauma is the in phrase I understand.' He smiled grimly, he had no time for those who tried to baffle people with medical jargon. He continued, 'It could of course have been the decapitation itself that caused his death. But without the body I can say with complete confidence that I don't have a bloody clue how he died, beyond the fact that the expression imprinted on his face suggests that it was a painful experience, so he was conscious when it happened. Find me the rest of him and I might be able to tell you more.'

Siobhan said, 'What about the weapon used to cut off the head, Professor?'

'Probably a blunt knife and an axe; the knife probably had a serrated edge. I can't be expected to carry out a proper examination perched on the top of a ladder. You will have to wait till I get the head to the mortuary.'

'Thank you, Professor,' she made no effort to keep the irony out of her voice.

'You're welcome, Siobhan. Now can I un-impale this ghastly thing and go and have my breakfast?

Prior looked at George Bailey, 'Have your people finished, George, can the professor have his head?'

'Yes guv, he'd better take it before the crows get at it. We've got photos and we've dusted for prints and that. We're just about done here at the scene.'

Prior turned back to the pathologist. 'The head is yours, Professor. I'd be obliged if you'd look at this soon; after you've eaten your breakfast of course. The press are going to make a big thing of this and at the moment I've got absolutely zilch to go on.'

Penhallon nodded and said in a more conciliatory tone, 'I understand, Matthew. I'll do the best I can but don't expect too much.' He climbed the metal step-ladder that had been stood in front of the gate. George Bailey held it steady whilst the pathologist placed a large, clear plastic bag over the head and lifted it off the spike. There was a gruesome sucking sound as it came loose.

Prior smiled grimly. 'I hope you enjoy your breakfast Professor.'

The pathologist glared at him but said nothing.

Prior turned back to his CSI. 'Well, George, anything at all?'

'Not a lot I'm afraid, guv. You've seen all the blood and gore around the gate. A few of the blood spots on the iron railing beneath the spike have been smudged; but no prints. Can't see any hairs or fibres except those on the dead head.' He smiled as his clumsy wording. 'If you see what I mean. No debris except the splinters you found on the cross rail. Find me the ladder and I might get a match.'

He paused. Prior waited for him to go on.

'I'd have to guess that whoever brought this thing here must have had a vehicle, especially as he seems to have used a ladder to put the thing on the gate. The vehicle was obviously parked where the blood trail begins, but it left no trace. Other than that, not a bleedin' sausage; no tyre prints, footprints, cigarette ends, no nothin'.'

Prior frowned in concentration. 'But the killer brought a ladder with him. That's something George. Must have had a roof-rack if it was a car, More likely he used a truck with all the blood there must have been. And that shows pre-meditation. He came pre-pared, this wasn't some spur of the moment thing.' He paused.

Then he smiled and added, 'There you are you see, George, there's always some-thing. Not a lot, but something.'

'Yes, guv. Can we get off now, my stomach's rumbling?'

'Why does everybody want to eat? Yes, go on, bugger off then.'

Bailey and Hinds walked off towards the plastic screen and began to disassemble it. As they had been talking an-other car had pulled up and two detectives got out; DCs Jean Wade and Fred Trimble, the elder brother of Charlie, the uniformed constable who had discovered the head.

Prior greeted them in a sharp tone. 'Nice of you to make an appearance. I hope we didn't get you out of bed too early.'

Wade smiled sheepishly. 'Sorry about that, sir, it was my fault. My mobile had a flat battery, so I didn't get the message.'

Prior opened his mouth to give her a sharp reprimand; then closed it again. Clear-ly, she had not been at home when she was called or would have answered her landline. She was a good detective and had not been on call and he guessed she'd slept at her boy-friend's place. His frown turned into a smile. 'Always a good idea to make sure it's charged Jean. It can save you a lot of embarrassment.' She nodded and gave him a weak smile in return.

They were joined by DS Quigley. 'We've searched the lane half-a-mile in each di-rection, sir; nothing. The mobile enquiry van is on its way.'

'OK. I want the force helicopter to help with the search; Siobhan's called them. We need to find the body. Old Penhallon couldn't tell us much from just the head. We've spoken to Sinclair up at the house. We can confirm the fact that he is an arsehole, be careful how you deal with him. I got the impression that he wasn't being totally honest with us about one or two things. But I hardly think it was him that put the head on the gate, he might be an arsehole, but I don't think he's a stupid arsehole.'

Quigley nodded, it was his nature to use words sparingly.

Prior scratched his head. 'I've got his permission to put the van on the estate. Go and see the estate manager, name's Callaghan. Talk to him about where to park it; we'll be away from the public and the press there. Oh, and make sure you all use the trades-man's gate in Lamb Lane, his nibs is fussy about who uses this one. Put a uniform on both gates; tell them to keep the press out. Get on with interviewing the farm workers and the staff at the house. Prepare a pro forma that's idiot proof, when did they last see Wright etc. etc. You know the form.'

Quigley nodded again.

'Then get some of the team down to the village, find out what you can. Siobhan and I are going to the lad's cottage; apparently he shared it with his girlfriend. Wait for me to confirm the ID before you release any information to anyone. And say nothing to the damned press until we've let the family know. I'll organise a statement when we get back. OK?'

'Yes, sir, leave it to me.'

5. Jenna Bligh.

'There is a remedy for everything except death.'

15th century proverb.

They drove the short distance to the village of Penwin. It was a working village with one pub and a few hundred mostly-modest dwellings. Too far from the coast for the second homes of the rich, it did not become sleepy hollow in the winter. And importantly, Prior thought, small enough so that everyone would take an interest in their neighbour.

They found the Wright home easily enough following the directions they had been given. It was an old miner's cottage, probably three hundred years old with three-foot thick stone walls painted white. It was one up and one down with a lean-to kitchen added almost as an afterthought. Its outer wall fronted directly onto the lane while the entrance door was at the side, down a narrow alley between the cottage and its neighbour.

Prior knocked and the door was opened immediately by a woman in her early twenties. She had a face like that drawn by a child; large wide-spaced blue eyes, a small button of a nose and wide generous mouth. Her light brown shoulder-length hair was flicked up at the ends. The whole effect was quite pretty. Her slim figure was clothed in a green cardigan and blue jeans; she wore pink fluffy carpet slippers on her feet. Clearly, when at home, she paid little attention to the dictates of fashion.

When she saw the grim expressions on the faces of the two detectives, her face dropped. 'No, oh please no.'

Prior produced his warrant card and introduced himself and his companion. He added in a soft voice, 'Are you Jenna?'

'Yes.' Her hand went to her mouth. 'It's about John isn't it? Please tell me he's all right.'

Prior said simply, 'May we come in please, Jenna?'

She nodded and stood back to let them pass, her hands moving defensively across her chest.

The doorway led directly into a small living room. It was dominated by an inglenook fireplace with recesses on either side. A wood-burning stove stood in the fireplace; a TV and music system sat comfortably in the recesses. A cheap but comfortable looking three-piece suite, a tiny coffee table and an old wooden sideboard were the only other furnishings.

In one corner of the room was an open door with a steep wooden staircase leading up to the first floor. In the rear wall was another open door leading to the small kitchen/diner. The walls were white-painted stone. There was no ceiling, just massive beams supporting the floor boards of the room above. Despite its cosy size, it looked an ideal home for a young couple just starting out on their own.

Jenna sat in the armchair with the two detectives on the settee facing her. Prior kept his voice soft, 'I understand that you live here with John Wright, Jenna, is that right?'

She nodded. 'Yes, yes. Tell me what's happened.'

'Please bear with me Jenna. When did you last see John?'

'Last night. He left the pub where I work at about ten. He said he was tired and was coming home.'

'Do you have a recent photograph of him, please?'

She got up and fetched a framed print from the sideboard. It showed a happy young couple sitting on a beach. Prior looked closely at the face of the man in the photograph; he glanced sideways at Siobhan, who nodded her confirmation. These were the moments he hated. He turned to face the young woman. 'I'm afraid it is bad news Jenna. I'm sorry to have to tell you that John has been killed.'

She burst into tears. Siobhan took a tissue from her pocket and handed it to her. Then the two detectives sat waiting patiently for her to deal with the initial shock. After a while her crying was reduced to the occasional sob. Through the sobs she said, 'What happened, how was he killed?'

This was the question Prior feared. He could hardly tell her he'd been beheaded. Instead he said, 'I'm afraid he was murdered.'

This brought another burst of tears. Eventually the two detectives managed to get her parents' phone number from her and Siobhan called them. When she'd finally recovered sufficiently to talk, Prior started the painful process of questioning her.

Over the next ten minutes he gently teased out of her the events of the previous evening. Wright had arrived home from work at about 5pm. The two had eaten a meal together. Then, at ten minutes to six, she had left to start her shift at The Hunters Arms. At about eight he had gone to the pub to play pool with his mate, Bob Parkin. At ten he told Jenna that he was tired and had left to return home.

She had finished her shift and walked home, arriving at about 11.30 to find the cottage empty. She had immediately become anxious and tried calling him on his mobile. She had rung three times without getting a reply. Next, she had run back to the pub only to find it in darkness. Returning to the cottage, she had sat on the settee not knowing what to do next. She had finally fallen asleep on the settee.

Prior had watched her reactions carefully and was convinced she was telling the truth. He probed deeper, 'Did you have any kind of an argument yesterday?'

'No, we were both in a good mood.' She began to cry again. Prior again waited patiently for her to stop.

There was a knock at the front door. Prior got up to answer it. He stepped outside and spoke to the caller in a soft voice. After a few moments he showed a middle-aged woman into the room. She rushed over to Jenna and embraced her. The two detectives waited patiently.

Only when she had settled down could they continue probing. Prior said gently, 'Just a few more questions, Jenna. Was the door locked when you got here?'

'Yes, I used my key to get in.'

'Was there any sign that John had been here after leaving the pub? Was his coat here for example?'

'No, nothing.'

'Did John go out with his mates much?'

'Yes of course. He played football for the village team; they often went out for boys' nights. But he always told me where he was going. He wasn't wild you know like some are, he was so reliable.'

'Did he have anything on his mind recently?'

She smiled through her tears. 'Yes we're going to have a baby; we were both so happy.' Then the import of her words hit her, she burst into tears again.

Her mother said, 'Isn't that enough, Inspector, you can see how upset she is?'

'Yes of course, Mrs Bligh.' Then to the daughter, 'Jenna, we can stop now if you wish. But if you can manage, I have just a few more questions.'

She nodded, wiping her nose with a tissue.

'Was there anything else on his mind recently, Jenna. Money worries, anything like that?'

'No, nothing. We'd started saving for the baby; John wasn't a big spender.' Then she smiled as a thought crossed her mind. 'He said he had a surprise for me.'

'Any idea what it was?'

'No, he was always surprising me with little things.' Her hand went to her throat where a thin silver necklace with a tiny pendant hung. 'He bought me this.'

Prior paused again. Then he asked, 'Do you and he have a car, Jenna?'

She shook her head. 'No, we both have push-bikes.'

'Is John's bike here?'

'I don't know. We keep the bikes in the shed.' She pointed over her shoulder to the rear of the house.

'Mind if I go and check?'

She shook her head.

Prior walked through the tiny kitchen and unlocked a back door. He found himself in a tiny paved yard. To one side was a wooden gate to a narrow alleyway. A wooden shed took up half of the yard. Otherwise it contained only rubbish bins and a washing line. He opened the shed door and looked in. There were two pedal cycles leaning against a work bench. There was little else in the shed except a few tools, a broken chair and some empty plant pots. He returned to the cottage.

As he walked into the living room he heard Siobhan ask, 'How far along are you Jenna?'

'Three months. Oh god, what am I going to do without John?'

Her mother put her arm round her and said, 'Don't you worry, love, you can come home and live with dad and me; we'll cope.' She looked at Prior over her daughter's head.

'Surely that's enough questions Inspector, give the poor girl a rest.'

'Yes of course Mrs Bligh.' He leaned forward and gently squeezed the daughter's shoulder. 'I'm so sorry for your loss, Jenna. I know its small consolation but we will do our very best to catch whoever did this to John. Go home with your mother now; I know you're in good hands. With your permission we'd like to have a look around the cottage before we leave. We'll shut the door behind us.'

6. The Cottage.

'Diligence is the mother of good luck.'

16th century proverb.

After the two women had left, Prior and Siobhan sat down again on the settee. 'Well, what do you think?' he asked.

She shook her head. 'She seemed genuine enough, there doesn't seem to have been any strife here. I think she was telling the truth.'

He nodded. 'Yes, but there has to be something in his life that will give us a clue why he was killed, he can't have been just a random victim. If it was some homicidal maniac, he's not likely to have chosen Wright as a victim. For a start he was a big strong lad, not the kind of person you'd choose to kill and decapitate without some good reason. And the village here, it's not the sort of place where you'd expect a maniac to be lurking waiting for some poor soul to come along, is it?'

She shook her head slowly. 'No, I agree. There has to be something that made him the specific target.'

'Well, let's reconstruct. He got home from work on the estate at about five. And it seems as though he had nothing on his mind. Surely if they were that close, she would have noticed if anything was bothering him. He ate a meal with Jenna then she went off to work. This is their regular routine by the sound of it. At eight he joins her at the pub and has a few pints with his mates. Then at ten he decides to go home and have an early night; again, nothing unusual if he's working the next day. As Sinclair said, the farm workers have an early start.'

She nodded.

After a short pause he continued, 'Somewhere between the pub and here he disappears. Seven and a half hours later his head is found on a spike, what, a mile away?'

She nodded again.

Prior scratched his head. 'It's just a ten-minute walk from the pub to here all through the lit village. Surely if there was some kind of a struggle, someone would have seen or heard something. Ten o'clock is not that late, most people would still be awake.'

'Maybe he went willingly. Maybe it was someone he knew and trusted.'

'That seems the likeliest explanation. Make a note to check if anyone else left the pub at about the time Wright did.'

She nodded and wrote in her notebook.

He continued, 'The next thing we know is that Jenna phoned him at 11.40. She said his phone just rang and rang, which means it was switched on. So, someone must have prevented him from answering it.'

'Or he was already dead by then.'

Prior nodded. 'Yes there's that possibility. Let's move on. The police patrol went past the gate at about 12.30 and the head wasn't there then. That means the time between 10 and 12.30 is unaccounted for, that's two and a half hours.'

'At least two and a half hours. We don't know exactly when the head was put there. Only that it was after 12.30'

'A good point. Yes, we need a time of death; that could be vital. Somewhere between 12.30 and 5.30 the head was put on the spike. So where was Wright between ten and that time? He can't just have disappeared.'

'Well, we know the killer had a motor vehicle, he must have taken Wright somewhere.'

Prior nodded. 'We need that time of death. Maybe old Penhallon will be able to pin it down closer once we have the body. We know when Wright last ate, so the stomach contents should tell us something.'

'That's if we find the body sir.'

'I thought you were an optimist, Siobhan.'

She smiled weakly. 'Just playing the devil's advocate.'

'Hmm, perhaps not the best choice of words in the circumstances; if anything looks like the devil's work, this does. Right, we'd best have a look round the cottage.'

They started in the living room. The young couple had been fond of music. There were over a hundred CD's on the sideboard; their tastes seem to have run to modern pop, rap, ballads and soul. Neither seemed to have read a great deal, they didn't even take a daily newspaper. The only reading matter was a few women's magazines on a shelf below the coffee table. In a drawer they found a neat pile of bills. Most were for household things and all were marked paid.

The kitchen proved no more rewarding. The contents of the fridge and larder showed their taste in food was simple; they were not into organic or vegetarian dishes. The general tidiness and empty draining board suggested that at least one of them was not frightened of domestic tasks. Nor did the rubbish bin hold any surprises.

They turned their attention to the bedroom. As they climbed the narrow stairs to the upper floor Siobhan said, 'This is the part of the job I hate, sir, going through people's personal things.'

'Me too, Siobhan. But we don't have a choice, so let's get on with it.'

'Yes, sir.'

The twin wardrobes and chest of drawers contained only a modest collection of his and her clothing. The tiny bathroom cabinet contained just toiletries and a bottle of aspirin, the laundry baskets simply dirty linen while the waste bin was empty.

A queen-sized double bed took up most of the space in the bedroom. It was covered in a white sheet and pillowcases and a pretty, floral-patterned duvet. It had been made since it was last slept in and smelled of violets. Sniffing a pillow Siobhan commented, 'I like the scented conditioner.'

He ignored her. On each side of the bed stood a small bedside cabinet. He said, 'You take the right, Siobhan, I'll take left.'

Pulling the top drawer open Prior found that he had Jenna's side if the bed. The drawer contained a packet of tampons and a box of paper tissues. There was nothing in there or the cupboard beneath that was in any way out of the ordinary. His mind wandered, thinking of other similar searches he had conducted. The contents of bedside cabinets were often an indication of how healthy a couple's sex life was; clearly this couple had needed no artificial aids.

His thoughts were interrupted.

'Sir, come and look at this.' She held a hardback book in her hands. Walking round the bed he took it from her and looked at the title - The Celts. The author was Nora Chadwick.

'Interesting' he said as he flicked through the pages. He stopped at some illustrations. 'Bingo!' he said. 'Look at this, Siobhan, ancient hill forts and Celtic settlements.' He read one or two lines from a page and added, 'Now what would a young farmhand who's supposed not to be too bright be doing with a book like this?'

Siobhan remained silent.

'And this is not a library book and it's not cheap either. For someone who apparently doesn't read much this is a bit heavy. And ancient history too.'

'And the honourable Mr Sinclair has an ancient hill fort on his estate, sir.'

Prior nodded, 'One he won't let the archaeologists dig up. Interestinger and interestinger as the good Sheerlock would say.'

'Did he struggle with the English language too sir?'

'Ha bloody ha. Well it's on Wright's side of the bed. I wonder if Jenna knows about this?'

'What if Wright found something on the estate?'

'Yes, that might explain it. But then he'd hardly go out and buy a book like this just because he found something interesting, would he?'

'Suppose it was something valuable? Perhaps that was the surprise he had for Jenna. Maybe he was killed to stop him digging.'

'What, you mean buried treasure? Don't be daft.'

'Have you got a better suggestion, sir?' She said in a haughty voice.

'Not at the moment but I wouldn't be surprised if it turned out to be a domestic after all; maybe he was bonking someone else.' He smiled. 'Maybe she was a librarian.'

Siobhan rolled her eyes at him. Then she said, 'A librarian with an axe, sir?'

He shook his head. 'No, but I certainly don't believe in buried treasure, not these days, not in the real world anyway. No, I'm not into theories on buried treasure, Siobhan.'

'Nor am I for that matter but there may be some connection between this Celtic stuff and Wright's death. This is the only thing out of the ordinary we've found so far.'

He looked at her and smiled. 'You're not just a pretty face, are you?'

'You do say the nicest things, sir, sometimes anyway.'

He laughed. 'Touché, Siobhan.'

'Perhaps we need more data before we speculate further, sir.'

'That's a very profound statement, sergeant. Why didn't I think of that?'

'Probably because you were too busy rubbishing my ideas, sir.'

They both laughed as they made their way down the narrow stairs.

7. Mobile home.

'The last thing we know in constructing a work is what to do first.'
Blaise Pascal 1623-62.

They took the right turn into Lamb Lane on the way back to the Sinclair Estate and entered through the tradesmen's gate. It was open and after rattling across a cattle grid, they found themselves on a well-worn track that crossed open farmland. On either side low stone walls divided the land into fields. To the right the land rose gradually. A footpath followed the line of one of the stone walls up the hill with styles crossing each dividing wall. The path disappeared over the brow of the hill some four hundred yards above them.

Prior pointed. 'That must be where the hill fort is, somewhere up there.'

Siobhan leaned forward to see past him. 'I can't see any trace of a fort, sir?'

'You won't from the ground; these sites are all grassed over. But from the air you can see the outlines of buildings and other structures that once stood there.'

'I didn't know you were into archaeology, sir.'

He smiled. 'Only from my armchair; the National Geographic programmes on the tele'.'

She nodded. 'It's not very public spirited of Sinclair not to allow a dig, is it? It's not as if he's short of land.'

'That's the landed gentry for you. They don't give much away unless there's something in it for them.'

'That's very cynical, sir.'

He glanced sideways at her. 'It's a cynical world, Siobhan. You heard what Charlie Trimble said about Sinclair, and you've met the man himself. I'd say that's typical of him.'

'But that's just Sinclair not the whole of the landed gentry as you call them.'

This time he smiled. 'It's amazing what greed does to people. I suppose there are one or two who are OK. But most of them...?' He left the sentence unfinished. They lapsed into silence.

To their left the land continued to fall away gradually. Fifty yards below them Prior caught glimpses of a stream meandering along the valley floor through the thick shrubs and trees that grew beside it.

'I suppose that's where his nibs does his trout fishing.' Siobhan said.

'Mmm. I wonder if he uses a worm on a hook?'

She smiled. 'Only the plebs do that, it's not cricket you know; got to give the fish a fair chance.'

'I would think that depends how hungry you are.'

Several buildings appeared ahead of them. First, there was a two-story stone house surrounded by its own small, fenced garden. Next there was a row of farm buildings with a tiny cottage behind. Fifty yards beyond these was the untidy sprawl of the manor house. Prior pointed to the small house. 'I suppose that's where the estate manager lives and the little cottage above the farm buildings is where the old cowman stays.'

They looked at the estate manager's house as they passed. Two Labrador dogs watched them from behind a garden gate, wagging their tails as they passed; otherwise there was no sign of activity.

Eventually they arrived at the farmyard. On one side was a long, low stone building with a grey-tiled roof, opposite was a row of barns. Parked in the yard was the police mobile trailer. There was no towing unit attached. It had obviously dumped the trailer and left. The trailer was supported by two sets of wheels, with jacks lowered at either end to keep it on an even keel. Electricity cables led from the trailer to one of the farm buildings. A row of cars was parked behind the trailer.

They parked and walked across the yard, careful to avoid the cow pats that seemed to be everywhere. Siobhan said, 'Nice of his nibs to find somewhere convenient for us to work from.'

Prior smiled but made no reply.

The door to the trailer led directly into a long narrow space filled with desks and chairs. One wall was covered in a long whiteboard on which was already written details of the victim and tasks allocated and completed. Several officers sat or stood about the office, some busy on computer terminals and telephones. Those not busy looked sheepish as Prior entered.

Prior nodded to them in passing, then walked straight to the desk occupied by DS Quigley, whose role in the enquiry was office manager. After nodding a greeting Prior added, 'We've identified the head; it is John Wright,' he placed the beach photo of the couple he'd got from Jenna Bligh on the desk. 'Siobhan will give you his other personal details. It's not going to be much fun when we ask his girlfriend to formally identify just a head but we'll face that hurdle when we come to it. What else have we got, Albert?'

'Not a lot, sir. No sign yet of the rest of the body. We've had the helicopter buzzing about and dog handlers have done a search along the stream, but they haven't found anything. Oh, and the press have besieged the front gate. We've taken statements from all the farm workers. They say Wright left the estate some time before five yesterday on his bike. In fact, one of the other lads cycled into the village with him. No one saw him after that.' As he spoke he handed Prior a pile of massages.

Prior nodded as he looked through them. 'What did the other farmhands say? Surely someone must know something.'

'No, sir. To a man they said that Wright was a nice lad and didn't have a care in the world. He didn't say anything to any of them about troubles at home and seemed happy enough yesterday.'

'What was his job on the farm?'

'He drove a tractor most of the time, sir?'

'I know that, damn it,' Prior said with a smile. 'I meant what kind of work did he do on the tractor.'

Quigley gave him a look that said, 'Well why didn't you say that.' But in fact, he answered, 'It depends on the time of year. This month he was cutting back the borders along the stream bed.'

'Out of interest what other things would he do on the tractor?'

'Well, sir, the tractor's got all sorts of attachments; anything from a plough, to a muck spreader or hedge trimmer; it's pretty versatile. But for the last week or so he was cutting back borders; if they weren't trimmed regularly they would spread into the fields.'

Prior was still reading his messages. Without looking up he said, 'Who do the farmhands think killed him?'

'None of them have any idea, sir.'

'Well, what did they say when asked?'

'They just said that: they had no idea.'

'Come on, Albert; don't tell me that a group of country folk don't have some theory about what happened. God, it's like trying to get blood out of a stone. What's the word going around?'

'Well, they're a superstitious lot, sir; they say it was a warning.'

'What kind of warning?'

'Not to dig up the past.'

'Are they saying that Wright was digging up the past?'

'No, sir, it was just superstition, as I said.'

'For god sake man, someone must have some ideas.'

Quigley simply shook his head.

'Has anything out of the ordinary happened on the farm recently?'

'Not according to them, no. All they would talk about was the old hill forts and burial sites.'

'Burial sites! Where did that come from?'

'Well, wherever there's a settlement. They have to bury their dead somewhere. Stands to reason, doesn't it?'

Prior ignored the question. 'And where is this burial ground?'

'As far as I know, the ancients around here built their settlements on the high ground where they were easier to defend and the burial site on the low ground.'

'I didn't know you were a historian Albert.'

'I'm not, sir but I do watch a bit of tele.'

'Let me get this right. Are the farmhands saying that there is a burial site somewhere on the estate?'

'As I said, sir, stands to reason. If people lived here, they died here; must be buried somewhere nearby.'

'And where exactly are they saying this burial site is?'

'Somewhere down by the stream.'

'Has anyone found any bones or remains?'

'Not as far as I know, sir, no.'

'And what do you make of all this?'

'Load of nonsense. Like I said, just superstition.'

'Most superstition is based on fact, Albert, something that actually took place long ago just gets distorted with time. I'd have thought they taught you that on the tele. I want all the people that mentioned burial sites interviewed again. This time get some specifics. Give the statements to Siobhan; she'll go through them. I've got a few phone calls to make, then I want a full briefing, bring everyone up to speed. But first I want something to eat. Send someone out for some pasties and doughnuts please, Albert. All detectives need doughnuts. I've seen that on the tele, doughnuts help you think.'

Siobhan said, 'Must be the sugar, sir.'

Quigley sighed deeply. 'Yes sir. What about the press?'

'Stuff the press. I haven't got time for them.'

Prior walked to the rear of the trailer where a door led through to a tiny cubicle. It contained a desk, two chairs and a filing cabinet. It was the Investigating Officer's personal office. He squeezed his frame behind the desk, picked up the phone and dialled a number. After a few moments he was put through to Superintendent Owen, his divisional commander. 'Morning ma'am, Prior here, or is it afternoon?' He looked at his watch, which said 12.10.

'Good afternoon, Matthew, good of you to find time to call. I've had the Chief Constable and half the nation's press on my back asking for information. What is happening?'

'Yes, ma'am, this is the first chance I've had to call you. Shall I brief you?'

'That would be nice.' Her tone was decidedly acerbic.

He spent five minutes detailing all that they had found and what the team had done in the past five hours.

When he paused she said, 'You have been busy. What are your thoughts on the killing?'

'Without a body we can't pin down the cause and time of death. By all accounts he was a nice guy in a stable relationship; his girlfriend is pregnant. No suggestion of rumpy-pumpy on the side; it doesn't look like a domestic. What little we have seems to lead us back here to the Sinclair Estate. But what we have is hardly evidence. The honourable Mr Cedric Sinclair is a bit hoity-toity but has given us the run of the estate. I'm running things from the mobile ops room here unless you have any other instructions.'

'No, Matthew you carry on as you are doing. What do the locals say about the death?'

Nothing useful, just a load of hocus-pocus about the past. The lad was well-liked, and his death is a mystery to them, or so they say.'

'So, you think one or more of them knows something?'

'Well, unless the killer picked his name out of a hat, someone must know something.'

There was a pause before she added, 'Tread carefully on the estate, Matthew. Sinclair is part of the county set and has a lot of influence. What are we going to release to the media?'

'As little as possible at this stage, certainly nothing about the ancients. Will you handle that, ma'am?'

'I'll make a statement today for you but you'll have to speak to them tomorrow. The less we tell them the more they will speculate.'

'Yes, ma'am. Hopefully by tomorrow we'll have a clearer picture.' As he was talking the door opened and Siobhan put a cup of coffee on the desk. He waved his thanks.

Owen continued, 'Have you got everything you need?'

'For the moment, yes. But I'll need for you to open the overtime budget. Oh, and I've only got the one DI. Pearce is on leave. Monk's not up to much but I'll have to leave him to run the main office.'

There was a moment's silence at the other end of the line as she absorbed what he'd said about his deputy. Then she said, 'OK, I'll keep a close eye on Monk. The overtime budget is open. But I want a daily accounting and update on progress, it's not a bottomless pit. What are your next steps?'

'I'm going to have a pasty and a doughnut. I've had no breakfast yet, ma'am. Then I'm going to retrace the victim's last day on Earth.'

She laughed into the phone. 'Careful the pasty doesn't choke you; and leave a bit for the piskies for good luck, it sounds as if you'll need it on this case. And bear in mind what I said, Matthew, tread warily with Sinclair, he's got a lot of friends in high places. I've already had the ACC crime on to me asking about the case. I'll try to keep him off your back, just make damned sure you keep me informed.' She referred to the Assistant Chief Constable responsible for the investigation of crime, Thomas Stapleton.

'Is that all the ACC said, ma'am?'

'Yes, what else did you expect him to say?'

Prior thought about his interview with Sinclair and the man's reluctance to talk about his guests of the previous evening. But after giving it a moment, he decided not to mention it. If nothing had come down from above he would leave well alone. He said, 'Nothing, ma'am, just wondered.'

'I know you, Matthew, and that pause tells me there's something on your mind. Now tell me, what is it?'

He heaved a sigh then took the plunge. 'This Sinclair. He lied to me when I asked him if he had any visitors last night. There's something he's hiding. It may have nothing to do with the investigation but then again it might have.'

There was a long pause before Owen said, 'Interesting. But what's that got to do with the ACC?'

'Maybe nothing. But why is he chasing you for information?'

'What's that famous saying, Matthew? Ours is not to wonder why.......'

The phone went dead.

Prior took a sip of his coffee then dialled his home number. His wife Jeanette was a freelance journalist who worked from home. In addition, she wrote speeches for politicians and after-dinner speakers. Most of her research she was able to do on the internet, so she needed no baby-sitter for their two young daughters.

She answered immediately, 'Matthew, you poor thing. I've heard it on the news. What kind of ghoul could have done such a thing?'

'Yes, love, it is a bit gruesome. We haven't got a clue yet, literally. I'm afraid I'm going to be late tonight.'

'That's a shame. It's the school's open night, and the girls were looking forward to showing you their work.'

'You'll have to give them my apologies. I'll make it up to them somehow.'

'You'd better. How's Siobhan taking this?'

'She's OK, I think.'

'Well you look after her; she's very sensitive you know.'

'What about me, I'm sensitive too?'

'You've got a skin like a rhinoceros. You make sure she's OK.'

'It doesn't feel like it when I'm shaving.'

'Very funny. Are you eating all right?'

'Yes, my love, I've just sent out for some pasties.'

'Good, make sure you eat. I'll see you when I see you. Love you.'

'Me too,' he replied.

As if on cue the door opened and Siobhan brought paper bags in and put them on the desk. He could smell the pasty and made a grab. 'God, I'm famished. Sit down, I've been told by Jeanette to look after you.'

'Yes, sir.' Siobhan sat on the only other chair in the tiny office and opened a paper bag. 'What did Owen say?'

He replied through a mouthful of pasty, 'More or less what you'd expect. But she is supportive, I must give her that. Oh, and she's opened the overtime budget, so you 'other ranks' can earn a few bob.'

'Oh goody, I can get a new outfit.'

Siobhan was single and lived in a tiny flat in Truro. She was a local girl, having been born in the nearby village of Tregallon where her father had been the village constable until his recent retirement. She had been an afterthought; her two brothers were more than ten years her senior. They had chosen a different path to their father; both worked at the nearby clay quarry. They were big burly chaps and played rugby for the village team. They doted on their baby sister and she had grown up a tomboy.

She had floated through school, showing no ambition or particular interest. Then, after a few years of drifting, she had applied to join the force. This had come as a surprise to her family. She had sailed through the entrance exam and took to policing like a duck to water. Her confidence and people skills made her a natural detective and she loved the work.

Sadly, she'd had little luck in the field of romance. Her self-confident manner and intelligence put off a lot of suitors. Her choice in men was of burly rugby-playing characters like her brothers. But, as she would say herself:' The only thing between a rugby players ears is distance'. None so far had held her attention for long. Nor was she keen to have children. Both her brothers had broods and she worked off her maternal instincts on them. This freed her to do what she loved most, chase criminals. And annoy me, thought Prior.

They chewed their food for a while. Then she asked, 'And Jeanette, what did she have to say?'

'She said I've got skin like a rhinoceros and should make sure you are OK.'

'That's thoughtful of her; you're a lucky man to have her.'

'Hmm. I'm surrounded by nagging women. What with her, two daughters, a superintendent and a sergeant, I can't seem to get away from you all.'

'Huh, you love it really.'

He finished his pasty and took a doughnut from a bag. 'Are you still seeing that guy, what's his name, Simon?'

'No, sir, I finished it with him. He made two short planks look thin; but he did have a nice butt'

Prior smiled. 'Anyone else on the horizon?'

'No, all the men I meet have got skins like a rhinoceros. And the best ones are already taken anyway.'

'Well you're not exactly ugly. It's time you settled down.'

'Did I detect some kind of a compliment there? You're slipping, sir, that's two in one day.'

'Don't change the subject and do as you're told.'

'Are you running a dating agency now, sir?'

He put his hands up defensively, 'All right, all right, forget I said anything.' Wiping his hands on a paper napkin he added, 'Seriously, are you OK with all this blood and gore?'

'Yes, sir, I think so. I'll let you know if I have any bad dreams. What about you?'

He smiled. 'You're right, I have Jeanette. I am a lucky man. And according to her I've got skin like a rhinoceros, remember? Anyway, enough of this chit-chat, we've got work to do.'

8. The Celtic Cross.

'If God did not exist, it would be necessary to invent him.'
Voltaire 1694-1778.

Prior had assembled his team of detectives in the mobile incident room. It was crowded and there were not enough chairs but they managed. He spent half-an-hour going over every detail of the case. Fifteen years as a detective had taught him a great deal. Both about detecting, at which he was very good but also about managing a team of detectives.

In cases such as this, where there were no obvious suspects, they must trawl their net over a wide area. No one man could do that alone. Tasks must be allocated to team members and if they were not fully conversant with every aspect of the case and properly motivated, coincidences and clues could easily be missed. He covered everything that they knew so far.

Then he turned to the speculation. 'OK we only have a few pieces of the jigsaw so far. We don't even have a body, just a head. Without the body we can't even pin down the time and cause of death. Nor have we any clue as to the motive. Nor has forensics been much help so far. Later DS Williams and I are going to retrace Wright's last known movements.

The rest of you will concentrate on two things. First, look for witnesses in the village. He left the pub last night at about ten. Did anyone in the pub leave at about the same time? Who did he speak to in the pub? Was anyone spotted loitering outside the pub at about that time? People will have been arriving and leaving the place throughout the evening. Find them and question them. People living in the village may have spotted someone or even a strange vehicle, so we'll do a house-to-house. Where was the victim between 10pm and the time his head was put on the gate? Anything you can find must be a help.' He paused. No one spoke.

'Then sometime between 12.30 and 5.30 this morning, his head was left on the spike. How did it get there? It was almost certainly brought in a motor vehicle, someone may have seen it on the move. There must be blood all over the vehicle used. Has anyone seen a vehicle with blood in it? And the place where he was decapitated. George Bailey doesn't think it could have taken place at the scene. There must have been buckets of blood when the head was chopped off.

Then at the scene, there is evidence that suggests the killer used a wooden ladder to reach the spike on top of the gate to impale the head. It's logical that he did, the spike is some eight foot from the ground. It is also logical to assume that the killer brought the ladder with him. And a ladder is not something that one could fit easily into a car. It follows that he probably used some kind of truck.' He paused again. Most of the team were making notes.

'Next, the body. Where has that been dumped? It could be somewhere nearby. It's not the sort of thing you keep in your boot for any longer than you have to. Without putting too fine a point on it, the thing would start to smell. We've checked for CCTV and security cameras but there are none in the village streets or the lane leading to the estate. Apparently, there is one outside the shop in the village. Check if it was on last night.

'Then there's motive. This was no random killing; someone wanted Wright dead. Who and why? Any rumour or bit of scandal we want to know about. We've interviewed the girlfriend and there doesn't seem to have been any strife there. But we could be wrong. Ask around, especially among his mates.

'There's a lot of speculation about digging up the past. Don't dismiss it out of hand; if someone mentions that then follow it up. I'm sceptical about that but we can't discount it. Follow it up.

'Stay alert and listen to what people tell you, I don't want anyone just going through the motions. Find something people. Now, are there any questions?'

'Yes, sir.' A voice at the back said, 'What about overtime, are we getting paid any?'

Prior frowned. 'If that's the only think on your mind man, you're in the wrong job. If you have to work late, you'll get paid for it. But don't expect it automatically. DS Quigley will authorise what's necessary. Now, any sensible questions?'

There was a buzz of conversation in the room, but no more questions were asked. Prior dismissed them, 'OK, get your assignments from DS Quigley. Now get on with it.'

He turned to Siobhan. 'I want to look at the place where Wright was working yesterday. And then there's your idea about buried treasure. I've got my wellies in the boot. We'll have to find you a pair. Let's try the estate manager.' They went to the estate office at the end of the long low building. The manager was not there but his secretary found a pair of boots that were several sizes too large for Siobhan. But, with a thick pair of woollen socks that Prior also carried in the boot of his car, she could walk in them.

Prior led the way down to the stream. Here the borders of the fields were defined by a dense growth of brambles and hawthorns. These had been vigorously trimmed on the field side, and recently. Beyond the rough hedgerow they could see a grove of trees that bordered the stream on both sides and continued to the boundary wall further on. They could hear the water gurgling its way along the bottomland. He led the way along the hedgerow towards the distant gate in Lamb Lane.

'What are we looking for, sir?'

'Buried treasure, Siobhan.'

'Oh goody. Shouldn't we have brought a spade? And don't we need a map with an X marking the spot?'

'Very funny. Listen this was your idea in the first place.'

'If we do find something, how will we recognise it for what it is?'

'I haven't a clue, signs of recent digging maybe?'

'But if there are signs, won't someone else have already seen them?'

He replied irritably, 'Yes, Siobhan, if they were looking for them. Maybe they did, maybe that's why Wright was killed.'

She clomped along behind him through the muddy ground, making heavy weather of it in her oversized wellies. After a while she said, almost to herself, 'I should have kept my big mouth shut.'

He laughed. 'Look on the bright side, all this fresh air will do you good.'

'Give me a stinking cold, more like.'

They had travelled some distance when Prior spotted something off-white among the brambles. He stopped and looked closer. It was a stone pillar no more than three feet high and half as wide. There was some kind of carving on its face. He frowned. 'Now, what is that? Help me move some of these brambles away, you've got gloves on.'

'These are fashion gloves sir, not gardening gloves.'

'Stop moaning and give me a hand.'

It was easier than he had expected. Without too much effort they managed to pull back some of the entangled branches and get a better view of the stone. It was some four feet from the edge of the brambles. 'That's odd, these branches are all loose. Someone has been here before us and just put the loose branches back to cover it.'

The stone was a dirty off-white colour. The bottom half was covered in moss but the top eighteen inches was clear of any growth. There were faint indentations on the face of the stone. 'Look at that, Siobhan. Someone has scraped the moss off here. There's some kind of pattern on it. Can you make it out?'

She peered into the channel they had cleared, 'Looks like a cross in a circle. But it must be very old, it's very faded.' Her interest had now been aroused. 'That's a Celtic cross, sir, I've seen them before.'

'What does it mean?'

'I haven't a clue.'

'That's useful. Listen, make a sketch of it, we can do some research.'

She took out her notebook and made a rough sketch.

Looking around him, Prior saw a spot where the brambles were not so thick some five yards further on. He walked to the spot and began to force his way through the undergrowth. Siobhan followed him gingerly. He said over his shoulder, 'Good job you've got trousers on Siobhan.'

'But I've got tights on underneath. I can feel the damned thorns scratching them and me.'

'Stop complaining, you can claim for a new pair of tights.'

'What about skin, sir? Can I claim for that too?'

He ignored her and continued to push his way through the brambles. They were about ten foot tall. Finally, after much struggling, he found himself standing among trees. They were of varying heights and species. He was no expert and only recognised a few of them. The stream ran past a few yards further in. On the far side the trees extended to the boundary wall of the estate.

'Are you any good at trees, Siobhan?'

'I hope you don't mean climbing them, sir.'

'No, you twerp, I mean at identifying them and telling their ages.'

She ignored the insult. 'I recognise a few of them; there are oaks, elms and some birch. Haven't a clue how old they are though.'

'But you'd agree it's what they call a mature forest?'

'Pretty small for a forest, sir; but the trees do look as if they've been here for a while.' She looked around her. 'No signs of digging.'

'Well, I didn't expect the whole place to be dug up. Let's look further along.'

They walked back until they were directly behind the stone cross and searched the ground. Nothing appeared to have been disturbed. Nor were there any irregularities in the ground that might indicate disturbance by human hand, either in the distant or recent past. 'Nothing,' he said, sounding disappointed. Then added, 'But someone definitely scratched the moss off that stone.'

'Perhaps they thought it was a milestone, sir. Just wanted to find how far it was to London.'

'Ha bloody ha. Where's your enthusiasm, Siobhan? After all we are following your hunch.'

'I withdraw my hunch, sir, unequivocally. My feet ache, I'm getting blisters and my legs are scratched to ribbons.'

'Serves you right. If you don't like the heat, you shouldn't come into the kitchen. Now we're here, let's look all the way along.' He led the way along the path heading towards Lamb Lane.

She groaned but followed him dutifully along the bank of the stream. Eventually they came to the estate wall where it bordered the lane. Here the stream rushed through an iron grill stretched across a stone arch that ran under the wall. Looking around, Prior spotted an area of disturbed ground close to the boundary wall. There was a large hole in the ground and beside it the stump of a tree that had been uprooted. To one side were heaps of sawn logs; sawdust was everywhere. 'Someone collecting firewood by the look of it, but why here?'

Siobhan pointed at the stone wall. 'It looks as if the tree roots were pushing the wall over. Probably took the tree out to stop the wall falling down.'

'Yes, I suppose you're right.' He paused then added, 'Well this is the only signs of digging we've seen.' He looked into the hole where the tree had once stood. 'It doesn't look as if anyone did more than uproot the tree, not the sort of hole you'd expect from treasure hunters.'

Siobhan replied without enthusiasm, 'No, sir.'

Forcing their way back through the hedgerow, they found a spot where something had been burned, an area of grass that had been scorched. Around its edge were a few small half-burned bramble branches. Prior looked at the patch. 'I suppose this is where Wright burned the stuff he'd trimmed from the hedge.'

She replied in a weary tone, 'That's interesting, sir. My feet are killing me.'

Prior laughed.

They made their way back along the line of the hedge until they were level with the farm buildings, looking around them as they went. They found no indication of the ground having been recently disturbed or any more stone markers.

Back in the trailer they sat changing their footwear. Siobhan rubbed her bare feet.

'Well that was fun, sir. What's next, mountaineering?'

'No, we're going to trace Wright's steps from the time he left here yesterday.'

'I hope that doesn't mean riding a push-bike.'

He smiled. 'I never thought of that. Perhaps we can borrow a couple and do the job properly.'

She groaned. 'Why don't I keep my big mouth shut.'

He laughed. 'Only kidding, Siobhan, we'll take the car.'

9. Penwin Village.

'Better to light a candle than curse the darkness.'

Peter Bendson.

They drove back to Penwin via the Lamb Lane gate, this time driving slowly once they had left the estate, taking note of the lie of the land. But there was nothing that raised their interest. Just high hedges on either side until the lane entered the village. Then the hedge was replaced by cottages, a few with large gardens that would look beautiful in the summer months but the majority old, more modest workers' homes.

Arriving in the village centre they came to a T-junction. To their right was the village shop and further on The Hunters Arms. They turned left and drove the short distance to the Wright cottage. Here the lane was very narrow and the nearest parking place some forty yards farther on. They parked the car then walked back to the cottage.

'Right,' Prior said, 'We'll walk to the pub and time the walk.' He looked at his watch, it read 5.20. 'Keep your eyes open for nosey parkers peeping from behind curtains. We could do with one or two of those.' They strolled along the lane keeping to the left as there was no footpath on the other side. They passed a few pedestrians and the occasional car drove along the lane, but generally, there was very little traffic.

Siobhan spotted the twitch of a curtain. 'There's one, sir, Albany Cottage. Shall we have a word?'

'Not now, Siobhan, make a note of the address and we'll come back. I want to time the walk.'

No more curtains twitched along the lane and they eventually arrived outside the pub. Prior looked at his watch - 5.28. 'Eight minutes, Siobhan, about what Jenna said.'

'Not much time for someone to disappear in, is it?'

'No,' Prior answered distractedly. 'Now where would the villain park his vehicle if he were lying in wait? There's nowhere here in the lane, it's too narrow.'

'There's the pub car park in the rear, sir.'

'Yes, I know. But don't you think someone waiting there in a vehicle would have risked being spotted? Surely he'd make sure he wasn't seen if he planned to kill someone?'

'Perhaps he wasn't planning to kill Wright, sir; maybe he only decided to do that later. Anyway, there's nowhere else, not nearby. And he'd have run the same risk of being seen parked here in the lane.'

The nearest place where on-road parking was available was 50 yards back along the lane towards the T-junction. They walked back that way, passing the shop on their left. It was here the road widened just enough so that several cars could park in row.

Prior shook his head in frustration. 'You know this doesn't make a lot of sense, it's all too public.' Siobhan made no reply and they continued walking. They passed the junction and approached Albany Cottage. Two of their detectives, Wade and Trimble, came out of the next-door cottage.

They joined them. 'Jean, have you and Fred done Albany Cottage?'

'Yes sir, old Mrs. Chivers.'

'What did she have to say?'

'Didn't see anything last night. But says that she heard the sound of a vehicle driving up and down. Says the last time she heard it was just after ten. She's sure of the time because the news had just started on the tele.'

'What kind of a vehicle?'

'What she actually said was that it wasn't a car, too big and too noisy.'

'You say up and down, how many times?'

'She says three or four, she only noticed it because it was quite noisy and went past so often.'

'Didn't she look out? I noticed her curtain twitch as we walked past.'

'No sir, she said she didn't.' Wade smiled, 'Said she was watching Strictly Come Dancing. Couldn't take her eyes off it.'

Prior grimaced. 'I suppose there's no accounting for taste. Anything else?'

'No, sir, she said it was a quiet night in the village, no disturbances, shouting or anything else that she noticed.'

Siobhan said, 'What about the other homes, anything there?'

'No sarge. No-one heard or saw anything unusual.'

'I think that's our problem. Motor vehicles pass all the time and we don't notice in the end, do we? What about the shop, anything there?'

'No luck there. They only have the security camera on when they're open and they close at six.'

Prior said, 'Does it show traffic in the lane?'

'Not clearly, it's pointed down to the door to the shop. You can just catch a glimpse of the road and anything passing on this side.'

'You had better have a look at yesterday's tape anyway, just in case the killer did a recce before the shop closed.'

'Right, sir, we'll call back now.'

'Thanks, you two carry on.'

Prior and Siobhan continued on their walk back to the Wright cottage. He frowned. 'The idea of the killer waiting in ambush looks less than likely, Siobhan. There's just nowhere where he could wait without being obvious.'

'No, sir. If I were going to abduct someone and chop their head off, I'd be damned careful no one saw me waiting to pick him up. Perhaps it all started innocently. Maybe the killer only decided later to kill Wright?'

'That's possible. But it's also possible it was the killer's vehicle Mrs. Chivers heard. Nowhere to park without being noticed so he kept on the move.' He shook his head in frustration. Then he added, 'I think we're clutching at straws, Siobhan. We need a new tack.'

'Like what, sir?'

'Like motive. Who wanted Wright killed?'

'And where do we look for that?'

'Let's have another chat with Jenna. Did you write her parents' address down?'

'Yes, sir, they live at the other end of the village, back past the pub,'

'OK, let's get the car and go see her.'

With a new sense of purpose they lengthened their strides and walked quickly to where they'd parked the car. This time they spent over an hour with Jenna Bligh and her parents. She had got over the immediate shock of losing the father of her unborn child and was able to answer their questions. In the bosom of her family she felt just a little more secure. Her father was a burly man with a gruff manner but obviously had a huge soft spot for his only daughter. His strength was transmitting itself to her.

They sat in the Blighs' comfortable living room and Prior made the interview more a conversation than an interrogation. Nevertheless, there was little more that they found out, other than confounding one of their half-theories. Jenna had known about the book on the Celts that Wright had been reading. He had borrowed it from a Tom Williamson who lived in the village.

Prior had asked, 'What was it that raised John's interest in the Celts?'

'He found some kind of a stone cross on the farm as he was cutting hedges. He was talking about it in the pub one night and old Tom overheard him. Tom's a member of the local Cornwall Society and John asked him about the cross. He used to be the gamekeeper on the estate and he remembered the cross. He said it was probably a memorial stone that are found here and there along old paths. He offered to lend John the book so he could look it up himself.'

'And did he - look it up I mean?'

She shook her head. 'No. He looked in the book but couldn't find anything on roadside crosses, only those at old burial sites. John wasn't much of a reader and found the book hard going.'

'Did he do any more research?'

'I don't think so, it wasn't that important, he was just curious.'

Jenna confirmed that several of John's friends had cars and a couple of them motorbikes. His best friend, Bill, drove his father's builders van and the football club's manager had a Transit van that he used to take the team to away matches so that they could have a pint after. Prior was careful not to make too much of this information as he didn't want to start a witch-hunt in the village.

When they left, the two detectives sat in the car discussing what little they had learned. Siobhan said, 'So it probably was Wright who cleaned the moss off the stone. But it was nothing more than natural curiosity, sir, nothing sinister.'

'I'm afraid you're right, Siobhan, unless of course some-one heard him talking about it and had more sinister motives. We'll have a look at all the motor vehicles she mentioned but that all seems a bit obvious.'

They sat thinking for a few moments. Then Prior voiced his thought, 'I may be clutching at straws again but how's this for a scenario? Suppose Wright had planned a surprise for Jenna and was buying something for her. Suppose he lied to her about being tired last night and had arranged to meet someone to pick up this surprise. Then whoever it was decided to kill Wright. Maybe they had an argument or something as you suggested earlier?'

'That would explain his disappearance from the village without a fuss. But why go to the ridiculous lengths that he did with the head?'

'I don't have the answer there. But why go to those lengths anyway. Why would anyone stick a head on a spike? Unless he was some kind of a nutter.'

'It comes back to that question every time, sir, doesn't it? Why stick the head on a spike? And why on the gates to Sinclair Estate?'

'As they say, that's the sixty-four-thousand-dollar question, Siobhan.'

'Where to next, sir?'

'The pub, let's pay that a visit.'

10. The Hunters Arms.

'A woman once drove me to drink, and I never had the courtesy to thank her.'

W.C.Fields.

The Hunters Arms was housed in two stone cottages knocked into one. Prior looked around as they entered. This was the only pub in the village and was clearly set up to cater for the tastes of both the young and the not-so-young. In one corner of the L-shaped bar was a pool table and two games machines. A row of high stools lined the bar. The remainder of the space was crammed with tables and chairs. A handwritten menu on a chalkboard drew Prior's attention; he'd only had a snack at lunchtime and no breakfast; and he was famished.

Looking around him he noticed that the pool table was not in use, there were just a dozen customers spread about the room, half of them reporters by the look of them. He spotted one of his team, DC Alan Waring, at the bar talking to the landlord.

Siobhan carried out her own inspection as she followed him to the bar. From the expressions on the customers' faces it was clear that they had identified the detectives for what they were. Not for the first time she wondered at this phenomenon, even the most law-abiding of citizens seemed able to do it. It was like some primitive instinct in man that he spotted even the hint or suggestion of danger as it approached.

Waring introduced them to the landlord, Derek Mason. His face wore a suitably grave expression. 'Makes you wonder what the world is coming to when something like this happens. And young John was not one of the wild ones. We have a few of those in the village. He were a steady lad.'

Prior made appropriate noises in response and ordered drinks. When they'd been served, the landlord moved away to serve another customer. Prior asked his DC what he had discovered.

'Everyone seems to be in shock, sir. No-one has a clue as to why it happened and why Wright was the victim.'

'What about witnesses, were any of these people in here last night?'

'You've probably guessed sir, half of them are reporters. But of the regulars, one or two were in last night. But this is the early crowd. I've spoken to them. Those that were here last night left before Wright arrived. I'm waiting for the late crowd now.'

'Are you on your own?'

'No, sir, Jane Foster is with me. She's out back talking to the smokers.'

'Good. What does the landlord have to say about the comings and goings last night?'

'Far as he can remember, no one left at about the time Wright did.'

'What about strangers?'

'No, sir none, just some of his regulars were in last night.'

Prior frowned. 'Who was Wright talking to when he was here?'

'He was playing pool with his mate, Bill Parkin.'

'And what time did Parkin leave?'

'About 10.30. Derek remembers it was a good half-an-hour after Wright left.'

'Parkin drives his dad's builders van. I want that checked for signs of blood. That still gives him time to have picked Wright up and taken him off somewhere.'

'Yes, sir.'

'Did anything out of the ordinary happen in the pub last night. Any arguments or fights?'

'Not according to the landlord. He said it was a quiet night. I'll ask the late crowd when they come in sir.'

'One other thing, Alan, one of the regulars is a guy called Tom Williamson. He's the ex-gamekeeper up at the estate. He's also something of an authority on local history. Have a word with him if he comes in. I'll want to speak to him as well at some time.'

Waring nodded and made a note in his notebook.

The door at the rear of the bar opened and Jane Foster entered. She joined them at the bar.

'Anything useful, Jane?'

'No sir. I've been talking to Norman the postman; they call him Storming Norman. He knows everyone in this village and the surrounding ones; he delivers the post in this area. But he's an early bird here, has a drink most evenings, gone by seven.' She smiled. 'He says he'd get hell from her indoors if he was late for dinner. I've asked him what the word is in the village but no one seems to have a clue about the murder. Some of the old-timers are talking about the ancients and curses but it's all superstition, nothing with any substance.'

'Are there any cults or groups hereabouts who are interested in the old ways?'

'I asked him about that. He says that most of the people in the village have families that have lived here for generations. They are all steeped in the past. But that's normal in a place like this.

But there aren't any weirdos around here. The nearest he knows are on the Lizard peninsular. Apparently there are some modern-day Druids there. And there are plenty of hippies and other weirdos about but they stick to the coast. There is a local group who meet in the village here once a month. They're not a cult or anything though, they're just a group of locals interested in Cornish history. Call themselves The Cornwall Society. Run by a guy called Miles, John Miles.'

Prior frowned and glanced at Siobhan, 'Miles? Didn't Sinclair mention a Miles who wants to dig on the estate?

And Tom Williamson who lent Wright the book; he's a member of this Cornwall Society.'

Siobhan nodded. 'Yes. Miles is a lecturer at Truro College. That's the contact number we have for him anyway.'

He turned back to Foster, 'Did Storming Norm give you an address for this John Miles?'

'Yes, sir, Gorse Cottage here in the village. It must be the same guy. Norman said that he lectures at the college.'

'Great. Siobhan and I will have a word with him once we've had something to eat.

Anything else Jane?'

'No, sir, that's it.'

'Well done, that's good work. The only other thing I can think of is something the girlfriend, Jenna said. Apparently Wright had some kind of surprise lined up for her. Ask this mate of his, Parkin, if he knew anything about that. If he doesn't come in tonight, make a point of seeing him tomorrow.'

She nodded. 'Yes sir.'

Prior turned to Siobhan, 'I'm famished. Shall we order something to eat?'

She nodded. 'A sandwich will do me, sir.'

Prior called the landlord and ordered a plate of sandwiches. Then he turned to his two DCs, 'You carry on with what you're doing. We'll find a table and watch for a while.'

They found an empty table in the corner of the room from where they could see the whole bar. Prior took a sip of his beer. 'We need for something to break, Siobhan. I don't remember a case where we didn't have a single suspect. Usually they're coming out of the woodwork. Is there something I'm missing?'

'If there is, I can't see it either, it's an uphill struggle. But I think you're right about one thing; I can't see someone lying in wait and abducting Wright forcefully. Apart from there being nowhere quiet to park, there doesn't appear to have been any disturbance here in the village. It just doesn't make sense.'

'Let's look at another scenario. Suppose he got to his cottage and was taken from there. Suppose it was someone he knew and let in. Then he was hit on the back of the head by whoever it was followed him in; Old Penhallon said that he had a contusion on the back of his head. Then he was bundled into a vehicle and taken away.'

Siobhan nodded thoughtfully. 'Yes, sir, that's one possibility. But he could also have agreed to go with him to some other location and got hit on the head later.'

Prior shook his head. 'No, if he had gone willingly he would have left a note for Jenna.'

'Maybe he thought he'd be back before she got home?'

'Or it was about the surprise he was going to give her and didn't want her to find out.'

'At risk of asking the obvious, if it was jewellery wouldn't he buy it in a shop?'

'Unless it was bent, that's something we have to look at. Make a note to get on to the local collator and find out who the local villains are. Wright wasn't exactly loaded, he might be tempted to pick something up on the cheap. But none of this explains why the killer put the head on the damned spike, does it?'

Siobhan smiled, 'Just what I was thinking, sir.'

'So we're back to square one.'

'To quote you once again, sir, not enough data.'

Prior looked up as a man approached their table. He was dressed in suit, collar and tie and a raincoat. He said, 'Excuse me are you the officer in charge of the investigation?'

'Who are you?'

'Ben Charles, The Mail. Can I have a word with you?'

'No.'

'I only want to ask you for a comment.'

'No, now kindly leave us in peace.'

The man shook his head, turned and walked away. Prior said to his back, 'Bloody vultures.'

Siobhan smiled. 'Did you learn that at charm school, sir? They should give you your money back if you did.'

Before Prior could reply the landlord's wife arrived with a large plate of sandwiches with an array of pickles on the side. Prior smiled. 'You've saved our lives, Mrs Mason. Thank you.'

She looked pleased at his comment. 'Must have been a long day for you, sir.'

'Yes it has. Before you go, can we ask you a few questions?'

'Yes, of course.' She sat down in an empty chair.

Prior took a huge bite of a ham sandwich. Through the mouthful he said, 'How well did you know John Wright, Mrs Mason?'

'Quite well. Since he'd been going out with Jenna he spent a lot of time in here.'

'Was everything all right between them?

'Oh yes. She's pregnant you know, they were both pleased.'

'So he wasn't one for other ladies then?'

'Not really, no.'

He picked up on her hesitation. 'While they were together, did he see anyone else?'

'I'm not one to speak ill of the dead, sir.

'I'm sure you're not, Mrs Mason. But this may be important, who was he seeing?'

'Well it wasn't like that. Just that there was talk, you know what country folk are like?'

'What were people saying?'

'Our cleaner, Carol, lives over in Grampian. She says that she once saw him with a girl.'

'When was this?'

'Oh, about a month ago I suppose.

'Where was this?'

'In Grampian I think, she didn't say and I didn't ask.'

'Have you heard anything else?'

'No, that's all I heard.'

'What about Jenna, anyone else in the picture? She's a pretty girl; some of the lads must be after her.'

'No, she loved him; weren't interested in anyone else. Mind you there were some that tried.'

Prior looked at Siobhan. She shook her head. He turned back to Mrs. Mason. 'Thanks Mrs Mason. And for the sandwiches, they're delicious.' She got up and returned to the kitchen.

There was one small sandwich left. Prior said. 'Do you want that Siobhan?'

'No, sir, you have it.'

He didn't ask again. When he'd swallowed the last mouthful he said, 'So, just a hint that Wright wasn't completely the innocent.'

Siobhan nodded. 'Typical man if you ask me. I'll get someone to follow that up with the cleaning lady, sir.'

'Such cynicism, Siobhan; don't forget, it takes two to tango. He took a last gulp of his pint. 'Right, let's go and have a word with this chap Miles. I'll get the bill. You tell Alan and Jane to carry on what they're doing.'

Siobhan smiled, 'Wow, not every day I get taken out to dinner by the boss. Thank you, sir.'

Prior smiled as he made his way to the bar.

11. The historian.

'Let the dead Past bury its dead.'

Longfellow, A psalm of Life

They found Gorse Cottage easily enough. It was tucked away in a narrow lane behind the church. Stone built, double-fronted and with a grey tiled roof, it sported a tiny porch where visitors could stand out of the rain while waiting to be admitted. Lights were showing from both the ground floor windows. A moment after Prior rang the doorbell a porch light came on.

The man who answered the door was in his late thirties. He was of above average height, slightly built, and his long brown hair was pulled into a pony tail. He wore blue jeans and a check shirt and had the appearance of an ageing hippy. 'Yes?' he said simply.

Prior produced his warrant card and introduced himself and Siobhan. 'Are you John Miles, sir?'

'Yes I am, what's the problem?' His tone suggested that the visitors had interrupted him in the middle of his favourite TV programme.

'No problem, Mr. Miles, we would like a word with you please, if it's convenient.'

Somewhat reluctantly he invited them in. A woman appeared in the corridor behind him. She was a large woman with chubby features and short curly fair hair. 'What is it John?'

He turned to her. 'It's the police Mary, they want to talk to me.'

'What on earth about?'

Prior answered, 'We are investigating the death of John Wright, madam. We think that Mr. Miles may have some information that will help our enquiry.'

Her frown deepened. 'We hardly knew John Wright. My John had nothing to do with his death.'

'No madam, we are not suggesting that he did. But he may be able to provide us with some background information.'

Miles said, 'It's OK, Mary. I'll talk to them in the kitchen.' She nodded reluctantly and stepped back to let them pass.

Miles led the way towards the rear of the house. The sound of a TV and children's laughter came through a closed door on his left as they passed. The door on the other side of the hall was open. Prior glanced in. An elderly woman sitting in a comfortable chair looked back at him.

Miles said, 'You look after your mother, Mary, I'll deal with this.'

'No,' she replied sternly, 'I want to know what this is about.'

Miles sighed and led the way through to a large kitchen. He pointed to chairs arranged around a pine kitchen table and invited them to sit down. He joined them but the woman stood in the doorway with her arms crossed over her large bosom. 'Now what exactly is this about?' she asked brusquely.

Prior looked at Miles. 'We understand you are a member of the village branch of the Cornwall Society, Mr Miles.'

'Yes, that's right, I'm the secretary.'

'And you lecture at Truro College?'

'I do indeed. I am a lecturer in the history department.'

'We understand that you applied for permission to carry out an archaeological dig on the Sinclair Estate. An ancient settlement?'

'Ah!' Miles almost sighed with relief. 'So that's what this is about. Yes, that was on behalf of the college.

'We are interested to know what you think you might find there.'

Miles smiled. Mrs Miles visibly relaxed. He said, 'There have been several aerial surveys carried out in the past five years. These cover the whole of the South West. Twelve sites have been identified as being late Bronze Age or early Iron Age settlements. Some eight have been excavated so far. Cedric Sinclair refused us permission to dig on his land.'

'What did you hope to find there exactly?'

Miles smiled. 'How much do you know about your ancient history, Chief Inspector?

'Very little, I'm afraid. But I'm willing to learn.'

There was a stirring in the doorway and Mrs Miles said, 'I'll leave you to it John, I'll be in the front room with mum.'

Miles nodded. As she left, he seemed to relax. 'We have Mary's mother staying with us, she's not well.'

'I see. I hope this isn't too inconvenient Mr Miles.'

Miles shook his head vigorously. 'Not at all.' He glanced along the corridor to check that his wife had gone out of hearing and added, 'Its welcome really, the old dear's a bit difficult.'

Prior smiled and nodded.

Miles continued, 'Now, your question. The University of the South West is co-ordinating a programme of excavations that is attempting to get a clearer picture of our Celtic history. We at Truro College are co-operating in this area.'

Prior nodded.

Miles scratched his chin. 'The Celts originated probably in Eastern Europe. By 3,000 BC they had spread across just about the whole of the continent. The latest thinking is that they arrived here in the British Isles around 2,000 BC, that is the late Bronze Age.'

Prior nodded encouragingly.

'They were farmers but with bronze tools, not that efficient. They mostly grazed cattle without a great deal of cultivation. The Iron Age started about 1,500 BC and brought changes with it. With iron tools and implements farming methods improved. People became richer and more settled. This in turn created a problem. The Celts were never organised into a nation of any kind; they lived in isolated tribes and were always fighting with each other. Now they had iron swords and spear tips and more to fight over, the fighting became even fiercer.

They lived in hill forts or 'rounds'. The more they had to protect, the greater the fortifications. In addition to wooden stockades they had lines of earthworks and ditches. Each tribe defended what was theirs from the tribes around them.

As time went by their lives became more sophisticated. What we are seeking to do is to map their development. Each new excavation adds to the knowledge we have of that development. Sadly, Mr Sinclair would not co-operate so we are not able to find out exactly what is there.'

'Yes, I gather he turned you down.'

Miles nodded. 'In the college library we have aerial photographs that clearly show the outline of a large settlement on the estate, in fact, on the hill above the house.'

It was Prior's turn to nod. 'What brought us here Mr Miles, is the nature of Wright's death. His head was cut off and impaled on a stake on the gate of the estate. I seem to remember that the Celts did that with the heads of their enemies.'

Miles smiled grimly. 'Yes, they did indeed, they were a bloodthirsty lot.'

'Two questions then Mr. Miles: why did they do that: and are there any local groups who might want to imitate that kind of behaviour: cults, that sort of thing?'

Miles shook his head. 'No, none that I know of. But your first question, why did they do that? Not that easy to answer. The Celts had no written language, so there are no records of their customs beyond what others have written about them and that's not always reliable. Historians have a theory. Most agree that they were a spiritual people and deeply religious. They believed that when their enemies were killed in battle, their spirits lived on. There is the suggestion that they put the heads of the bravest on their gateposts to have the spirits of the slain keep their enemies at bay. It is also thought that they put some heads in their wells. When they drank the water from the wells they would drink the courage of the slain.'

Siobhan screwed up her nose in distaste, 'So this could be a warning, Mr Miles, telling their enemies to keep out?'

Miles grinned and shook his head. 'My field is ancient history. I can't tell you what modern man might do. I can tell you that there are no cults in this area. The nearest are on the Lizard peninsula and they certainly don't kill people, let alone cut their heads off'

Siobhan probed deeper. 'What about ancient burial sites? Where would the Celts have buried their dead?'

'Somewhere outside the round but nearby. The dead would have a place set aside for them, just as we do today.'

'How would you recognise the burial sites?'

'Stone. They usually covered the bodies in stone coffins. A death was considered permanent it was customary to bury the person's belongings with him. Life was temporary so they lived in wooden dwellings, until much later when they turned to more solid building materials.'

Prior intervened. 'So, if they were rich there might be treasure in the graves?'

Miles smiled. 'When the very rich were buried, maybe, but such finds are very rare. It wasn't only in Egypt that grave robbers operated. And there weren't that many Celts that were very rich. As I've said they lived in isolated groups and the groups were rarely large. There are a few places in Europe where such rich finds have been made but only a very few.'

'I'll be frank with you Mr Miles; we are looking for a motive for the killing. If there was a rich burial site on the estate and people were fighting over it, that might be a motive, might it not?

'Anything's possible I suppose. Without examining the site I couldn't answer that question. But I think it unlikely.'

'One other thing, we found a stone cross in a bramble patch down by the stream. What would be the significance of that?'

Miles frowned. 'What kind of cross?'

Siobhan turned to the page in her notebook where she had sketched the cross and showed it to him.

He nodded. 'The design is quite old I would say.' He paused, then added, 'Hmm, interesting.'

They waited for him to go on.

Miles eventually looked up. 'Yes, the design could be pre-Roman.'

'And the significance?'

'Well, the circle almost certainly represents the sun and the crossed lines the summer and winter solstices and equinoxes. Impossible to say its actual significance. These things have been found wherever the Celts lived. Without a close scrutiny of the whole area I wouldn't be able to say why it is where you say it is.'

'Couldn't you make a guess?'

'Hardly, Chief Inspector, hardly. I am a scientist and we try not to make guesses. I'd say the design is probably pre-Christian.' He pointed to the drawing, 'You see this is a simple cross in a circle. When the Christians came they extended the upright arm below the circle to resemble the cross of Jesus.' He paused. Then he shook his head and added, 'But why it's in that location, I've no idea. It could be for any number of reasons.'

Prior sat for a few moments but could think of no other questions to ask. He glanced at Siobhan, who shook her head. He smiled. 'Thank you, Mr Miles, you have been very helpful.'

Miles returned the smile. 'One piece of sky in a jigsaw puzzle hardly gives one a clue as to the picture. That's why we want to excavate the site. The more pieces we have, the clearer the picture.'

Prior nodded. 'I see your point. Thank you for your time.'

As they got up to leave, Mrs Miles appeared as if by magic to usher them out of the cottage.

Walking back to their car Siobhan said, 'You can see who wears the trousers in that household.'

Prior nodded. 'There is another way of putting it. He might actually wear them but she tells him which pair to put on.'

It was Siobhan's turn to smile. 'I'll remember that one, sir, some of the men I meet haven't got a clue how to dress.' She paused for a moment. Then in a more serious tone, 'His information wasn't worth a lot was it?'

'No, not as far as the case is concerned. Interesting though.'

'First we'll check back at the pub, then home to get some sleep.'

*

An hour later Siobhan arrived at her small flat in the centre of Truro. She was too tired eat or drink. She just quickly brushed her teeth and flopped onto her bed. But sleep wouldn't come immediately. Her mind kept pulling up pictures of the head on the stake. Eventually she dropped off but the image appeared in her dreams. When the alarm went the next morning, she woke feeling washed-out and still tired.

12. Home affairs.

'All things one has forgotten scream for help in dreams.'

Alias Connetti 1905-94

Wednesday night.

Prior looked at his watch as he arrived home, it said 11.32pm. He had been on the case for over 16 hours. Weariness made his shoulders droop as he walked to his front door. He took a deep breath as he crossed the threshold and entered the comfort of his home.

The house was silent and just a dim light showed through the open doorway on his right. He tiptoed into the room and saw his wife, Jeanette, sleeping on the couch. He paused for a moment to look at her. She was his best friend. But there was an enormous bonus for him; she was the most beautiful woman he had ever met. Smiling at the thought, he knelt down beside her and kissed her cheek. She stirred but her eyes remained closed. 'Is that you, Matthew?'
'I hope so or there's something you're not telling me.'

She frowned and slowly sat up. 'I'd certainly find the time, wouldn't I? Why are you so late?'

'Sorry, love, it's this damned bodiless head. We haven't got anywhere with it yet.'

'You must be tired.'

'Yes, knackered,' he replied. 'How are the girls, how did it go at the school?'

'They're fine. They were disappointed you weren't there. They're both doing well with their studies.'

'That's good. I'll make a fuss of them over breakfast.'

'What time is it? I'll make you something to eat.'

'No need, love. I had a sandwich in the pub. It's just after 11.30.'

'I thought I smelled drink on you.' She said it with just a hint of recrimination.

'Yes, the village pub was the last place the victim was seen alive.'

'It's horrible Matthew, who could have done such a thing?'

'I think this is going to be a difficult one; we haven't got a clue at the moment, literally.' He paused and then added, 'Are you coming to bed, I'll lock up?'

He went around the house checking the windows and doors, then mounted the stairs. He went into each of his children's rooms, pulling their duvets up to their chins and kissing their foreheads. Then to the bathroom where he took a long hot shower.

When he and his wife were lying side by side in their bed, she turned towards him. 'Do you want to talk about it love?'

'Not really, I just need a big hug.'

She snuggled up to him. 'Is that all you need?'

He kissed her gently on her forehead. 'That's all I've got the energy for.'

Nothing more was said. She held him close, softly stroking his hair. Within a few minutes he was asleep. When she heard his gentle snoring she carefully disengaged herself, turned over and went to sleep. She stirred several times during the night when she heard him groaning but he didn't wake. When the alarm woke him the next morning he had no memory of the demons that had visited him during the night.

Suddenly a weight descended onto his chest. 'Daddy, daddy, wake up. Miss Harris says she likes my work. Why weren't you there?'

He groaned. 'You're getting too big to leap on me like that tiger, you'll break something.' He sat up and gave her a hug. 'Mummy told me how well you are doing. I'm very proud of you and Samantha. This weekend I'm taking you all out for lunch and you can choose the restaurant. '

'Goody, goody, MacDonald's.'

There was a groan from the bed beside him. 'Now look what you've done.'

Prior laughed. 'I thought you liked the occasional beef burger.'

She kicked him under the bedclothes. 'Not that kind of burger, thank you.'

'What kind of burger do you like mummy?' Natalie asked with a child's innocence.

'Homemade ones, Natalie.'

Their other daughter, Samantha, appeared in the doorway. Prior held out his arms, 'Hello princess, have you got a hug for me?'

She ran forward and hugged him. Natalie, the eldest, was ten going on sixteen, her sister, Samantha a shy eight. Prior sat her down on the bed and swung his feet to the floor. 'Right, if you ladies will give me ten minutes to shave, you can tell me about your schoolwork over breakfast. Now, you two go and clean your teeth, give mummy five minutes to wake up.'

Over breakfast he listened to their happy chatter whilst he munched his toast. He knew from experience that these twenty minutes of sanity would sustain him during the day to come.

Then the phone rang.

Natalie jumped up shouting, 'I'll get it. Let me get it.' She picked up the receiver and said in a fair imitation of Patricia Routledge's tone. 'The Prior residence, Natalie speaking.' Prior shared a smile with his wife.

The child held the phone out towards her father. 'It's for you, daddy, it's a woman.'

The spell was broken. He went to the phone. 'Prior,'

'Hello, sir, Inspector Fields here. We've found a body; it washed up at St Mawes. It has no head; we think it must be John Wright.'

Watching him, Jeanette saw his expression change. Into the phone he said, 'Give me the details.'

He listened as Fields gave him the exact location. 'Right, I'm on my way. Phone DS Williams and have her meet me there.'

He kissed the girls and whispered into his wife's ear as she hugged him, 'They've found the rest of the body, I must go.'

She kissed him. 'Phone me when you can. Try to be early tonight and bring Siobhan with you. You two have to have a proper meal.'

His protective shell disappeared again for a moment as he gave her a huge smile. 'I'll do my very best. You girls have a good day.'

Then he was gone.

13. The torso.

"You know,' he said very gravely
'It is one of the most serious things
That can possibly happen to one
To get one's head cut off."
Lewis Carroll. Through the looking glass.

Thursday 8am.

As he drove to St Mawes, Prior was thinking about where
the body might have been put in the water. St Mawes stood
on a headland opposite Falmouth. Between the two ran the
Carrick Roads. But this was not a single river mouth; it was
part of an intricate system of rivers, streams, broads and
marshes that eventually fed into the English Channel at the
Fal Estuary.

When the world's major landmasses were being formed
in the distant past, the tectonic plates of Northern Europe
had rubbed together and pushed up a range of rock formations in this part of the land. Later, at the end of the

last ice age, sea levels had risen, cutting the British Isles off from continental Europe. The sea began pounding at the newly-formed coastline. Over the millennia, it had eroded many of the softer rock formations, leaving a broken, fractured coastline.

The result is a palaeontologist's dream. Further east in Dorset and Devon is a stretch called the Jurassic coast. In South Cornwall the line between land and sea is less distinct and in places the sea penetrates deep into the land between the rocky outbreaks. The Carrick Roads itself was formed when the melt from the last ice age flooded the huge valley carved out by a glacier from an even more ancient ice age.

The coast is a navigator's nightmare, both on the sea and on land. At sea there are hundreds of shipwrecks along the treacherous coast. On land there are few direct routes between any two places. St Mawes is only nine miles from Truro as the crow flies. But by road it is twice that. The narrow lane meanders back and forth as it skirts the complicated system of waterways and marshland between. Prior had no doubt that the torso would have been deposited in the water somewhere along the route he was driving. But where exactly was almost impossible to calculate. This close to the coast, the waterways and marshland were tidal and it was difficult to calculate how far a body would have travelled once in the water. There were so many variables; the state of the tide when the body went in; the height of the tide which varied even in each month; whether the body had been weighted down with anything or had snagged somewhere along its travels. He quickly gave up trying to pinpoint where the torso might have been put in. Even an expert could have made only an educated guess.

Trying to think positively, he consoled himself with the thought that at least finding the body might enable them to discover the cause of Wright's death and a closer approximation of the time of it. The fact that they knew when Wright had eaten his last meal would help. The stomach digests food at a measurable rate, a process that ceases abruptly with death.

As Prior entered St Mawes he turned right towards the castle. He knew from visiting the place with his family that it had been part of the old maritime defences along the coast. Together with a sister fort, Pendennis Castle, on the headland the other side of the Roads, it commanded the entrance to the whole of the estuary.

He smiled as he remembered the history lesson he had given the girls. Reading from a tourist brochure, he'd told them it had been built in the mid-sixteenth century by Henry VIII as defence against Catholic France and Spain. It had led to a long and complicated explanation as to why they would want to invade England and why Henry had had so many wives.

His mind came back to the present as he descended the steep hill towards the old fort. To his right were the Carrick Roads, to the front and left, the open estuary. The surface of the water had been whipped into whitecaps by the stiff autumn breeze. The tide was in full ebb and was racing towards the sea to his left. Ahead of him was the round stone fort. It was now a tourist attraction and a car park had been built beside it.

There were three police vehicles and an ambulance already in the car park. A uniformed constable stood talking to a small group of people who had obviously gathered to catch a glimpse of the washed-up torso. Prior never ceased to wonder at the public's morbid curiosity. He turned into the car park and switched off the engine. As he got out the constable approached him. Not recognising him, Prior produced his warrant card and introduced himself.

The constable pointed. 'The body's down there, sir, on the beach.'

Following his pointed finger, Prior saw below him a rocky ledge just above the waterline that jutted out from the steep bank beneath where they stood. A group of uniformed police and medics surrounded a shape draped in a tarpaulin, lying on the rocks.

Prior nodded and looked around him. The rocky beach would not be visible from the road above. 'Right, get those people out of the car park, this is not a peep show. And the only people you let in are my team, the CSIs and the pathologist. I'll send you some help. I do not want to even smell the media when they arrive. You can bet your bottom dollar they will be here soon like the pack of vultures they are. Keep them back on the road, do you understand?'

'Yes sir.'

There were no stairs leading down to the narrow beach; Prior scrambled down the steep bank cursing as his shoes and trousers were soon covered in mud. He found himself on the narrow rocky ledge just inches above the waterline. The rocks were wet and slippery. Clearly they had only been uncovered by the falling tide in the last hour or so.

One of the uniformed figures approached him, the stripes on his sleeve identifying him as a sergeant. Prior introduced himself, 'Get your constables up there and keep the public back out of sight. The damned media will be here soon, determined to get pictures. Make sure they don't get near. I don't want anyone interfering with my forensic team while they are doing their job.'

The sergeant nodded diplomatically and went to do his bidding.

Prior turned to the medics. 'What can you tell me?'

'Well, apart from the missing head, he has a wound in his chest. Probably a stab wound but don't quote me.'

Prior nodded. 'Anything else?'

'He hasn't been in the water long; the crabs and fish haven't had much of a go at him.'

Prior nodded again and looked up at the car park which was now empty. He lifted a corner of the tarpaulin. The body was fully clothed. A pair of trainers, socks and blue jeans covered the lower half while above that was a crew neck sweater and Anorak. This matched the clothes Jenna had said Wright was wearing two nights ago. The head was indeed missing with the neck ending in jagged edges. The skin had been turned a dirty off-white colour by immersion in the water.

Replacing the tarpaulin he turned to the police sergeant. 'Has the clothing been searched?'

'No, sir, we waited for you.'

'Good, we'll leave that to my SOCO. Who discovered the body?'

'A woman walking her dog, just after dawn.' He looked at his watch, 'About an hour ago sir.'

Prior nodded. 'Are you familiar with the tides, sergeant?'

'Yes, sir.'

'Suppose the body was put in the water something over 24 hours ago. Any idea where it might have been put in?'

The sergeant blew out his cheeks and shook his head. 'Upstream somewhere. Beyond that, your guess is as good as mine, sir.'

'How can you be certain it was upstream?'

'Ninety-nine percent certain. It's the configuration of the coast here. The castle here is on a promontory that juts out, so when the tide's flowing it pushes the water across to the other side of the Roads. Anything floating in on the tide is dumped on the beach across there. Only when it's ebbing is it pushed to this side.'

'That makes sense. If your life depended on it, sergeant, where would you say the body was put in the water?'

'One of the tidal rivers that flow into the Roads. More than that I couldn't say even if my life did depend on it.'

'OK, thanks, I gathered that was the case but I had to confirm it.'

Ten minutes later Siobhan arrived closely followed by the CSIs, George Bailey and Sally Hinds. Siobhan looked tired, yet freshly turned out. Her hair was still wet from the shower. She too had mud smears on her slacks from the scramble down the bank.

He smiled at her. 'You were right yesterday about the mountaineering, Siobhan. Still, you can claim for the dry cleaning.'

She nodded without returning his smile. 'Morning, sir, what do you want me to do?'

'Have a look at the grisly remains then you can go back up to the road. There's a woman there who discovered the body. We'll need a statement from her.'

She opened her mouth to speak, then closed it again.

He turned to the SOCO'. Bailey was his usual cheerful self. 'A day at the seaside at the public's expense guv. I'm glad I moved down here, we don't get to do this in the big smoke. What's new?'

Prior smiled. 'If you stop rabbiting I'll tell you. Washed ashore, probably from one of the rivers feeding into the Roads. It looks like our body, the clothes match. If there ever was any doubt. The locals haven't touched it but the medics have done their thing. The clothing hasn't been searched, we've left that to you. See if there's any identification on him. Oh, and there should be a mobile phone. It's up to you if you need a tent but don't make a three-ringed circus out of it.'

'Gotcha, guv. Leave it to us. You just enjoy the view.'

Prior smiled again. Bailey managed to lighten his mood even when standing over a headless corpse.

Professor Penhallon, the pathologist, arrived. Forewarned, he was dressed in overalls and Wellington boots. Having conducted his examination he said to Prior, 'You know, Matthew it's not often I have to declare the same person dead twice. But I have to say for the record that this piece of the corpse is just as dead as the head was.'

'No surprises then Professor?'

'None that I can see, we'll find out more at the autopsy. Apart from the lack of a head, the only obvious wound is that in his chest. Looks like a knife wound but we'll see when we look inside, won't we?'

'When will you do the post-mortem?'

'Now that we've got the body and the head, we'll do them together. First thing tomorrow morning, I've got a full day today.'

'Is there no way you can do it today?'

'Strange as it may seem, Matthew, the coroner has priority over even you. I have an inquest to give evidence at, a fatal accident the other side of St Austell. I also have a morgue full of bodies and my assistant is off sick with the damned flu. You will just have to wait your turn.'

'OK, I'll see you in the morning Professor.'

Penhallon gave him a grim smile. 'Don't be late Matthew or I'll have to start carving without you.'

Prior did not appreciate Penhallon's morbid humour any more than DS Williams did but made no comment. He spent another hour at the scene then left to drive to Truro. He despatched Siobhan back to the mobile enquiry van on the Sinclair Estate. As he reached his car, several cameras were turned in his direction and questions were shouted at him. The press had arrived in force. There were a dozen of them at the entrance to the car park, held back by the uniforms he had posted there. He ignored them and they reluctantly made a path for his car as he drove through.

Prior had a particular aversion to the media. Early in his career a friend and colleague had committed suicide partly as the result of an article in a Sunday newspaper. That incident remained in his mind and had been reinforced several times since. The words of an old detective who had been his mentor had stuck in his mind: 'Their job is to sell newspapers and TV programmes. They have little interest in the truth, only in what will grab the public's interest and increase their circulation. I wouldn't trust them any further than I could throw them.'

As Prior drove, his mind was busy processing the new information revealed by the finding of the body. He now knew that the victim had three wounds: a bruise on the back of the head, a stab wound in the chest, and the decapitation; probably inflicted in that order. The lad's wallet, containing just a single £5 note and a bank debit card, had been found in his back pocket and he had been wearing a cheap wristwatch. In his jeans pockets was just some small change, a house key and a handkerchief. His mobile phone was missing.

What did this tell him? Not a great deal that he didn't already know or had worked out. The blow to the head was probably inflicted when he was abducted, the other wounds probably later, but he still didn't have a clue where or why. The other stuff on the body told him nothing. Perhaps the missing mobile phone was significant but it could just as easily have slipped out of his pocket when he was put in the water or at some time during the abduction. He gave a deep sigh and concentrated on his driving.

14. The Assistant Chief Constable.

'If you gently grasp a nettle it'll sting you for your pains;
Grasp it like a lad of mettle, an as soft as silk remains.'

16th century proverb.

Arriving at Truro Police Station, Prior went straight to his office to check on his deputy, DI Monk. The man was nowhere to be found and Prior noted the in-tray was filling up. Going into the general CID office, he spoke to Bill Medway, one of his DSs. 'Where's Mr. Monk, Bill?'

'Said he'd be late in, sir, making a call on the way.'

Returning to his office, he checked Monk's diary. There was no appointment for this morning shown in it. Prior had a frown on his face as he went upstairs to Superintendent Owen's office. She greeted him warmly and poured him a coffee. She was as particular about the coffee she drank as she was about most things and made her own brew of a mellow Columbian bean that she ground herself.

Patricia Owen was in her mid-forties and destined for the very top in her profession. She had a reputation that she had earned, learning her trade as she rose through the ranks. A good administrator, she was as at home with her constables as she was with politicians. She pushed the people who worked for her to their limits but not beyond; in return she looked after their welfare. She was liked and respected by all who came in contact with her. She had a trim figure, a plain face and wore her grey-black hair short.

There was much speculation in the lower ranks about her love life. The general consensus of opinion was that she was a lesbian. As far as Prior was concerned that was her business. He considered her a friend as well as a colleague. But strictly within the limits imposed by their roles in the force. As his divisional commander she pushed him just as hard as she pushed all those under her command.

When they were both seated in comfortable chairs, she said, 'So Matthew, you've had a busy 24 hours. Tell me what you have.'

He spent two minutes bringing her up to date, then summarised, 'There's nothing so far to indicate a motive or a suspect. Apart from a few slivers of wood on the iron crossbar on the gate and the wounds to the corpse we have no forensic evidence. And, after he left the pub at ten that night, there are no witnesses as to where he went. There's still the autopsy, of course, that might come up with something. But, as the body was in sea water for over twenty-four hours, I don't think we're going to get much more from that other than the time and cause of death.'

He paused and sipped his coffee. 'The only things we have remotely resembling clues are: one, the bizarre display of the severed head and its location; two, his missing mobile phone as it wasn't found on the body; and three, a promise he made to his girlfriend that he had a surprise for her.'

'Not very promising then,' Owen responded. 'What are your next steps?'

He took another sip of the excellent coffee before replying, 'I'm going to find out more about the victim and about the Sinclair Estate. There has to be some connection. The other thing we can't work out is whether Wright was abducted or willingly went off to meet someone. Siobhan and I spent time in the village and there's nowhere that you could effectively set up an ambush without the risk of being spotted. You know what country folk are like and no-one seems to have seen anything. There was no sign of a struggle at the cottage but he did take a blow to the back of his head at some stage. So we're looking at the possibility that he voluntarily went to meet someone elsewhere then got clobbered.'

'Why would he do that do you think? Didn't you say that he told his partner that he was going to have an early night. Why would he lie to her?'

'Yes, ma'am. But all we have to go on is this surprise he was preparing for her. Maybe he would have told her a little porky if he was going to collect her surprise.'

'It's a bit thin isn't it, Matthew?'

'About as thin as it gets. We're almost clutching at straws, ma'am but there's nothing else to go on except the connection with the estate.'

Owen nodded slowly and sat thinking for a moment. 'A couple of things, Matthew. The press conference; I've arranged it for five this afternoon. Mr Stapleton wants you to brief him before it starts. He wants you to prepare a statement to give them and he wants to see it beforehand. I know you haven't much time for reporters but you can't avoid this one.'

'Yes, ma'am I realise that. Is Stapleton going to be there?'

'No, he has another engagement but he insists on speaking to you before it starts. That's the other thing, Matthew. He's a personal friend of Mr Sinclair. Tread very carefully. He wants you to meet him here in my office at 4.30.'

Prior simply nodded, keeping his thoughts to himself.

Owen smiled, reading his mind. She continued on another vein, 'Is there anything else you need?'

He smiled wanly. 'Apart from divine guidance, you mean? No, nothing I can think of.'

'There's one thing that comes to my mind Matthew, a psychological profiler. I'm wary of the mumbo-jumbo some of them put about but this bizarre display of the severed head must have some significance.'

Prior's reply was diplomatic, 'I suppose that's possible, ma'am.'

She frowned, anticipating his cynicism. 'I have someone in mind, just give her a chance; I've had good reports on her contributions elsewhere.'

'I'll do my best, as long as she doesn't get under my feet. And I think you're right about the significance, there may be even an historic one. We've already had a word with the historian from Truro College who wants to excavate on the estate. He confirmed this is something the Celts used to do with the heads of their enemies.'

'OK, you've got your hands full; I won't delay you any longer. I'll arrange for the profiler to come and see you.' She smiled. 'Perhaps she'll be as good as the guy on TV. What's his name, the one in Wire in the Blood?'

Prior smiled with her, 'Or Cracker. He was good although both of them seem to have a few personal problems. Perhaps it goes with the job.'

They both laughed as Prior left her office.

He drove to the mobile incident room parked on the Sinclair Estate. Quigley handed him a sheath of messages.

He took them without glancing at them. 'Albert, send a team back to the Wright cottage. Siobhan and I had a look around but this time I want it gone over properly. See if there's anything we missed. Where is she by the way?'

'She took a walk up the hill sir. Said she was going to look for a fort or something.' He grinned as he said it.

Prior returned the grin. 'I hope she remembered her wellies this time.'

He walked to his tiny office, reading the messages as he went. Squeezing himself behind the desk he picked up the phone and dialled the ACCs office. He was put through immediately.

'Matthew, how are you?'

'Well, sir and you?'

'Fine, thank you. How is your enquiry going?'

'Slowly, sir, not much to go on, I'm afraid.'

There was a moment's silence at the other end of the line, then, 'A delicate matter, Matthew. You know I wouldn't dream of interfering with your enquiry, don't you?'

'Yes, sir,' Prior replied, knowing full well that he would.

'I've had Mr Sinclair on the phone. He's very concerned about the incident. Tread very carefully Matthew, he has a lot of influence in the county.'

'Yes sir.' Prior was determined not to help Stapleton say what he was going to say.

At the other end of the line Stapleton cleared his throat. 'Mr Sinclair seems to have got the impression that you view him as a suspect.'

'Him and everyone else. At the moment there is very little to go on. We have to consider the fact that the head was impaled on his gate and that the victim worked there as having some significance.'

'Yes, of course. But I'm sure that Mr Sinclair had nothing to do with the murder, aren't you?'

Prior made no reply.

'What possible motive could he have?'

'I've no idea, sir. But then I can't find anyone with a motive at the moment.'

'What I'm saying is that you should be very careful how you deal with Mr Sinclair.'

Now we are getting to the nitty-gritty, Prior thought. He chose his words carefully, 'I wouldn't be doing my duty if I didn't look into all the possibilities, sir.'

'You know damned well what I'm saying, do not do something that might damage your career. The man is obviously above suspicion. I know him personally, he is not a murderer.'

'I hear what you say, sir.'

'Keep me informed of your progress. I'll see you at 4.30 in Owen's office.' The line went dead.

Prior slammed the receiver down. 'Damn, damn, damn!'

He looked up to see Siobhan standing in the doorway. Keeping a straight face she said, 'Is it safe to come in, sir?'

'Don't you bloody well start, Siobhan; that was the ACC telling me that his friend, Sinclair wouldn't dream of killing anyone. He warned me off. How am I supposed to carry out an investigation without upsetting anyone?'

'Did he say who Sinclair's visitors were on the night of the murder?'

'No. And I was so damned angry I forgot to ask him if he had.'

Siobhan paused for a long moment. Then she said, 'Not a good time to tell you then sir, Mr Sinclair would like to see you.'

'Well he can bloody well wait until I've had a cup of coffee.'

He sat back in his chair with a sigh. But there wasn't much space and his head hit the wall. 'Ouch!' He rubbed the back of his head and looked at Siobhan.

She stood, suppressing a smile.

Eventually he grinned. 'Politicians, the landed gentry and reporters. What a wonderful world it would be without them.' They both laughed, relieving his tension.

DC Waring appeared behind Siobhan with two cups of coffee. She moved aside and he deposited them on Prior's desk. 'Thank you, Alan,' Prior said.

Waring smiled and quickly left.

Prior looked at his DS. 'So, Siobhan, I hear you've been walking in the hills, hunting for treasure no doubt. I notice you brought your wellies this time.'

She smiled and sat in the only other chair in the cubicle. 'Enervating sir, the fresh air I mean.'

'Enervating? Where'd you pick that one up? What did you find up there?'

'Just a few bumps and hollows, sir.'

He smiled, 'Bumps and hollows, eh? That's interesting. No buried treasure though?'

She ignored his innuendo and said primly, 'No but there are signs of digging.'

'Really? Tell me more.'

'There isn't much more to tell. I found a patch of disturbed ground. It looks as if someone dug a large hole then refilled it. That's all.'

'It wasn't grave-shaped was it?'

'No, roughly round, about eight feet across.'

'Hmm. I wonder who did the digging?'

'Me too. Do you think there might be something in this treasure theory?'

'Who knows? I still haven't got a bloody clue what we're dealing with here, have you?'

She shook her head. 'There is something else, sir.'

'Yes?'

'While I was up there, Sinclair came along with his dog. He was quite huffy, asked me what I was doing up there. That's when he told me he wants to see you.'

'That's interesting, especially after the conversation I've just had with the ACC. I think I want a record of this meeting. I'll take the tape-recorder.'

Sinclair received them in the same room as he had on their first interview. But that was the only similarity to the first meeting. They were offered no refreshments and the man's manner was abrupt to say the least. He was dressed in the manner of the country gentleman. Brown shoes, twill trousers and a dogtooth jacket over collar and tie. The whole ensemble was in soft shades of brown and screamed 'look at me, I'm a rich landowner'. While those in cities and towns followed the dictates of fashion, those in the country lived comfortably in the past.

Sinclair offered no greeting, opening the conversation with, 'How is your investigation progressing, Chief Inspector?'

'It's rather early to say, sir. But we are getting a clearer picture of what occurred.' He produced a small tape recorder and placed it on the table between them. 'I hope you don't mind if I record our conversation, it saves my sergeant making notes.'

This seemed to put Sinclair on the back foot. He said, 'Am I to take it that I am a suspect in this enquiry, Chief Inspector?'

'Not at all, sir. It was you that asked to see me, this is not an interrogation. The tape recorder is simply a labour-saving device to make sure we don't forget anything.'

Sinclair paused for a moment clearly seeking a reason to object to the tape recorder. Just as clearly he was unable to find one. Then he asked, 'Do you have a suspect?'

'Several at the moment, sir.'

'And where is your investigation leading you, Chief Inspector?'

Ignoring the question, Prior asked. 'Might I ask you a few questions, sir?'

'I know nothing at all about this murder. You would be better advised to be out looking for the killer.'

'Yes, sir, but you asked to see me, remember? And you might be able to help give us a direction in which to look as this clearly has some connection with your estate.'

Through his teeth, Sinclair said, 'What exactly is it you want to know?'

'You mentioned yesterday that you had refused permission for some archaeologists to dig on the estate?'

'Yes, what has that to do with your enquiry?'

'Yet someone has been digging up on the hill. Have you any idea who that was?'

Sinclair's face visibly reddened with anger, 'I can't see what on earth that has to do with Wright's murder.'

'Nor can I at the moment, sir, which is why I'm asking the question. Do you know who was digging up there on the hill?'

'I have neither the time nor the inclination to satisfy your idle curiosity. If that's all you have to talk about, this interview is over.'

'Professional curiosity, sir, not idle. The head was spiked on your gate. I have no choice but to follow that line of enquiry.'

'No one is digging on the estate and that's an end to the matter. Now you have completed your interviews with the farm workers, I see no reason for your caravan to remain on the estate. Please have it removed.'

'Immediately, sir, I'll have the towing unit come and take it away. Thank you for your co-operation.' He was careful to say this without any intonation.

'Enough of your sarcasm, Chief Inspector, your Chief Constable will hear of this.'

'Thank you, sir. I'll see that he gets a copy of the tape.' Prior picked it up and switched it off.

Prior saw immediately from the expression on Sinclair's face that he had won a victory; there was nothing on the tape that could come back at him.

When they reached the fresh air, Siobhan said, 'Well, he's had a change of heart.'

'Yes, I wonder why? I wasn't rude to him; he must have something to hide.'

'Perhaps he's too used to the serfs tipping their caps to him.'

'No, I think it's more than that, he was on the attack as soon as we arrived. I'm glad I thought to bring the tape recorder.'

Away from Prior's investigation a series of phone calls took place. These culminated in Superintendent Owen being summoned to ACC Stapleton's office.

The moment she walked through the door the ACC said, 'I think you should remove Chief Inspector Prior from this investigation.'

She frowned, 'On what grounds, sir?'

'On the grounds that the man is completely lacking in tact. I've had a complaint from Mr Sinclair.'

'What was the substance of the complaint, sir?'

He says that Prior was extremely rude to him and treated him like a suspect.'

'In what way, sir, specifically.'

'He insisted on taping the interview and questioning him as if he were a criminal.'

'Matthew Prior may have a few rough edges, sir, but he's a damned good detective. I'll ask him for the tape and see what it contains.'

'Bring the tape to me Patricia. And let me give you some advice. Don't go out on a limb for Prior; you have a promising career ahead of you.'

Owen bristled. 'My career, as you put it, sir, is based on my integrity. I will not do anything to compromise that. But nor will I condemn an officer under my command without a proper enquiry. If I take him off the investigation without good cause that would damage his reputation. I'll let you have a copy of the tape. The original, I'll give to the officer assigned to investigate the complaint, if it's a formal complaint that is.'

Stapleton looked at her for a long moment. 'There's no need to bother the Chief, Patricia. Just bring me the tape. And be very careful, Superintendent, we all need friends in order to get on in this job. Make sure you choose the right ones.'

Owen smiled to herself, although her face showed no sign of it. There obviously was no official complaint, simply an attempt to tap into the old boys' network. She knew that the Chief Constable would not stand for such nonsense. She said, 'I'll bring you a copy, sir. As you know, the original must be considered evidence and should remain with the investigating officer.' She got up and left the office without another word.

Returning to her office she made careful notes of the interview. She was shrewd enough to know that her immediate superior could easily damage her prospects. She also knew how to defend herself from any frivolous allegations. Putting that aside, she too was curious about Sinclair's change of heart. Did he indeed have something to hide?

15. The Press Conference.

'There are laws to protect the freedom of the press, but none that are worth anything to protect the public from the press.'

Mark Twain.

Thursday afternoon.

Prior arrived at Truro Police Station precisely at 4.30. He went directly to Superintendent Owen's office. The ACC was already there. He nodded curtly in response to Prior's formal greeting. The expression on his face was, to say the least, not friendly. Owen's greeting was warmer. She offered him a coffee and invited him to join them at her low coffee table.

Once they were all seated, Stapleton started, 'Superintendent Owen will conduct the press conference Chief Inspector. I have another engagement. She will invite you to make a statement, I hope you have one prepared.'

Prior replied, 'Yes, sir,' and handed copies to both senior officers. He took note of the fact that he was no longer 'Matthew'. Each read the statement through. Watching Stapleton as he read, Prior noticed a thin film of sweat on his face.

Stapleton looked up. 'This is very bland. Is there nothing else you can tell them?'

'Like what, sir? This is basically all we know.'

Owen intervened, 'Matthew, I think we want to avoid speculation if we possibly can.'

'Yes, ma'am, what do you suggest?'

Stapleton intervened, 'What about the girlfriend? Isn't it likely that she is involved? Isn't that usually the case?'

'In a majority of cases, sir, yes, but there's absolutely no evidence of that in this one. All the evidence we have suggests they had a happy relationship.'

'You've had two full days, Chief Inspector, surely you've come up with something. What have you been doing all that time?'

Prior took a twenty-page report from his briefcase. It was a computer print-out from the murder file detailing every action taken by his team. 'Here is my progress report, sir. I think we have been very thorough. If you think there's anything we've missed, sir, I'd be obliged if you'd point it out to me. There is absolutely no evidence that points to anything in Wright's social life that gives us a sniff of a motive for killing him or to a possible killer.' He paused but Stapleton said nothing.

He continued, 'In fact, his relationship with his partner seems to have been a very happy one, they were both looking forward to becoming parents. There are no indications of rivals for either of their affections and no evidence at all of strife between them. Everyone we've spoken to, including the girlfriend say they were a happy couple.' He carefully avoided saying that the few clues that had pointed to the Sinclair Estate.

There was silence for a long moment. Then Owen tactfully changed the subject. 'I've made arrangements with the profiler, Matthew, I'll bring her along to see you in the morning.'

'Thank you, ma'am. at Mr Sinclair's request we've moved the caravan off the estate. It is now in Penwin Village. We're using the village hall for interviews.'

Stapleton spoke, 'Caravan, Chief Inspector; isn't that a bit flippant?'

'Yes, sir, I suppose it is. That is how Mr Sinclair described the mobile enquiry unit when he told us to move it.'

Stapleton's face reddened. 'I have told you to leave Mr Sinclair out of this enquiry. You will not mention him to the press and any enquiries from them in that direction will be dealt with by Superintendent Owen.'

'I understand that fully, sir. I understand also that you want the tape of my interview with Mr. Sinclair.' He leant forward and put a tape on the table.

Owen quickly picked it up and said, 'I'll make a copy of that, Matthew, and let you have the original back for the evidence file.'

Prior turned to the ACC. 'There is one other thing, sir, something we need to know. I realise I am treading on delicate ground here, but I wouldn't be doing my job properly if I ignored it. Mr Sinclair had guests on the night of the murder; he declined to tell us who they were. As I am not permitted to contact him, I wonder if you might find out who they were and find out if they saw anything when they left through the front gate that night. It is important to narrow down the time the head was mounted there. If they could confirm the time they left and the fact that the head wasn't there then that would help.'

Stapleton glared at him. He said nothing for a long moment. Then, through gritted teeth, he said, 'I will deal with that.'

Owen looked at her watch. Then she said diplomatically, 'It's getting on towards five, sir, hadn't Matthew and I best get to the conference room?'

Stapleton seemed to be having great problems hanging on to his composure. He said, 'Yes, you had better go. Be very careful what you say, Chief Inspector. You could very easily damage your career if you say anything rash to the media.'

Prior took a last sip of his coffee and said nothing. He wondered what was important enough to keep Stapleton away from the conference but was wise enough not to ask. He had pushed the man as far as he safely dare.

*

The conference room was packed. Twenty seats had been arranged facing a low stage and TV cameras and microphones installed. Every seat was filled and in addition a dozen or so more reporters lined the walls. Owen led the way to the stage and she and Prior sat down behind a desk facing the assembled reporters. Cameras focused and lights flashed. Owen cleared her throat, 'Detective Chief Inspector Prior is the officer conducting this enquiry. He will make a short statement then I will invite questions.'

Prior looked at the faces in front of him, then down at his notes. 'As you are no doubt aware a severed head was found impaled on a gatepost at the entrance to the Sinclair Estate at 5.32am on the morning of the 12th. It was identified as the head of John Wright of Penwin Village. At 7.10am this morning the remainder of the corpse was found on a beach below St Mawes Castle. There is a stab wound to the chest that is the probable cause of death. The family have been informed. The autopsy will take place at 9am tomorrow.'

He looked up at the faces in front of him almost defiantly. He was not comfortable thrust into the spotlight with a doctored script. He continued, 'I would like to appeal for witnesses. Mr. Wright was last seen alive at 10pm leaving The Hunters Arms in the village of Penwin. Anyone who saw him subsequently is asked to contact us. In addition anyone who saw a van or a truck in the village at about that time or later between the village and Stag Lane is asked to come forward. The body was most likely placed in one of the rivers feeding into the Carrick Roads. Again, anyone witnessing a strange vehicle anywhere in that vicinity should contact us.

He chose his next words carefully, 'Not to put too fine a point on it, there must have been a great deal of blood spilled, so anyone finding bloody clothing should contact us. All contacts will be treated in the strictest confidence.' He then gave the contact number and finished with a thank you.

The moment he finished speaking there was uproar as thirty-odd reporters each tried to make themselves heard. Owen called for order and said, 'If you have a question, please raise your hand.'

She pointed to a man in the front row who had his hand raised.

The man stood, 'John Harris, Daily Telegraph. 'Chief Inspector, what was the motive for this killing and the bizarre display of the severed head?'

Prior nodded. 'We are considering a number of possible motives.'

Harris who had remained on his feet, said, 'Does that mean you have no idea of the motive?'

Prior kept his cool and there was no inflection in his voice as he replied. 'That means precisely what I said, Mr. Harris. We are considering a number of possible motives.'

Owen pointed to a woman in the second row. She stood, 'Sue Porter, BBC News. 'Is this the work of some religious cult?'

'That's one possibility.'

'What are the others?'

'I'm sure you don't expect me to reveal details of my investigation particularly at such an early stage of the enquiry.'

There was more uproar. Owen waited for it to subside. Then she pointed to a man at the rear of the room who was already standing.

'Bob Miller, News of the World. What you are telling us, Chief Inspector, is that you haven't a clue, isn't it?'

There was a chorus of support from those around him.

Prior waited for it to subside then said, 'I'm sure you heard my answer to the last question; the same answer applies to this one.'

Yet more chaos. Over the noise Miller shouted; 'So it's true, you haven't a clue. Are you sure you're capable of conducting an enquiry like this, you can't have too many murders like this to investigate down here in the sticks?'

Prior waited patiently again for the noise to subside. 'Fortunately we don't get many murders like this anywhere in this country, Mr. Miller, not even in the big cities. In fact, to my certain knowledge, this incident is unique in modern times.'

Owen added, 'Detective Chief Inspector Prior is one of our most experienced detectives, I have every confidence in his ability.'

Well at least she hasn't hung me out to dry was the thought that flew across Prior's mind.

Above the hubbub in the room Miller shouted, 'Why don't you give us something to print? What are you hiding?'

The room fell silent, awaiting his reply.

Prior felt the desperate urge to lick his dry lips, he resisted it knowing the impression it might give. After a long pause, he said between gritted teeth, 'Strange as it may seem to you, Mr. Miller, my priorities are slightly different to yours. My job is to solve the murder and bring the culprit to justice, not to increase the circulation of your newspaper. Now I have told you what I can at this stage and I have nothing to add.'

The room erupted again. Owen waited until it had quietened down. Then she pointed to another man.

He stood and said, 'Phillip Baird, The Times. What is the significance of the location of the severed head? Why was it put on the gatepost of the local landowner?'

Owen put her hand on Prior's arm. She whispered, 'I'll deal with this.' Then into the microphones, 'As far as we know, there is no significance. We think it was chosen at random. We are confident that the landowner has no connection with the killing.'

Baird said, 'Isn't it true that the victim worked on the estate, is that not a connection?'

Owen didn't flinch away from the question. 'This is a small rural community Mr. Baird, many local people work on the estate. We do not see that as significant at this stage.'

Prior seethed inside. Here was Owen toeing the party line and making the local force look like a bunch of idiots.

A woman was next. 'Jill Matthews, The Sun. 'When can we expect an arrest, Chief Inspector?'

'At this stage I'm not prepared to comment. We await the results of the post-mortem and forensic tests.'

Matthews asked her supplementary question, 'I understand the victim's girlfriend is pregnant; how is she taking this?'

'Not well. She's understandably very upset. Fortunately she is very close to her parents and they are caring for her.'

Matthews tried to squeeze in another question but Owen overruled her. She pointed to another man.

He stood, 'Charles Rivers, ITV News. Chief Inspector, your superintendent suggests that there is no connection with the Sinclair Estate, do you share her view?'

Prior said slowly and clearly into the microphones, 'At this stage we have no reason to suspect there is any connection with the estate.'

'But you've no reason to dismiss the possibility, have you?'

Faced with this direct question, Prior was caught truly on the horns of a dilemma; should he publicly disagree with Owen or should he lie. Finally he replied, 'I have no further comment to make on the matter.' Then he sat there thinking he'd taken the coward's way out.

The next question was from a reporter from another of the tabloids. 'Why are you so reluctant to share any information with us, Chief Inspector? Is it because you are frightened of revealing your own incompetence?'

Prior took a deep breath and let it out slowly.

Beside him, Owen whispered, 'Careful, Matthew, don't rise to the bait.'

The room fell silent, waiting for his reply.

Finally he spoke through his teeth, carefully enunciating his words. 'I'm sure your bullying tactics are successful when questioning some poor victim of crime but they won't work with me. This is not about my ego, it's about catching some vicious killer before he kills someone else. Now can we move on, I don't have time for this nonsense?'

The room erupted again. The reporter who'd asked the question went red in the face and shouted something in reply. But it was lost in the general hubbub. Owen thumped the desk until the noise finally subsided. When it had she said in a calm voice, 'Are there any more sensible questions?'

This was met with complete silence. After several seconds she said, 'Thank you for your attention,' and stood up to leave.

Prior followed her to her office, his face still flushed with anger. He plonked himself into one of her comfortable chairs and let his breath out slowly.

Without a word, Owen placed a cup of coffee in front of him. Then she spoke, 'Well done, Matthew, you kept your cool; although you walked pretty close to the line at the end there.'

His took a welcome gulp of his coffee. 'I have to say ma'am, I feel as if I have one hand tied behind my back.'

She nodded. 'You are of a rank now where you must add diplomacy to your armoury. My advice to you is to follow the evidence. Anything controversial, bring to me before you wade in. I was being perfectly honest when I said that I have every confidence in you.' She paused, and then continued, 'Now drink your coffee and get home to see your family, I'm sure you haven't had much time for them recently.'

As he stood to leave she added, 'Matthew, don't push Stapleton too far, he could do a great deal of damage to your career. If anything further comes to light that points towards Sinclair or the estate bring it to me at once, don't wade in yourself. I promise you that I will look into it. It will not be pushed under the carpet.'

Prior sighed deeply. 'Yes ma'am, thank you, I'll do that.'

16. Dinner for three.

'They are ill discoverers that think there is no land
When they can see nothing but sea.'

Francis Bacon 1561-1626

Thursday evening.

Prior got home at 6.30 feeling completely washed out. As he opened the front door his two daughters rushed to greet him and his spirits rose. He swept them both off their feet, one in each arm.

'Daddy, daddy, we saw you on TV,' this from Samantha, usually the quiet one.

'And how was I?'

'Very stern, like you are when we do something wrong.'

He laughed. 'It was all those reporters; I should have sent them to bed early.'

He carried the two girls into the kitchen where he found Jeanette. She kissed him, 'So, the hero returns, I was proud of you, Matthew.' She took a pace back and gave him an appraising look. 'You need a shower and you didn't phone. Where's Siobhan?'

'Huh! You sound like my superintendent. Yes ma'am; no ma'am, three bags full ma'am. Sorry I didn't get the chance to phone and Siobhan will be here at seven.'

She smiled as he put the girls down. 'I could see you were seething inside but you didn't quite lose it.'

Natalie asked, 'What's seething, mummy?'

'It means angry but trying not to show it, just like I am sometimes with daddy.'

The child laughed. 'We always know when you are seething mummy, you bang things.'

Prior laughed too. In those few minutes, much of the tension of the day had drained out of him. He said, 'That'll teach you to seethe more quietly, mummy, won't it? Right ladies, I'm going to have a shower then you can tell me about your day.'

Precisely ten minutes later he rejoined them in the kitchen. He had showered and changed into jeans, an open necked shirt and a cardigan. The two girls were eating their supper at the kitchen table. He sat with them and listened to their chatter while they ate. Nothing more was said about his enquiry until the children had finished. They then rushed into the lounge to play on a computer game.

He picked up their plates and put them into the dishwasher. 'Would you like a drink love?'

'Yes please Matthew, why don't you open a bottle of red?

He opened a bottle of Hardy's Cabernet Sauvignon and poured two glasses; a cheap quaffing wine but just barely drinkable, as Jeanette's father described it. Prior's father-in-law was something of a wine buff and had taught him how to be a little discerning when searching the bargain shelves of the supermarkets. Prior was secretly pleased to find that the Australians were good at something other than coarseness and cricket. Sipping his wine, he said, 'Anything I can do?'

'No, it's all ready, it's a casserole.'

'Great, I'm famished.'

'Now tell me what's on your mind Matthew.'

He smiled. 'You can read me like a book. What chapter are you on?'

'The one that starts, 'I've got something under my skin.' Isn't that the case?'

'Yes, you're right as always. It's a good job I've no interest in other women, I wouldn't stand a chance of getting away with it.'

'No, you wouldn't, and I'd have your balls off if you did. Now, stop prevaricating and tell me what's bothering you. Is it the case?'

'Prevaricating? Everyone seems to be throwing long words at me today.' He smiled. 'Siobhan went for a walk on the estate, said it was enervating.'

'You're still prevaricating Matthew, answer the question.'

'Yes love.' He paused, then said, 'In a way it's the case but not the investigation. The damned ACC, Stapleton, he's stuck his oar in.'

'Really? Owen sounded quite supportive at the press conference. She seems to be behind you.'

'Yes, she's stuck squarely in the middle, has to toe the party line and support me at the same time. I suppose I should be grateful that she's there. Some superintendents I've met would throw me to the wolves when the ACC tells them to. He's warned me off the Sinclair Estate.' He went on to tell her of the events of the day.

Before she could comment, the doorbell rang. She looked at her watch. 'That'll be Siobhan, I'll get it.' He sat sipping his wine, listening to the two women chatting in the hall. They had met at a police social function months ago and had immediately become firm friends. This pleased Prior as it made his life much easier. There was no rivalry between the women in his life nor any petty jealousies.

He heard Jeanette say, 'We're in the kitchen.'

He got up to greet Siobhan. They had quickly learned to adapt to the potential conflict between the formality required on the job and the more relaxed attitudes on social occasions. Quite simply, he was 'sir' at work and 'Matthew' away from work. He greeted her with a peck on the cheek and handed her a glass of wine.

Jeanette said to Siobhan, 'Matthew was just telling me about the case. How are you coping with all this blood and gore?'

'I'm OK thanks, Jeanette, despite having to work with his nibs here.'

'Just thank god you don't have to live with him.'

'I think you're very brave, Jeanette.'

'Oiy! Do you two mind not discussing me as if I weren't here. When can we eat?'

'Just as soon as you lay the table, dear, we'll eat in the dining room.'

'I see it's a posh one, is it.' He left to do her bidding.

Jeanette was a good cook, in fact she had many talents. With a good degree in English Literature she had started her professional life as a journalist. Then a brother had gone into politics and had asked her for help with his speeches. She found she had a talent for writing them and soon she was writing for many of his colleagues, as well as continuing her career as a freelance journalist.

She had met Matthew at a dinner party and the two had immediately become friends. That was twelve years ago. Friendship had quickly blossomed into romance and they had been happily married for eleven years. During her first pregnancy she had started working from home. This had proved no barrier to her career and she fitted the work in between the duties of housewife and mother. She kept up-to-date with world events with her computer and thoroughly researched all of her subjects.

Their combined incomes enabled them to afford every modern labour-saving device on the market. The only help she got in the home was a cleaner, who came two mornings a week, and from Matthew when he was there. His career had blossomed apace, not least because of her support. As the Americans so simply put it, 'it worked for them'.

The three friends chatted gaily over dinner, talking about everything but the case. When they'd finished eating Prior got up to clear things away.

Jeanette said, 'Leave that to us, love; you put the girls to bed and then we'll have coffee.

Half an hour later they sat drinking coffee in front of an open fire. The women had declined liqueurs but Prior indulged himself with a glass of decent brandy given to him by his father-in-law.

Jeanette produced a sheaf of papers. 'OK, dogged detectives, pin back your ears. Whilst you two have been scouring the undergrowth for clues I've been doing some research on your Celtic Cross.'

Prior said, 'How did you know we found a Celtic cross?'

'Just because you can't find time to phone me doesn't mean my friends can't. Siobhan told me.'

Prior shook his head with a satisfied smile on his face. 'OK professor, the floor is yours.'

She then proceeded to tell them much of what they had learned from Miles but went deeper. 'It seems the Celts learned everything by rote, poetry and song, not much of which has survived sadly, as they had no written language. But a lot of their culture has survived, more than you might think incidentally.'

Prior nodded encouragingly.

She continued, 'The only things written about their history before about 300AD was written by others. And, as the Celts weren't the friendliest of people, not much of that is complimentary. What is obvious is that without a written language, symbols were important to them. And one of their symbols was something resembling a primitive cross.

But it differs from the Christian cross as the poles are of equal length and are surrounded by a circle.

Historians are fairly sure the circle represented the sun or moon; and the cross the lines of the summer and winter solstices and the equinoxes. The Celts were particularly concerned with the calendar, it told them when to plant their seed and collect the harvest.'

Prior interrupted with a smile on his face, 'You're talking about agriculture are you?'

'Typical man,' Siobhan intervened, 'assuming that everything has a sexual connotation.'

Jeanette laughed, 'You're right about men Siobhan. But for once he's not wrong. Their priests, the Druids, were deep into fertility rites as well. They had young women jumping across fires to encourage conception.'

Prior laughed. 'That's a damned good idea, I think we should bring that back. I can think of a few women I'd like to see jumping through flames.'

Jeanette grinned. 'And more than a few men I know would benefit from that, especially if we made a very big fire. But back to the cross. Now, most people think that Christians rejected everything pagan. But that's not quite true. The word pagan incidentally, comes from the Latin; it meant villager or peasant. Country folk were much slower to take up the new faith than the townies. They stuck to the old religions.

But even among the townies there were some symbols and practices people were reluctant to give up, so the sneaky Christians incorporated them into their faith. As far as the Celtic cross is concerned they simply extended the upright so it resembled the Christian symbol. There are lots of other examples of old practices incorporated into Christianity. About the only thing Christians wouldn't accept was human sacrifice.'

'A bit hypocritical of them, wasn't it?' Siobhan said. 'When you think of witch hunts and crusades, they probably killed more people than the pagans ever did.'

Prior frowned. 'Aren't we getting away from the subject?'

Siobhan replied, 'We can digress if we like Matthew, we're not at work you know.'

'Huh, sorry I spoke.'

Jeanette looked at them with a smile of her face. 'Do you two want to hear about my research or not?'

Prior held his hands up in front of him. 'Sorry, please tell us more, Jeanette.'

'OK. Now, where was I? Oh yes. So, later on, the Celtic cross became acceptable as a Christian symbol.'

'You mean like the cross of Jesus?'

'Not exactly, Matthew. People like to think in absolutes but things don't always happen that way. What is interesting is that many stone Celtic crosses have been found at early Christian burial sites all over Europe.'

'This more or less confirms what Miles told us. Except that he added that as the upright doesn't extend under the circle the one we found is probably pre-Christian.' Siobhan offered. 'But this still doesn't tell us what its presence signifies.'

'Unfortunately, Miles is right but they have also been found alongside paths used by the ancients.'

'You mean like shrines?' asked Prior.

'That's the problem according to what I've found so far with my research, no one quite knows. What is interesting though is that stone ornaments do usually seem to be associated with the dead. You know my friend Julie Davis, Matthew?'

He nodded.

Then to Siobhan she explained, 'Julie and I were at uni together and she now lectures on history at Bristol. She says that all the early settlements and houses that people lived in were made of wood. Yet all the burial chambers found are constructed in stone. She suggests this signifies that life was seen as temporary, death as permanent.'

Siobhan frowned, 'That's what we were told by Miles. But where does that leave us?'

Jeanette smiled. 'I haven't quite finished yet. You say there's a hill fort on the high ground on the estate?'

'Yes, I walked up there today. Local archaeologists want to dig there. Miles was the man who wrote to Sinclair asking for permission to dig on the site. Sinclair refused. '

'Well, if people lived there, they must have buried their dead nearby and they usually did that on the lower ground.' She sat back with a smug expression on her face.

There was silence in the room for a while as Prior and Siobhan absorbed this. Prior scratched his head. 'So, what you're saying love is that the stone cross might indicate a burial site or at least a path leading to one.'

'That's what I think, yes.'

Siobhan shook her head. 'That's more than Miles was prepared to say. You know everything about this case points to the Sinclair Estate. We keep looking elsewhere but we keep being drawn back to the estate.'

'And we've been warned off by the ACC.' Prior added.

'Why do you think that is Matthew? Do you think he's involved in something crooked?' from Jeanette.

'No love, he's not very streetwise but I don't think he's bent as such. But it's clear that Stapleton and Sinclair are hiding something, it's not just those with their noses in the air closing ranks.'

Prior got up and refilled their coffee cups. Jeanette asked, 'So, deadly duo, where do you go from here?'

Prior sighed. He turned to Siobhan. 'Did you tell Jeanette that you found traces of someone digging on the hill? When you were being enervated, remember?'

She nodded and looked at Jeanette. 'He doesn't like me using long words. I think he feels intellectually challenged.'

Jeanette laughed. 'I think you're right, he had a go at me earlier because I said he was prevaricating.'

'Oh, he does that all the time at work, Jeanette, prevaricate I mean.' The two women laughed.

When it had died down, Siobhan said, 'What was interesting was that Sinclair should happen along as I was there.'

Prior prompted, 'So you don't think that was a coincidence then?'

'Huh! Aren't you the one who's always telling me there are no coincidences in murder cases?'

He grinned. 'Hoist by my own petard. What did he actually say to you up there?'

'He asked me what I was doing there.'

'What did you tell him?'

'Said I was taking some air. That was when he told me he wanted to see you.'

'Where were you in relation to the patch that had been dug when he approached you?'

'I'd just walked away from it.'

'So he must have seen it?'

'Yes, I'm certain he did.'

'Yet he denied that fact that anyone was digging on the estate. Why, what is he hiding?'

Jeanette intervened, 'Where was this patch that had been dug in relation to the fort?'

'Well, I didn't actually find a fort; just some bumps and hollows. But it was right in the middle of those.'

'Then he told you all to get off the estate. Surely there must be some connection.' She frowned. 'But surely you don't suspect Sinclair of the murder Matthew, especially since the head was put on his gate?'

'No love, I don't. But I can't help wondering what he's hiding.'

Siobhan looked at her watch. 'I'd better be going. My boss is a stickler for punctuality. I don't want to be late in the morning.'

'No, you don't, are you OK to drive or shall I call a taxi?' Prior added with a grin.

'No, I'm fine.'

*

Later, when Prior and Jeanette were lying next to each other in their bed, she said, 'Be careful Matthew, I'd hate to see you sacrifice your career over this case.'

'You don't expect me to back off do you?'

'No, I don't. But I do expect you to tread carefully. You can be quite stubborn you know.'

'Determined love, not stubborn.'

She smiled and snuggled up to him. 'That's what I love about you, your determination.'

He turned towards her. 'Shall I show you what I love about you?'

'I hoped you might say something like that.'

It was some time before they both got to sleep. Prior had no bad dreams that night.

17. The Autopsy.

'The cobbler to his last and the gunner to his linstock.'

18th century proverb.

The third day of the investigation dawned bright and clear. The clouds that had shrouded the land all week were gone, blown away by a north-easterly. But the wind had come all the way from Siberia and there was an icy feel to it.

Prior enjoyed breakfast with his young family uninterrupted by urgent phone calls, then at 7.45 set off for Penwin. He felt refreshed and alert after a good night's sleep and was determined to get his teeth into the case. The village hall that he'd commandeered was on the edge of the village, accessed by a narrow lane. It had a spacious car park and the enquiry van had been drawn up next to the building leaving plenty of room for his team's cars to come and go. Electric cables ran through the window of a toilet in the building to the trailer, providing power for the computers and lights and recharging the van's batteries.

Entering the trailer, Prior saw just DS Quigley and two of his DCs had got in before him. The uniformed officer who had manned the van overnight was just leaving. Prior acknowledged his greeting as he passed and headed straight for the coffee machine. Pouring a cup, he pulled up a chair beside Quigley's desk.

'Morning, sir,' Quigley greeted him. He was a burly man in his early fifties only a year or two away from retirement. His enthusiasm for physically chasing villains on the streets had waned over the years but his brain was still sharp. He was a good organiser and had an excellent memory. He was also familiar with this part of Cornwall, having spent much of his service at Truro, a valuable asset in what was a small tight-knit community. He made an excellent office manager.

Prior returned his greeting adding, 'Any response to our appeal?'

'Couple of nutters and just one interesting call, sir. A woman. Wouldn't give her name; said we should look into the goings on at the manor house.'

'What kind of goings on?'

'She wouldn't say, but the village bobby has added something that might be useful. He says that there have been two occasions he's seen a Truro taxi with young women in the back leaving the estate in the small hours.'

'Really? Is that recently?'

'In the last couple of months. Last time was about three weeks ago.'

Prior frowned. 'That's very interesting. According to the local gossip Sinclair only got married in order to get a son, then he ditched his wife. Now he lives alone. He must have some way to satisfy his lust. Perhaps he has prostitutes brought in. This could be what he's so anxious to hide.'

Quigley nodded.

Prior continued, 'Now, I wonder who this woman is, the one who phoned in, obviously someone local. We know that Sinclair is not very popular locally. Until he took over, his family had always looked after the people who worked on the estate. Cedric is a different animal, doesn't do any more than he has to for the folk around here.'

Suddenly he slapped the desk. 'Got it! I knew there was something we missed. Charlie Trimble said that his wife got the local gossip from the woman who cleaned up at the big house. I'm sure he said her name was Chivers. Then we were looking for a busybody in the village and Jean Wade found one, her name was Chivers. I'll bet she's the one that phoned. And she will know what goes on at the house. We need to have another word with her.' He paused for a moment, thinking.

'But we have to tread carefully, we've been warned off anything to do with Sinclair. If she has a loose tongue, word could get back to him that we've been asking her questions, then the shit will hit the fan. Damn it! How can I carry out an enquiry with one hand tied behind my back?'

Quigley said nothing, waiting for him to go on.

Prior's mind was busy. Another thought occurred to him and he smiled. 'OK, let's leave her for the moment. One thing we can do is follow up the taxi report. Find out from the constable if he knows which cab company it was, Albert. The pick-ups must have been arranged by phone. The company must keep records and the drivers will remember that kind of a fare. But tread carefully, I don't want any harassment charges.'

He paused again, frowning in concentration. Finally he spoke, 'What we need is a lever that gets us back onto the estate, this may be it.'

Quigley nodded again without comment.

'Have we found out anything else about Sinclair?'

'Not a lot, sir. Just confirmation of what you got from Charlie Kimble. Cedric's not half the man his father was. The old man gave a lot to local charities and funded lots of the village activities. Cedric put a stop to all that. He doesn't give a shit about the villagers, treats them all like serfs. And he's about as popular in the village as the bubonic plague.'

Siobhan had appeared at Prior's elbow. 'Morning, sir, morning Albert. Who doesn't give a shit?'

Quigley pulled a face. 'Sorry Siobhan, didn't see you come in.'

Prior grinned. 'Your chivalry is wasted on her, Albert; she swears worse than you do.'

He turned to her. 'Good morning, Siobhan. Apart from the usual nutters the appeal for witnesses has come up with something interesting. The high and mighty Sinclair apparently has a penchant for young women. Two have been seen leaving in a taxi in the small hours. Albert was just confirming that Sinclair isn't popular with his serfs, doesn't treat them too well.'

'That smells distinctly malodorous, sir. But does it help us with our enquiry?'

'Malodorous, sergeant? Yet another long word, you're beginning to sound like a walking bloody dictionary.'

'Yes, sir, trying to better myself, not that there's much chance of that round here. But seriously, I don't see what his bad habits could have to do with the murder. Aren't we treading on dangerous ground, having been warned off by the top brass?'

'Yes. That's what makes me even more curious. He paused and smiled, 'Besides, it's fun isn't it, living dangerously? We'll just have to be discreet with our enquiries.'

He turned back to Quigley. 'Anything else happen overnight?'

'Just the reports from yesterday, sir. All of Wright's friends have been interviewed and their vehicles examined. All clean as a whistle. And Liz and Fred spent a couple of hours turning over Wright's cottage. That's clean too.'

Prior looked at his watch. 'You've just got time for a coffee, Siobhan, then we must be off to the PM.' Then to Quigley, 'The Super is bringing over a profiler. I forgot to tell her I'll be at the PM. Give Owen my apologies and tell her about the young women in the taxis. No need to tell her what we're doing about it unless she asks. What she doesn't know she won't worry about. You can give the profiler a briefing. Give her what details she needs. We'll be back as soon as we can.'

Truro public mortuary was housed in an impressive grey-brick building over a century old. Modernisation had taken place over the years but the autopsy room in the basement was much as it had been in the early days of forensic science. It had white-tiled walls and a concrete floor that sloped gently to the centre, where there was a large drain.

Most of the furnishings and equipment were modern but Prior always had the feeling that he was stepping back in time when he entered there. The two detectives arrived suitably garbed. Professor Penhallon and his lab assistant were already there, robed and ready to go. Prior's nose twitched as it picked up the pungent aromas of formaldehyde, burnt bone and disinfectant that permeated the room; despite the air conditioning unit's efforts, the smell never completely dispersed.

In front of them were two stainless steel tables. On one was the severed head, on the other the torso. Penhallon greeted them in his familiar caustic tone. 'Matthew, Siobhan, how good of you to come. Perhaps now we can start.'

Prior looked at his watch. They were five minutes early but there was no point in telling the old pathologist this. He said, 'Fine, Professor shall we leave the carving to you?

Penhallon gave him a glare, switched on the tape recorder he carried in the breast pocket of his robe and spoke into the tiny microphone that hung beside his mouth from a harness worn on his head. First, he identified the body parts, stating where and when they had been found, and identified those present at the autopsy. Then he declared the corpse to be that of a male in his mid-twenties, apparently healthy apart from having no head. He cackled to himself at this remark. Prior knew from experience that Penhallon's secretary of many years knew which bits of the recording to put in his formal report and which to leave out.

Next Penhallon measured the length of the corpse and the severed head. He said, 'Five-eleven to six-foot-tall when all in one piece; difficult to be more precise when some butcher has cut his head off.' Next he examined the neck from different angles. 'Hmm, some kind of long flat blade used to sever the tissue of the neck, probably a kitchen knife with a serrated edge. And he didn't do it too well. Not a clean cut, several cut marks in the tissue where he carved away at it. Lots of bone chips where the vertebrae are parted. Must have used a damned axe here, and it took him more than one blow.'

Prior felt Siobhan stir beside him. He touched her elbow and whispered softly, 'No need for both of us to stay through all this. Why don't you go and get a cup of tea, Siobhan?'

She shook her head. 'No, sir, I'll see it through.'

Penhallon looked up. 'Please don't chatter when I'm working, it disturbs my concentration.'

He moved to the chest wound and placed a small ruler beside it. He stepped back and nodded to his assistant, who took two photographs of it. Then Penhallon said, 'Hmm, seven centimetres in length and not a clean entry wound. I'd say you are dealing with a particularly cold-blooded sod here, Matthew. It looks as if, having stabbed the knife into the chest, the killer then manipulated it from side to side to drive it deeper. I'll be able to tell you more once I'm inside.'

Siobhan stirred again but when Prior looked at her she avoided eye contact.

Penhallon continued, 'No more marks on the torso. But look here, Matthew, at the wrists and ankles. There are rope marks here. He was tied up and this happened before he was killed, hence the bruising.'

He lifted the right hand and manipulated the fingers. 'Two of his fingers are fractured; compression fractures by the feel of it.' A pause as he examined the flesh on the fingers. Then, 'Yes, look here on the skin. These marks were made by a vice or a pair of pliers.'

'Are you saying he was tortured, Professor?'

'Well I don't think he will have enjoyed the experience.'

'I mean, could this have been an accident?' Prior said irritably.

'Hardly. I can't see how this could have been anything but deliberate, the other fingers are undamaged.'

Siobhan spoke, her voice shrill, 'For god sake. You're saying this poor man was tied up and then tortured. Then a knife was ground into his chest and his head sawn off. This is sick. I've had enough.' She turned and left, letting the door slam to behind her.

Neither man said anything. Penhallon continued with his examination while Prior stood by, stoically watching the pathologist at work. He remained in his position at the foot of the two tables throughout the autopsy. There were one or two occasions when he almost faltered, once when Penhallon used a circular saw to cut through the ribcage, another when he made an incision in the skin at the rear of the severed head before peeling forward the hair and exposing the skull. All the while Penhallon commented on his work, interspersing the comments with his dreadful humour. Prior gritted his teeth and stayed to the bitter end.

When it was over he went in search of his DS. He found her in the tiny kitchen the mortuary staff used to make tea and coffee. She looked up as he joined her. Her face was pale and wore a sad expression. 'Are you OK, Siobhan?'

'Not really sir, no. But I'll cope.'

Prior slumped into a chair beside her. 'Good. You know, it doesn't matter how many of those you've been to, you never get used to it.'

'I think I'd have been all right except for his stupid attempts at humour.'

'One thing you should remember, Siobhan. We all have to find a coping mechanism for these occasions. Old Penhallon uses his morbid humour. Bear in mind he does several of these each week.'

'I know, sir, but I kept thinking what the poor lad went through. It just got worse and worse as it went along.' She paused. 'Was it worth staying the distance?'

He nodded. 'I suppose you could say that. I've now got a clear idea what happened that night. We've pinned down the time of death a bit. Penhallon said it was between midnight and two in the morning. He confirmed that before he was killed he was hit over the head with something. All Penhallon can tell us is that it had a blunt edge, probably a tool of some sort. Then he was tied up and tortured. The rest you know.'

'The lividity is all down his back; he was obviously laid out flat for some time after death. Then, after the head was chopped off, the torso was put in the water.'

'The poor lad, sir, having to go through that. What on earth was the killer after?'

Prior shook his head. 'The only thing I can think of is some kind of information. But I haven't a clue what. I expect that when we find out what that was, we'll know who killed him.'

'But this is dreadful. We're no closer to finding the killer.'

'I wouldn't say that. We have eliminated a lot of people. And I think we now have a focus, the Sinclair Estate.'

'Huh! We've been warned off the estate, sir, remember?'

'But I think we might find a lever. Let's go and talk to this taxi firm. I'm sure Albert will have found out which one it was by now.'

18. Handycabs.

Friday 1pm.

As they left the building Prior phoned Quigley on his mobile and gave him the provisional results of the post-mortem. Quigley had news for Prior. Owen had dropped off the profiler and had wanted to see him. Her message was to contact her urgently. Prior knew she wouldn't be bringing him good news.

To Quigley he said, 'Have you got details of the company operating the cabs seen near the Estate?'

'Yes, sir, it's called Handycabs, their office is in Truro.'

Prior had seen their cabs about. They were distinctive white Fords with the company logo and phone number in green lettering on the sides. Quigley also confirmed that they operated under a car hire licence rather than a Hackney carriage licence. The distinction was significant. It meant they could not cruise the streets looking for business but had to be booked in advance. This meant that there would be records of the hirings.

Prior said, 'OK. If Owen calls again, you haven't been able to contact me, is that clear.'

There was a pause before Quigley replied, 'Yes, sir.'

'Good, I'll contact her as soon as I've visited Handycabs, but as far as anyone else is concerned you don't know where I am, OK? Oh, and one other thing. Give the profiler access to the murder file, I'll be back to see her as soon as I can.'

There was another pause before Quigley replied, 'Yes, I've got that, sir.'

Handycabs office proved to be in a narrow street behind the cathedral. It stood between an estate agent and a shoe shop. Several of its cabs stood in the reserved parking bay in the street outside. The premises had clearly been a shop in a previous existence. Its frontage was one large plate glass window with a glass panelled door to one side. The bottom two-thirds of the window and the door had been papered over so that passers-by could not see what went on inside. The same green logo and telephone number on the cabs was painted in large letters above the shop.

As the two detectives entered they were confronted by a high counter dividing the space into two. On the public side the only furniture was a long, upholstered bench. Three men sat on it reading newspapers. Behind the counter a young woman sat at a desk on which were two telephones and a radio transceiver. In the far corner of the space was a small partitioned office.

The woman and the three men all looked up. Their expressions went from hopeful to something else when they identified them as detective rather than potential customers. Prior produced his warrant card and asked to see the manager. The woman got up and went to the office and said something through the open door. A man emerged. His skin was the colour of milky coffee and his features Indo-Asian. He looked at the two visitors and walked to the counter with a worried expression on his face.

He said, 'I'm Mr Rhanji, the manager, how can I help you, sir?' He spoke without trace of an accent.

Prior produced showed him his warrant card and introduced Siobhan, adding, 'Can we speak to you in private please?'

Rhanji lifted a flap in the counter and led them to his small office. There was just enough room for his desk and chair and two visitors' chairs. He invited them to sit. Prior closed the door and took a seat.

He said, 'We are investigating a murder and need some information from you, Mr. Rhanji.'

'Really? Yes of course, anything you want.'

'Do you keep records of people ordering cabs by phone?'

'Yes, sir, everything is recorded.'

'Pick up points and destinations?'

'Yes, sir.'

'How is this information recorded?'

'It's all on my computer sir. We keep the records for six months in case of any disputes.'

173

'So, if I gave you a location, you could tell me every time you have either picked someone up or dropped them off there?'

'Yes, sir, for the last six months.'

'Good Mr Rhanji. The location we're interested in is Sinclair House on the Sinclair Estate.'

'Oh yes, sir, Mr. Sinclair is a regular customer, he has a monthly account.'

Prior couldn't believe his luck. 'Can I see your record of trips to and from Sinclair House please?'

Rhanji pressed some keys on the computer. The screen flickered for a moment then a page of details appeared on the screen. Rhanji twisted the screen round so the detectives could see it. Prior's eyes flicked down the page. The entries started six months ago and filled the whole page and beyond.

He nodded and said, 'Can we see the most recent entries please.'

Rhanji scrolled down to the second page. The detective's eyes became riveted to the last four entries. He exchanged meaningful glances with Siobhan but said nothing. The entries covered the night of the murder. And the pick-ups from the estate were during the period when the head had been impaled on the gate

The entries read: -

| 8/10 | 9pm | Lrl Ave. | (1) | - 9.20pm | Sinc. |
| Est. | £10 c | NM | | | |

| 8/10 | 9.30pm | Bl St. | (2) | - 9.50pm | Sinc. |
| Est. | £10 A | CP | Acc. Sinc. | | |

9/10	2am	Sinc. Est.	(1)	-	
2.15am	Lrl Ave	.£10c	NM		
9/10	2am	Sinc Est .(2)	-	2.20am	Bl St.
£10A	TB	Acc Sinc.			

Rhanji ran his finger across the page and explained. 'The first column is the date and time; the second the pick-up point; the third the time of arrival; next the destination; then the fare and whether cash or account; the initials are the driver; and the last entry is the person whose account this is to be charged to.'

Prior frowned in concentration; 'So the first entry tells us that a single fare was picked up at 9pm on the 8th October at ..., what does Lrl Ave mean?'

That's Laurel Avenue, here in Truro, sir.'

Prior's heart skipped a beat. He knew someone very close to this investigation who lived in Laurel Avenue.

Rhanji interrupted his thoughts. 'You see, sir,' he traced his finger along the line. 'He was taken to The Sinclair Estate, arriving at 9.20pm. He paid £10 cash and the driver was NM; that's Norman Miles, sir.'

Prior nodded, 'And Bl St., what's that?'

'That's Blake Street, Truro, sir.'

Prior nodded again. Brian's Escort Agency, Truro's one and only knocking shop was in Blake Street. Suddenly it all fell into place. He glanced at Siobhan again and saw she had a smile on her face. She nodded, confirming that she had reached the same conclusion.

Turning back to Rhanji Prior said, 'Just to be absolutely sure that I have this correct, Mr Rhanji, these entries say that on the evening of Tuesday the 8th of October three fares were picked up; one in Laurel Street and two in Blake Street; all three were taken to The Sinclair Estate. Then at 2am that same night, all three were brought back to Truro. Is that correct?'

'Yes, sir, that is correct.'

Prior nodded yet again. He was beginning to feel like one of those toy nodding dogs you used to see in the backs of cars when he was a child. He was also feeling much relieved. It was now crystal clear why they had been barred from the Sinclair Estate. He continued to check his understanding of the entries with Rhanji, 'And these initials are the drivers. Can we have their full names and addresses please?'

Rhanji gave them and Siobhan wrote them down.

'Are these drivers on duty now, Mr Rhanji?'

'No, sir, they work the late shift, they will be here at 6pm.'

Prior couldn't stop yet another nod. 'Can I have a print out of all these entries please?'

Rhanji nodded. 'Is everything in order sir?' He seemed very eager to please. He pressed some keys and the printer beside the computer whirred and spewed out the pages.

Prior gave him a reassuring smile. 'Yes, it is, Mr Rhanji, if every company kept records as thoroughly as you do our job would be much easier.'

Rhanji positively glowed. Then another thought struck him. He said, 'Are my drivers in trouble, sir?'

Prior shook his head; it was a relief from constantly nodding. 'On the contrary, but they may have seen something relevant to our enquiry, so I need to speak to them.'

Rhanji licked his lips. 'Is this about the head on the gate, sir?'

Prior gave him a stern look. 'I'm sure you realise Mr. Rhanji that I can't talk about our investigation.' He paused for effect, then added, 'I need just one more thing from you Mr. Rhanji. When these drivers book on duty tonight, I need to interview them. Can I do that here?'

The man nodded enthusiastically, 'Yes of course sir, you can use this office.'

'Thank you. And it's best they don't know in advance what this is about. I want their answers to be spontaneous. Can I rely on your discretion?'

'Yes, of course, I won't tell them anything.'

Prior gave him a beaming smile. 'Mr. Rhanji you have been very helpful, thank you for your co-operation. We'll see you again at six.'

As they left the office Prior noticed that only one of the drivers remained sitting on the bench; no doubt the other two had gone to collect fares. Certainly the phones had been busy during their visit. Business was obviously brisk.

When they were outside Prior led the way quickly to the car. Only when they were both seated and the doors closed did Siobhan speak, 'So that's why Sinclair wouldn't tell us about his visitors, he was bonking toms that night.' By toms she meant prostitutes.

Prior smiled. 'You sound like George Bailey, Siobhan, I'm sure you mean he was entertaining two young ladies.'

She laughed. 'If you say so, sir. I wonder who the other person was, the one who was picked up in Laurel Avenue?'

He looked at her. 'So you don't know who lives in Laurel Avenue?'

'No sir, do you?'

He nodded, 'One Thomas Stapleton, Assistant Chief Constable of this force.'

There was a long intake of breath. Then she said, 'You're joking, sir, Stapleton?'

'Yes. I had to send a car for him one night when we had a midnight raid on a club. He lives in a swanky big house called 'The Pines'. This explains a great deal. He wasn't protecting Sinclair, he was looking after his own skin.'

Clearly the implications were beginning to sink into Siobhan's mind. 'Jesus, sir, the shit's really going to hit the roof now. What are we going to do?'

'It's the fan, Siobhan, not the roof. But the answer to your question is, nothing at this moment. We've got to make damned sure the flying shit doesn't hit us. We don't know for certain it was him, although I'd bet my mortgage on it. We will have to tread very carefully. Let's have a closer look at that list.'

They spent ten minutes poring over the Handycabs computer print-out. A pattern quickly emerged. Since the records begun in May, on every second Tuesday fares had been picked up in Blake Street and carried to Sinclair

House. Some hours later they had been returned to Blake Street. Siobhan had not needed to ask about Brian's Escort Agency as it was known to every police officer in the city. It had been raided several times over the years when public pressure demanded some action. But it was generally tolerated by the local police.

Both detectives knew that banning prostitution would have been like Prohibition in the United States. Where there was a demand, there would always be someone willing to supply it. If you pushed the industry underground you created more problems than you solved. The prissy puritans who were always campaigning against prostitution didn't have a clue about the urges of men, including, no doubt, some who regularly attended their church. Much more likely they tried to deny that such urges existed even though they felt them too. It was rather like ostriches putting their heads in the sand whenever they saw a lion approaching.

The incidence of sexual assaults on respectable woman would rocket if there were no prostitutes available to satisfy the lust of men who couldn't satisfy it in the normal way. Better the evil you know, then at least you can exercise some control over it.

The 'Brian' who ran the business was, in fact, a woman in her fifties, an ex-prostitute who had seen a niche in the market and opened the house of ill repute ten years ago. Punters could either go to the brothel itself or could order the girls to be sent to them - provided always that they paid in advance. They could even use their credit cards to make payment. Prior had no doubt that Sinclair also had an account with Brian. All of this would go towards providing what he needed to screw Sinclair down very tight and get him and his team back onto the estate to pursue the murder enquiry.

Seven times in that six-month period, a single fare had been picked up in Laurel Avenue and taken to The Estate and returned to Laurel Avenue later that night. These journeys corresponded with the Blake Street pick-ups. All were on Tuesdays when the Brightons visited Mrs. Brighton's mother. It seemed that Stapleton's itches were not quite as frequent as Sinclair's.

Prior sat back in his seat, his mind racing ahead. He took a deep breath. 'Right, this is how we work this. I want you to do CRO checks on the three drivers and Rhanji, and a collator's check on Handycabs. But for god sake be careful. Don't let anyone know what you're at, understand?'

Siobhan nodded, 'Yes, sir.'

'And get hold of a photo of Stapleton in plain clothes. Get a group shot with him among a crowd. He attends so many damned functions you shouldn't have any trouble. We can use that to show the drivers and see if any of them recognise Stapleton in a crowd.' He looked at his watch. It said 1pm. 'In the meantime, we don't say a word to a soul.'

'What are you going to do, sir?'

'Carry on as normal. Until we have concrete evidence, we have to carry on as if nothing has happened.'

Siobhan had a deep frown on her face. 'This worries me, sir. Suppose we find the evidence and no-one believes us?'

Prior nodded. 'That's precisely why we have to tread so carefully. So far all we have is a bad smell.' He smiled. 'To use your word, malodorous. But we are perfectly justified in following this line of enquiry. Any activity at Sinclair House around the time of the murder must be relevant. Let's just gather the evidence for the moment. Let me worry about the politics.'

She nodded. 'What I don't understand is how Stapleton thought he could get away with it.'

'I've been thinking about that. If he had the itch, he had to get it scratched somewhere and he could hardly go to a brothel or pick a girl up on the streets as someone might have spotted him. Once he found out that Sinclair had a similar itch, it must have seemed like the perfect solution. Doing it on an isolated country estate away from prying eyes must have seemed ideal. Who's going to suspect? He could tell anyone who found out where he was going that it was to play poker or something? He must have told his wife something like that.'

'What do you think will happen to him sir, if it's what we think it is?'

'Consorting with known prostitutes and obstructing justice? Even if it's nothing to do with the murder, he'll be lucky to keep his pension. This is dynamite, Siobhan.'

She said nothing as she absorbed the implications.

'OK, it's back to the ranch. Just make damned sure you keep shtum about this.'

'Shtum, sir, what's that?'

'It's foreign for keep your big mouth shut.'

She laughed. 'I didn't know you spoke foreign, sir.'

He gave her a smile.

Then a frown replaced the smile on her face. 'What about Superintendent Owen, sir? Shouldn't we tell her?'

It was at that precise moment Prior's mobile phone rang. He looked at the caller ID, it was Owen. He answered it 'Yes ma'am.'

'Where are you Matthew?'

'In Truro, I've just completed an enquiry.'

'Come and see me, now.' The line went dead.

No please on the end, no 'where have you been I've been looking for you'. This royal summons was decidedly ominous.

Siobhan was looking at him. She saw the expression on his face. 'Trouble, sir?'

He shook his head. 'I don't know, Siobhan, but I think so. Owen wants to see me now.'

Siobhan raised her eyebrows but said nothing more. Her face however bore a worried frown.

*

Five minutes later Prior pulled the car into the Truro Police Station yard. He told Siobhan to wait in the canteen and went straight up to Owen's office.

Her secretary looked up as he passed and said, 'Go straight in.'

He knocked on Owen's door and opened it. She looked up from her desk and beckoned with a finger. 'Shut the door behind you.'

He did so. She didn't get up from her seat but pointed to the chair opposite her. The signs were now all bad. No offer of coffee and no comfortable chair.

Without further preamble she said, 'I've got some bad news for you, Matthew, the Chief wants you off the case.' His heart dropped. He opened my mouth to tell her what he'd just discovered but closed it again. He had to play this hand close to his chest until he had the evidence. After a moment or two he managed to say, 'On what grounds ma'am?'

'He says the ACC thinks you are not capable of handling a case of this magnitude.'

The bile was rising in Prior's gullet. 'And that's it, I just step aside with my reputation ruined?'

She gave him a hard look. Then slowly shook her head. 'No, Matthew, that's not it, as you put it. I took him a copy of your murder file and managed to convince him you have been very thorough so he's given you another couple of days. Now we are both out on a limb.'

He took a moment to consider this information. Clearly Owen had gone in to bat for him. It looked as if both their careers were now on the line. Now he was itching to tell her what he'd found out at Handycabs, but you don't accuse a senior officer of breaking the rules without the evidence to back it up. Instead he simply said, 'Thank you ma'am.'

She smiled grimly. 'Now, tell me what developments there are in the case.'

Prior scratched his head, thinking how much he could tell her. In the end he said, 'Will you be you at home later this evening Ma'am?'

She frowned then nodded. 'Why?'

'I'm interviewing important witnesses later this afternoon. Once I've seen them I'll be in a better position to brief you properly.'

Her frown deepened. 'Why can't you tell me about it now?'

I looked her straight in the eye. 'Because I don't have evidence to back up what I think. I need you to trust me ma'am, just for a few hours more.'

She sat tapping her finger on the desk for what seemed an age. Finally, she looked up and nodded. 'OK, I'll expect to hear from you later this evening.'

He smiled his thanks and left her office as if walking on eggs.

19. The profiler.

'Where observation is concerned, chance favours the prepared mind.'
Louis Pasteur 1822-95

Arriving back at the enquiry van, Prior saw a tall thin woman sitting beside DS Quigley. She looked about fifty and was clearly not concerned with the dictates of fashion. Her steel-grey hair was cut short and there was no trace of make-up on her plain face. Rimless wired spectacles did nothing to soften her stern appearance.

She wore a blue polo neck sweater and blue jeans. The sweater revealed her best features, Prior thought, a magnificent pair of mammary glands. He tore his eyes off them as she rose to be introduced. Then he noticed her eyes. There was an amused twinkle in them as if she was enjoying some private joke; his face reddened as he realised what it was.

Quigley introduced them, 'Jessica Bloomfield, sir, this is Detective Chief Inspector Prior and DS Siobhan Williams.'

Her handshake was firm and there was just the merest hint of a smile on her lips.

He said, 'Call me Matthew please Ms Bloomfield. My apologies for not being here to greet you. I'm sure my sergeant has told you, we were at a post-mortem.'

'It's Miss, Chief Inspector, and please don't apologise, I understand the pressure you are under.' She spoke with no trace of an accent, carefully enunciating her words.

Siobhan put the oily paper bag she was carrying on Quigley's desk and shook Bloomfield's hand.

Looking down, Bloomfield said, 'I see you've brought your lunch with you. Don't let me disturb that. We can talk once you've eaten. Mr. Quigley here has given me plenty to read.'

Prior smiled his thanks. 'If you don't mind then, I'm famished. We'll be just ten minutes.' Grabbing two mugs of coffee he and Siobhan disappeared into his office.

Between bites of Cornish pasty Siobhan said, 'I wonder how long it's been going on, sir, with Stapleton I mean.'

'If there's an enquiry, I'm sure they'll find out. But we need to concentrate on how this affects our murder investigation. One thing I'm curious about is this woman who made the phone call; no doubt this Mrs. Chivers. If she was on the estate on the night of the murder, she could be a valuable witness. Remind me to make sure Albert follows that up once we get back on the estate.'

He continued, 'Anyway we've a more immediate problem. We must make sure we're ready for this evening. I'll have to spend time with Miss Bloomfield. I want you to do some checks on this cab company. And do CRO checks on Rhanji and the drivers whose names he gave us. And don't forget the photographs. But be discreet whatever you do, we don't want this blowing up in our faces.'

'Yes, sir.'

'Then take a couple of hours off. I'll pick you up at half five and we'll see what comes up. I'll have to spend some time with this profiler.'

'Great, I can do some shopping and some laundry.'

They finished their lunch and she slipped out quietly.

Prior called Quigley into his office and learned that Superintendent Owen had stayed only briefly when she had brought the profiler and she had not enquired too deeply into the progress of the investigation. She knew nothing of the anonymous call or the women in the taxis. He thanked the old DS and invited Bloomfield to join him in his office.

When they were seated he said, 'Right, tell me what you need.'

'The first thing I need is to know what your expectations are of me.'

He scratched his head. 'I suppose I hope that you might help identify the kind of person we are looking for.'

She nodded but said nothing. Prior waited too. The silence lengthened.

Finally, she prompted him, 'But you are not convinced that I can help you, are you?'

'I have an open mind.'

This time the smile spread to her lips. 'Do you?'

He smiled back at her. 'The one thing I don't expect you to do is to analyse me.'

'Is that what you think I'm doing?'

'Perhaps you'll be kind enough to tell me what you are doing. What I need are answers not questions. I do have a murder to investigate.'

She broke eye contact with him for the first time and looked down at her hands. 'And you'd like my help?'

His patience were beginning to wear thin. 'Yes. If you can help that is.' he snapped. Then, in a more conciliatory tone, he added, 'Miss Bloomfield, I'm having a hard day. First, I had to watch a pathologist cut and saw up a corpse. He told me that the victim had first been hit on the back of the head; then tied to a chair and tortured; then stabbed to death and beheaded. Then my investigation led me into territory I'd rather not go into. Now you are sitting here asking me questions when what I need are answers. I'm not finding that very helpful.'

She sat back in her chair. 'OK you are resisting me, that's quite natural. I'll tell you what I do then you can decide if I can help.'

'Thank you.'

She sat for a moment organising her thoughts. 'There is a great deal of mumbo-jumbo spoken and written about offender profiling. Let me tell you in simple language how I might be able to help your enquiry. Essentially I am a healer. At best, I help people deal with their troubled minds. It is an inexact science and my success rate is not especially high. But by studying people's minds I have acquired some knowledge of how minds work.

I and my colleagues worldwide communicate freely with each other so are constantly adding to our shared knowledge. Patterns emerge, and we are able to categorise people from those patterns. People become predictable to a degree. This applies to psychopaths and sociopaths, just like everyone else.' She smiled, 'Sometimes their unpredictability is predictable if that makes sense.'

Prior nodded.

She continued, 'Behaviours can be used to identify individuals, particularly those with troubled minds. Usually there is some behavioural history that is documented somewhere. In the case of criminals, often the person will have had previous contact with the police. That may help us trace them.'

Prior nodded, 'Thank you, now I understand a little better. What do you need?'

'At this stage just access to all the information you have on the death and the events leading up to it.'

'No problem, we'll link you into our computer. You are welcome to use this office if you wish, I'm seldom here.'

'Thank you, Chief Inspector, no. I would rather be in the general office where I can be in touch with events as they unfold.'

'Matthew will do Miss Bloomfield; Chief Inspector is quite a mouthful.'

She smiled. 'So is Miss Bloomfield, please call me Jessica.' She paused, then added, 'There is one more thing.'

'Yes?'

'There is an area of research that fringes on what we are doing here.'

'And what's that?'

'Instincts, Matthew.'

'Instincts? You mean like knowing not to put your hand in a fire?'

'No, that's learned behaviour, our instincts tell us to put our hand in the fire. It's called curiosity. I mean detectives hunches.'

'What about them?'

'Have you ever been curious about the phenomenon?'

'Not really, I haven't had the time.'

'Will you indulge me on this?'

'If I have the time, I do have a killer to catch.'

'And it is your hunches that may help you catch him. There is no other time that one can study the phenomenon except on the job. Indulge me please, Matthew. Do you have a hunch about this case?'

'Maybe, yes.'

'Will you share it with me?'

He sat looking at her without answering.

She said, 'You are not willing to share it with me?'

'Not at this stage, no.'

She stood up. 'I understand, we'll talk again.'

As the door closed behind her Prior picked up the phone and dialled a number.

Owen answered. He said, 'I've spoken with Jessica Bloomfield and given her access to the murder file.'

'And did you spend some time with her?'

'Yes, we've just had half-an-hour together.'

'Do you think she'll prove helpful?'

'I hope so, ma'am.'

Owen laughed. 'Non-committal as usual.'

'I'll try to keep an open mind ma'am.'

'Make sure you do. Give her a chance.'

'Yes, ma'am. And thank you.'

'What for?'

'For sticking up for me with the Chief.'

'I look forward to hearing from you later this evening.'

He put the phone down, opened the office door and called, 'Albert, spare me a minute.' As Quigley got up and walked towards him, Prior cursed to himself. The presence of Bloomfield was already disrupting the office routine. 'Come in and close the door, Albert.'

'Yes sir. '

When the old DS was seated Prior said, 'First let me tell you about the autopsy. Time of death between midnight and 2am. Cause of death a stab wound to the chest. He was also hit on the back of the head before he was killed, probably with some kind of a heavy tool. But here's the interesting bit. Wright was tortured before he was killed; the killer used a pair of pliers or something like that on two of his fingers. It seems he wanted some information from Wright. And it seems he may have got it, as he stopped after two fingers.

So I think this rules out a crime of passion. Clearly the killer wanted something from the lad and having got it, killed him. We still don't have any idea why he put the head on the gate and there has to be a reason for the killer doing that.'

Quigley nodded. 'So we're back to the estate, sir, and we can't go there.'

'Don't worry about that for the moment, Albert, there may be a way. I'll know more by this evening. This profiler, what do you make of her?'

Quigley smiled. 'How honest do you want me to be?'

'Tell me what you think.'

'I think she's a waste of space, sir. And she's already getting under my feet.'

'Humour her, Albert, give her what she wants. Now, I'm going home for an hour.

Siobhan and I have a call to make later; we're following up on this taxi lead. If anyone asks, you know nothing about it, do you understand?'

'Yes sir. Is this to do with the night of the murder?'

'I'll tell you later. But at this stage you keep shtum about it, even the fact we're questioning them. It's important Albert, do you understand?'

'Yes, sir.'

'Good. You can reach me on my mobile if you need me. Keep the team on their toes. I'll see you in the morning.'

20. The Call Girls.

'Man with all his noble qualities…. still bears, in his bodily frame the indelible stamp of his lowly origins.'

Charles Darwin 1809-82

Prior picked up Siobhan at her flat sharp at 5.30. She handed him a sheet of paper. It was the CRO checks on the three drivers they were going to interview, and Rhanji the manager. Prior sat and read it before they moved off. The taxi trade in the UK is an interesting one. Since the days of horse-drawn cabs, the Hackney Carriage Act had regulated those that plied for hire on the streets of the cities. Only persons of good character were granted a licence.

To the layman this may have seemed an unnecessary piece of bureaucracy. But the reality is that unscrupulous cab drivers can take advantage of innocents by inflating fares or prolonging routes. And they often operate on the fringes of crime. Even the more scrupulous ones usually know where drugs can be purchased and prostitutes found, to say nothing of illegal gambling joints and other fringe entertainments.

But the demand for cabs increased and the minicab industry thrived. The only difference between a licenced cab and minicab is that the former can stop in the street when hailed by a potential customer whereas minicabs must be booked in advance. The integrity of its drivers was, however, open to question; all they needed to operate was a driving licence and the appropriate insurance.

The list prepared by Siobhan showed that only one of the three named minicab drivers had had no previous brushes with the law. Prior was relieved to find that Rhan-ji, the manager, also had a clean record. His co-operation would be necessary to obtain the evidence they sought and his integrity might be questioned in any subsequent court action.

Prior looked up. 'What about the company, Siobhan, Handycabs?'

'Been operating for six years. The collator says there has been the occasional dispute with drivers and fares. But there's nothing on the company itself. Apparently Rhan-ji has been co-operative whenever he's been approached. He's always got rid of dodgy drivers when we've suggested it. For a cab company, it's surprisingly clean, sir.'

'Good, that should help.'

They arrived at the Handycabs office at 5.55pm. There were several drivers milling about on the public side of the counter as the shifts were about to change.

Once again the looks the two detectives received quickly changed from hopeful to suspicious as they were recognised for what they were. The dispatcher behind the counter recognised them and lifted the flap to let them pass. Rhanji was standing at his office door. He invited them in.

Prior thanked him. 'Are the drivers we want to interview here?'

'Two of them I've seen yes, sir. I'm sure the other one will be here shortly.'

'Have you told them we want to interview them?'

'No, sir, you asked me not to.'

'Good. Do you mind if we interview them in here?'

'Not at all. I can work from the dispatcher's desk.'

'It's important that the ones we've interviewed don't chat to the ones we haven't yet seen. Is there some way you can organise that?'

'Yes, sir, we get a lot of calls this time of day. I can send them out as you finish with them.'

Prior smiled. 'We appreciate your co-operation, Mr Rhanji. Please send the first one in.'

A stocky man in his sixties entered. Prior invited him to sit and turned on the tape recorder. He introduced himself and Siobhan then got straight down to business. 'We are conducting a murder enquiry and need to ask you some questions. First, can I ask your name?'

The man gave it as Norman Mills. This was the one driver with a clean police record.

Prior said, 'I understand that you took a fare to the Sinclair Estate on the night of the twelfth/ thirteenth of this month, Mr Mills. Is that correct?'

Mills licked his lips. 'Er, Tuesday? Yes, that's right.'

'What time was that?'

'About nine o'clock.'

'Where did you pick up this fare?'

'Laurel Avenue, here in Truro'

'Can you remember which house?'

'Yes, it was number five; he was outside waiting for me. I dropped him back there later.'

'What time was that?'

'Sometime after two in the morning, something like that.'

Prior looked into the man's eyes. 'Would you recognise this man if you saw him again?'

Without hesitation Mills replied. 'Yes, he was a good tipper I've picked him up a few times.'

'Does he always go to the Sinclair Estate when you pick him up?'

'Yes and he always wants picking up later.'

'You say a few times, how many exactly.'

Mills frowned. 'Four or five I think, I can't be more exact that that.'

'Over what period of time, Mr. Mills?'

'Can't say exactly. Probably over the last three months or so.'

Prior produced a photograph. It had been cut from a magazine and showed a group of twelve men in evening dress. The caption at the bottom had been cut off. 'Do you see that man here, Mr Mills?'

Watching this, Siobhan became tense waiting for the answer.

Mills pointed to one of the figures. 'Yes sir, it was that man there, the big one.'

'Are you absolutely sure it was that man you took to the Sinclair Estate on the night of the twelfth and picked him up at two in the morning from the estate?'

'Yes, sir, he gave me a £5 tip and we've done the trip several times as I said. I'd recognise him anywhere.'

'Can you remember what he was wearing that night?'

'Light-coloured raincoat, dark suit and collar and tie.'

Prior looked at Siobhan. She nodded, 'Tell me Mr. Mills when you picked him up to take him home from the Sinclair Estate which gate did you use?'

'The front gate, the one in Penwin Lane.'

'Was that coming and going?'

'Yes, of course.'

'And did you notice anything strange about the gate when you were leaving?'

He shook his head vigorously, 'Do you mean was there a head on it?'

She nodded.

He smiled. 'No definitely not.'

'Remind me sir, what time was that.'

'Just after 2am.'

Prior took over the questioning, 'Have you taken other fares to the estate or picked them up there, Mr Mills?'

'A few months ago, I picked up two girls from there, brought them to Truro. That was late at night too.'

'Thank you, you've been very helpful. I just need for you to sign a statement for me before you go.'

'Is this man the killer then, sir? Is he the one that put the head on the gate?'

Prior smiled. 'No, we don't think he had anything to do with the death. We are just checking on everyone who visited the estate that night. They might have witnessed something. It would be helpful if you didn't speak to your colleagues until we've interviewed them, or anyone else for that matter. We'd like to keep our enquiry confidential for the moment. Did you see anyone else at Sinclair House that night?'

'Two young girls, they were waiting for a cab. I told them one was on its way.'

'Anyone else?'

'Well there was a man in the doorway of the house but I didn't see his face.'

The next driver they interviewed was Claire Pearson, a chubby woman in her forties. She had bleached hair and a well-worn face. Prior noted from Siobhan's list that she had previous for prostitution and shoplifting but nothing recent.

As she sat down, she said, 'This is about the other night, is it?' She spoke in an aggressive tone.

Prior ignored her question and made the same introduction he had made to Mills. She gave her name and added, 'So this is about the other night.'

'What about the other night, Mrs. Pearson?'

'I took two girls up to the house, that's all I know.'

'What night was that?'

'Tuesday.'

'What time did you pick the girls up?'

'Picked 'em up at 9.30.'

'You said the house, which house?'

'Sinclair House, on the big estate.'

'Where did you pick them up?'

'In Blake Street.'

'Where in Blake Street?'

She looked at the table. 'Just in Blake Street, they were standing in the street.'

Prior waited until she looked up. Then he said sternly, 'Do yourself a favour, Mrs Pearson. I've told you this is a murder enquiry. You've kept out of trouble for some time now, no need to get back into bad habits. Just tell us what you know then we'll leave you in peace.'

He paused, then asked the question again, 'Where exactly did you pick them up from?'

She took a while to answer; eventually said, 'Brian's Escort Agency.'

'What were their names?'

'Why do you want those?'

'Just tell us their names, they're not in any trouble.'

'Mary and Sarah, that's all I know.'

'And the time you picked them up again?'

'Just after half past nine.'

'There that wasn't so difficult, was it? We just need you to sign a statement and then you can go.'

When she had done so, Prior told her to keep her mouth closed about the enquiry and thanked her for her help.

When the door closed behind her Prior said, 'Now for the difficult one. This Bolton has done time for blagging. There's no way he should be trusted in a cab.' He used the slang term for armed robbery.

Trevor Bolton was a huge man of about forty. He wore an open necked shirt and a leather jacket. The top of a tattoo showed on his neck and on the little finger of his left hand he wore a gold signet ring. He looked the stereotypical self-styled hard man. Having made eye contact briefly with each of the detectives, he aimed his gaze above their heads, avoiding their stares.

Prior introduced himself and added, 'I'm conducting a murder investigation and need to ask you some questions. State your name please.'

'I know nothing about no murder.'

'You are not a suspect as far as we know, if you were we'd have given you a caution. But you were near a crime scene on the night in question. All we want is a record of your movements that night. But first of all, state your name.'

Bolton said nothing, continuing to look over their heads.

Prior sighed inwardly. He'd played this game with several so-called hard men. In their own minds they had built this image of how strong they were and tried to convince the world that it was true. But the result was usually the same.

After they strutted their defiance for as long as they could, they caved in quickly. He gave Bolton a full twenty seconds, then he said, 'OK, you want to play hard, we'll continue this at the police station.'

Bolton looked at Prior. His face showed the thought processes that were going on inside his head. Finally, he licked his lips and said, 'Trevor Bolton.'

Once he'd showed how hard he was, he crumbled quickly, if reluctantly. He told them that he'd picked two girls up at Sinclair House at just after 2am and dropped them off at Blake Street in Truro. He had seen nothing unusual, certainly not a head on the gate of the estate. Bolton signed his statement and left.

*

Once the door had closed behind him, Prior looked at Siobhan. 'Whew! We were lucky it was Mills that picked up Stapleton. I doubt the other two would have picked him out on that photograph. Even if they had, with their records they would not have made very reliable witnesses.'

'This is a bit out of my league, sir. What do we do with this now?'

'I drop you home and go to see Owen. I dump it on her lap then go home myself.'

'Isn't it a bit sad, sir? I've no love for Stapleton but he's thrown away his career over a prostitute. What on earth possessed him?'

'That's a good question. He's got a wife and two grown-up kids. This will destroy more than his career. As I said earlier, he obviously had some itch that he had to scratch. Probably thought he'd be safe on Sinclair's private estate, just bad timing on his part that someone chose that night to put the head on the gate. He either had to tell us about his visit or bluff it out. I've no doubt that Sinclair phoned him after we spoke to him and told him to deny being there. Once he'd taken that path there was no turning back. It explains why he didn't chair the press conference. He didn't want his face plastered all over the tele.'

'Do you know his wife, sir?'

'I've met her, yes. Can't say I know her. She didn't come across as the loving type. Cold as a fish, not that I'm suggesting she deserves something like this.'

'What'll happen to him now?'

'That's up to the Chief Constable. He'll have to get an ACC from another force to carry out an enquiry. Stapleton will probably be suspended pending the result.'

'And then?'

'Then it depends on how careful we've been, collecting the evidence. He could be charged with falsifying evidence as the time the head was put on that gate could prove crucial to our case. But that's a worst-case scenario. I expect he'll go quietly, take early retirement. It's a shame really. If he'd owned up straight away, he'd probably have got away with a slap on the wrist. I don't imagine for one moment he had anything to do with the murder. But, there you go, Siobhan, it doesn't do to try to bully or bluff your way through things.'

Leaving the office, they thanked Rhanji for his help and went to Prior's car. He used his mobile to phone Owen. She was at home. 'I've got something I need to talk to you about ma'am and it won't wait till the morning.'

'OK, Matthew, you know where I live.'

Prior dropped off Siobhan and drove to Owen's home. She answered his ring immediately and let him in. She said, 'I've made coffee, Matthew, go into the lounge and I'll bring it through. Prior sank into an armchair and opened his briefcase. He put the tape recorder on the coffee table and rewound it. Owen came through from the kitchen, put a tray on the table and poured two coffees.

'OK, talk to me,' she said.

Prior started, 'Apart from nutters, there was just one interesting response to our appeal for witnesses to the murder. It was a woman's voice; she wouldn't give her name but I've no doubt she's one of the women who cleans at Sinclair House, a Mrs. Chivers. She said we should look into goings-on at the house.

Owen remained silent, listening intently.

Prior continued, ' At the same time the village constable in Penwin told us he'd seen taxis leaving the estate late at night with young women in the back. He recognised the cab company. I had no choice but to follow it up.'

She nodded. 'Of course.'

'This morning Siobhan and I went to see the manager of the cab company. He gave us this, ma'am.' He put the schedule of pick-ups and drop-offs at the Sinclair Estate on the table in front of her. He pointed to the entries for the 12th and 13th.

She looked up, 'Two pick-ups at 2am? What does this mean?'

'We interviewed the drivers who made those pick-ups just before I called you, ma'am. I taped the interviews.'

Her eyes were still riveted to the schedule. Her finger was on the line indicating the pick up at Laurel Crescent, destination the Sinclair Estate. She looked up. 'And this one?' Clearly she had worked out from the simple abbreviations that this was Laurel Crescent

'That's also on the tape, ma'am.'

She nodded grimly. 'Let me hear the tape.'

He played her the tape. The only time he interrupted was when reference was made to the photograph.

There he stopped the tape and put the photograph on the table pointing to Stapleton. 'This is the man the driver identified as the man he picked up.'

She sat back with a grim expression on her face. 'Play me the rest of the tape.'

He did so.

There was a long pause. Finally she said, 'Who knows about this, Matthew?'

'Just DS Williams and me. DS Quigley knows we were making the enquiry but not the result.'

'Does the cab driver, what's his name, Mills?' Prior nodded. 'Does he know who his fare was?'

'Not as far as we know ma'am; we didn't tell him and the photograph we used doesn't identify him.'

'Well done, Matthew, we can do without the scandal this will bring if it gets out.'

There was silence for several moments. Owen broke it. 'How does this effect your investigation, Matthew?'

He scratched the back of his head, 'Other than helping to pin down the time the head was put on the gate, I don't think it does. Although it does explain a few things.'

'Such as?'

'Why Sinclair didn't want us sniffing around the estate. And why Stapleton supported him. It also explains why he didn't chair the press conference.'

'Did you take formal statements from the drivers?'

He handed them to her.

'Thank you, Matthew, you've been very thorough as always. You realise the implications of this? I'll have to take this to the very top. In the meantime you and Siobhan must not say a word to anyone.'

'No problem there, I'm conducting a murder enquiry not a witch hunt.'

She smiled, if a little grimly for the first time since he had arrived. 'I'm glad I had faith in you Matthew. You've done exactly the right thing. Now leave all this with me and get home to that lovely wife of yours. The Chief is not going to be very happy but that's life.'

'I don't think any of us are happy about it, ma'am. None of us like to see a colleague hung out to dry, even if he is an arsehole.'

She laughed. 'I'll forgive your choice of words just this once, Matthew. In fact I might even agree with you.'

Prior looked at his watch as he arrived home, 9.30, yet another long day. Jeanette was in the lounge reading. He kissed her and said, 'Would you like a drink love, I need one.'

'Yes, a G and T. Then you must tell me what happened today.'

She listened without interruption as he did so. Only when he'd finished did she speak, 'You poor love. It isn't bad enough you have a gruesome murder to deal with. Now you have this. What will happen to Stapleton?'

He told her what he expected would happen. She nodded and sat thinking.

'How did Siobhan deal with the post-mortem this morning?'

'Not well, it was a bad one.'

'It's a rotten job, especially for a woman.'

He snuggled up to her on the couch and said, 'I'd get hung for saying that, equal opportunities and all.'

She smiled. 'You probably would but I won't.'

'Humph! Typical woman take every advantage you can.'

'It makes up for all those muscles you men are always parading in front of us.'

'Do you want to see my muscles?'

'Not at the moment, I'm enjoying my G and T.'

He went to pull away from her. She said, 'But behave yourself and you might get lucky later.'

He replaced his arm around her shoulders. 'Behaving myself now, ma'am.'

21. The Village Constable.

'When constabulary duty's to be done,
A policeman's lot is not a happy one,'

The Pirates of Penzance.

Day five was another bright day, although the early morning temperature was not much above zero. As he drove to Penwin, Prior tried unsuccessfully to concentrate on the murder enquiry. He couldn't get the Stapleton affair out of his mind. He knew that at some stage he would be summoned to see the Chief Constable, who would want to hear the evidence straight from the horse's mouth.

Normal procedure when an officer is accused of bringing the force into disrepute is to appoint an investigating officer of at least equal rank to the accused. In this case someone from another force would have to be brought in as officers of that rank were rather thin on the ground in the Devon and Cornwall Constabulary. The Home Office would have to be informed and there was a danger that politics would interfere further with his murder enquiry.

He was determined that should not happen. But a Chief Inspector was pretty low in the pecking order and would not have much say in the matter. His best bet was to get the case solved as soon as possible. That meant he must concentrate his mind. And that was his problem; it was a catch-22 situation. The politics threatened to inhibit his clear thinking and he needed a great deal of clear thinking to solve the case.

Arriving at the enquiry van he saw that Owen's car was there before him. 'Shit!' he said under his breath; it might be too late already. He found her sitting drinking coffee with DS Quigley.

She greeted him with a tired smile. She'd obviously had a long night. 'Good morning Matthew, get yourself a coffee we must talk.'

He grabbed a cup from the machine and followed her to his tiny office.

As soon as they were seated, she began, 'It's been a busy night. Stapleton has been suspended. The Chief has asked for his resignation. He's given Stapleton the option. If he goes quietly that will be an end to the matter, subject of course to the result of your murder enquiry.'

Prior nodded but said nothing knowing that there was more to come.

She continued, 'I'm being pressured to take you off the case. The Chief wants to bring in Detective Superintendent Ward.'

'Can I ask why, ma'am?'

'He is suggesting that you might have a conflict of interests, particularly as Sinclair has complained about you.'

Prior was struggling to hold his temper. 'So I'm being penalised for doing my job.'

'No, Matthew you are not. I said that was what the Chief suggested. I told him I didn't agree with him. Fortunately you taped your interview with Sinclair, there's nothing on the tape that suggests you behaved anything but properly.' What she didn't say was that she had threatened to resign herself if the Chief Constable took that action. 'The investigation is still in your hands. But it does mean that you will be under a microscope. Don't let me down, Matthew.'

Prior heaved a sigh of relief. She had gone in to bat for him again. 'Thank you ma'am,' he said with feeling.

'No need to thank me, Matthew, I have every confidence in you. Just hang on to your temper. And get me a result.'

He smiled, realising she had put her career prospects on the line for him. 'I'll give it everything I have.'

'I know you will. Now, tell me how the investigation is going.'

He took a deep breath and said, 'I think I mentioned on the phone yesterday that Wright was tortured before he was killed.'

She nodded, 'Do you have any idea why?'

'I can only guess. He had some information the killer wanted.'

'What kind of information?'

'That's the question. I think that when we have the answer to that we'll know who the killer is.'

There was a long pause. She broke it, 'What do your instincts tell you about the case, Matthew?'

He smiled. 'That's the same questions your profiler asked me. Don't laugh. Buried treasure.'

'I'm not laughing. What evidence do you have? And what did you tell Jessica?'

'You asked me about my instincts, ma'am, not about evidence and I didn't tell Jessica anything.'

'Don't play games, Matthew, what makes you think that?'

He frowned and considered his answer. Finally he said, 'The only thing we've found that's out of sync with the victim's lifestyle is a serious book on the ancient Celts we found it in his bedside cabinet. It's an authoritative work by an academic. Everything else we've found suggests that Wright was a simple soul, not especially bright. For the life of me I can't see him ploughing through that, let alone understanding it. So why did he have it?'

Clearly it was a rhetorical question. Owen remained silent.

He continued, 'Coupled with that, when DS Williams and I had a walk where Wright had been working on the estate just before he died, we found something interesting. It was a small stone column with a Celtic cross carved on it. It was in the middle of a patch of brambles that Wright had been cutting back on his tractor. What was interesting was that someone had scraped the moss off the carving. The third thing is that archaeologists had applied to Sinclair to dig on his land and he'd refused them permission.'

'Interesting. Anything else?'

'Now we find that Wright was tortured before he was killed. What on earth could he have known that was worth torturing and killing him for? And why stick his head on a spike?'

Owen's brow was now furrowed as she thought about this information. Eventually she asked, 'Is there anything else, evidence-wise?'

'Circumstantial and thin. More a guess than evidence.'

'Tell me about it.'

'When Wright disappeared from the village the night he was killed, it was between the pub and his cottage. We timed it, an eight-minute walk and all through the brightly lit village streets. Now Wright was a big strong lad and parking in the village is a nightmare. No one saw or heard anything, so it seems likely that wherever he went he went willingly. This coupled with the fact that he told his girlfriend that he had a surprise in store for her leads me to the thought that perhaps he went to meet someone that night and lied to his girlfriend about having an early night.'

'And that's all you have?'

'Yes, ma'am.'

She sat thinking for a few moments. She looked up. 'What's your next step?'

'I want to search the Sinclair Estate properly to see if there is anything to this buried treasure theory. We also need to re-question all the people who work on the estate. Maybe one of them has some idea what Wright found. Someone must have some idea of what was going on.'

She smiled wanly. 'On top of this Stapleton business that might raise a few hackles. Let me have a word with the Chief Constable.'

'I want to search the house as well.'

'On what grounds?'

'Sinclair is hiding something. I want to know what it is.'

'Surely all he was hiding was his sexual trysts. You'll need more than that and you know it.'

He returned her smile. 'Yes, ma'am. The other thing I want to do is have a word with the guy that leant Wright the book. He was the gamekeeper on the estate before he retired. I'd like to see what he thinks of the buried treasure theory.'

'Good, go ahead with that. In the meantime I'll try to get you back on the estate.'

'Thank you, ma'am. And thank you for your backing.'

'Just get me a result, Matthew.'

When Owen had gone, Prior sat at his desk poring over statements. It was now day four of the enquiry and he was no closer to solving it than he had been on day one. He had sent Siobhan off to Grampian Village to sniff around. It was where Wright had grown up and there was just the chance that someone there might know something about his past that would be useful. It was also where he had been seen with another woman. He sat reviewing the evidence in the hope that he might find some inconsistency. He was beginning to lose hope of that happening.

There was a light knock on his door. 'Come in,' he called.

The door opened to reveal a uniformed constable. He had his helmet in his hand and wore a pair of cycle clips on his ankles. He said awkwardly, 'PC Gibbons, sir, you wanted to see me.'

Prior frowned for a moment, not recognising the name. Then it came to him. 'Are you the Penwin village constable, Gibbons?'

'Yes, sir, that's me.'

'Come in and sit down. You can take your cycle clips off, nothing's going to run up your trouser leg here.'

Gibbons squeezed his large frame into the only other chair in the room. Then he looked round for somewhere to put his helmet as the desk was covered in papers. 'Put it on the floor, man,' Prior said impatiently.

Gibbons did so and took off his cycle clips.

Prior pushed the pile of statements on his desk to one side to make room for his elbows. He leant forward. 'How long have you been in the village?'

'Three years, sir.' He was a big man in his late twenties and looked uncomfortable squeezed into the small space. He didn't seem to know what to do with his cycle clips and fiddled with them with his hands.

Prior smiled, conscious of the fact that he was making the man nervous. He tried a gentler tone, 'Relax, Gibbons, I just wanted to have a chat.'

The youngster returned the smile and his body slumped a little in the confined space.

'It was you that saw these young women leaving the estate in a taxi, right?

Gibbons nodded.

'How comes you were on patrol at that time of night?'

'Mr Sinclair complained to the Inspector, sir. Said there were people prowling around the estate. I do a couple of late shifts each week anyway so made a point of riding up there, just to check the gates and that.'

'When did he make the complaint?'

'Must have been about a week ago, sir.'

'What did he actually say about the prowlers?'

'Well, it were Inspector Bradley he actually spoke to. It were he who told me to check for intruders.'

'Did you find any?'

'No, sir. Penwin Lane is quiet at the best of time, let alone at night. The road doesn't lead anywhere, see, except back to the main St. Austell, Truro road. At night you don't see a soul.'

'Where did you actually see the taxis?'

'First time just as I was leaving the village, that were months ago, it were coming towards me. Second time I saw it coming out of the gate to the estate.'

'The one in Penwin Lane?'

'Yes sir.'

'Do you still do these night patrols?'

'Yes, sir, twice a week.'

'You didn't happen to do one on the night of the twelfth did you?'

Gibbons smiled, 'No, sir, unfortunately not.'

'And have you ever seen anyone on these patrols.'

'Not really, sir, no.'

Picking up some doubt in this reply he probed deeper, 'You're sure, no-one at all?'

'Just the night duty area car, sir. Oh, and old Tom Williamson walking his dog.'

'Really, where exactly did you see him?'

'Just outside the village sir, in Penwin Lane.'

'Did you speak to him?'

'Yes sir, of course. He said he couldn't sleep so he took his dog for a walk.'

'Was he carrying anything?'

'Just his stick,, he don't walk too well.'

'When was this exactly?'

'A week ago today.'

'And what time?'

'Just after midnight, I think.'

Prior wrinkled his brow. 'What do you know about this man, Gibbons?'

'Used to be the gamekeeper up at the estate. Retired five years ago, I think. Lives in a cottage in the village with his son. Just the two of them.'

'Isn't he some kind of historian?'

'I don't know about that, but he does ramble on sometimes about the past.'

'How many times did you actually see him at night, Gibbons?'

'Just the once sir.'

'Which way was he walking when you saw him?'

'Back towards the village.'

'Didn't you ask him where he'd been? You were looking for prowlers weren't you?'

'Yes, sir. As I said, he just told me he couldn't sleep so took his dog for a walk.'

'And you're sure he wasn't carrying anything other than a walking stick?'

'Yes I'm sure. I even looked inside his coat. He wasn't carrying anything.'

'Did you report this at the time?'

'No, sir.'

'Why on earth not?'

Gibbons hesitated nervously. 'Well sir, he weren't doing anything wrong. And no crimes had been reported. And he were nowhere near the estate, he were just walking his dog.'

'How far from the estate was it that you saw him?'

'He was only just outside the village, sir, best part of a half-a-mile from the estate.'

Prior nodded, he could see Gibbons' dilemma. People did walk their dogs at night; there was certainly no law against it.

He changed tack. 'Back to these intruders Sinclair complained about. There's nothing in the crime books about intruders. What were they supposed to have been up to on the estate?'

'Don't rightly know sir, he spoke to the Inspector.'

'Ask Inspector Bradley to call me, will you?'

Gibbons nodded. 'Yes, sir.'

'So you spotted no-one else on all those patrols, just old Tom and his dog?'

'Just him and the taxis, sir, that's about all.'

'Have you ever been called up to the estate?'

'Just the once. Ben Stevens, one of the farmhands, had a fall and broke his leg. I had to do an accident report so he could claim the insurance.'

'Who did you speak to?'

'Just Stevens, sir, and Mr Callaghan, the farm manager.'

'Do you know the villagers that work up at the house?'

'Yes, sir, Mrs. Chivers does the cleaning and Sally Mc-Grath helps in the kitchen.'

'Does the butler, Brighton, come into the village much?'

He shook his head, 'Hardly at all Mrs. Brighton comes into the shop now and again but I think they have most stuff delivered.'

Prior paused; he was fast running out of questions. 'What's the word in the village about the murder, Gibbons, what are people saying?'

Gibbons shook his head, 'Nobody seems to have a clue, sir. John Wright wasn't wild like some and he was well liked.'

'Does anyone have any idea why this might have happened?'

'Not to Wright, sir, no.' He hesitated as if he had more to say.

'What else were you going to say?'

'Well I don't want to speak out of turn, sir.'

Prior smiled. 'You're not giving evidence here. Tell me what people are saying.'

Reluctantly, Gibbons told him, 'Well sir, Mr Sinclair upset a lot of people in the village. Sacked a lot of the locals when his father died and some of them had to move out of their cottages. They were tied cottages see, tied to the estate. Mr. Sinclair wanted to sell them. And without jobs the farmhands couldn't afford to buy them. He ain't very popular in the village.'

Prior nodded. 'I can imagine. Anything else you can tell me?'

'No, sir.'

'OK. Just remember in future when you do a stop in the street, whatever the outcome you record it, understand?'

The PC nodded.

When Gibbons had left, Prior sat thinking about what he'd been told. It didn't amount to much in terms of the investigation. Sinclair was obviously unpopular locally but he wasn't the victim, one of his farm workers was. Prior sighed and looked at his watch. It was approaching noon and he had promised to take his family out to lunch. He'd decided to take the rest of the weekend off and spend time with them.

22. The Weekend.

Happy is the hare at morning
As it cannot read the hunter's thoughts.

W.H. Auden.

The joy on his children's faces when they all arrived at Mc-Donalds was reward enough for keeping his promise to them. He managed to put all thoughts of the enquiry out of his mind. When they were all seated at a table with their trays of food in front of them, Natalie said importantly to her sister, 'Mummy has chicken nuggets because she only likes home-made burgers.'

Prior and his wife exchanged looks. He wondered how much longer they could get away with innuendos. The girls were growing up fast and they took everything in. After lunch they drove to Falmouth. It was a typical winter's day, cold but bright. As they walked along the road above the harbour, Prior was reminded again of the case. Across the Carrick Roads he could see St Mawes Castle. The rocky ledge below, where they had found the torso, was under water. The tide was running fast.

Noticing the change in his mood, Jeanette said, 'What's happening with the case, Matthew?'

He looked at her, 'Not much at the moment, love, this Stapleton affair has thrown us a bit off balance.'

'So you've heard nothing more about that?'

'Owen says that he's been suspended and asked to resign. Let's hope that will be an end to it.'

Natalie interrupted them. She said, 'Look daddy, look. What's that big ship there?' It was a large vessel in battle-ship grey but carried no armaments.

Prior said, 'Some kind of supply ship, princess. Takes food and provisions to the fighting ships at sea.'

'What sort of provisions, daddy?'

He went into a long explanation and the murder was pushed to the back of his mind once more.

The next 24 hours passed peacefully. On Sunday morning they drove to the Eden Project and spent three hours wandering through the tropical and sub-tropical plants. Then home where Prior prepared the Sunday lunch, helped by Samantha who already had an interest in cooking. It was only in the evening when they were sat in front of the TV that his peace was interrupted. The phone rang.

23. Another death.

'However many ways there are of being alive, it is certain that there are vastly more ways of being dead.'

'There's been another killing, sir.'

Prior sighed heavily, 'Where this time?'

'On the Sinclair Estate, sir.'

'What?' Then after a moment, 'Give me the details.'

'I've only got the bare details, sir. Sergeant Green from St. Austell called it in, he's at the scene. He said it's by the stream.'

'OK, phone DS Williams. Tell her I'll pick her up in twenty minutes. Tell her to bring her wellies. And inform DS Quigley. Tell him to get the team together. Tell Sergeant Green not to disturb the scene any more than he has to.'

Prior put the phone down and beckoned Jeanette. When they were out of the hearing of the girls, he told her the news.

She frowned. 'I'm getting fed up with this Matthew; there must be better ways of earning a living.'

He shrugged his shoulders. 'It's what I do best, love. It would kill me sitting behind a desk.' He leaned towards her and she offered only her cheek to be kissed, a sure sign of her displeasure.

It was already dark outside as he walked to his car. Those few discordant words from Jeanette had affected his mood more than the news of the killing. There had been a few crises in his marriage about the demands of his job but they had weathered them all so far. Nevertheless he knew there was a limit to how much she would take.

As he started the car and drove the short distance to Siobhan's flat, he struggled to get those thoughts out of his mind. She was waiting for him on the pavement. She had dressed for the occasion, wearing blue jeans, a sweater and a fashionable donkey jacket. She carried her Wellington boots in her hand.

She got into the car beside him, slamming the door. 'This bloody job is ruining my love life, sir. I was on a promise tonight. Wouldn't it be nice if murderers and crooks worked office hours?'

'Think of the positives, more overtime. You'll be richer than I am.'

'Yes. And never get the time to spend it.'

He gave her a hard glance. 'Stop moaning and get your mind on the job. By the sound of it we've got another crime scene.'

She laughed, 'It was the job I had my mind on sir.'

He couldn't help but smile.

There was a line of cars parked along Penwin Lane on either side of the entrance to the estate. 'Here we go again, the vultures are gathering.' One or two of the more eager members of the press moved forward as their car approached. Prior ignored them and drove straight to the gate. The uniformed constable on duty recognised him and waved him through. Prior saw that it was Gibbons, the village constable. He wound his window down and said, 'Keep the vultures out and take your bloody cycle clips off, you're not on your bike now.'

The young PC smiled wanly. 'Yes, sir. I forgot.'

Prior drove across the bridge over the stream and up the tree-lined drive till he reached the open ground. On his right he could see lights shining through the trees. He pulled onto the grass verge and parked behind an ambulance and two police cars already there. He got his Wellingtons from the boot, put them on, then brandishing a torch he led the way along the field beside the bramble hedge towards the lights.

Yellow police tape marked a gap that had been made in the brambles; a uniformed constable stood guarding the entrance to the gap. He recognised the detectives and nodded them past. Forcing their way through, they saw to their left a group of uniforms and a man in a Burberry coat. Prior recognised him as Callaghan, the estate manager.

Halogen lamps illuminated a grim scene. In the harsh light they saw a body lying across the path, its head close to the edge of the stream. It lay on its back but the face was unrecognisable, even as a face. Prior swallowed hard to keep down his Sunday lunch. He heard Siobhan gasp for breath beside him. 'Take it easy, Siobhan, let me deal with this.'

As they neared the scene, Sergeant Green met them. 'Evening, sir, Siobhan. This man here, Callaghan, found the body at about 5.30. He says it's Mr Sinclair, his boss. Though how he recognised him is beyond me, he's in an awful mess.'

'Has the body been moved?'

'No, sir, the paramedics examined it, other than that we haven't touched it.'

Prior nodded and looked around. Two uniformed constables, two paramedics and the witness stood with hands in pockets on the path close to the body. Prior gave Green a hard look and took him along the path and out of the hearing of the others. Then in a quiet but angry voice he said, 'What the hell are you doing here, having a picnic? This is a crime scene. Get those people,' he waved his hand at the group by the body, 'out of here.'

Green opened his mouth to speak; then closed it again.

Prior added, 'Tell the witness to wait on the other side of the hedge and the two PC's to go and help Gibbons keep the press at bay. Get them off that path. Did it never occur to you that the killer may have left footprints?'

The sergeant turned away, shamefaced. Prior raised his voice and called after him, 'And tell your man in the field that no-one other than my team and the pathologist comes through the hedge. Do you hear me?'

Green turned his head. 'Yes, sir.'

As the group pushed their way back through the hedge Prior glared at them. Only when they had disappeared from sight did he turn his attention to the scene.

He gingerly approached the body, keeping to the grass that fringed the path. He knelt down beside the corpse. Broken teeth showed through torn lips. One eyeball was dislodged and lay on what had once been a cheek. A mess of blood, raw flesh and bone splinters hid the other eye. The skull had been beaten with such savagery that it was impossible to tell where the face ended and the hair began. Blood pooled beneath the head and ran down into the stream. In the harsh lights it looked black and had the consistency of oil.

Beside him Siobhan spoke, 'My god, this is worse than the first. What kind of an animal are we dealing with?'

'An animal wouldn't do this, Siobhan, only human beings are this cruel.'

The body was clothed in sturdy walking boots, twill trousers tucked into woollen socks and a green Burberry jacket buttoned to the neck. After a moment or two Prior stood up and took a pace back, a whole host of thoughts filling his mind. Finally he spoke, 'Murder weapon, what did the killer use?'

Knowing it was a rhetorical question, Siobhan remained silent.

'And what was Sinclair doing here, just taking the air or did he have a purpose? Did the killer lay in wait or did Sinclair surprise him? In which case what was the killer doing here?'

Siobhan looked around her. Along this stretch the stream and the path beside it ran fairly straight. 'I doubt he was ambushed, sir, there's nowhere really to hide. You can see for some distance in either direction, or at least you could in the daylight.'

Prior nodded. 'What time did it get dark today, Siobhan?'

'Some time after five, I think.'

'Make a note to check with the Met Office. It could be important.' He frowned. 'And what was Callaghan doing here I wonder.'

'Maybe they were both checking for intruders. Perhaps Sinclair disturbed one.'

Prior considered this, then shook his head. 'No, an intruder would simply run away when disturbed, not beat the guy who discovered him to death, not like this anyway. The killer must have hit him a dozen times after he was dead. What kind of intruder would be that savage? It doesn't make sense.'

'There's an awful lot of anger here, sir.'

'Yes, a whole lot more than you'd expect from a simple poacher. But what the hell else would an intruder be looking for?' He smiled grimly. 'Jessica will have a field day with this one.'

Siobhan shivered. 'What could have set this off, sir? I mean something must have triggered this maniac to start on this terrible rampage.'

'Who knows what goes on in troubled minds, Siobhan? But it does confirm what everyone has been telling us, Sinclair was not very popular locally.'

'Is that what they call British understatement, sir?'

Prior smiled grimly and made no reply.

He looked around. 'I wonder where the intruder got onto the estate. We must find out from Callaghan if the gates were open this afternoon. I think we'll have to search the whole area but that will have to wait till the morning.'

'Where are we in relation to the Celtic cross, sir?'

'I think it's about twenty or thirty yards further along, we'll check when we have some light.' He paused then handed her his torch. 'You have a look along the path Siobhan, I'm going to have a word with Callaghan. And mind where you put your feet.' She rolled her eyes at him in the darkness.

Prior found Callaghan chatting to the constable on the other side of the hedge. He was a stocky man in his forties, dressed in a heavy combat jacket, corduroy trousers and the inevitable green Wellington boots. His thick, dark brown hair was covered in a smart flat cap.

Prior started, 'Bit of a shock finding your boss like that, Mr Callaghan?'

'That's an understatement, Chief Inspector. I only recognised him from the ring on his finger.'

'How's that, sir?'

'On the third finger of his right hand, he wears a signet ring with the family crest on it.'

Prior nodded. 'How did you happen to be down here?'

'Walking the dogs, usually do in the late afternoon.' His speech was articulate but with a soft West Country lilt.

'Were the gates open today?'

'No, we keep them closed on Sundays.'

'No one working today then.'

'Only the lads doing the milking, they only stay a couple of hours. In the winter we keep the cattle in on a Sunday.'

'Do you usually take your walk down here by the stream?'

'Sometimes, not always.'

'Which direction did you come from?'

'From the Lamb Lane end. The dogs spotted him lying there, they went mad.'

Prior nodded. 'I'm sure they would have. Where are the dogs now Mr. Callaghan?'

'I left them up at my cottage when I went to phone the police.'

'Did Mr Sinclair often walk the estate?'

'Now and again, not regularly.'

'When did you last see him alive?'

'Just before lunch, about midday? I was in the office doing the books, he just popped in.'

'Any particular reason?'

'No, just for a chat.'

'How did you get on with him?'

Callaghan took a moment to choose his words, 'If I'm honest, he wasn't the easiest man to work for. But I did my job and he let me get on with it, generally speaking.'

'Generally speaking?'

'Well he'd occasionally blow his top about something or other. But he'd soon get over it.'

'What sort of thing did he blow his top about?'

'Usually something one of the hands had done or not done properly; or when one got out of line.'

'In what way out of line?'

'Well, if he thought they were slacking or giving him lip.'

'He wasn't very popular, was he?'

'Not very, no.'

'Why did you put up with him?'

Callaghan gave him a hard look. 'I can't afford my own farm and management jobs are hard to come by. With the acreage we have here, this is a plum job.'

'What will you do now?'

'That depends on the son. He's in the army and I can't see him running the farm. Hopefully he'll keep me on.'

'Did Sinclair take much part in the running of the farm?'

'Not the actual running, no. He was more interested in the business side. He did the planning and left the rest to me, as long as it turned a profit.'

'And did it? Turn a profit I mean.'

'A good profit, yes. We've got a fine herd of milkers and they produce good heifers; the lambs fetch a good price in today's market; and there's good growing land on the other side of the hill.'

'Did he have many visitors?'

'I wouldn't know about that, Chief Inspector. I just run the farm.'

'Did you not go up to the house much?'

Callaghan smiled sardonically. 'No. If he wanted me he'd come down to the office or call me. And I'm only the hired help, had to use the kitchen entrance. He didn't socialise with us.' There was bitterness in his tone.

'And what did go on up there at the house, Mr Callaghan?'

'I've no idea. He was a private man, didn't encourage those who worked for him to interfere with his social life.'

'So you wouldn't know if he had any visitors, this morning for example.'

'No, my house is tucked well round the back, can't see the front drive from my place. And the hands and I all use the Lamb Lane gate to come and go.'

'OK, Mr Callaghan, thank you. We'll talk again.'

'Can I go back to my house now?'

'Yes, of course. I'd be obliged if you are available later to make a formal statement.'

'OK, I'm not going anywhere. What about informing his son and his solicitor?'

'We'll sort that out, thank you.'

Prior was thoughtful as he walked back to the murder scene. The CSIs had arrived and taped off the area around the body. And the pathologist was standing talking to them. 'Good evening, Professor, what do you have for me, anything beyond the obvious?'

'Someone didn't like the man, Matthew.'

'I think I'd already gathered that, anything else?'

'He's dead.'

Prior sighed, 'You're a mine of information this evening, Professor, I think I'd already guessed that too.'

Penhallon smiled. 'Ah but mine is the official verdict. In fact he's very dead. If the first few blows hadn't killed him, each of the next half dozen would have. The killer was very thorough.'

'That's useful, any ideas on the murder weapon?'

'Something rounded I would suggest, perhaps a rock or a large stone.'

Prior nodded at the stream. 'Lots of those around. So the killer probably didn't bring a weapon with him, just picked up a stone and started whacking him?'

'That's your department, Matthew. But not many people carry large stones around with them. This particular one will be covered in 'blood, snot and gore' as the fiction writers would have it. You should recognise it when you find it.'

Prior nodded slowly. 'And it will no doubt be all over the killer's clothing too I expect won't it?'

'Very likely, Matthew, such an attack does tend to cause something of a splash, although he may well have disposed of the clothing by now. This happened at least two hours ago.'

Prior looked at his watch. It said 6.30pm. 'So before 4.30pm. What's the earliest time it could have happened?'

Penhallon leant down and lifted one of the corpse's hands and let it drop. 'Not much in the way of rigor mortis, I'd say not more than three hours ago.'

'Anything else you can tell me?'

'Not really, no. Do you know who the victim is?'

'Yes, he's the landowner, one Cedric Sinclair.'

'Really? Perhaps the serfs are in rebellion.'

'Maybe so, Professor, maybe so.'

'Well, I can't spend all evening chatting Matthew, my dinner has already been delayed. I think it's about time you caught this fiend, he's interfering with my digestion. My morticians will collect the body and I'll do the PM tomorrow. I'll let your sergeant know the time.'

Prior smiled. 'Perish the thought that you should have an upset stomach, Professor: You should try living on a diet of pasties and doughnuts. Life at the sharp end is not easy.'

Penhallon smiled grimly. He pointed to the corpse. 'Well at least that's one thing this fellow won't have to worry about any more, his digestion.'

Siobhan had listened to this exchange without saying a word. The moment she judged Penhallon to be out of hearing she said, 'What a callous bastard that man is, he really gets under my skin.'

'As long as that isn't literally, you'll survive, Siobhan.'

'And you encouraged him sir. I'm surprised at you.'

'OK, that's enough Siobhan, let's move on.'

He turned to Bailey, who was hovering nearby. 'Anything George?'

'Not much guv. With the heavy mob trampling around there's more footprints than bare ground, Gawd only knows if any of them are the killer's. Can't see any sign of a murder weapon nearby. We'll do a wider search in the morning.'

'What did he have in his pockets?'

'Wallet with about fifty quid in it and a few credit cards, and a hanky; nothing else.'

Prior frowned, 'No keys, pens, correspondence?'

'No.'

'OK, we'll leave the body to the morticians. We'll start sharp at dawn tomorrow and search the whole area.'

He turned back to Siobhan. 'Right, let's get up to the house and see what the butler has to say. I wonder why he hasn't been down here for a peek?'

24. The butler

'There was one poor tiger that hadn't got a Christian.'

Punch 1875.

As they walked up the hill to the house, Prior said, 'This man Brighton seems a cold fish. Let's put a bit of pressure on him this time. Follow my lead; we'll see where it takes us.'

'Yes, sir.'

A light was shining above the grand entrance door to the house. 'Those damned lions are still sitting there, Siobhan.'

'Yes, sir, they're made of stone, they tend not to move a lot.'

'Just as well, there seems to be enough happening on this estate as it is.'

'Well, I don't think they committed the murder. Sir, Sinclair was clubbed not mauled.'

'I expect you're right.'

Prior rang the bell and the door was opened almost immediately by Brighton. He was wearing the same outfit they had seen him in at their first meeting. He opened the door wide and invited them in. 'Terrible news, sir. Who could have done this dreadful thing?'

Prior thought to himself, this man says the right words but there is no feeling in the way he says them, it's as if he's commenting on the weather. He put the thought to one side, 'Yes, Mr Brighton, terrible news indeed. We need to ask you some questions.'

'Come through to the kitchen, sir.'

They followed him to the rear of the large hallway and through an oak-panelled door. It led into a huge kitchen. All the appliances were new, finished in stainless steel and white enamel but the furniture was from a different era. Pine cabinets lined two of the walls and a massive table of the same wood occupied the centre of the room. The patina of the wood suggested that it was very old. Around the table were six sturdy-looking pine chairs of similar age. There was no sign of Mrs Brighton. Everything was neat and tidy and a coffee machine, half full, gave off a pleasant aroma.

Brighton invited them to sit and offered coffee. They both said yes. Once it was poured, Brighton joined them at the table.

'When did you last see Mr. Sinclair alive, Mr. Brighton?'

'That would be just after lunch, sir, about 3pm.'

'Did he say that he was going out?'

'No sir, he didn't discuss his plans with me.'

'Was he alone?'

'Yes sir.'

'Did he have any visitors this morning?'

'No sir, not to my knowledge.'

'Surely you would have known if he had, wouldn't you?'

'Probably, sir, yes.'

'What about yesterday?'

'No, sir.'

'What about phone calls, any of those over the weekend?'

'Not that I recall, sir, no.'

'And you would know wouldn't you, don't you usually answer the phone?' Prior had noticed a phone on the wall of the kitchen.

'Yes, sir. If the master doesn't answer in the first three rings, I answer it. But he does have a mobile phone.'

'And the land line hasn't rung the whole weekend as far as you know?'

'That is correct, sir.'

'And where is his mobile, do you know?'

'It's probably in the sitting room, sir, if he didn't have it with him when he went for his walk.'

'Would you please check if it's there?'

Brighton nodded and left. He returned in a few moments brandishing the phone. Prior thanked him and pocketed it. 'We'll check if it's been used over the weekend and return it.'

He continued, 'So it appears that he had no calls over the weekend. Is that normal, did he not have many friends?'

'He did have a circle of friends, but he spent a great deal of time alone.'

'What did he do when he was alone?'

'He read, sir, quite extensively.'

'Did he have any special hobbies, pastimes?'

'His reading, sir, and he studied the stock market.'

'So he had large investments, did he?'

'That I wouldn't know, sir, he didn't discuss his business with me.'

'What did he discuss with you, Mr. Brighton?'

'Just the running of the house, sir.'

'What family did he have?'

'A son, sir, Reginald, he's in the Grenadier Guards.'

'And where is he at the moment?'

'He's with the regiment, sir; I understand they are in Afghanistan.'

'Do you have a number to contact him?'

'Yes, sir, through the regimental depot.'

Prior asked him for the number and Siobhan noted it down.

'What about other relatives?'

'None close, sir, no siblings. Two distant cousins but he was not in contact with them.'

'What about the son's mother, is she still alive?'

'I believe so, sir. But she left some years ago. The master had no contact with her.'

'What about the son, surely he kept in contact with her?'

'Very much so, sir, he spent many of his leaves with her. But the master wouldn't allow her name to be mentioned in the house.'

'Why is that?'

'It's not for me to say sir.'

'Mr Brighton, the man has been murdered, that won't wash any more. Why would he not have her name mentioned?'

Brighton licked his lips and looked uncomfortable. 'The divorce was acrimonious, they didn't get along.'

'Why not?'

Brighton fidgeted in his chair. 'The master was not the easiest of men to get along with. His ex-wife got a large financial settlement. He was quite bitter about her.'

Siobhan asked, 'What about when they were married, how did they get along then?'

'Things deteriorated soon after Reginald was born. They were not a good match.'

Siobhan probed deeper, 'How did the son feel about this?'

Brighton was by now sweating, clearly he found this subject uncomfortable. 'He didn't have a happy childhood, madam.'

Prior took over the questioning, 'How often did the son visit here in recent years?'

'Not often, sir.'

'Once a month, once a year?'

'When he was stationed in England, sir, maybe twice a year.'

'When was the last time he was here?'

'About three months ago, just before he was sent abroad.'

'Who will inherit, Mr Brighton?'

'I don't know the contents of the will, sir, but I imagine Mr Reginald will, naturally.'

'So there is a will?'

'I imagine his solicitor will know about that, sir.'

Prior asked for and was given the solicitor's details.

He changed tack again, 'So, Mr Sinclair spent his time reading and studying the stock market, nothing else? Didn't he have a profession of any sort? What did he do for exercise?'

'No, sir, he had a large portfolio of stocks and shares and he supervised Mr Callaghan running the estate. He used to walk a lot and fished the stream in the summer.'

'Who are these friends he had?'

For the first time Brighton hesitated. 'I didn't pry into the master's private affairs, sir.'

'I'm not suggesting you did. But you were his bloody butler man, you must have known the people he entertained. Who were they?'

Brighton licked his lips. 'His doctor, sir, and his solicitor.'

'And who else?'

'A Mr Stapleton, sir.'

'Yes, we know about him. Who else?'

'I don't know of anyone else, sir.'

'When was the last time he entertained people here?'

'About two weeks ago, sir.'

'Who did he entertain then?'

'Mr Peterson and Mr Stapleton.' Prior noticed that, for the first time he'd dropped the sir.

'And who served them dinner?'

'I did.'

'No women?'

Brighton licked his lips again; he was by now very uncomfortable. 'No sir, just the two gentlemen.'

'What about Tuesday, there were people here then?'

'Tuesday is our evening off sir, we visit Mrs Brighton's mother in St Agnes.'

'So you visited her last Tuesday. What time did you get back?'

'Six in the morning, sir, we stay the night with her.'

'Why so early?'

'We have to prepare the master's breakfast and make sure everything is tidy.'

'How did you get onto the estate Mr. Brighton?'

'We always use the staff entrance, sir, in Lamb Lane. This was all in the statement I gave your officers on Wednesday.'

'The master, as you call him, wasn't up when we wanted to speak to him. What time did he usually get up?'

'Usually around 7.30.'

'And was everything tidy last Wednesday morning?'

Again Brighton licked his lips. 'Yes sir, it was.'

'You are lying to me Mr. Brighton, try again.'

'No, sir, that's the truth.'

'No sir, that's not the truth. Try again.'

Brighton remained silent.

Siobhan took over the questioning again, 'What time did you leave on Tuesday, Mr Brighton?'

'In the afternoon, about five.'

'Who cooked dinner for Sinclair then?'

'Mrs Brighton prepared a meal as usual. The master simply had to heat it in the microwave.'

'And the next morning, weren't there signs that he had entertained people, dirty glasses for example?'

Another pause before he answered, 'A few madam, yes.'

Prior stepped in again. 'So there were people here Tuesday evening and everything wasn't tidy. How many dirty glasses?'

'Just a few, sir.'

'How many had lipstick on them?'

'None that I noticed, sir.'

'Mr. Brighton, it really is time you stopped prevaricating. The man is dead and we must find out who killed him. We know that Mr Sinclair entertained young women that night so there is no point in being evasive. Now, what do you know about the women he entertained?'

Brighton sat up straight in his chair. He took a clean white handkerchief from a jacket pocket and deliberately mopped his face. For the first time there was emotion in his voice when he said, 'Nothing, sir. It was not my business to know, a servant does not question his master's business.'

Siobhan took over again, 'Did Mr Sinclair have a daily paper delivered?'

'Yes, madam, from the shop in the village.'

'How did they get into the estate; the gates were closed?'

'Through the Lamb Lane gate The delivery van rang the bell. there is a remote control in Mr Callaghan's home, one in his office and I have one here.'

'Was the paper delivered this Wednesday?'

'Yes, I'm sure it was, they are very reliable.'

Prior said, 'Tell me Mr Brighton, what newspaper did he take?'

'The Times sir.'

'Really? And did you iron it for him each morning?'

Brighton managed a glimmer of a smile despite his discomfort. 'No, sir.'

Prior looked at Siobhan. Her eyes rolled to the top of her head in exasperation.

Prior half-suppressed a smile. 'How long have you worked for the Sinclairs?'

'Twenty-eight years sir.'

'Always as the butler?'

'No, sir, I started as what used to be called a footman. I became butler just ten years ago when my predecessor retired.'

'How did you get on with Mr Cedric?'

'Get on with him?' Another hint of a smile crossed the man's face. 'I am a servant sir, servants don't 'get on' as you put it with the people they serve.'

'Mr Sinclair was unpopular with the other workers on the estate. Why was that?'

'It's not my place to say, sir.'

'The man is dead Mr Brighton, this is no time to be coy.'

'I have little to do with the farm workers, sir.'

'What about the cleaning staff?'

'They are not encouraged to chatter, sir.'

'But they must say something, you must have some kind of conversation with them.'

'About their work, yes, sir. Not about our employer.'

Siobhan said, 'Who looks after the money used to run the estate?'

'That would be Mr. Callaghan.'

'What about the housekeeping?'

'Money is paid monthly into a housekeeping account. Mrs Brighton draws from it as necessary. The utility bills are paid by standing order.'

There was silence for some moments as the two detectives began running out of questions. Prior finally broke the silence, 'Who do you think killed Mr Sinclair, Mr Brighton?'

Brighton had recovered his cool. He looked Prior straight in the eyes and said, 'I'm sure I've no idea, sir; probably an intruder.'

'Do you get many intruders on the estate?'

'Not to my knowledge but that would be Mr Callaghan's department. I only look after the house.'

'I know whose department it is man, but unless you're some kind of zombie you must have some idea of what is going on around you.'

Brighton sat looking at the table in front of him. 'I've told you what I know, sir.'

'I think you had better wake up, man. This is a murder enquiry not some bloody game, just answer my questions.'

'I am doing so, sir, to the best of my ability. My responsibility is the house. Mr Callaghan looks after the estate.'

Siobhan said, 'What do you do in your spare time, Mr Brighton?'

'Spare time, madam? Mrs. Brighton and I watch some television and I read.'

'Prior smiled. 'What are your favourite programmes?'

'We watch the National Geographic and Discovery channels mostly.'

'Where do you sleep?'

Brighton pointed to the door behind him. 'Mrs Brighton and I have a small sitting room and bedroom here on the ground floor, madam.'

'What did you do after you served Sinclair's lunch today?'

'Mrs Brighton and I had our lunch sir.'

'Then what?'

'Then we sat and watched the TV, sir.'

'Until what time?'

'Until Mr Callaghan phoned with the dreadful news.'

'And what time was that?'

'About 5pm, sir.'

Prior looked at Siobhan, who shook her head. 'Thank you, Mr Brighton, we'd like to talk to your wife now.'

'Yes, sir, I'll fetch her.'

Mrs. Brighton was a petite woman of about fifty, a few years older than her husband. She wore a modest navy-blue dress and a neat pinafore. Her plain face was topped by steel-grey hair pulled into a tight bun at the back of her head. Prior thought just how little had changed over the years in remote places like this. Her husband disappeared quietly through the door to their living quarters. Prior invited her to sit down. She did so primly on the edge of the seat.

The two detectives spent twenty minutes with her. But she was as unforthcoming as her husband. When they finally ran out of questions they were no further forward with the investigation. She had confirmed what Brighton had said but added nothing.

They left the house the way they had come and walked back down the hill to where Prior's car was parked. As they walked he said, 'Well, that was a waste of time wasn't it?'

'Yes, sir. I loved your comment about a zombie, the butler's about as animated as the stone lions.'

'Makes you wonder what these people get out of life. A diet of service and nature programmes, a pretty grey existence.'

'I think that's the right word to describe them, grey. Except one thing; did you notice he dies his hair?'

Prior smiled. 'We all have our little vanities, Siobhan. I suppose the interview did give us a better perspective on Sinclair's life. Seems pretty boring to me. He seemed to have spent most of his time lording it over the serfs. Not surprising he couldn't sustain a relationship and turned to prostitutes to satisfy his lust. But that doesn't tell us who killed him or why. What amazes me in this day and age is how this place remains the same as it has been for centuries. Time just seems to have passed it by. Everyone knows his place and knuckles his forehead to his nibs.'

'Well someone used more than a knuckle this time. What's next on the agenda, sir?'

'Two or three things come to mind, Siobhan. Tomorrow morning I want the estate searched, every inch of it. We'll start with the bottom land along the stream. And the house. I want that searched from top to bottom.'

'We'll need more men sir, there must be a thousand acres and the house is huge.'

'Yeah, I'll get on to division, they'll have to arrange that. But you and I will concentrate on people. Tomorrow we'll speak to this Tom Williamson and have another go at Callaghan.'

*

Prior was home by 10.30, Jeanette was reading in the lounge. Prior kissed her and said, 'Are the girls all right.'

'Yes, they're fine. It was good you found time for them at the weekend, Matthew, they had a great time.'

He smiled. 'So did I love. Is there anything to eat?'

'Yes I'll make you a sandwich. Come and sit in the kitchen while I make it and tell me about this new murder.'

They sat for an hour chatting. When he finally got to bed, Prior's sleep was again disturbed by demons and he tossed and turned throughout the night.

25. The search.

'The rain it raineth on the just
And also on the unjust fella
But chiefly on the just because
The unjust steals the just's umbrella.'

Lord Bowen.

Monday morning limped into being, damp and miserable. The wind had changed direction and overnight a band of rain had swept in over the Atlantic. Prior's mood matched the weather as he drove to the Sinclair Estate. It was as if the fates were conspiring against him on this case; everything that could hinder his investigation seemed to be doing so, even the damned weather. At first light a search team was to scour the woods along the stream. Another team of dogs and their handlers would search the remainder of the estate.

He was faced with a catch-22 situation. The rain would inhibit the search. But it was forecast to last throughout the day. And the more it rained, the more likely any evidence left by the killer would be washed away so there was no point in delaying the search.

He ignored the press still camped outside the gates. The traffic constable manning the gate didn't recognise him, so he had to wind the window down and identify himself. He showed his warrant card and was waved through. He quickly negotiated the drive past the big house to the farmyard behind. Here chaos reigned.

Overnight the enquiry van had been returned to its spot beside the farm manager's office. A coach was parked behind the van containing the twenty uniformed officers who would conduct the search. They sat miserably waiting to be briefed. Two small vans complete with four handlers and dogs were parked beside the coach. The dogs were excited at the smell of the cattle in the barn opposite and were barking continuously. Cows in the milking shed made nervous by the sounds of the barking added their mournful lowing to the noise and Prior couldn't hear himself think. Heavy rain fell on the scene, making everyone miserable at the prospect of spending the next several hours wading through the resultant mud.

He stopped beside the first dog van and knocked sharply on the window. The uniformed sergeant inside wound the window down. Prior shouted above the noise of the animals, 'Have you got no more sense than you were born with? Take your damned dogs down the road where they can't smell the cattle. Otherwise we'll have a stampede when they come out into the yard. Then you and your men come to the enquiry van and I'll brief you'. Without waiting for a reply he stomped off to the enquiry van.

His team were gathered in the van drinking coffee. With DS Quigley was Inspector Brian Clark, in charge of the search team sitting in the coach. All conversation stopped as Prior entered. He took off his raincoat and shook it. The expression on his face did not invite a greeting. He grabbed a cup of coffee and stomped over to Quigley's desk. 'Inspector Clark, there's no damned room in here to brief your men, so we'll have to do it on the coach. But first I'll brief the dog handlers, they've got a bigger area to cover.'

The door opened and the four dog handlers came in looking bedraggled, there was a sergeant and three constables. Prior sat them down around a desk and produced a map of the estate. As he briefed them he traced the boundary of the estate with his finger. Then he said, 'I realise it's a huge area but most of it is open land so that shouldn't be too difficult, except for one or two bits of land. To the right of the bridge near the front entrance there's a tract of wilderness without even a path through it. And I understand there's another patch of woodlands at the top of the estate. Both of those areas need to be searched too. I'm told nobody uses these areas now but we can't ignore them.

Look for anything out of the ordinary. A murder weapon would be handy. The latest victim was clubbed to death, could have been a rock or a large stone. The other thing is any sign of digging. One theory is that something has been

buried somewhere down on the bottomland, so any disturbance in the ground has to be looked at.

Otherwise, concentrate your search around the perimeter
of the estate. Look for any sign left by an intruder or anything out of the ordinary. The other team are going to look
along the stream between the Stag Lane and Lamb Lane
gates, that's where the body of the estate owner was found.
Take a radio with you and keep in touch. Any questions?'

The sergeant said, 'Dogs won't be able to pick up much
scent in this rain but we'll do our best, sir.'

'That's all I can ask of you. If there are no more questions, get started.'

Next he gave the detectives their assignments as they
huddled around his desk. Jane Foster and Alan Waring had
drawn the short straws; they would accompany the search
team down by the stream. Four others would go up to the
house, interview the cleaning staff and sift through Sinclair's papers and possessions.

As he was finishing, Prior heard the lowing of the cattle
as the farmhands drove them out to face the elements. He
stood by the window watching the herders persuading the
reluctant beasts to leave their warm barn.

Beside him, Siobhan commented, 'I don't think they are
any keener than we are to go out in the rain.'

Prior ignored her. He turned to Inspector Clark. 'Right,
let's get your lot moving.'

He briefed the team in the coach. The briefing was suc-
cinct. He gave them details of the two murders and the

probable murder weapon for the second of them. He outlined the area to be searched and the theories about possible motives for the killings.

He finished by saying, 'If you find anything at all, don't touch it. Call one of the detectives who will accompany you. Just make sure you look before you tread anywhere. I'll have your balls if I find you've destroyed any evidence.' Then he realized that a third of the search team were women. He smiled. 'That includes you women, even if you haven't got any.' There was a murmur of laughter in response.

There was a shuffling of feet and a soft buzz of conversation. Prior turned to the Inspector and nodded. The search team began filing out of the coach.

Returning to the van, Prior spent ten minutes discussing the various lines of enquiry and possible scenarios with his two DSs.

Quigley scratched his head. 'I can't get my head around this intruder theory, sir. What was he doing wandering about the estate on a Sunday afternoon?'

'What do you mean?'

'Well, it's a funny place to find a burglar, a long way from the house and it wouldn't have been a poacher.'

'Why not?'

'They operate at night, not during the day when there are people about. Besides, there's not much down there to poach unless he was tickling trout.'

Prior smiled grimly. 'Do people really do that? But it's a good question, Albert, what was he looking for?'

Siobhan coughed then said, 'I wonder if he was looking for buried treasure, sir?'

Prior gave her a hard look. 'Or maybe he was panning for gold in the stream. We've been down that road Siobhan and this is not the Klondike. There are only a very few sites in the whole of Europe where Celtic chieftains have been buried with the trappings of wealth. Not only that but the likelihood of it remaining undiscovered after all this time is remote. I don't think it's likely.'

'Well, with respect, sir, it's you that's always telling me not to dismiss something because it's unlikely. Besides, what else could the intruder have been looking for?'

'OK, OK, supposing you're right? We found no signs of digging down there, did we?'

'No, sir, but we were hardly thorough. Perhaps the search will come up with something.'

There was a long silence that Siobhan finally broke. 'The only sign of the ground being disturbed was that tree stump that had been dug up. Supposing Wright found something among the roots?'

'That's possible but wouldn't he have dug further if he had? And the intruder was nowhere near the Lamb Lane wall.' He paused. 'But it may be worth another look. That's if there's anything left after this damned rain. The holes will be full of water.'

'Perhaps the intruder knew that Wright found something but didn't know exactly where. He might have been looking for the spot.'

'Perhaps that's why he was tortured in the first place, to get that information, maybe he lied to the killer.' Then he shook his head. 'Too many maybes. Callaghan said that he walks along the stream occasionally. Let's question him again.'

There was another pause that was finally broken by Quigley. 'What about this butler, sir, bit of an oddball isn't he?'

'Yes, he is, Albert, what are you suggesting?'

'Don't really know, sir. But if he wanted to kill his master, he wouldn't do it in the house, would he?'

Prior smiled. 'Sounds a bit Agatha Christie-ish doesn't it? He's worked on the estate for over twenty years. And, while there are lots of local people who have lost their jobs, he and his wife have still got theirs. I can't see a motive. And he has an alibi for the time of Wright's death, he and his wife were visiting her mother that night. Whilst I wouldn't dismiss him, I wouldn't put him high on my list of suspects.'

Siobhan laughed, 'Well at least we have eliminated the stone lions from the enquiry, sir, no claw marks on the body.'

'Very funny, Siobhan. Now, be serious, what are the other possibilities?'

'The inevitable one. Perhaps the two killings are not related.'

Prior sat for a moment before answering. Then he shook his head, 'No, there are no coincidences in murder cases. We must concentrate on the connection, the location. Wright was working down there the day he died and Sinclair was killed there.' Another thought struck him. 'What happened to our profiler, Albert?'

'Academics don't do weekends, sir.' He looked at his watch. 'And it's not nine-o-clock yet. These people are not early risers.'

Prior smiled, 'Perhaps she can't find us now we've moved the van. Has anyone told her we're here now?'

Quigley smiled to, 'That's a thought sir, I'll give her a ring.'

At that moment the door opened and Superintendent Owen walked in. The three detectives stood to greet her. She signalled with her hand for them to remain seated. 'Don't let me disturb you. I thought I'd come and see how things are going. The population seems to be thinning out a little around here. When you have a moment we must have a chat, Matthew.'

'Yes ma'am, we were just having a council of war. We've about finished anyway. I've got a uniform team searching the bottomland, and a dog team looking over the rest of the estate. My detectives are up at the house.'

Quigley asked, 'Would you like some coffee, ma'am?'

'That depends what it is.'

'Colombian dark roast, ma'am.'

She sniffed the air. 'I'll risk it. Milk, no sugar please.'

Prior took her into his tiny office.

When they were seated, she said, 'The Chief Constable has been on to me already this morning. How will this killing affect the Stapleton affair?'

'Too early to say. At first glance it looks as if Sinclair disturbed an intruder on the estate. I think I told you there was a report some weeks ago of an intruder. It's possible the two incidents are not related.'

'Well, he wants a daily report. Let me have one by six each evening until you solve these crimes.'

'Yes, ma'am.'

'Do you think the two murders are related?'

He nodded, 'I'm sure they are. Two murders virtually in the same place in the course of one week have to be related. We're a bit short on evidence but my gut tells me they are. I think the location is the key.'

'What do you think is going on here then?'

'I'm fairly sure that when we discover the motive, we'll discover the killer.'

She sighed. 'OK, brief me on what you have.'

He spent the next ten minutes bringing her up to date with the enquiry. When he'd finished, she nodded. 'I can't think of anything you've overlooked, keep at it. Now this profiler, what has she come up with?'

Prior smiled, 'It seems she doesn't do weekends, ma'am and she's not here yet.'

'Well let me know if she comes up with anything useful. Now I'll let you get on.'

The door had hardly closed behind her when it opened again. Siobhan's head appeared round it. She said airily, 'Everything all right, sir?'

'Yes. Any reason why it shouldn't be?'

'No, sir, just asking.'

He grinned. 'Come in and sit.' He filled her in with what Owen had said; 'Just politics, Siobhan. The Chief Constable's concerned that the press might get hold of the Stapleton connection. He's worried about the force's reputation.'

'Yea, I can see his point. The problem is they do seem good at digging up the dirt.'

Prior's grin widened. 'Perhaps we should give them a shovel and send them down to the stream.'

She laughed.

At that moment the radio on his desk crackled and a voice said, 'Mobile control from Kilo 93, message over.'

He picked it up and looked at Siobhan. 'That's one of the dog units.' Into the radio he said, 'Go ahead Kilo 93.'

'We've found something you'll want to see, sir. There's a derelict cottage in the woods the other side of Lamb Lane. Looks as if it used to be the gamekeeper's place. There's a mass of dried blood in one of the rooms.'

26. The killing ground.

'The only thing necessary for the triumph of evil is for good men to do nothing,'

Edmund Burke.

They took Prior's car. Turning left out of the Lamb Lane gate they followed the lane up the hill. The rain was less intense but a heavy drizzle continued to fall. Prior's brow was furrowed as he peered through the windscreen wipers at the road ahead. 'If this is what we think it is, Siobhan, Sinclair may have contributed to his own death. If he hadn't thrown us off the damned estate, we would probably have found this cottage already and been closer to solving the case. Let's hope we find some evidence there.'

Siobhan remained silent, her eyes on the road ahead.

At the top of the hill, the lane veered left, bisecting the estate. Soon a few trees appeared on their right, these quickly thickened into a wood. Prior saw the uniformed figure of one of the dog-handlers waiting beside a three-bar gate. Prior stopped the car beside him and got out, popping the boot as he did.

'The cottage is about a hundred yards up that track, sir. PC Golding is waiting there for you. The windows are boarded up and it's dark inside, you'll need a torch.' As he was speaking he pointed behind him to a gap in the trees.

It was narrow and overgrown but Prior could just make out twin tyre tracks. The tracks were old and there was no sign of recent use. Prior nodded, but before moving off he examined the gate. It was fastened by a simple latch, rusty from lack of use. He opened and closed it a couple of time. It was stiff but still worked.

He looked at the dog handler. 'Was this open or closed when you arrived?

'Closed, on the latch, sir.'

'Any sign of a padlock or chain?'

'No, sir.'

'Did you see any new tyre marks on the track?'

'No, just the old ones. The ruts are compacted earth but they're full of water. No telling what's underneath. But there's definitely no visible sign of any recent marks.'

Prior turned to Siobhan. 'We'll need evidence suits and a torch Siobhan, they're in the boot.' He turned back to the handler, 'OK wait here for my CSI team, they're on their way.'

Prior led the way up the track, keeping to the grass verge. 'This bloody rain, even if the killer's vehicle had left tyre marks they will have been washed away by now.'

Siobhan didn't answer; there was nothing to say.

The cottage came in sight. It was typical of old Cornish workmen's homes, built of local grey granite and with a slate roof. There were signs of years of neglect. Several tiles were missing from the roof, while those remaining were covered in lichen and moss. The ground-floor windows were boarded up and thick weeds grew everywhere.

Standing beside the front door was PC Golding, holding his dog on a tight leash. As they approached, the dog whined and pulled at the leash. The handler stroked it and spoke softly, comforting the animal. He looked up as they approached. Seeing Prior's eyes on the dog he said, 'It's the blood, sir, he can smell it.'

Prior looked at the handler and smiled for the first time since leaving home that morning, although it was more like a grimace than a smile. He said, 'Well he's earned his keep today.'

He looked at the door. A padlock was hanging from the metal plate that anchored it to the door post. But the ring welded to the metal plate that should have been screwed to the door was hanging from the padlock. Looking at the door he saw splintered wood where the screws had been. The splinters were fresh, not weathered by long exposure to the elements. There was the mark of a crowbar on the door that had obviously been used to pry off the metal plate.

Seeing the direction of his gaze, Golding said, 'That's how we found it, sir.'

Siobhan spoke for the first time since they'd left the enquiry van, 'If this is the old gamekeepers cottage, it will have been empty for five years, sir.'

Prior nodded. 'It probably is. And it looks as if no-one has been here until recently.' He turned to Golding. 'Did you both go into the cottage?'

'I did sir, but only just inside the door. My dog went mad when he smelled the blood. I didn't go any further. I came out and called you.'

'Good, well done.' As he talked, Prior was putting on his evidence suit.

He took a deep breath and gently pushed the door with his gloved hand. It opened directly onto a square-shaped room. The interior was dim, the only light coming from the doorway in which he stood. The first thing that hit him was the smell that assailed his nostrils, a mixture of mould, damp, mildew and something else. Only when the dog started whining again did he realise what it was. Blood.

Over his shoulder he said, 'OK, Golding, take your dog away from the smell, he's done his work. Have a look around the outside of the cottage, see if there's anything out of place.' Then to his DS, 'Give me the torch, Siobhan.'

He shone the torch into the room. A large fireplace dominated the wall to his left. There were closed doors set into the other two walls which he guessed led to the kitchen and staircase. Most of the floor was covered in an old, threadbare, mildewed carpet. An ancient wooden cabinet stood against a wall, its surface streaked with white mould. The only other furniture was a sturdy-looking, upright wooden chair that lay on its back in the centre of the room.

But it was the carpet itself that drew his attention. A large black stain covered two-thirds of it around where the chair lay. Prior knew that this had to be the killing ground. This was where John Wright had been tortured, stabbed to death, then decapitated. This was where he had bled out.

Behind him, he heard Siobhan sniff. 'So this is where it happened, sir.' Her voice trembled a little. 'This is inhuman, what kind of man could do this?'

Prior grunted, then loudly cleared his throat. 'Yeah.'

He took a deep breath and stepped into the room, the plastic overshoes on his feet making a strange crinkling noise on the stone floor. Careful not to tread on any prints in the dust on the floor, he walked gingerly to the point opposite the upturned chair.

There he squatted down and concentrated the torch beam on the scene in front of him. Apart from the pool of blood and the chair, the only other thing he saw were lengths of plastic-covered wire lying in the blood. He counted them. There were four, one for each of Wright's arms and one for each of his legs.

Prior swayed as a wave of nausea passed over him. This was worse even than finding the severed head. The upturned chair and the twisted lengths of wire casually dropped on the blood-soaked carpet triggered his imagination. His mind drew up a vivid picture of what had taken place here. The victim, tied to a chair while the killer tortured and then butchered him. He shook his head, trying to dispel the image from his mind.

He stood up and moved to the door on one side of the room. Careful not to smudge any prints that might be there, he lifted the latch and swung the door open. A staircase led to the upper floor. A thick layer of dust on the stairs told him that no-one had used them for a long, long time. He moved to the other door at the rear and opened that. It led to a kitchen, the dust on the stone-tiled floor telling him no-one had been there recently either.

He took one final look around the room before moving back to the front entrance. There was nothing else to see. Siobhan hadn't moved from the doorway. He said softly, 'OK, Siobhan, we'll leave this to George and Sally.'

Outside again, he took a deep breath of the fresh, clean, cold, rain-laden air. He spoke, almost in a whisper, 'I sometimes think I should have been a second-hand car salesman.'

Siobhan smiled wanly. 'No sir, salesmen have to be nice to people, you're far too grumpy.'

The two detectives stood in silence for some minutes, each thinking of the horrors that had taken place in the cottage behind them.

Finally, Prior saw movement on the track, his two Crime Scene Investigators trudging towards him. Dressed in their familiar green evidence suits and carrying their bright metal tool cases, they might have been moonwalkers coming to collect rock samples. But the expressions on their faces showed that they were very conscious of the grisly task ahead of them. Even the normally chirpy George Bailey could not find a joke to lighten the gloom.

27. The dungeon.

'Three may keep a secret if two of them are dead.'

16th century proverb.

Meanwhile Inspector Brian Clark had assembled his men down by the Lamb Lane gate. He split them into two groups. There was no bridge over the stream at this end of the estate. He kept just six to search the nearside and sent the rest out into the lane to walk over the bridge and climb over the wall back onto the estate. There was much cursing and swearing as they did so but worse was to come for them.

They started on a high. Twigs and other debris had built up against the grill under the arch where the stream, made into a torrent by the heavy rain, rushed into the tunnel under the wall of the estate. Among the debris they found Sinclair's flat cap. Clearly it had fallen into the stream where he had been attacked and been carried here by the current. One of the men used a stick to fish it out and handed it to DC Waring, who put it in an evidence bag.

Thereafter they had found nothing of any consequence. The going on the nearside of the stream was difficult. The ground undulated and was muddy and the men slipped and fell frequently. In the undulations there were boot marks. But the rain had blurred the tread from the boots that had made them. Without such tread there was no chance of identifying the footwear that had made the prints.

On the far side of the stream things were much worse. Here the forest had been left to its own devices for God knows how many years. A thick layer of dead rotting leaves covered the forest floor. As their boots disturbed it, the foul smell of decay permeated the air around them. At first this prompted jokes about police canteen food, but this soon degenerated to mere curses and swearing.

But they did as they had been instructed and poked and prodded their way along, searching for anything that might indicate that someone had recently been there. The sum total of their finds was a few empty crisp packets and plastic shopping bags snagged on branches where the wind had blown them. But that was all. There was no sign of a murder weapon or even a cigarette end along the whole stretch of ground.

The men's spirits revived as they reached the drive at the main entrance to the estate. And, as they made their way wearily back to the farmyard, they whistled the theme tune to the film, Bridge over the River Kwai. Reaching their coach, they broke out the Thermos flasks as Inspector Clark reported their limited success to DS Quigley.

The other pair of dog handlers had had even less success. One abandoned Wellington boot, a single woollen sock and a wet, snotty handkerchief had been all they had discovered. But when he later heard this news, Prior was not dismayed. He had hoped for a better result but had not expected it.

Returning from the killing scene at the old gamekeeper's cottage, Prior and Siobhan had gone up to the house. They entered through the back door that led directly into the kitchen. DC Jean Wade was sitting at the table with one of the two women who did the cleaning at the house.

Wade looked up as they entered. 'Fred is down in the cellar sir, there's something there you ought to see.'

Prior nodded and followed her pointed finger to a door in the corner of the room.

On his previous visit he'd thought it to be the entrance to a larder or cupboard. But, opening it, he found a stone staircase leading down into the bowels of the earth. A bare electric light bulb hung from the ceiling halfway down. In its dim light he saw an open doorway at the foot of the stairs. They made their way down the stairs and through the doorway.

They found themselves in an old wine cellar. Rows of wooden wine racks ran down each side of the cellar. All but the first few rows were empty of bottles and covered in dust and cobwebs. Several dozen bottles half-filled the first few racks. Only a light film of dust had accumulated on these.

Lifting a bottle from the first rack, he wiped the dust off the label and looked at it. '1989, St Emilion.' Looking at others in the rack he saw bottles with labels he didn't recognise but with similar vintages. He thought, 'Hmm! Expensive stuff, I suppose you would expect that from the landed gentry.'

'Didn't know you were a wine buff, sir. How much is that a bottle?'

'I'm not but Jeanette's father is. He's introduced me to a few wines. Work it out for yourself Siobhan, these are not just wines of the region, these are château wines; and they are well aged. I'd guess they're upwards of fifty quid a bottle and that's a conservative guess.'

'If it's more than a fiver in the supermarket, I move to the next shelf.'

He smiled, 'So do I, but I don't own a thousand-acre estate. These people have different values.'

He looked at the second full rack. Here there were white wines and rows of vintage champagne. He didn't recognise the labels but knew they were more expensive than anything he might afford. 'He certainly wasn't a cheapskate when it came to wine. I couldn't afford to even sniff this stuff.'

'Most of it tastes the same to me, sir. I don't know what people make all the fuss about.'

'That's because you're a pleb, Siobhan. There are some people who say that you can judge a man's character by the wine he drinks.'

'Snob values, a load of nonsense. I judge a man by his butt, that's a much better guide.'

Prior laughed. 'I'll make sure I walk behind you in future.'

'There's nothing wrong with your butt, sir, but it's spoken for.'

He shook his head, 'Don't know what the world's coming to when a man is judged by the shape of his rear end.'

'A good strong butt is far more useful than a bottle of wine, sir. Anyway, how do you judge a woman?'

'That's neither here nor there, sergeant, get your mind back on the case.'

She smiled triumphantly. 'Yes, sir, getting my mind back on the case now.'

It was clear that both had recovered their spirits quickly after the horrors of the gamekeeper's cottage and this repartee was part of their way of doing so.

They made their way down the passageway between the empty wine racks. Another door stood open ahead of them. Passing through that, they found themselves in a second cellar. This contained just a wooden bench, two upturned wooden barrels and some broken furniture. All was covered in dust and cobwebs. Yet another open doorway faced them at the other end of the space.

As they approached it, DC Trimble appeared in the doorway. 'Thought I heard voices, sir. You might want to see what's through here.' As they passed through the doorway, he added, 'I think this is the recreation room.'

In front of them was a huge four-poster bed. The stone wall behind it was draped in velvet curtains. Pink silk sheets and pillows were the only coverings on the bed. To one side was a clothes rack. Hanging on it were several costumes, everything from a schoolgirl's uniform, through that of a traffic warden, to metal-studded leather bikers' gear. Masks and other headgear lay on a shelf above.

On the other side of the room was a large wooden cross with iron shackles at each end of the crosspiece. Two leather whips hung from nails on the wall. On a tripod behind the door, stood a video camera, beside that a TV and DVD player.

'Wow! Some recreation room.' Prior said.

Siobhan pulled a face. 'I think I prefer ping-pong.'

'Don't you see yourself as a biker, Siobhan?'

'Maybe, but there's no bike here, sir.'

'Just use your imagination, go vroom vroom.'

'You're always telling me I have no imagination, sir.'

Trimble had been with the team long enough to know of the banter that went on between these two. He also knew enough not to take part. He just stood there with a big smile on his face. Seeing the smile, Prior said, 'What are you grinning at?'

Trimble replied innocently, 'Me, sir? Nothing, sir.'

Also with a smile on his face Prior said, 'Have you found any DVDs?'

'Yes, there's four in a rack under the TV.'

'Well put them in an evidence bag and seal it. I don't want a load of lewd detectives watching porn films. And look in the camera, there may be a disc in there. I remember watching a film where the ace detective forgot the one in the camera. Until the end of the film that is, when they looked on the disc and it revealed the identity of the killer.'

'Do you think this has anything to do with Sinclair's murder sir?' Trimble asked.

'I'll keep an open mind on that. Get George Bailey down here when you can; he's got another job on at the moment. DS Quigley will tell you when he's free. In the meantime, keep this place locked, and hang on to the key.'

'Yes, sir.'

Siobhan wiped her finger over the surface of the DVD player, 'No dust. I can't imagine his nibs doing the hoovering, can you? One of the staff must clean the place.'

'Good point, Siobhan. It seems that Sinclair's sex life must have been an open secret, what with cleaning women and taxis full of prostitutes going back and forth. I think we can forget blackmail as a motive, I expect half the village knew what he was up to down here.'

She smiled. 'Perhaps Brighton worked the DVD player, sir.'

Prior returned the smile. 'Can't somehow see him in the schoolgirl's uniform, can you?'

'Might make a good biker, though?'

'I won't ask about his butt.' Turning to Trimble, he said, 'How did you get in here Fred, was the place locked?'

'Yes, sir. The butler gave me a whole bunch of keys on a ring, they're for all the cellars.'

'You didn't see where he got the keys from by any chance, did you?'

'Yes, they were in a small key cupboard on the kitchen wall, he got them from there.'

'So, he had access and so did the rest of the staff.'

Prior stood with a thoughtful expression on his face. 'What about the rest of the house; was anything found do you know?'

'As far as I know nothing interesting as yet, sir. Just the stuff you'd expect to find.'

'How much of the house is actually in use?'

'Only the east wing sir the west wing is in a bit of a state, full of damp and crumbling brickwork. In the east wing there are four bedrooms made up. One was Sinclair's, one his son's and two guest rooms.'

'And on the ground floor?'

'Sitting room, drawing room, library, dining room and study, sir. Oh, and the butler's quarters, kitchen and utility rooms at the back of the house.'

'What about papers, accounts, that sort of thing?'

'Desk in the study, sir, full of stuff, Ben Grimshaw's going through it now.'

'And valuables, family silver, that sort of thing?'

'Plenty of that, sir, lots of silver in the dining room. Then there are all sorts of collections of pottery, crockery, and there are paintings all over the place. There's a safe in the study but we can't find a key. The butler says Sinclair always carried it with him'

Prior frowned, 'I don't remember any keys being found on the body, do you Siobhan?'

'No, sir, definitely no keys.'

'So, it might have been a burglar after all, if he took Sinclair's keys.'

'If it was, what on earth was he doing down by the stream and in broad daylight, sir? And the silver and all the goodies are still here in the house. It doesn't make sense.'

'There's not much in this case that does, Siobhan.' Then to Trimble, 'Fred, there must be an inventory of house contents somewhere for insurance purposes. Find it and do a stocktake. Find out what, if anything, is missing.'

Trimble nodded soberly, not looking forward to the huge task.

Prior looked at his watch. 'Damn, we have to get to Sinclair's PM. Old Penhallon will do his nut if we're late.'

28. The Sinclair Autopsy.

'They that sow the wind shall reap the whirlwind.'

16th century proverb.

On the way to Truro they stopped at the village shop in Tresillian and bought pasties and doughnuts. As they sat in the car munching them, Siobhan said, 'I'm beginning to look like a pasty.'

Prior replied through a mouthful of food, 'Look on the bright side, the poor bloody miners had to sit in a freezing cold mine shaft eating theirs.'

'This case is getting me down, we don't seem to be getting anywhere with it.'

He replied testily, 'Just be patient Siobhan. Wait and see what George comes up with at the gamekeeper's cottage. We just have to keep plugging away, something will break eventually.'

'You've got more patience than I have.'

'By the way, Jeanette wants you to come to dinner tomorrow night, there's someone she wants you to meet.'

'Please tell me she's not matchmaking.'

'She's not, unless you've changed your sexual preference. This is a woman she was at uni. with.'

'Oh, sorry.'

'No need to apologise. But isn't it about time you found a steady partner. Then you wouldn't be so bloody miserable all the time.'

'I suppose if I had the odd evening off it might help. Anyway, steady partners don't always make you happy. The ones I've found were always complaining about the hours I work'

'You've only got to tell me when you have a date, I can manage without you.'

'Huh! I'll remind you that you said that the next time I ask for a few hours off. Who is this friend of Jeanette's?'

'She's a history buff, lectures at Bristol. Jeanette told you about her. She's interested in the ancient Brits and the Celts.'

Siobhan laughed. 'You know the job should pay Jeanette a consultant's fee, she does most of your research for you.'

He laughed with her. 'Yes, I'm very lucky in more ways than one, she takes an interest in my work.'

'How are the girls?'

'They're fine.' He wiped his hands on the paper bag the food had come in and started the car. They drove to Truro Public Mortuary.

Penhallon was robed up and ready to start the autopsy He glared at them, 'Good of you to come Matthew, May I make a start now?'

'You don't usually ask for my permission, Professor.'

'It isn't your permission I'm seeking, it's your attention. Now please be quiet, I need to concentrate. By the way, I have some toxicology reports for you from the Wright corpse, remind me afterwards.'

'Wonders will never cease, I was beginning to think the lab had ground to a halt.'

Penhallon glared at him but said nothing more.

The autopsy was straightforward. There were no surprises and for once it was not accompanied by Penhallon's funereal humour. Cause of death was a fractured skull, one of the several fractures that he had found but impossible to say which one. There were no defence wounds. Otherwise the corpse was free of disease or illness and bore no other significant marks or injuries. Prior thanked Penhallon and said, 'The toxicology report, Professor?'

'Oh yes, it's in my office.'

They followed Penhallon to his first-floor office. His large desk was surrounded by files, bones and anatomical specimens. The pathologist shuffled through a pile of papers on his desk. 'Now, where did I put the damned report?' Finally he came up with a single sheet of paper. 'Here it is.' He held it out. 'Amphetamines, Matthew. The lad Wright was on amphetamines, or speed as the Plebeians call it.'

Prior's eyebrows rose. 'Really? So, he wasn't the saint everyone says he was. Can you tell us if he was addicted?'

'Probably not, there's no tissue damage and there were only small traces in his system. I'd guess either he was just an occasional user or he'd only just started using the drug. You know it's very addictive, if he'd been on it long it would have affected his behaviour. His lady friend would have noticed I'm sure.'

'Now where would he have got speed from?' Prior voiced his thoughts.

'You are supposed to be the detective Matthew, detect, find some clues or something. I just look at the cadavers. There are no traces of anything else in his system.'

'Thanks, Professor.'

Prior was deep in thought as they left the mortuary. While, on the face of it, today had produced a great deal of evidence it didn't seem to bring him closer to solving either murder. He knew that Sinclair's death would cause more pressure from above than that of Wright, who had been a mere farm worker. Those in the corridors of power became fidgety when someone from their own social class was the victim. He was running out of time. If the case didn't break very soon, the Chief Constable would bring someone in over his head. Whilst Owen had faith in him, she was only a superintendent and would eventually have to give way to pressure from above.

He did not hear Siobhan ask. 'Where to now, sir?' She repeated the question.

His mind came back to the present. 'What? Oh, I want to pay a brief visit to the station, then back to the farm.'

Once they were in the car, she asked, 'How does this affect the case, sir?'

Again he'd been only half listening. He shook his head as if to clear it. 'You mean the drugs? He didn't earn a great deal and he was saving for the birth of his baby. There's no way he could afford drugs unless he was getting additional cash from somewhere. We've gone through his life with a fine toothcomb, he had no other legitimate source of income: Which means he must have come by it illegally. Now where on earth would he get money from?'

'What about blackmail, sir?'

'From what we've heard about him I don't think he was bright enough to blackmail anyone, do you? Anyway, who might he blackmail?'

'I was thinking perhaps Sinclair with his dungeon. But you're right, the lad wasn't very sharp.'

'Sinclair's sexual trysts were an open secret, hardly blackmail material.' He frowned. 'So we come back to the bloody Sinclair Estate. He must have found something there and sold it. But he had no money on him and there was no trace of any extra cash in his bank account. And this surprise he had for Jenna, presumably that would have cost him something.'

'Perhaps the killer took it off him.'

'That's possible but if he had a large amount he'd hardly be likely to carry it around with him.'

'What makes you think it was a large amount, sir?'

'Well it must have been worth killing for. And remember he was tortured before he was killed. You'd hardly go to those lengths for a few quid would you?'

'So we are back to buried treasure.'

'But where the hell was it buried, damn it? And where is it now?'

Siobhan wisely didn't answer him, and they made the rest of the journey to Truro Police Station in silence.

Prior parked in the station yard. He said to his companion, 'Get yourself a coffee, Siobhan, I just want to see how Bob Monk is coping.' Making his way up to his office, he noticed the door was closed. Looking through the small glass window in the door, he saw DI Monk leaning back in his chair with his feet on the desk. He was reading the Daily Mirror.

Opening the door, Prior stomped into the office. 'I see you're busy, Bob, has crime suddenly come to a stop?'

Monk quickly swung his feet to the floor. 'Afternoon sir. No, I've been busy; I'm taking a late lunch.'

'I see the in-tray is filling up, anything urgent in there?'

'No, sir. I'm working on that. How's the enquiry going?'

'Slowly. What's happening on the division?'

'Just the usual stuff, a few car thefts and a spate of shop-lifting.'

'Don't you think you might shorten your lunch break then and do some detective work?'

'Yes, sir.'

Prior sighed. Monk had only a few years to go before his pension and had no prospect of further promotion. It was difficult to motivate him other than by constantly looking over his shoulder.

He took a few minutes to gather his thoughts before continuing. 'At the moment I'm under a great deal of pressure investigating not one but two murders. One grabbed the public's eye because of its ferocity and the other high profile because of the victim's local standing. I come in here and see a full in-tray and you sitting with your feet on the desk reading a newspaper. I give you fair warning. If you don't pull your finger out then I will come down on you like a ton of bricks. Do I make myself clear?'

Monk gulped, 'Yes, sir.'

'I repeat, when I do get this inquiry finished and get back here, I do not want to find a crime wave and a full in-tray. Now, get off your fat arse and get busy.' Without waiting for a response, he turned and left the office.

Going to the canteen he joined Siobhan. She could see that he was not in the best of moods and said simply; 'Ready when you are, sir.'

When they arrived at the enquiry van, they were told that the old gamekeeper, Tom Williamson, was on his way to see them.

29. Old Tom.

'The mill cannot grind with water that is past.'

17th century proverb.

Tom Williamson was a grizzled old man in his seventies. He was short and wiry, his legs bowed as if from a lifetime of carrying heavy weights which gave him a rolling gait. He carried a stout stick with a curved handle and leant heavily on it as he walked. His full head of grey hair was neatly trimmed and his lined weather-beaten face clean shaven. Clearly, he had spent much of his life outdoors.

He was dressed like a farm worker. His clothes were clean and his boots polished. Overall, he had a wholesome appearance, that of a man who cared for himself and retained his dignity despite advancing years.

Beside him was his dog, his constant companion. It was a black and white Border Collie, its whiskers and snout as grey as the old man's hair. It was as if the animal was attached to him by an umbilical cord. When Williamson walked, the dog walked; when he stopped, it stopped; and when he sat, it sat without bidding. Prior had no doubt that the animal slept beside the old man's bed at night.

As PC Trimble helped him up the steps to the enquiry van, DS Quigley made as if to tell him not to bring the dog in but Prior said, 'No, Albert, that's OK.' Prior had watched through the window as the old man had walked across the yard. Two farm workers mucking out had greeted him warmly. He had acknowledged their greetings with a smile and a nod.

Prior stepped forward to meet him. 'Mr Williamson, thanks for coming. I'm DCI Prior and this is DS Williams.'

The old man nodded. 'Tain't no trouble, Brian here gave me a lift.' His voice was deep and gravelly, and full of the rich brogue of the Southwest. Looking into his eyes, Prior saw a bright sparkle that told him the old man's mind was still sharp, despite what the ravages of time had done to his body.

They interviewed him in the general office. He sat on the edge of an upright chair, his back stiff as a ramrod. His walking stick was planted firmly on the floor between his widespread knees, his hands cupped over its curved handle. He politely refused the offer of refreshments and Prior started the interview.

'I understand you were the gamekeeper here on the estate, Mr Williamson?'

'That I were. Until the old Mr Sinclair passed away five years ago.'

'Did you live on the estate then?'

Williamson smiled. 'I 'ear you were at my old cottage this morning. There's talk in the village there's been goin's on there. Yes, I were born there. My father were gamekeeper before me.'

Prior returned the smile. 'So the village grapevine works does it?'

He nodded. 'Ain't much goes on around 'ere we don't get to 'ear about.'

'Do you know what those goings on were?'

The old man's eyes sparkled. 'I expect it's something to do with the two killings.'

'What makes you think that, Mr Williamson, what's the word in the village?'

'Village talk is mostly tittle-tattle, they don't know nothin'.'

'And you, what do you know? I suspect it's a bit more than they do.'

'No, I know no more than they do. But I got my thoughts on what it likely is.'

'Please share those thoughts with me Mr Williamson.'

Another smile. 'You're the big detective, I'm just an old gamekeeper. Tain't nothin' to do with me.'

Prior could see that the old man was just sparring with him. He moved on. 'You'll know the estate well then.'

'Better'n most, yes.'

'Tell me what exactly does a gamekeeper do?'

The old man's eyes twinkled. 'You're not a countryman are you, lad?'

'No, I'm a townie I'm afraid.'

'What a gamekeeper does is make sure the birds breed and the predators and poachers don't get too many of them.'

'So you reared the birds. What kind of birds were they?'

The old man cackled. 'Pheasants. No, I didn't rear them, they're wild. But they ain't native to this country and they ain't used to foxes, stoats and weasels. They nest on the ground, see? And if someone don't keep the predators down, the eggs get taken.'

'What about poachers, did you have trouble with them?'

'There were a few that tried, yes, but I was on to their tricks and we didn't lose many birds.'

'How many birds were there on the estate?'

'Back in my father's time there were a couple of thousand nesting birds. But the numbers got smaller and smaller as they put more land under the plough.'

'What happened to the birds when you retired?'

An angry spark appeared in the old man's eyes 'Who said I retired? Got sent packing I did. When the old master died, his son Cedric weren't interested in the birds. Changed everything he did. Got more machines in to farm the land and sacked half the workers. Weren't no better up at the house. Stopped entertaining, except those young floozie's. Closed up most of the old house and sacked most of the staff. What happened to the birds you say? They scattered far and wide and predators got most of them, that's what happened to them.'

'Seems a shame.'

'Damned shame, you ask me. A lot of the villagers packed up and moved away. Not much employment round here except on the land and at the clay works.'

Prior paused. He had started that line of questioning to try to relax the old man but had inadvertently struck a raw spot. He turned to Siobhan.

She nodded. 'I understand you're interested in history Mr Williamson?'

The old man's sharp gaze moved to her. 'My family have lived hereabouts for as long as anyone can remember. Don't seem right to forget about them.'

'I meant ancient history, the Celts.'

'Well, they're our ancestors, aren't they?'

Siobhan softened her tone, 'Yes I suppose they are. Didn't they have a settlement here?'

'Top of the hill, yes.'

'What do you think about the people who've been trying to dig on the site?'

'T'aint right, that's what I think.'

'But won't that give us more knowledge about their way of life?'

'What will a few bits of pottery tell us? The important things were handed down by word of mouth. Fathers told their sons and they told theirs. No need to go digging up the ground where they lived.'

Prior intervened. 'Where did they bury their dead, Mr Williamson?'

The old man gave him a sharp look. 'Why do you want to know that?'

'Two people have been murdered. One who worked on the estate and the other its owner? If that had anything to do with what's buried on the estate, we need to know.'

For the first time the old man became evasive. 'I don't know nothing about their deaths.'

'I'm not suggesting you do. But I think you know a lot about goings on here past and present. Is there a burial site on the estate?'

'I expect so. If people lived here, they must have buried their dead somewhere.'

'You spent the best part of your life here. Did you find any burial sites?'

'I never done no digging.'

Prior sighed. 'That's not what I asked, Mr Williamson. Did you come across any evidence of burial sites anywhere on the estate?'

Anger showed on the old man's face. 'You're just like the rest of them, no respect for the dead. The old people believed that when someone died they went on a journey to the next world. So it was natural that what they might need on the journey be buried with them. Robbing those graves is wrong and I'll have no truck with it.'

Prior did not back off. He looked the old man in the eye and said, 'You're wrong about one thing, I agree that the dead should be left in peace. But that doesn't justify killing the living. Young Wright seems to have been a nice lad. All

I'm trying to do is to find out who killed him. And if it had something to do with the past I want to know about it. Now, will you help me or not?'

The old man did not respond. He sat looking straight ahead of him with a determined expression on his face.

Siobhan said softly, 'The stone cross in the brambles, Mr Williamson, what is the significance of that?'

He looked at her sharply. 'Marks the boundary between the living and the dead.'

'What exactly do you mean?'

'I mean that the ground above that cross was for the living and below it was for the dead to rest in peace. That's why no-one cuts down the trees there.'

'So the old Celts did bury their dead along the bottom-land?'

The old man's expression softened. 'I expect they did and it ain't right that folk want to disturb their graves.'

'I agree with you. Do you know anyone that does want to?'

'There's some that think there might be valuables there.'

'And who are these people?'

'It's just talk. I don't know anyone who wants to dig there.'

'No-one?' Prior asked.

'That's right no-one. Just villagers' idle chatter in the pub.'

'Was Wright one of these people?'

'No, he were just curious about the cross. He found it when he were cutting back the brambles. Asked me what it meant. I lent him a book I had, explained what the Celtic cross meant.'

'Did he ask anything else?'

'Didn't get a chance, did he? He were killed two days later.'

'Do you have any idea who might have killed him?'

'I don't know and I don't want to know. T'aint any of my business.'

There was silence for a long moment. Then Siobhan said, 'You walk your dog late at night Mr. Williamson, where do you go?'

'With my legs, I can't go far. Just around the village.'

'Do you ever get as far as the estate here?'

'No, that's too far for me these days.'

Prior intervened, 'Do you meet anyone on your walks?'

'Hardly, country folk go to bed early. They're up at the crack of dawn, not like town folk.'

'You say hardly. Who have you met on your walks?'

The old man cackled. 'Met young Gibbons the constable a couple of time. He thought I were a poacher, asked me what I had under my coat.'

'Anyone else?'

'Not walking, no.'

'What about driving, people in motor vehicles?'

A look of distaste spread over his face. 'You mean the taxis taking those floozies back and forth to the estate? I've seen them a few times.'

Prior looked at Siobhan, who shook her head. Neither had any more questions for the old gamekeeper. Prior thanked him for his time and PC Brian Trimble took him out to his car to ferry him back to the village.

When he had left Siobhan said, 'A bitter old man but I can't see him killing someone as fit as young Wright and sticking his head on a post, or pounding Sinclair's head with a rock.'

Prior shook his head. 'Nor can I.'

'So we are no further forward, sir?'

He gave her a hard look, 'You've been in the job long enough to know, Siobhan, these cases are sometimes a hard slog. We are eliminating people as we go and that's all we can do until we get a clue as to what this is about.'

She said, 'Perhaps we should consult a medium, sir. We've already got a profiler. And what about a clown and an acrobat, we might as well have the whole circus?'

Prior's frown turned to a grin. 'I'm not sure about the clown, Siobhan, people might think we're not taking this enquiry seriously. And we haven't seen the profiler since Friday'

They both laughed.

As if bidden, Jessica Bloomfield chose that moment to walk through the door.

30. The Profile.

'In the country of the blind the one-eyed man is king'
16th century proverb.

Prior greeted her, 'Jessica, good to see you.' He didn't add 'at last'.

She acknowledged his greeting, 'I wondered if you'd still be here at this time of day, Matthew. Another murder, very worrying.'

'Yes, we're still here Jessica, policemen do tend to work long hours. And yes it is terrible, another murder. It might be helpful to have your opinion on that as well as the first one if you have the time. Especially to see if you think they are connected.' He didn't make too much of an effort to be civil.

Unabashed, Bloomfield looked at Siobhan, 'And police women too by the look of it. I did some work on the first murder over the weekend. I'll look at the evidence on this latest one and let you have my conclusions.'

Prior said, 'We are just about to have an ideas session. The whole team will be present. Perhaps you'd like to sit in.'

'Yes, I'd find that interesting, thank you.'

Prior gritted his teeth to stop himself from making further comment. The murder enquiry was not being conducted for her entertainment; she was supposed to be giving him ideas. He managed to say, 'Any contribution you make will be welcome.'

*

Prior had assembled his whole squad, his two DSs, six DCs and the two CSIs. Each found somewhere to sit facing Prior. He stood beside the whiteboard that showed details of the investigation. Jessica Bloomfield found a seat at the back of the van.

Prior called them to order. 'OK, pay attention. We now have two murders within a week, both with strong connections to this estate.' He pointed to the whiteboard where details of the victims were shown, including stark photographs of the victims. 'Two brutal murders. The killer, if it is the same man, is totally ruthless, So far we have no eye witnesses, no obvious motives and very little forensic evidence. Every line of enquiry that we have pursued seems to have ended in a dead end, no pun intended.' He paused. There wasn't a sound in the room.

'It's time we came up with something. Someone out there must know something and we have to find that person and put some pressure on them. This is a small rural community and, unlike the big towns, the animals outnumber the humans. In places like this everyone knows everyone else's business. Now, you are the people who have been talking to those who live and work locally. You are the ones who must have picked up both the verbal and non-verbal signals. You know my rules with these sessions, anything goes. We've explored the evidence trail, now we're down to our instincts. No one will rubbish whatever you bring up here.' He paused again to let the words sink in.

He continued, 'OK, motive, means and opportunity. Let's look at motive first. First, who had a motive to kill John Wright? There was a buzz of people wanting to answer. Prior held up his hands and nodded to DC Fraser. 'Jane, what do you want to say?'

'How's this for a scenario, sir? Wright is working on the estate and finds something valuable. Someone learns of this and kidnaps him. Then he tortures him to find out where he has hidden the find. Then he kills him once he has the information.'

'OK, what did Wright find?'

'Obviously something valuable sir.'

'Yes, but what?'

Fraser grinned. 'If I knew that sir, you'd have to promote me.'

When the laughter had subsided, Prior said, 'OK what are the possibilities?'

Siobhan said, 'Buried treasure?'

Prior allowed the hubbub that ensued to continue for a few moments and then held his hands up again. 'Jessica, you wanted to say something?'

'Yes, Matthew. My question is, 'what is valuable?' She paused then answered her own question. 'Perhaps we should look beyond intrinsic value and think of aesthetic worth.'

'Would you like to expand on that, Jessica?'

'Things a historian might value that the average man in the street might miss.'

Prior nodded. 'But Wright wasn't especially bright. If he found whatever it is, how would he have recognised its historical value?'

'Maybe he didn't but was curious enough about his find to take it to an expert.'

Siobhan looked sceptical. 'What, then the expert tortured him then killed him? Does that mean we should be looking for a historian?'

There were a few murmurs of agreement around the room.

Bloomfield shook her head and smiled. 'I'm sure there are historians who would kill for such things but, no, that's not what I mean. But if someone local thought the find might be of intrinsic value, they might kill in order to get it.'

Siobhan insisted, 'But we've searched the whole area and we found no sign of a burial site or of anyone digging, or anything else for that matter. And we've questioned an expert at Truro College who says that, even if there is a burial ground, it's most unlikely there's anything of value in the graves.'

Bloomfield said, 'That doesn't mean there are no graves. With all due respect to the searchers, perhaps it's something only a trained archaeologist would spot.'

'Then how did Wright find this grave?' asked Siobhan.

'Maybe he stumbled across it simply by chance,'

Prior held his hands up again for quiet. 'That makes sense. But we do need an expert to come and look at the area. I've got someone coming to see me tomorrow night who's an expert on the ancient Celts. She has agreed to come and have a look around the next morning.' He paused then said, 'OK, let's move on. Any other ideas?'

Trimble said, 'What about the S & M dungeon, sir. Might that be connected to the killing?'

Prior nodded. 'I can see the possible connection to Sinclair but what about Wright?'

'Who was on the DVDs we found, sir?'

Prior smiled. 'We're having them looked at. I'll let you know Fred.'

Quigley said, 'I'm pretty sure we've found out all there is to know about Wright. There doesn't seem to have been a lot of side to the lad. There's nothing to suggest that he had any sexual kinks. The only thing we've found about him is that he was into amphetamines.'

'Wasn't there some talk about him being seen with another woman sarge?' Foster asked.

'Yes, there was Jane. But that was followed up. It turned out to be a cousin of his visiting his parents. She's happily married with two kids and lives in Barnstaple. No hanky panky there.'

Prior added, 'We'll follow up on the drugs. Otherwise, the only mystery about him is the surprise he had planned for his girlfriend. Perhaps he did find something on the estate and sold it. That would explain how he could afford the speed. I think Sinclair's sexual exploits are simply a co-incidence. '

'But surely we can't ignore them, sir?' Trimble insisted.

'No, we can't and nor shall we. But let's wait until we see who was on the DVD, then we might be able to tell if it's connected. In the meantime, let's move on here.'

Siobhan said, 'What about blackmail as a motive, sir?'

'What about it Siobhan?'

'Well, suppose Wright was blackmailing Sinclair over his kinky sex in the dungeon and Sinclair decided to kill him rather than pay him?'

'You forget, Sinclair was busy at the time Wright disap-peared, he has an alibi. Anyway, Sinclair's sexual activities were no secret locally. half the damned village knew about them. '

Siobhan smiled. 'Yes I forgot about that, he was playing ping-pong when Wright was killed wasn't he?'

Prior let the ensuing laughter continue for a moment, then brought them back to the matter at hand. 'OK, any-thing else?'

DC Jean Wade said, 'Yes, sir. We are assuming it was an outsider who killed Wright just because the head was brought to the scene from the outside. Couldn't it have been someone on the estate doing that to throw us off the track?'

'Yes, of course it could, Jean. Everyone is on our list of suspects. But the same question applies, who and why? And why put the head on the gate when that would only draw attention to the estate?'

No one volunteered an answer.

'Could Sinclair have arranged to meet someone down by the stream, sir?' Wade asked.

'That's possible, of course. But he had no visitors over the weekend or any phone calls as far as we know and why down there?'

There was a long silence. Everyone seemed to have run out of ideas.

Eventually Bloomfield said, 'Would this be an appropriate moment to share my thoughts with the team, Matthew?'

'It would indeed, Jessica, the floor is yours.' Prior sank into a seat and Bloomfield walked to the front of the room.

She stood looking at the detectives for a long moment, her hands clasped in front of her. She was dressed as she had been the previous Friday and Prior smiled to himself as he noticed the eyes of the males in the audience focus on her generous breasts.

Finally she started to speak. She told the team basically what she had already told Prior about her work. Prior watched her audience as she spoke. It was noticeable that the men's eyes gradually moved from her breasts to her face. Clearly she knew how to hold an audience.

She continued, 'Each of us is unique, each of us does things differently, even the most simple of tasks. Take handwriting for example; we each hold the pen differently and our writing is individual to us. There are people who analyse handwriting and identify the characteristics of the person who did the writing. It's the same with most tasks, including murder; each person will commit the act according to his or her personal characteristics. Some people are impulsive and act without thought while others are methodical and never act without forward planning. The same characteristics that dictate how we write or kill will be present in just about everything we do.

There are, of course, constraints when we commit murder. In the vast majority of cases, we don't want to get caught and punished although there are exceptions. What weapon will we use? What location will we choose? How will we dispose of the body? Will we prepare an alibi? Will we act alone? How strong are we? What skills do we have? There are many, many variables. But each choice made by the killer can tell us something about them.' She paused again to check that her audience were still with her. To a man, they were.

She continued, 'Then we have to consider the kind of person who might take the life of another. Murder is defined as the unlawful killing of another. The decision as to what is unlawful is purely arbitrary. We each have a moral code that helps us decide what is right and what is wrong. The Bible tells us it is wrong to kill, the text makes no exceptions. Yet on occasions the law says it is right to kill, say in wartime, in self-defence or the defence of another. So, it could be argued, the law is at odds with morality.

It follows therefore that sometimes our minds are at odds with the law. Often the circumstances we find ourselves in dictate our actions. How often has each of us said, 'I could kill that man or woman'? But, fortunately, the vast majority of us do not carry through with the thought. Some of course do.' She paused and smiled. 'Otherwise you lot would be out of a job.' There was a buzz of subdued laughter. Prior looked around him. The whole team were now hanging on her every word.

She continued, 'I could go on to tell you about psychopaths and sociopaths but I don't think they are especially relevant here, so I will get to specifics about the Wright murder. First, I can confirm that the killer is local and probably lives within five miles of the estate. He knows the area well and deliberately chose his spot to display the head.

Over the weekend I drove around the whole area. There are several spots where the head could have been displayed more easily, at less risk, and where it would have been seen by a greater number of people. The location was not random and the head placed there for a reason. I believe that reason was as a warning to others, keep off.' One or two of her audience stirred.

She continued, 'Before you ask, I don't know whether it was to keep off the estate or to do what Wright did. I suspect it may have been both.

Next the killer. He knew his victim but I don't think he was close to him. This is not the action of an angry lover or rival but neither was the victim chosen at random. John Wright was his target.

The killer's age? Anywhere between 25 and 50, but I would think more towards the top end of the scale. This murder was carefully planned and executed and the head impaled on the spike for a purpose. My experience leads me to suggest that this was not the act of an impetuous youth. The killer executed his plan coolly before, during and after the act. I doubt an elderly man would have had the strength to subdue the victim and do what he did and yes, I'm sure it is a man.

The vehicle used, obviously there was one. We are dealing with several different locations some distance apart; the site of the torture, killing and decapitation; the positioning of the head; and the disposal of the torso. I know you have already considered the vehicle.

It could just as easily have been a car as some kind of truck as the body could have been carried in the boot. But he used a ladder. There is evidence of a ladder being leant against the gate. Analysis of the wood shavings found confirm that they had only recently been rubbed from the ladder itself, otherwise there would have been more weathering of the slivers of wood found. I am convinced, therefore, that a ladder was used to put the head on the spike. Unless the car used had a roof rack, it would have been difficult to transport in a car. I doubt the killer would have risked hiring a truck, too easy to trace. I suspect therefore that the killer had access to a truck of some sort.'

The victim was tortured before he died. I've spoken to the pathologist who conducted the autopsy. He confirms that there was no trace in or around the victim's mouth of a gag of any sort having been applied. When someone is tortured, he will no doubt make a great deal of noise. This suggests that the torturer found some isolated spot where the screams of the victim would not be heard. It might be that he lives in such a spot; certainly he would have to have access to one. I know we are in the countryside. Nevertheless the killer would not take the chance of being disturbed. It is something to consider.'

Prior interrupted her, 'Jessica, you are obviously not aware that this morning we found where Wright was tortured and killed. It was an isolated cottage about half-a-mile from where the head was displayed. Our CSI here will brief us on what was found there in a moment.'

'Thank you, Matthew, I will be very interested to hear what was found at that scene. In the meantime, I'll move on. The method used to kill the victim. A knife ground into the victim's chest; cold and efficient; a determination to get the job done. Callous you might say, I would agree. The fact that the wound was inflicted to the front of the chest, probably with the victim's eyes upon him all the time, tells us something. The killer set himself a task and methodically and determinedly went about that task until it was complete.' She paused and smiled. 'Perhaps some of you will see similarities here with work of the detective. You need to be methodical and determined, hopefully without the callousness.'

There were a few titters from her audience.

'The decapitation. Performed with the same determination but without expertise. I don't think we are dealing here with a serial killer. The killing was necessary to effect his purpose and not an end in itself. The displaying of the severed head I have already dealt with; a crude warning to others who might stand in the way of his overall purpose. It may have had an additional meaning, resentment. Resentment against the estate owner or the landowning gentry. This too could be significant. The disposal of the torso in the nearest river was simply a means of getting rid of unwanted baggage. He had no further use for it.

Just a word about sociopaths. There is a spectrum of sociopathic behaviour that stretches from that of Ted Bundy at one extreme to Sister Teresa at the other. Depending on the circumstances, we are all capable of selfish behaviour; sociopaths display extremely selfish behaviour. What the layman tends to forget is that most of us think and act somewhere between the two extremes. And although not consistently throughout our lives, in extreme circumstances, we do extreme things. Do not think that you are looking for some kind of freak who will give himself away when you confront him.

I doubt that this man will display sociopathic behaviour in his everyday life. He may well have a wife and children and he will probably appear normal in other circumstances. The one characteristic he may display in his everyday life is a certain coolness toward others. I don't think he will be someone who people warm to. But many sociopaths are good actors which is why they are difficult to catch.

I think this man set his mind on what he would do and put all other thoughts aside. I do think that he bears some resentment towards society or sections of it. This enables him to ignore society's rules of behaviour when it suits him. As I've said, this resentment may be directed at the Sinclair Estate, hence the positioning of the severed head. Or it may be more general. It might be against the privileged classes as a whole and he is using this estate as an example. It may also be that he has a sense of history; our distant ancestors displayed severed heads as a warning to others. Certainly something in his past or something he has learned will have triggered this particular action.

One thing that may help to find him is that, in the past he may have displayed abnormal or abhorrent behaviour. His resentment will be deep rooted and could well have resulted in displays of cruelty earlier in his life. This may have brought him to the attention of police in the past. But this is not necessarily so, it could easily have gone unnoticed or unremarked upon. In the past it may have been confined to cruelty to animals. But please bear in mind that in his everyday life this man may appear to be kind to animals and children. Clearly he is clever and in most circumstances will control his behaviour and show no sign of abnormality.

To summarise then. The physical prowess required to do what he did leads us to the obvious conclusion about his age and build; he is neither a small man nor a frail one. He lives locally and has access to some kind of vehicle larger than a saloon car. I was going to add that he had access to some isolated place where he could be sure he would not be overheard but it now seems that you have discovered that.

He has some connection with the Sinclair Estate, either past or present. He carries a great deal of resentment, enough to make him kill. He knew the victim but was probably not close to him. His everyday behaviour probably gives no indication of what is going on in his mind.

That's all I have at the moment but I see that things have moved on since my last visit. I have had no chance to look at the scene of Wright's death, nor the second murder, or to consider whether the two are connected. Although at first glance it seems extremely likely that the two murders are. I will be pleased to answer any questions that you may have if I am able to. Thank you for your attention.'

The spell was lifted and there was a shuffling of feet and a buzz of conversation in the room.

Prior cleared his throat. 'Jessica, thank you. If any of us had any doubts as to the usefulness of your contribution, I'm certain they are now dispelled. Can I ask a question? Do you think that the killer is employed on the estate?'

'Thank you for those kind words, Matthew. Employed on the estate? Maybe he is or once was but not necessarily. The influence of the estate obviously extends beyond its walls and the people actually employed there. I'm afraid I cannot be more precise.'

Siobhan asked, 'Jessica, this information the killer extracted from Wright. Have you any idea what it might have been?'

Bloomfield smiled. 'Beyond saying that it will have been something that he saw as necessary to complete his overall purpose, no. This is more your field of expertise. What information might he have had that would be useful to someone else?'

Siobhan returned her smile. 'If we knew that we'd all be at home now eating dinner.'

Various team members chimed in with questions but raised nothing that took them any further with the investigation.

Prior moved on, 'OK, George what did you find at the old gamekeeper's cottage?'

Bailey gave his report in his own imitable style. The essence of it was that he had found some valuable forensic evidence. First he dealt with the negatives. He'd found nothing useful on the gate in Lamb Lane or on the track leading to the cottage. From there on the news was more positive.

He'd examined the plate holding the padlock ring prised from the door. It was of a softer metal than the crowbar used to prise it loose and he was certain that shavings from the plate would have adhered to the crowbar. Find him the bar and he might give you a match.

Next, the stone floor of the cottage. He'd found two partial shoeprints. The patterns on them were sufficient to provide a match when the shoe that made them was found.

Adhered to the overturned chair, on the pieces of flex and in the pool of blood, were flakes of dried skin and body hairs that would provide a match with the body or bodies that had left them there.

Prior brought the session to a close. The one positive outcome of the day was that they now had some forensic evidence that might help identify the suspect when one emerged. He thought about what Jessica had said concerning resentment towards the Sinclair Estate. This was of limited value, as just about the whole of the local community seemed to resent something about the place and Sinclair himself. It seemed, despite Bloomfield's fascinating contribution, it brought them no closer to identifying the killer. He looked at his watch, 8.30, another twelve-hour day. He phoned Jeanette and told her he was on his way home.

31. Tuesday Morning.

'Where the carcass is, there shall the eagles be gathered together.'
16th century proverb.

Prior's alarm woke him at 6.50am. He lay for a moment luxuriating in the warm bed. Sleep had cleared his mind and he was planning the day ahead. He thought about the lecture that Bloomfield had given his team. On reflection, he realised that she had not told him a great deal more than he already knew. But she had provided a focus, put a better perspective on who they were looking for. Before her talk, the mass of information his team had accumulated had threatened to swamp him. Now he could see some order and the way forward.

Jeanette beside him surfaced more slowly in the mornings and it was only when the back-up alarm went off at 7am that she kicked him. 'Shouldn't you be up, Matthew?'

'Yes, love, I'm getting up now.' He pulled back the covers and put his feet on the floor.

Twenty minutes later he was in the kitchen brewing the coffee and listening to the local news on the radio. In the background he could hear the sounds of Jeanette getting the girls ready upstairs. As he put the cereal dishes out, he smiled; domestic bliss.

Then something the newscaster was saying caught his attention. 'Concern increases over the two murders committed on the Sinclair Estate near Truro. First, the brutal slaying of a farmworker and the macabre display of his severed head on the gate to the estate, then, less than a week later, the clubbing to death of Cedric Sinclair, the estate owner.

A police spokesperson says that enquiries are progressing, no doubt a euphemism for the fact that the investigation team has made no progress in identifying the killer or killers and bringing them to justice. A resident of the nearby village of Penwin said, 'We are all worried in the village, who will be next?' The detective leading the investigation was not available for comment.'

Prior's good mood evaporated. He cursed and switched the radio off.

The imminent arrival of his family was heralded by the noise of their feet on the stairs and their excited chatter. Prior brought his mind back to the present and shouted, 'Is that a herd of elephants I hear coming down the stairs?'

Samantha was first through the kitchen doorway and said, 'Good morning, daddy, elephants live in the zoo not in our house.'

Quickly following her, Natalie said importantly, 'Only a few of them live in the zoo, Samantha, most of them live in the jungle.'

'Well, the noise you two make causes me to wonder whether some have escaped.'

His day had started. After a coffee and a slice of toast, he kissed his family goodbye and set off to work.

It was a grey overcast day but the rain had stopped. On the Sinclair Estate everything was dripping wet and it would take days to dry out, even if there was no more rain. Nevertheless, Prior was determined to revisit the scene of the most recent crime.

After a coffee and a chat to Quigley, he and Siobhan put on the Wellington boots and picked their way carefully across the field to the bottomland. With all the recent traffic the ground underfoot had been churned into a sea of mud. They gingerly made their way through a gap in the brambles.

Clumping along behind him Siobhan said, 'What are we looking for, sir?'

'Sherlock Holmes often revisited the scene of crime, Siobhan, and he always solved his crimes. We are not looking for anything in particular but for anything we might find.'

'What kind of answer is that, sir?'

'Would you rather I told you to shut up and eat your ice cream? I'm looking for inspiration not a bloody wet blanket.'

'Well, if there are any blankets down here they'll definitely be wet.'

'Very funny, now concentrate. There has to be something down here that will give us a clue why two people were murdered. Now, apply your mind.'

'Yes, sir, applying my mind now.'

Slipping and sliding, they walked the short distance to where Sinclair's body had been found. Prior stopped and looked around. The place was now becoming familiar; he could even recognise some of the trees and their configuration. He looked at the stream below him. There was no way one could describe its path as meandering, unless of course you were a poet with license.

For much of the 600-yard stretch between the main gate to the estate and the Lamb Lane wall it ran fairly straight. Only the occasional rocky outcrop on either bank caused it to change course around them. It varied in width from just a few yards at its narrowest point to ten in the straight stretches. In these wide stretches it was no more than three foot deep and its stony bed could clearly be seen. In places at the bends the current had gouged out deeper pools where the water eddied.

Prior was not a fisherman but guessed it was in those pools that trout sheltered from the current when recent rains increased the flow. He said, 'I've often wondered about this trout tickling lark. How do you find the bloody fish to tickle them?'

'That's because you're a townie, sir. You have to creep up on them. You don't understand the mysteries of the countryside.'

'How do you creep up on a fish? They're in the water and you're on the bank.'

'For a start you don't talk or make noise, they can hear you. They can also see your silhouette. They're not as stupid as you think.'

'Well they can't be very bright if they let people tickle them to death.'

She laughed. 'I've got an uncle who knows how to do it. Fish have parasites and they rub themselves against stones when they itch. You have to get the fish to think your hand is a stone. Then, when they rub against your hand, you flick them onto the bank.'

'Stones don't have fingers, Siobhan. That proves the fish are stupid.'

'Yes, sir. So are some people, particularly those with closed minds.'

He smiled. 'Ouch! I suppose I asked for that.'

'You even said please, sir.'

He shook his head. 'Sometimes I despair as to what will happen to you when you have another boss who doesn't appreciate your humour.'

'Why, you're not thinking of moving on are you?'

'Huh! If we don't solve these murders soon I may not have the choice.'

There was silence for a long moment. Then he said, 'Back to business. Let's try to reconstruct, Siobhan. Sinclair had a quiet weekend with no visitors and no phone calls. He ate his Sunday lunch, then sometime after three he decided to go for a walk. Now, he was dressed smartly in collar and tie, jacket and cavalry twill trousers, his Burberry jacket, flat cap and walking boots. What does that tell us?'

'Isn't that what the gentleman farmer wears on a Sunday afternoon? I don't understand your question, sir.'

'Well, he was certainly not dressed for a dig, was he?'

'Ah, I see. No, he wasn't, and as far as we know he didn't have a shovel with him.'

'OK smart-arse where was he going?'

'Just for a stroll, sir, to help his lunch go down?'

'Good, so he was out for an innocent stroll. That's a start. Now, why here and what route did he take to get here?'

Siobhan looked around her. 'Well that gap we came through wasn't there on Sunday, the uniform made that when they got here.'

'Good, now you're thinking. Go on.'

'As far as I remember, there aren't any gaps as such along the whole of this stretch, unless you want to force a way through. And as you say, he wasn't dressed for that, was he?'

'Indeed not. So where did he get onto this path?'

'Probably where it meets the drive, that's the most direct route from the house.'

'OK, let's walk to there then follow his route.'

They made their way along the path the 100 yards to the point where the stream passed under the drive near the main gate. Climbing the slope, Prior stepped out onto the drive, He looked across to the other side. The path did not continue. On that side there was just a solid wall of brambles.

'So, the only convenient access to the stream is along this stretch, the other side is just jungle.'

'I wonder if there are wild animals on that side, sir?'

'Be serious, Siobhan. Now, where's the most likely place an intruder who didn't want to be seen would enter the estate?'

'The wall in Penwin Lane is eight feet high. I think it's only six feet in Lamb Lane.'

'Just what I was thinking. And the gate is even less and far easier to climb over, even when it's locked. And that entrance is further from the farm buildings and not visible from them. Lamb Lane is also quieter than Penwin Lane, so it makes sense he came onto the estate there, agreed?'

'Yes, sir.'

'Let's walk back along the stream, the way Sinclair probably did.' They turned and re-traced their steps. They had walked for some 60 yards before there was a small bend in the stream and the path alongside it. As they rounded the bend, the spot where Sinclair's body had been found came into sight for the first time. They stopped for a moment.

Siobhan pointed and said, 'If the killer was there when Sinclair got to this point, why the hell didn't he try to get away? Intruders usually try to escape, not club to death someone who happens to see them. He must have seen Sinclair coming some way off.'

'Yes. So he was either caught with his trousers down or knew that Sinclair had recognised him, so decided then to kill him.'

Siobhan screwed up her nose, 'I can think of only one reason he might have his trousers down, sir, and fortunately there is no evidence of that having happened. But if all he was doing was trespassing, why kill the person who discovers you? Trespass is not a hanging offence.'

'No, it doesn't make a lot of sense. Maybe he was here to kill Sinclair in the first place.'

'But there's no way he could know that he would be here. That doesn't make sense either.'

'This whole bloody case doesn't make sense.' He paused, deep in thought. 'Let's assume it was a chance encounter. Having been seen and knowing that Sinclair would recognise him, he decided to kill him. But why was he here in the first place? He had to have been searching for something.'

'We just keep going round in circles.'

'Let's walk along to Lamb Lane, see if there's anything at all that's out of place.'

The path undulated slightly as it followed the course of the stream. At places it was as high as five foot above the water level, at others just one. The occasional rocky outcrop broke up the symmetry of the plants and trees. Some of the trees growing close to the stream had their roots exposed by the rushing water. They passed the occasional fallen tree trunk in various stages of decay. Clearly no-one had harvested the timber or cleared the land for many years. Other than the well-trodden path, there was no sign of man's interference.

Prior remarked, 'By the looks of it, this place won't have changed much over the years.'

Siobhan nodded. 'Just as old Tom said, no one worked this land, they left the dead in peace.'

'What dead, we haven't found any except for Sinclair?'

'Ah, as Jessica said, sir, perhaps we wouldn't recognise an old burial site if we saw one.'

They reached the Lamb Lane wall without seeing anything out of the ordinary. Here was the only evidence of man's interference with nature, the uprooted oak. The stump still lay where they had first seen it, the pile of logs beside it. The hole from which the stump had been uprooted was half-filled with rainwater.

Prior scratched his chin, 'Wright must have used chains to haul this out with his tractor, one hell of a job. I know because I once took out the roots of an apple tree from our garden. That was hard enough and it wasn't a fraction the size of this brute.'

Siobhan replied, 'Ah, but you didn't have a tractor did you.' She paused then added, 'I suppose it is possible Wright found something among the roots, sir.'

'We've already covered that, Siobhan. It's possible but there's no sign of that.'

'So, we are none the wiser.'

'Didn't Sherlock Holmes say, if you eliminate the impossible what you have left must be the answer however improbable it is?'

'He wasn't real, sir. Besides what are we left with?'

'A good question, what we need is a good answer.'

'Changing the subject. Those DVDs, shouldn't someone be looking at them?'

'I've given them to Owen, Siobhan, because of the Stapleton connection. If there's politics involved let her deal with it.'

'Don't you think Sinclair's dungeon might have some bearing on things, sir?'

'I discussed that with her. She knows what's what. If there's a connection, she'll spot it and let us know.'

'You're very trusting, sir, I'd want to see for myself. Another thing, what about Sinclair's missing keys?'

'Yes, why steal them unless you're going to use them? And there appears to have been no burglary at the house, another mystery. There's a locksmith coming this morning to open the safe.' He looked at his watch, it said 9am. 'He should be there now.'

'And the house contents, sir, did we find an inventory?'

'Yes, that's all in hand. Peterson, Sinclair's solicitor, has it. We're seeing him at ten.'

'Oh goody, I can take off my wellies.'

Prior laughed. 'I'd wait until I got back to the van if I were you. OK let's go back across the fields it should be easier going.'

As they walked Prior said, 'Don't forget tonight Siobhan, Jeanette's expecting you at seven.'

'That should be fun, yesterday a psychology lesson, today a history lesson.'

'You are a bloody cynic. We learned something from Bloomfield, didn't we?'

'Yes sir, I must admit she's good, no mumbo jumbo. But who fits the profile on our list of suspects?'

'The butler, the estate manager, half the farmworkers and half the local village.'

'That's useful then, narrows it down nicely.'

Prior laughed. 'Let's see if she comes up with anything useful after she's looked at the Sinclair murder.'

32. The Solicitor.

'The cat would eat fish but not wet her feet.'

13th century proverb.

Charles Peterson was a man in his early thirties, immaculately dressed and well groomed. Prior had expected someone older, probably from watching too many old British films, he thought, when the family solicitor is usually ancient. When asked about the contents of the will, he replied simply, 'Everything goes to the son, Reginald.'

'No bequests to faithful retainers, that sort of thing?'

'You mean Brighton and his wife? No, Cedric's father looked after them in his will. He left them a fund to provide them with a good pension when they retire.'

'Tell me, are the estate finances in good order?'

'Well, the value of Cedric's estate is, of course, confidential. But I can tell you the estate is in very good order.'

'The house contents, I understand you have an inventory?'

'Yes, my clerks have already started checking the contents.'

'What are those contents worth?'

'A considerable sum of money.'

'Can you be more precise. I'm sure you realise the reason I ask is to establish if it would be worth a burglar's trouble. What about stuff that's easily portable?'

'The contents are insured for several million pounds. There is a lot of silver and one or two ornaments. But the main worth is in the paintings and antique furniture, most of which is not easily portable. Brighton tells me that Cedric's keys are missing. Unless he brought a furniture van, I'm not sure what the thief hoped to gain. The family jewellery and heirlooms are kept safely in the bank.'

'Do you know what is in his safe?'

'Not really, no. But I can tell you he did not keep a lot of cash in the house. And all the deeds to property and stock certificates are kept at my office or the bank.'

'Any idea then what a thief may have been after?'

'No idea at all, the Sinclair family have had this estate since the eleventh century. Cedric wasn't a collector. When the west wing was closed, he had all the valuable paintings and furniture from that part of the house put into secure storage. There was a codicil to his father's will that prevented the sale of things that have been in the family for generations. Not that Cedric had any reason to sell anything, he was quite comfortable.'

'How did you get on with him?'

Peterson gave him a suspicious look. 'Fine.'

'Is that a diplomatic 'fine' or did you socialise with him?'

'I mean fine, he was a friend as well as a client.'

'He didn't have too many friends, did he?'

'That's not something I'm prepared to discuss.'

'Well you should get prepared, this is a murder enquiry and we need to look into the victim's background.'

'If there's anything I can help you with without betraying client confidentiality, I will, Chief Inspector,' Peterson replied officiously.

'Your client is dead, Mr. Peterson, and we are trying to find out who killed him.'

'My firm represent the family, Chief Inspector, family matters are confidential.'

'To a degree yes, but Sinclair's social life is not.'

'If it infringes on the family's standing, it is.'

Prior glanced at Siobhan. She nodded. 'What interests did you share with Mr Sinclair, sir?'

'Interests? I had dinner here once a month to discuss his business affairs. We met occasionally in Truro. We are both members of certain clubs and associations. My firm have looked after the family's affairs for generations.'

'We are talking social life here, sir. What did you share with him socially?'

'We met on several social occasions.'

'Such as?'

'The occasional dinner party, that sort of thing.'

'Are you married, Mr Peterson?'

'What is the relevance of that question?'

Prior intervened, 'Were you aware of Sinclair's sexual proclivities?'

'Cedric was divorced, Chief Inspector, to my knowledge he was not sexually active.'

'Do you know about his recreation room?'

Peterson frowned. 'What do you mean recreation room?'

'So you don't know about the dungeon in the cellars then? Set up for masochistic and sadistic sex. Whips and brass-studded leather, the whole works. '

'I have no idea what you mean.'

'I mean that he was a sexual deviant, Mr Peterson.'

The man licked his lips. 'What he did in the privacy of his own home, Chief Inspector, was his affair. None of what you've told me is illegal, is it?'

'No. But he was murdered and murder is illegal. This may have relevance to his murder.'

'I have no knowledge of such matters. And if you seek to defame the Sinclair family name, Chief Inspector, you tread on dangerous ground. The laws on slander and libel are quite specific.'

'They are indeed Mr. Peterson. But they do not apply when the matters raised are true and there is evidence to support that truth. But that's not the issue here. I have no intention of making this information public. I repeat, I am trying to find out who killed this man.'

'I understood that he was killed by an intruder?'

'Then you know more than we do at this stage. I realise you must toe the family line Mr. Peterson, but the man is dead. If you know of any people who were involved with Cedric in these activities you should tell me.'

Peterson made no reply.

After a pause Siobhan said, 'Do you know anyone who had reason to kill him?'

'No, most certainly not. He was a major local employer and benefactor, a pillar of the community. The family have provided employment and welfare to the local community for generations.'

Prior intervened. 'I do wish you would stop suggesting that we are attacking the man or his family. However, the facts are that when his father died five years ago, Cedric sacked half the workforce on the estate and stopped supporting local charities. He also threatened to sell the houses out from under his tenants unless they were prepared to pay huge rent increases. Nor does he contribute to any local charities. Despite what all his ancestors had done. Hardly the actions of a benefactor. No-one but no-one in the village has a good word to say about him.'

'Then you have a direction in which to pursue your enquiries, Chief Inspector. Now, if you have no further questions, I have a busy day ahead of me.'

Prior sighed deeply then shook his head. 'Thank you for your co-operation, Mr Peterson. Please inform me if you find that anything is missing from the house.'

Peterson would inform them the next day that nothing at all appeared to have been stolen.

As they walked back to the van Siobhan said, 'What an arsehole, sir.'

'Very succinctly put, Siobhan. Typical of his profession, protect his client's reputation even beyond the grave.'

'But surely in a murder case he should co-operate.'

'The king is dead, long live the king. The Sinclair family are his clients and they live on. Young Reginald is now his client. We'll get no help from Peterson.'

After a pause he said, 'Anyway let's move on. I've got to go and see Owen. Make an appointment for us to interview Callaghan this afternoon. I'll see you then.'

'I hope you're not going to watch naughty DVDs, sir, not with the superintendent.'

Prior smiled, 'You've got a dirty mind, Siobhan. Besides, I'm perfectly safe with Owen.'

'So the rumours about her are true, sir?'

He looked at her sternly. 'That's not somewhere you want to go, sergeant. She's very good at her job and a friend of mine. Watch what you say.'

After a moment she replied. 'Yes, sir, I'm sorry. I was out of line.'

Prior's frown turned into a smile. 'No harm done. There's something for you to do. Draw up a list of those people who fit Jessica's profile and see which of them had the opportunity for both killings. I'll see you later.'

Arriving at Truro Police Station, Prior went first to his own office. The office was empty again. Of human presence that is, the in-tray was overflowing. With a sigh, Prior sat and flipped through the files, reports and memos it contained. He picked up the phone. When it was answered, he said, 'Find me DI Monk and send him up to my office.' Whilst he waited for the man to appear, he sorted the pile according to the urgency of the various contents. He'd nearly finished when there was a quiet knock on the door. He shouted, 'Come in.'

Monk was a large man who enjoyed a drink. His grey suit was in need of a press and his tie had stains on it.

Prior said, 'What have you got on at the moment, Bob?'

'Still looking into the spate of car thefts, sir.'

'What have you found?'

'Not a lot, I'm afraid, none of the informants have come up with anything.'

Prior spread his hands over the three piles of paperwork in front of him. 'What about this lot?'

Monk wiped his nose with the back of his hand. 'Haven't had a lot of time for that, sir.'

Prior glared at him. 'Rubbish, you've just left it for me. Well, I've got news for you.' He pointed to the urgent pile. 'This lot is urgent. You sit here and deal with it now and don't bloody well move from this desk until it's clear.' He pointed to the other two piles. 'Then I'll give you 24 hours to clear this other lot. I'll be back tomorrow to check that you've cleared it. And don't just shuffle it around, deal with it. Understand?'

'Yes sir, but....'

'No buts, deal with it or I'll have you up before the superintendent. You've still got a few years to go to your pension and you are still subject to discipline. Either perform or face the consequences. Do you understand?'

'Yes, sir.'

'Now I've got to make a phone call, get out and come back in five minutes.' Monk left the office sheepishly.

Feeling better now that he had vented his anger, Prior picked up the phone. He dialled Force Headquarters. When the phone was answered he said, 'Drug Squad, DI Chalcott please.'

A moment later a voice at the other end of the line said, 'DI Chalcott.'

'Ben, Matt Prior. How are you?'

'Weary but well Matt. What can I do for you?'

'The head on the stake murder, the victim was on amphetamines. Where would he have got them around Truro?'

'Truro? Probably the Starburst Club or O'Henry's, there's a lot of the stuff about. The national squad are looking at a big supplier in Bristol. He's flooding it all over the South-west.'

'Who should I talk to locally?'

'DS Bill Truscott is your man. He's good. I'll get him to contact you, save you chasing him.'

'Thanks, Ben.'

'No problem. How's that lovely wife of yours?'

'She's fine thanks, how's your love life?'

'Bit up and down at the moment, nothing permanent.'

'Keep your chin up Ben, Thanks for your help.' He put the phone down. He knew not to probe too deeply; Chalcott had recently gone through a messy divorce and his romantic life was going through a bad patch.

Prior walked up the flight of stairs to Owen's office. The door was open and she looked up as he appeared. 'Matthew, come in and close the door. I gathered you were in the building, sound travels you know?' She smiled as she spoke.

'Sorry ma'am, but you know the problem.'

'I do, indeed, Matthew. We have a few dinosaurs I haven't yet managed to weed out. You seem to be able to manage that one OK.'

He returned her smile. 'That's one aspect of management I can cope with, ma'am.'

'Don't underrate yourself. You're a very good manager when it comes to motivating the troops in every respect. While you're busy with these murders, I'll keep my eye on Monk for you. Now, tell me how things are going with the case.'

'Thanks, ma'am, I appreciate that. The investigation? Not well I'm afraid.' He went on to detail the progress his team had made. Then he asked. 'Anything useful on the DVDs?'

'Not to your investigation I'm afraid. But confirmation of what we already knew, two very sick minds. It is hard enough to understand the behaviour but I can't for the life of me understand why they would film themselves in action. I'm keeping the discs in my safe. If they do become relevant to your investigation, they will be there.'

'Thanks ma'am, have you told the Chief?'

'Yes, he appreciates the fact that you brought them to me. That was wise of you. I think you earned a few brownie points there. Now, have you got time for lunch?'

Prior looked at his watch, 12.15. 'Yes, I've got an hour.'

They went to the senior officers section of the station canteen and enjoyed a plain but wholesome meal. Police canteens were not famous for their cordon bleu cuisine, but some excelled at shepherd's pie and the like.

Whilst they were eating, Owen said, 'Matthew you must talk to the media, it won't do your career any good avoiding them. They are making snide comments about you, the investigating officer. What is your problem with them?'

'It goes back a long way. They caused the death of a good friend of mine. I have no time for them.'

'Caused a death? I know some of them can be a bit careless as to whom the drivel they write might hurt, but I don't know of any instances where they've caused a death.'

'What about Princess Di, ma'am? I've no doubt it was the so-called paparazzi chasing her car that contributed to the fatal accident.'

'Maybe you are right. Tell me about your friend.'

'It isn't just the media I hate, barristers are just as bad. When I got out of training school, I was posted to Exeter as a probationer. There was another young PC, Bill Griffiths, just ahead of me. He was a very good policeman from the job's point of view but should never have been in the job. He was far too sensitive for his own good.

'He dealt with a hit and run where a car mounted the pavement and killed a young girl. A witness got the car's number and Bill arrested the driver, a young guy who thought he was Jack the lad. When he appeared at court his barrister persuaded him to plead guilty to causing death by reckless driving. In mitigation, the brief said that a tracking rod had failed on the car that caused the swerve, claiming it wasn't entirely the driver's fault.

'The Crown's brief had dozed off. Had he been awake, he would have known that, in the opinion of the vehicle examiner, the tracking rod only broke when the car hit the kerb. So the broken rod was caused by the reckless driving not the other way round. Obviously, with the guilty plea the vehicle examiner was not required to give evidence. But if the damned barrister representing us had read his brief properly he would have seen that it was not mechanical failure that caused or even contributed to the accident.

'Without an argument from the Crown, the judge was lenient and six months later Jack the lad was free. But he had been disqualified from driving for five years. A week after he was out, Bill saw him driving the same car that he had killed the girl with, an old Ford Capri. Bill was driving what we used to call a Panda car in those days. He gave chase. Jack the lad decided to make a race of it and lost it again on a bend. He went head-on into a bus.

'Killed himself; fortunately no one else was injured. Bill went sick with depression. He couldn't cope with the thought that he had, without any intention of doing so, contributed to the someone's death.

'Then the Sunday papers got hold of the story. A reporter with the brains of a mule wrote a story saying that Bill should never have given chase, claiming that he had some kind of vendetta against Jack the lad. He suggested that, as

Bill knew the disqualified driver's address, he should not have chased him but should have gone to his home later and arrested him. Can you imagine, ma'am, the questions that would have been asked if Bill hadn't gone after him?'

Owen nodded, 'Yes the driver could have claimed mistaken identity or something similar. A judge would have asked why he didn't give chase at the time. That's to say nothing of the fact that he might have killed someone else in the meantime which is why he was disqualified from driving in the first place.'

'Exactly. Anyway, Bill read the article then swallowed a bottle of sleeping pills. He never woke up.'

Owen nodded slowly, 'Now I understand, Matthew. But you can't condemn the whole of the media; most of them do have some integrity.'

'Yes, of course. But at a press conference how do you tell one from another? There are sure to be a few from the gutter among them. There are one or two I trust and will speak to. But en masse? No, I'll say as little as I can.'

Owen smiled sympathetically. 'OK, now I know, I won't press you on that. Just try to be as forthcoming as you can and control that temper of yours.'

He nodded and looked at his watch. Looking up he said, 'I'd better go, ma'am, I've lots to do.'

33. The Callaghan Interview.

'A nod's as good as a wink to a blind horse.'

18th century proverb.

They interviewed Callaghan in the estate office. This was housed at the end of the long narrow building beside which the enquiry van was parked. The doorway was no more than six foot high and Prior had to duck as he entered. Once inside he looked around him.

The office looked as if it hadn't changed much in the past few centuries. The building itself must have been at least 200 years old and most of the furnishings could easily have come from the same period in time. The walls were white-painted stone. A huge fireplace stood on one side of the room with a wood-burning stove sitting comfortably in its centre. A neat pile of logs stood beside it and a cheerful fire burned in the stove. Old-fashioned framed windows in the far wall looked out onto a field of grass that sloped gently towards them from the brow of the hill 100 yards above.

Wooden shelves lined one wall. The shelves were filled with farm records gathered through the ages. The bottom three shelves contained rows of leather bound ledgers. Above those were rows of box files and on the top two rows, plastic-bound files containing computer printouts: A working reminder of the advance of technology.

On the wall on either side of the fireplace hung leather harnesses and saddles. On the floor were two sacks labelled fertiliser and several large tins, the contents of which Prior could only guess at. In stark contrast, two modern steel tables contained a computer and printer, piles of farming magazines and booklets advertising fertilisers and animal feed. The room smelled of a combination of leather, wood smoke and fertiliser and, despite the clutter, had an air of tidiness about it.

Callaghan sat behind a scarred oak desk in front of the windows. He rose to greet them as they approached. He was dressed in what Prior imagined to be more or less the uniform of the estate manager. Tan shirt in some soft fabric, woollen tie and brown hacking jacket. Beneath that he wore corduroy trousers and polished brown boots. The dress set him above the farm workers but did not compete with the elegance of the landowner. Everyone knew their place in the hierarchy of the country estate.

They shook hands and the two detectives sat in comfortable leather-seated, upright wooden chairs. They politely declined Callaghan's offer of refreshments. On the wall behind the estate manager was an oil painting of cattle grazing in a field. In the background of the painting were an old stone church and a row of thatched cottages. The ornate wooden picture frame had a patina of considerable age. In Prior's mind the painting was symbolic, men came and went and technology brought new farming methods, but the scenery on the farm remained very much the same.

He brought his mind back to the matter at hand. 'I hope our presence hasn't caused too much disruption to your work, Mr Callaghan.'

'No, Chief Inspector, everything is running smoothly.'

'Good. We have a few more questions if you don't mind.'

'Not at all.'

'There has been talk of intruders on the estate. Do you know of any?'

'No, I don't. Mr Sinclair told me of his concerns about that but I've found no evidence of an intruder.'

'What about the farmhands?'

Callaghan shook his head. 'No one has reported anything to me.'

'So, to your knowledge there have been no intruders?'

'To my knowledge, no, but something must have made Mr Sinclair think we had.'

'What about the old gamekeeper's cottage in the woods at the top of the estate?'

Callaghan waited for Prior to say more. When he didn't Callaghan said, 'I'm sorry, I don't understand. What about it?'

'Someone has been there recently.'

Callaghan looked vexed. 'I gathered that you and your men were up there yesterday. But I don't know what about.'

'When was the last time you were up there?'

Callaghan frowned in thought. 'Well, I was in the field above the wood just the other day. But I haven't been in the woods for weeks.'

'What took you there?'

'Nothing really, just walking the dogs and checking that everything was OK.'

'And was it?'

'Yes, as far as I could see.'

'Have you ever been in the cottage?'

A firm shake of the head. 'No, it's been unoccupied since before I arrived here.'

Prior changed tack. 'My sergeant noticed that someone has been digging up on the hill. What can you tell us about that?'

'Digging?' He frowned. 'Ah yes, rocks, Chief Inspector. You know in this area there are rocky outcrops all over the place. On the farm most of the small ones were removed years ago. But there was a small outcrop of rocks in the top field that I'd been meaning to get dug out for ages. I expect my predecessors didn't have the equipment to shift it. We get a good yield of hay from that field and rocks play havoc with the cutter blades, you know. I finally got round to that last month.'

'You say an outcrop of rocks. So they couldn't have been put there by someone in the past?'

'No, rocks occur naturally hereabouts, I'm sure they were put there by nature.'

Siobhan said, 'Isn't that the place where there used to be a hill fort?'

Callaghan smiled. 'So we're told. Lot of nonsense as far as I'm concerned. And Mr Sinclair would have none of it.'

'You mean you don't believe it's there?'

'It may well be there. But this is a working farm and I agreed with Mr Sinclair. We're far too busy to have people digging the place up.'

Prior intervened, 'Sinclair wasn't a very compromising man, was he?'

'Well, it's his land; or rather was. Up to him what happened on it.'

'What about his son, do you know him?'

'Mr Reginald? Not very well, met him once or twice, seems a nice lad.' He smiled, 'Hope he is anyway, he's my new boss.'

Siobhan asked innocently, 'Is he like his father?'

Callaghan shook his head vigorously. 'No, chalk and cheese apparently. The hands who've been here for years say he's more like his grandfather.'

'So you're looking forward to working for him?'

'I'm hoping we'll get on, yes.'

Prior moved on, 'What about the land down along the stream. Isn't there some kind of burial ground there?'

'Depends what you mean by burial ground. People have lived on this land for thousands of years. Stands to reason they had to bury their dead somewhere. If you dig deep enough, you'll find bones all over the place.'

'Have any been found since you have been here?'

'No human ones to my knowledge, no.'

Siobhan said with a laugh, 'No buried treasure then?'

'I doubt that very much. You know we Cornish folk are a superstitious lot, piskies and giants all over the place according to some. No harm in it but it's all nonsense. No, there's nothing down there but trees and rocks.'

Prior tried a new tack. 'Why do you think Wright and Sinclair were killed?'

'Damned if I know. But it wasn't over anything buried in the ground, that's for sure.'

'Was Wright a good worker?'

'Very good, conscientious and did as he was told.'

'Was it him that took out the roots of the tree down by the wall?'

'Yes. They were beginning to lift the wall so it had to go.'

'So that was on your instructions?'

'Yes, of course. But it was Mr Sinclair that first spotted the problem.'

'Has there been any other digging at all along by the stream?'

Callaghan gave Prior a sharp look. 'Not in my time there hasn't. The hands don't like disturbing things down there. They are a superstitious lot, as I said.'

'Do you often take your dogs for a walk down there, Mr. Callaghan?'

'From time to time, yes, I like to walk all over the estate from time to time just to see that everything's in order.'

'Have you found anything lately that's not in order?'

'No, not a thing.'

'Well there have now been two murders on the estate, something is very much not in order.'

Callaghan frowned. 'I don't follow. I thought Wright was killed elsewhere and his head left on the gate?'

'But Sinclair was killed by the stream. You should know, after all it was you that found the body.'

'Yes, are you saying the two killings are connected?'

'So you think the killings were just a coincidence, do you?'

'I don't know what to think, Chief Inspector. But surely Mr Sinclair was killed by an intruder.'

'Really, what makes you think that?'

'Well it was Sunday, there was no-one on the estate except the Brightons, the old cowman and me'

'What were you doing Mr Callaghan, between the hours of three and five on Sunday?'

'I had a late lunch and then I dozed off in front of the TV.'

'Can anyone verify that?'

'No, I live alone.'

'Not married then?'

'Was once but not now.'

'No woman friends then?'

Callaghan bristled. 'I do have a friend that I see occasionally but I don't see what that has to do with this matter.'

'Where were you on the night that Wright was killed?'

'Your officers have already asked me that. You have my statement.'

'Remind me what's in it, Mr Callaghan.'

'I went to bed at about ten and woke up just before six.'

Prior paused before asking his next question. 'Who do you think did the killings?'

Prior watched Callaghan's eyes as he answered. 'I've absolutely no idea. It certainly wasn't me.' He looked straight at Prior without wavering.

'Why do you think they were killed?'

'Again, I've no idea at all.'

Prior looked at Siobhan who shook her head. He said to Callaghan, 'Thank you, you've been very helpful.'

Back in the van, they sat around Quigley's desk drinking coffee. Prior frowned, 'Well, that doesn't take us much further forward. If we believe Callaghan, all our theories about buried treasure are out the window.'

Siobhan said, 'He seemed believable for most of the interview. But did you notice, when you asked about digging down by the stream he gave you a sharp look?'

Prior nodded, 'Yes, Siobhan, I noticed that.'

'What do you make of it?'

'Could be something I suppose. There again it could just have been annoyance at what he considered a load of nonsense. I was watching him very closely. If he was lying he's very good at it. But there was something about him that didn't quite ring true.' He turned to Quigley. 'Albert, I know we've done checks on his background, get someone to dig deeper, see what they can find.'

Quigley nodded.

There was silence for a few moments. Then Prior spoke, 'Loose ends, Albert, what does the computer tell us that are still outstanding?'

'Lots of little things, sir: Sinclair's missing keys; Wright's missing mobile phone; Cornwall Society's asking permission to dig; Wright's surprise for Jenna; drugs. Oh yes, Inspector Bradley phoned. Apparently Sinclair phoned the station twice, last time about two weeks ago, complaining about intruders on the estate. Bradley asked him if there was any description of these intruders. Sinclair got snotty, said that if he knew what they looked like, he'd have told him. So Bradley didn't ask any more questions.'

Prior nodded slowly. 'Right, not much we can do about the keys or the mobile unless they turn up. As far as the dig's concerned, I've got a historian coming to dinner tonight. She's a friend of my wife. She's agreed to come and have a look around on the estate tomorrow. Hopefully she'll be able to tell us if there's any likelihood of buried treasure.' He moved on. 'Wright's surprise for his girlfriend? I'm not sure what more we can do about that. Any ideas?'

Siobhan shook her head. 'Well Jane and Alan searched the cottage and we spoke to Jenna. And none of his friends knew anything about it. I'm not sure what else we can do.'

'What we can do is go over the ground again, but we'll send different teams, fresh approach and all that. Albert, send Fred and Jean to have another look at the cottage and Jane and Alan to talk to Jenna. That just leaves the drug angle. A DS Truscott will come here looking for me. If I'm not here, fill him in and get what you can from him.'

Quigley said, 'I know Bill Truscott, he knows all there is to know about the local drug scene. I'll have a word with him, sir.'

'Good and get PC Gibbons to come and see me again. I want to ask him about drugs in the village.' Prior smiled and added, 'Make sure he takes his damned bicycle clips off before he comes in.'

Quigley smiled too and made a note.

'And send someone to see this Miles bloke again, the one from Truro College. Ask him if he's thought of anything else useful.' He looked at his watch; it said 4.30. 'Now,' he said, 'I'm going to call it a day. I'll be here in the morning with Doctor Davies, the historian. Siobhan and I will take her to have a look down by the stream.' To Siobhan he said, 'See you at about seven?'

She nodded.

34. Julie Davies.

'The dwarf sees further than the giant when he has the giant's shoulders to mount on.'

Confucius.

Prior arrived home to find the children watching TV and Jeanette working on her computer in the dining room. The house did not have a separate study, but the dining room had ample space for her work station. She had set it up beside the glass sliding doors that led to the spacious garden. When she lacked inspiration, she could simply swivel her chair and gaze out at the superb views.

The house was on the very edge of Truro and on the top of a hill. The land at the bottom of the garden fell away sharply. Across the valley stood another hill with a ridge that ran away at an angle. At the far end of the ridge stood the old engine house of a long-defunct tin mine. Built of local granite, it stood as a monument to the past. A tall chimney stood beside it, once the outlet for the smoke from the coal burning steam engine used to pump the water out of the mine far below the ground.

For thousands of years Cornwall had produced most of the tin used across the whole of Europe. Mines had sprung up all over Cornwall, providing employment for the local people and riches for the mine owners. But this had begun to decline around 1860, when the rich seams of tin bearing rock started to run out.

When the mines were in operation, the engine rooms had contained the winding gear for the cages that took the miners down into the depths of the earth where the tin ore was found. Digging it out with just hand-tools was back-breaking and dangerous work. There had been many tragedies in the history of the mines.

There was much folklore associated with the industry. The local people were deeply superstitious and believed in the little folk; in Cornwall these were known as the Pobel Vean or piskies, dwarfs that lived all over the land and under the earth. Many thought that the evil dwarfs who inhabited the mines were responsible for these tragedies. When they were angry they threw stones at the miners, often causing cave-ins. Miners tried to appease them by leaving pieces of their lunch for the dwarfs to eat.

The mines had given birth to the humble Cornish pasty. Those working underground taking a meal break during their long shift, simply downed their tools and opened their lunch boxes, these contained pasties cooked by their wives. The pasty was a meal in itself, meat, potatoes and vegetables cooked in pastry. Some of the wives added jam or apple at one end so their lucky husbands had a two-course meal. It was wedges of these pasties that the miners left for the dwarfs. Invariably these offerings would be gone by the next morning: The superstitious miners insisted it had been the dwarves that ate them and not the rats that also infested the mines.

Prior leant over behind Jeanette and kissed her neck.

'Mm,' she said, 'that's nice. Why are you home so early?'

'Not you too? I came home early to spend some time with the girls, but they are more interested in Shrek.'

She giggled without looking up from her work. 'Well you must admit he's more attractive than you. Listen, I must finish this speech for Leonard, I promised it for the morning.' Leonard Truscott was her brother, the MP for West Cornwall.

'Really, what's his topic?'

'He's the guest speaker tomorrow evening at the Truro Chamber of Commerce dinner. His topic is corruption in high places.'

Prior laughed. 'That should be good. He doesn't know about Stapleton, does he?'

'Not from me he doesn't. But he smelled something fishy about his sudden retirement.'

'This puts you in a difficult position doesn't it, love, knowing what you do?'

She swivelled her chair to face him. 'Not really, Matthew, Leonard is an honourable man. He knows better than to pump me for information about your job. If he wants to know something from you, he'll approach you directly.'

Prior shook his head. 'I wasn't suggesting otherwise, my love. I was simply saying that it must make things difficult for you when writing his speeches.'

'Not really, no. He's given me the theme of his speech and I have simply researched my normal sources; newspaper articles, the internet and court reports. Stapleton isn't an issue.' She paused. Then she added, 'What would you say about Stapleton if he asked you?'

'Nothing, I'd refer him to the Chief Constable.'

'Then there isn't an issue, is there?' She looked at her watch. 'I've got to finish this before I start dinner.'

'OK, you get on. Is there anything I can do?'

'Yes, peel the potatoes, that'll save me time.'

'Huh, I should have stayed at work.' Nevertheless, he went to the kitchen and did as she had asked.

*

Julie Davies and Siobhan arrived within a few minutes of each other, just after seven, by which time the children had eaten their supper and the adults' dinner was ready but for the final touches. Introductions were made and the children went upstairs to play. The four adults sat in the lounge drinking aperitifs.

Siobhan gave Julie an appraising look. She was a tall woman in her mid-thirties. Her black hair was cut short and she wore a minimum of make-up. Her eyebrows were natural but neatly trimmed. She was dressed smartly in cashmere

341

sweater and slacks. The overall impression was fashionable but tending towards practical. She made little effort to add to her attractiveness. Siobhan wondered about her sexual persuasion but concluded that it was none of her business.

Jeanette was the perfect hostess and made the conversational running until her guests had relaxed. Then she left them to it and went to finish the cooking. Prior kept their glasses topped up and the atmosphere soon became jovial. Having got the small talk out of the way, Julie turned to Siobhan, 'I understand you and Matthew are working on the head on the stake murder. It must be rather grisly.'

Siobhan replied, 'Yes, it was a bit shocking to begin with. Your field is ancient history I understand.'

'Medieval history actually, the ancient stuff is more of a hobby.' She smiled, 'My idea of the perfect weekend is digging up bones and pottery shards and sleeping in a tent. Jeanette emailed me the photos of the stone cross you found. I think it's very old. I can't wait to have a close look at it in the morning. Do you think it has some bearing on the murder?'

Prior joined the conversation. 'We think it might. The second murder happened fairly close to it and the first victim had been working nearby the day before he died. But I don't want to spoil your dinner. Perhaps we can give you the sordid details after?'

'What a good idea. I do love Jeanette's cooking and don't want to spoil my appetite. I can smell my favourite starter, kidneys and bacon.'

Soon after, Jeanette called them to the dinner table. Prior and their guests knew that she was an innovative as well as accomplished cook. The starter was her own recipe; finely-diced lambs' kidneys, bacon, mushrooms and onions, cooked in a wok and served with hot pitta bread. Prior served a light rosé, wine with it that did not seek to combat the rich flavours. This was followed by Beef Wellington accompanied by boiled potatoes and steamed green vegetables. To drink with it Prior had opened a bottle of full-bodied claret from the Medoc region of France.

Julie complimented them, 'The meal was magnificent Jeanette and the wine did it proud. Thank you both.'

Siobhan added, 'If ever you both get fed up with what you are doing now, open a restaurant. I'd be there as often as I could afford it.'

Jeanette smiled at the compliments. 'I don't think that's a good idea, I wouldn't like him under my feet all day. But thank you both for the nice words. I think that we spend so much time worrying about calorie control, it's nice just occasionally to please our taste buds and say damn to the balance.'

Jeanette was not into exotic desserts and served rich Farmhouse cheddar with biscuits and fresh fruit as the final course. Then, the three women cleared up while Prior settled the children in bed; they were sleeping in the same room, as Julie was staying overnight and the house had only the three bedrooms.

It was 9.30 before they all gathered together again in the lounge with coffee and liqueurs. Julie said, 'Right, time for me to sing for my supper. I've done some research on the Celtic stone and the Sinclair estate. I think Jeanette has already told you the probable origins of the Celtic cross.

Not having a written language made things very difficult. It took their priests, the Druids, at least 15 years as apprentices before they were fully fledged priests. You can imagine, with no books, everything had to be learned by rote.' She paused. Prior and Siobhan looked at each other but said nothing. Neither was inclined to tell Julie that that they had heard most of this before.

She continued, 'There's also a lot of mythology surrounding the Celts. Legends passed by word of mouth, often fearfully, became an established part of their mythology, beliefs and folklore. Now it is difficult to separate legend from fact. But that's true of most of the people in the world at that time. And it took a long time for some of the legends to die out. Look at the epic poems of the troubadours in the Middle Ages. Some of those refer to very ancient celebrations and events.' She paused and smiled. 'In fact that's true of people, period. Who knows what legends we'll leave behind us and how much truth there will be in them?'

She nodded at Prior and Siobhan. 'You two would know about that. People's memories are selective, people see what they want to see as often as not, even witnesses to crime.'

Prior nodded, 'That's very true, we often get big discrepancies in what two different people who witnessed the same incident say they saw.'

Julie continued, 'So, almost all that we know of the Celts is from what others have written about them and, of course, from archaeological finds. This presents us with a few problems. The Celts were not the friendliest of folk and what others wrote was not always very complimentary or necessarily very accurate. And the Celts lived in wooden structures, which have left little trace. We actually know more about their dead than we do the living. They tended to bury them in stone burial chambers some of which have survived intact.' She paused to check their attention hadn't strayed; it hadn't.

Prior nodded encouragingly.

'The design on the stone then. The outer circle almost certainly represents the sun or the moon, the lines across it probably the summer and winter solstices and the two equinoxes. Many of the ancient civilisations studied astrology, as the seasons were particularly important to the farmers. Knowing when to plant their seeds and harvest the crops was vital. We're fairly sure that their religious beliefs were very strong. The Druids were very influential in their daily lives.' She paused again.

Siobhan took the opportunity to interrupt, 'You say astrology, don't you mean astronomy?'

Julie nodded. 'That's a moot point. The ancients studied the heavens but they lacked instruments and depth of knowledge to claim it was a science. But they could see that the sun influenced their lives, maybe even the moon too with the tides. Whether you describe it as ology or onomy depends on your viewpoint.'

Siobhan nodded.

Julie continued, 'Where was I? Oh yes. Then along came the jolly old Christians, who tried to convert everyone to their faith. And they weren't very tolerant. Anyone who wouldn't play ball didn't last long. But old habits die hard and many people, particularly countryfolk; whilst more or less accepting the new religion, clung to some of the old customs. So, instead of fighting against some of the deep-rooted customs, the Christian priests incorporated them into the Christian way of life.

Many historians believe that's how the Celtic cross became a Christian symbol. The Christians accepted many of the old ways. Of course, they drew the line at human sacrifice. The fact that later they slaughtered so many people in the name of the religion makes something of a mockery of that. But back to the point. A great many so-called pagan rituals and symbols were incorporated into the church. That's probably how we got Halloween by the way.'

Siobhan interrupted, 'Really? How did that come about?'

'You have to understand that the Celts believed there were several gods. There were two in particular that were very influential. They looked over them during different seasons of the year. In summer or Samradh as they called it, and autumn or Foghamhar, the god of growth, Beltane, looked down on them. In winter or Geinredh and spring or Earrach, the goddess Samhain took over the mantle.

Samhain arrived on the 1st of November and bonfires were burned to welcome her the night before; the celebrations went on for three days. The feast was actually called Samhuinn and was a magical time. It was thought to be the time when the veil between the world of the living and that of the dead was lifted. It was a time when ghosts and spirits returned to the Earth and wandered about.

In Celtic settlements everyone knew their place and the hierarchy was strictly enforced. But just for the three days of this celebration, they relaxed and people went crazy, men dressing as women and women as men. Children went from home to home asking for food. This is almost certainly the origins of 'trick or treat' still celebrated in many countries. It really was a crazy time.

That's also where we get the word bonfire by the way. The feast coincided with the end of the harvest season. In those days farmers couldn't buy in fodder for the winter. They realised that they couldn't keep all of their domestic animals alive on the fodder they had harvested and collected. So they slaughtered the ones they had insufficient winter food for, cured the meat and burned the bones, bone fire – bonfire, simple as that.

But back to the feast of Samhuinn. Even after taking on the new religion, country folk still lit their bonfires and had their feast at the end of October. So, some bright spark in the Christian church introduced All Saints' Day or All Hallows as it came to be known. This was put into the calendar at the beginning of November and celebrated on All Hallows eve, the 31st of October. All Hallows eve became Halloween'

Siobhan said, 'Amazing! So that's why there are witches and ghouls and all sorts associated with that date. Tell us about some of the other things please, Julie.'

Prior said, 'Aren't we getting away from the Celtic cross?'

Jeanette stuck an elbow in his ribs. 'You're not at work now Matthew, I'd like to hear about the other stuff too.'

He smiled and rubbed his ribs. 'Sorry I spoke.'

Jeanette said, 'Please go on Julie, take no notice of this ignorant hulk.'

Siobhan added, 'Yes, he's always shutting me up at work, well done, Jeanette.'

The three women laughed and Prior put on a pained expression.

Julie continued. 'The use of candles in church, not just for lighting but in a religious context, was practiced before Christianity. The Celts used to carry them in processions and during religious ceremonies. So there's another thing that was incorporated into the new faith.'

She looked at Matthew.' I'll save the rest till later. Right Matthew, back to your Celtic cross and what it symbolises. That's a difficult one. In the Middle Ages its use became simply decorative and the design more ornate. But because there is no written evidence, historians are still not sure what its exact significance was to the Celts. Most educated guesses are that it had something to do with burials. The very old ones have mostly been found at burial sites.'

'So, the fact that there is one on the estate probably does signify there is a burial site nearby.' Prior said.

'Not so fast, Sherlock. It could be but I wouldn't bank on it.'

Siobhan said, 'The old gamekeeper who used to work on the estate said this one marked the boundary between the land where the people lived and that set aside for the dead, could that be right?'

Julie paused for a moment before replying. 'I'd like to say yes and it might well be true, but we can't be certain. If your gamekeeper's family have lived there for a long time, it could be that he heard that from his father and his father from his grandfather etc. etc. etc.

But the problem with word of mouth is that meanings can change. Do you remember the experiments most of us did at school, whispering a message around a circle? 'Send reinforcements we're going to advance' becomes 'send three and four pence we're going to a dance' if you're not very careful.'

Prior asked, 'If you had a look at the stone could you tell how old it is?'

Julie smiled. 'There are ways we can tell the age of the symbol by the tools used to carve it. The style used may also give us a clue as they became more stylised as time progressed. The design of this one looks quite old. But exactly how old? That's a difficult one.'

Jeanette asked, 'If there was a burial site nearby, what would you see now?'

'Depends who was buried. We know that the Celts buried their chieftains in large stone chambers. But for the majority that would only be the size of a large coffin. Only the rich and powerful were buried with their wealth; some of the wealthiest even had their horses and funeral carriage buried with them. So their chambers were much larger. They were lined with stone then the whole thing covered by a large mound of earth, only the stone-lined entrances would be visible.'

'And the mound, surely? Was anything valuable buried with them?' Siobhan asked,

'Yes, the mound should be visible. Sometimes valuables have been found. But these chambers are extremely rare and, just like the pyramids in Egypt, in most cases grave robbers will have made off with anything valuable in the meantime.'

'Back to the living, Julie, did your research suggest that there was a settlement on the Sinclair estate?'

'Yes, it's well documented. Aerial photographs clearly show the outline of some kind of settlement up on the hill. But it has never been excavated.'

Prior nodded, 'Yes, we interviewed the historian who asked if the local college could do the dig. The landowner, who's the second murder victim, turned him down flat. Was it a large settlement as these things go?'

'Not especially, no.'

'So it's not likely to have had a big chief?'

Julie smiled. 'I see where you're going. No, it's most un-likely there would be a large burial chamber with lots of goodies in it down by the stream. Most unlikely.'

Prior turned to Siobhan, 'So bang goes your buried treasure theory.'

Unabashed, she replied, 'Well at least I had a theory, all you seemed concerned with in the Wright murder was who was bonking who.'

They all laughed.

Julie said, 'Tell me about your investigation, I love detective stories.'

Prior turned to Siobhan, 'You tell her, Siobhan, and I'll put some more coffee on.'

Jeanette said, 'No Matthew, I'll do that. You carry on with your discussion.'

Prior spent the next ten minutes giving Julie details of the two murders and where their investigation had taken them. In the meantime, Jeanette refilled the coffee cups.

Julie sipped hers and said, 'So you have a real life psychological profiler on the job. Is she anything like Cracker?'

Siobhan answered, 'No, thank god. She doesn't smoke or drink as far as I know and she's quite slim.' He smiled and added, 'Well, apart from her chest measurements. But she does talk a lot of sense. We had a session yesterday and she told us how she works. One thing especially. She said that we leave our signature on everything we do and that signature gives indications as to our characters and habits. Whether we are tidy or not, methodical or haphazard, cool and calculating or impetuous, that sort of thing. I found her fascinating.'

Prior said, 'I agree, what she said was fascinating. But whether it will help us identify the murderer remains to be seen. To be fair, I suppose she has provided us with a better focus.'

The discussion drifted on to other things and half-an-hour later Siobhan decided it was time to go home. This effectively ended the evening and Jeanette took her friend Julie to Samantha's room where she was to sleep. They said their goodnights, and everyone prepared for bed.

A little later Prior snuggled up to Jeanette and said, 'Are you tired, love?'

She nudged him with an elbow and said, 'Behave yourself, Julie is just the other side of the hall.'

'Yes, dear,' Prior sighed and rolled back to his side of the bed. After just a few minutes he was snoring loudly.

35. Going over old ground.

'The more you stir it the worse it stinks.'

16th century proverb.

Julie Davies was up with the lark the next morning. Even had she been of a mind to lie in she would have found no peace, the sounds of the girls getting ready for school would have woken the dead. Fifteen minutes later she joined the family for breakfast looking fresh and well rested. She had a way with children and managed to draw Samantha out of her natural shyness. Natalie needed no such drawing out and swapped banter with her father with Jeanette acting as referee. As a result, the next 20 minutes passed noisily and quickly before Prior and his archaeological consultant set out for the Sinclair Estate.

Arriving at the Penwin Lane gate, they found that the media's vigil had diminished somewhat. There were only two cars left in the lane. One lone cameraman clicked away at them through their car window as they turned into the estate.

Ignoring him, Prior drove to the farm yard and parked behind the enquiry van. For once most of his team had arrived before him, including Siobhan, who greeted Julie warmly. Prior made the introductions to the rest of the team, then he, Julie and Siobhan sat at Quigley's desk drinking coffee while the old DS briefed him on what had happened overnight. Apart from the report from the Sinclair family solicitor confirming that nothing appeared to have been stolen from the house, this amounted to very little. So, as soon as they had finished their coffee, they set off to explore the bottomland.

Julie had come prepared and wore a warm duffle coat over a woollen sweater and jeans. The two detectives had by now learned what attire was suitable for the terrain and had dressed accordingly. They all put on Wellington boots before setting off down the hill. Overhead, the grey clouds had moved away and it was a bright, chilly late autumn day.

Arriving at the bramble hedge, Julie knelt to examine the stone cross. Prior and Siobhan stood by expectantly. After several moments she stood up and backed away from the hedge and looked around her. Only then did she speak. 'The primitive design suggests it is more than 1800 years old. After that, the designs became more elaborate and the shaping of the stone itself smoother. Remember we're talking Iron Age here. I'm amazed it has lasted this long.

It certainly does look like some kind of demarcation marker, being where it is. The one thing we don't know is if the line of the hedge has changed much over the 18 hundred or so years that the stone has stood here. Looking at the lie of the land, I don't think it will have. It does seem a natural boundary.'

After a pause, she continued, 'If it hasn't changed then the old gamekeeper is probably right. The ground above the cross was for the living. Anything below it was sacred, the land of the dead. We know that the Celts did revere their ancestors and were anxious that they be left in peace.' After a pause she said, 'Show me where the tree was taken down. Matthew.'

They walked along the line of the hedge to the Lamb Lane boundary. As they walked Julie said, 'You know the stone could well have been one of a row, the others may have disappeared over the centuries. The aerial photographs of the settlement clearly show that there were two distinct paths from the hill down to the bottomland. One leads towards the house and probably continued where the drive is now. The other comes down this way.'

Siobhan asked, 'How on earth can you tell that?'

'Well, when generations of feet have trodden the same path for hundreds of years, the ground beneath becomes compacted. Even after a further thousand years or so, a shallow depression remains marking the path people walked. That can be seen from the air.'

They reached the wall and the uprooted tree. Julie looked around for some minutes. She found a stick and poked the bottom of the hole where the tree had once stood. She said, 'It's rocky down at the bottom here. That's why the roots spread sideway and undermined the wall; they couldn't penetrate deeper. Sorry to disappoint you but I can't see anything else here.'

They moved through the gap in the hedge to the stream then began walking back along the path beside it.

Prior asked, 'What are you actually looking for, Julie?'

She pointed to the undulations in the ground. 'These humps. If any of them are man-made they will probably be more symmetrical than the others. Nature tends to be more haphazard. And obviously any stone slabs as distinct from naturally occurring rocks would show they were put there by man.'

They moved on again till they reached the point where Sinclair's body had been found. Prior pointed out the spot and Julie studied the area on both sides of the stream, her face a picture of concentration. Then she squatted and, taking off a glove, dug gently among the dead leaves that carpeted the ground on either side of the path. Here, under the trees, only the occasional patch of scrub grass grew where little sunlight penetrated in the summer months. 'Well, there's nothing that distinguishes this spot from anywhere else along here, is there?' Having previously made his own close inspection of the spot, Prior agreed with her.

They moved on again and eventually reached the gravel drive close to the main entrance to the estate from Penwin Lane. Climbing the slope to the gravel, Julie stopped and looked back. Then she looked across the drive where everything grew wild.

She asked, 'Is it only that stretch you are interested in?'

Prior said, 'Yes, there's no evidence of any recent activity on the other side and there's no path there.'

'Nothing recent maybe, but that doesn't mean the Celts didn't use the land there; maybe even to bury their dead.'

Prior scratched his head. 'Perhaps we should look there then.'

He led the way looking for a place where the undergrowth was not so thick. Finding a spot, he forced his way through and descended the slope until he reached the level of the stream. Here there was no discernible path and the ground was covered in brambles and other shrubs fiercely competing for space. He looked around for a way forward but could find none that would be easy.

Julie said, 'The only way I could tell you if there are burial chambers here is if the undergrowth was all cut back. I don't think there's any point in scratching ourselves to pieces on the brambles if I can't find what you're looking for.'

Prior nodded and looked at Siobhan. 'I agree, what do you think, Siobhan?'

'Unless you've got chain saw I can't see us getting any further. Anyway, there's no way the killer came down here, he would have had the same problem we have.'

'OK, let's go back then.'

Julie nodded, 'Can we walk back on the other side of the stream?' Crossing the driveway, they forced their way through the brambles that bordered the drive on the road side of the stream, then descended the slope. Here, under the trees, the ground vegetation quickly thinned out.

Looking up Prior noticed that the trees were at their thickest here. In the summer, when the trees had leaves, they would form a solid canopy. The ground here would be constantly in shade. Accordingly there were only patches of the stubborn scrub grass, fallen rotting tree trunks and the occasional young sapling that broke up the sea of rotting leaves.

Squatting, Julie once again ran her fingers through the detritus on the ground. She went down several inches before it became soil. She stood and said, 'Interesting, this is probably as close as we get in this country to natural forest. Presumably, no-one ever comes here.'

Prior nodded, 'Except my search team, they searched all along here on Monday. Not that they found anything except a few empty crisp packets blown here on the wind.'

They walked on, avoiding the swampy patches between the undulations where the rainwater had accumulated having nowhere to run off. Reaching the spot opposite where Sinclair's body had been found, they paused again. Five yards from the spot a towering yew tree grew close to the stream, its roots exposed by the current. Julie pointed. Among the roots could be seen a slab of off-white rock. 'That could be the roof of a burial chamber. But don't get too excited, even if I'm right it would hardly have been a large burial chamber, the ground around it is virtually flat.'

'But it could be a grave?' Prior probed.

'Yes, but the only way you will find out for certain is to cut the tree down and clear the roots. Even then I doubt you'll find what you're looking for. I think you can forget about buried Celtic treasure anywhere along here.'

They made their way slowly back to the end wall but found nothing that interested Julie. There was no way to get out at that end of the strip of land and they had to retrace their steps to the drive.

Walking back up the hill to the van, Julie shook her head, 'Well, I'm sorry, Matthew, you'll have to think again about a motive for your murders. I expect there are graves along the stream but nothing large enough to contain much other than old bones and maybe a few shards of pottery. And they would only be of interest to the odd archaeologist and historian. Nothing of much value there to the layman.'

Reaching the van, they sat and drank more coffee. Julie was having lunch with Jeanette before driving back to Bristol. Prior thanked her and asked Siobhan to drive her back to Truro.

Once she had gone, Quigley said, 'PC Gibbons will be here at about eleven, sir. You remember you asked to see him. And DS Truscott has been in touch. I looked in your diary and saw you didn't have much on, so I asked him to be here at lunch time.'

'Thanks, Albert, in the meantime I'll have another look at the case file.'

36. Mumbo jumbo.

'I knew a man who when he wrote a letter he would put what was most material in the postscript, as if it had been a bye matter.'

Francis Bacon 1561-1626

Prior sat in his tiny cubicle reading through the murder file. Since first finding the head there had been so many cul-de-sacs down which his team had gone. Each one had ended in a brick wall. Now that the buried treasure theory had apparently proved another dead end, he wondered where they would go next. Sinclair's murder seemed to have added nothing to their knowledge beyond concentrating their efforts on the estate.

On the file he noted that the solicitor's stocktake of Sinclair House had revealed nothing missing. Why then had Sinclair's keys been stolen he wondered, making a note to flag this for future action. Otherwise Prior gained nothing new from his reading.

There was a gentle tap on his office door. Pleased at the interruption, as he was going nowhere with the file, he called, 'Come in.' The door opened to reveal Jessica Bloomfield.

She said, 'Do you have five minutes, Matthew.'

He looked at his watch; it said 1050. He said, 'Just about Jessica, please come in.'

She did so and squeezed her long frame onto the visitor's chair. 'They don't exactly provide you with luxury, do they, Matthew?'

'No, but it's quiet and away from the distractions of the CID office. There I'm at everyone's beck and call and it's difficult to concentrate.' He looked at the papers in her hand and asked, 'Do you have something for me?'

She nodded, 'Yes, I hope so. I've looked at the second murder and have some thoughts on it.'

'Tell me about them please.'

'First I looked at it in isolation, then in relation to the first killing.'

'Do you think they were committed by the same person?'

'I'm not totally convinced, no, but I am working on that assumption. They were committed in very different circumstances and by different methods. One carefully planned and executed, the other impromptu so to speak.'

Prior smiled grimly. 'An interesting way of putting it. Please go on.'

'Clearly the killer did not go to this spot prepared to kill. He did not take a weapon with him. He improvised. He picked up a large stone or rock that he most probably found at the location. So he was surprised by the arrival of Sinclair. This suggests he was there for some other purpose. And that purpose was important to him. His reaction when disturbed was extreme to say the least. There was no question in his mind of fleeing from the scene. This indicates his purpose in being there was paramount; he would brook no interruption.'

Prior nodded. 'That's the conclusion we came to. We first considered the possibility that they had arranged a meeting at the spot or that the killer had arranged an ambush. But we discovered from our enquiries that it was most unlikely that anyone could have known of Sinclair's intentions to take a walk.'

It was Bloomfield's turn to nod. 'The man you are dealing with would have come fully prepared in those circumstances. Even had he no preconceived plan to kill Sinclair, he would have prepared himself for that eventuality.'

Prior waited for her to continue.

She said, 'Moving on to the manner of the attack. It was frenzied. He went straight for the kill. The lack of defensive wounds suggests that the attack was unexpected. I think that Sinclair knew his attacker and may not have been surprised by finding him there. Clearly he was surprised by the violent reaction. This leads me to the conclusion that in previous meetings between the two the killer had been passive, maybe even subservient; an underling maybe.'

'An employee maybe?'

'Possibly but not necessarily. We have also to take account of Sinclair's arrogance. He was, after all, the lord of the manor and expected subservient behaviour from those around him both on the estate and off.'

'Wait a minute, Jessica, here I was hoping you had narrowed the field but then you widen it again. Sinclair treated all the local people as serfs. That's why they all resented him.'

'All I can say with confidence is that they did not behave as equals. Sinclair would have been more careful in such circumstances, I'm sure.'

Prior was becoming impatient. This woman was getting to him. First she zeroes in on something then backs away from committing herself. This was going nowhere. He said, 'What I need, Jessica, is something about the killer that sets him apart from others, something that points to a particular suspect. Nothing you've said so far does that any more than our own enquiries have done.'

Bloomfield sighed. 'Perhaps you are expecting too much of me. Would you like me to go on?'

Trying to keep the resignation out of his voice, he said, 'Please do.'

'From the pathologist's report it is clear that any one of the blows struck would have been sufficient to kill the victim. But the killer didn't stop, he delivered at least a dozen more blows, most of these when the victim was on the ground. Such frenzied attacks are usually as the release of pent-up anger and frustration. The continued beating served no other purpose. The killer was releasing his anger. I've no doubt that when he finally stopped he felt a sense of relief.'

'As you say, Jessica, clearly.'

A sardonic smile spread over Bloomfield's face. 'Your cynicism is showing, Matthew.'

'More likely my frustration Jessica. There have been so many dead ends in this case my patience is wearing thin. Now you must forgive me, I have another appointment and have to get on. You have obviously put a great deal of thought into this and I must thank you for that.'

Bloomfield started gathering her papers together. She said, 'This man is on a mission, Matthew, a mission he is determined to fulfil. Any obstacle he meets, he will remove. And he is gaining in confidence. There was no effort to remove the body from the scene of the attack. This means the scene no longer has relevance to him or his purpose.'

Prior snapped, 'Then why was he there in the first place?'

'Maybe the place once had relevance. Perhaps it had been important but no longer was. By the way we haven't had an opportunity to talk about your instincts, Matthew, a shame.'

He forced a smile. 'Yes, perhaps when we have the killer in custody? Thanks again for your input.'

She left without another word.

As the door closed behind her, movement in the yard outside drew his eyes. It was PC Gibbons walking across the yard. Despite his frustration, Prior grinned as Gibbons stopped and removed his cycle clips. Seeing Prior's face at the window, the young constable grinned back at him.

A minute later Gibbons knocked at his office door. Prior invited him in and when he was seated asked, 'Drugs, do you have a problem in the village?'

Gibbons shook his head. 'No, sir, not really. Bit of cannabis now and again but not a real problem.'

'Are you sure, no amphetamines, speed?'

'Haven't seen any of that, sir. I've caught one or two of the lads with small amounts of cannabis they got from clubs in Truro but nothing stronger.'

'So there's no dealing in the village?'

'Absolutely not, sir, I'd know if there was.'

'Young Wright seems to have got hold of some speed; there were traces in his system. Where do you think he would have got that?'

Gibbons shook his head slowly. 'Not from the village, sir, I'm certain of that.'

'OK, thanks Gibbons. Anything else happening in your neck of the woods?'

'Very quiet, sir. Couple of the local yobs vandalised a stained-glass window in the church after getting drunk one night. Other than that nothing.'

'Any talk about the murders?'

'Plenty of talk, but nothing worth reporting.'

'OK, thanks for coming in Gibbons. Nice to see you without those damned cycle clips, you've even got creases in your trousers. Keep up the good work.'

Gibbons left, grinning like a Cheshire cat.

At noon DS Truscott arrived. Prior knew him slightly but the drug squad kept a low profile working odd hours, so they hadn't met often. He was about thirty and wore his dark hair long. Designer stubble covered his handsome face and he wore blue jeans and a leather jacket that helped him melt into the background of the club scene in Truro. Prior asked him where Wright might have got amphetamines and got the expected reply, the Starburst Club and O'Henry's already mentioned by DI Chalcott.

Prior said, 'How big a drug problem do we have?'

'Depends on your point of view guv. Nothing like the big cities but we've got all the hippy types and dropouts along the coast. But they tend to stick to themselves. We've had one or two who have tried to sell to our youngsters but mostly they don't, it draws our attention to them. Otherwise, there's just the odd bit in the discos.'

Prior nodded. 'I'm sure you have a few informants. Put the word out that we want to know who supplied speed to young Wright. You might be lucky and come up with something.' He handed Truscott a photo of Wright. 'Show this around. See if anyone recognises him. Will you do that for me?'

'Of course, guv. I'll get onto it straight away. I'll get back to you.'

*

Reginald Sinclair had arrived back from Afghanistan. He received Prior and Siobhan in the same room his father had. But the atmosphere was very different. The new owner of the Sinclair Estate greeted them warmly. If he was upset by his father's death, he didn't show it. Even the butler, Brighton, had the hint of a smile on his face as he showed them in. Clearly the young man had a different relationship with the staff.

The young Sinclair was certainly not a chip off the old block either in appearance or character. He was as tall as Prior's six foot and built like a rugby prop. His face had a healthy tan from his time in the hills of Afghanistan. There was a slight facial resemblance to his father around the eyes. They were set close together and his nose was thin and straight, but his face was chubbier and his lips more generous and he smiled easily. He was dressed casually in blue jeans, open-neck shirt and V-necked pullover. His handshake was firm but not challenging.

Prior said, 'Thank you for seeing us, Mr. Sinclair. I'm sorry for your loss.'

'Thank you, Chief Inspector. I won't pretend that we were close. But he was my father. I'm sorry to lose the old dog in such a fashion. And so early, he was only 49 you know?'

'Yes sir, it is sad.' He paused and then added, 'I wonder if you'd mind answering a few questions?'

'Of course. Anything I can do to help.'

'What was the last communication you had with your father?'

A wan smile crossed Sinclair's face. 'That sounds very Cromwellian, Chief Inspector. We didn't correspond regularly. I think the last communication we had was a card from him on my birthday; that was two months ago.'

'Did he send a message with the card?'

'Only good wishes, Chief Inspector.'

'Nothing at all since?'

'No, we didn't see eye to eye on most matters, so we tended to keep our conversations to a minimum.'

'And the last time you actually saw him?'

'It must be six months ago. I spend my leaves with my mother.'

'Where would that be, sir?'

'Dorset. She married again after the divorce. I have two half-siblings.'

'I see, so you won't be aware of anything happening here on the estate?'

'Well, that's not quite true. Mrs Brighton writes regularly, she keeps me in touch with what's going on here.' He paused, and then added, 'When my parents divorced I was very young, Chief Inspector. The Brightons have no children of their own. Mrs Brighton and I have always been close.

'I see.'

'I am not sure that you do, Chief Inspector. My parents' divorce was quite acrimonious; there was even a dispute over which I should live with. Father won the dispute so I stayed here. But those were not good times. My father was a difficult man and had little time for children. To be brutally honest I think he only married my mother in the first place to produce an heir. He had a sense of family duty but he was hardly a family man. Mrs Brighton was like a surrogate mother to me.'

'Thank you for being so frank, sir. Are you aware of any enemies your father may have had?'

'Enemies? No. He wasn't popular locally but I wouldn't say he had enemies as such. You see, when my grandfather died, father set out to make the farm more profitable. Grandfather had a great sense of his responsibility to the local people. He probably employed more people on the estate than was absolutely necessary. Father brought in more machinery and halved the workforce. It was not a popular decision. He also reduced the house staff; he didn't do much entertaining. He and I had a disagreement over that decision, after that I didn't spend much time here. But I can't imagine any of the workforce feeling strongly enough to kill him.'

Prior diplomatically made no mention of the dungeon and the kind of entertaining that had gone on there. He asked, 'What about neighbours or business rivals?'

'No, Chief Inspector. He was a difficult man and had few friends but no enemies that I know of.'

Prior tried a new tack. 'Who stands to gain from his death?'

The young Sinclair smiled. 'You mean other than me? No, there were no bequests to others and, other than me, he had no close family so everything comes to me. I suppose that makes me a suspect?'

'In theory, yes, sir. But I think we've already eliminated you from our enquiries, Afghanistan is a long way from here.'

'Who do you suspect, Chief Inspector?'

'As far as we can gather, no one knew of your father's plan to take a walk down by the stream. We think maybe he was just in the wrong place at the wrong time. Maybe he surprised an intruder.'

'What would an intruder be doing down there? There are a few trout in the stream but not much else, hardly anything to encourage intruders.'

'We think whoever it was took your father's keys. Did he keep anything valuable in the house, anything that would not appear on the inventory of house contents?'

'You mean did he have a secret collection of valuables or something? No, he wasn't a collector of anything.'

'Would you necessarily know if he was?'

Another smile. 'A good question, as I didn't spend much time here. But he wasn't the type. He enjoyed good food and wine but was not a collector, no.'

Siobhan asked, 'Do you know of any ancient burial sites on the estate, sir?'

Sinclair looked surprised for a moment at the change of tack. After a moment he shook his head. 'No, I've never heard talk of anything like that. There is a hill fort in the top field, so we're told but father wouldn't allow it to be excavated.'

'Nothing down by the stream then, sir?'

'Not to my knowledge, no. Someone who might know is the old gamekeeper, Tom Williamson. He's retired now but lives in the village.'

'Yes, thank you. We have interviewed him but he's not very co-operative.'

Sinclair smiled again, 'I can well imagine that, he didn't like the thought of people digging up the past.'

There was a pause, then Prior asked, 'What will you do with the estate now?'

'I'm not sure at the moment. You know my family have been here for nearly a thousand years. I don't think I would sell it. There are also the workers to consider. But I'm not keen on living here myself. There are a few months to go on my tour in Afghanistan. I will have to go back and complete that. I'll make a decision when I return to England.'

Prior smiled. 'Are you not interested in farming?'

'I don't see myself as the gentleman farmer, no. But Callaghan seems to be doing a good job. Whatever I do, I'll let him continue to run things for the time being.'

'And the staff at the house?'

'That's another difficult one.' He smiled, 'Not much call for butlers these days. But someone has to care for the house and they have been very loyal. I don't anticipate making too many changes.'

Prior got up to leave. He said, 'Thank you for your frankness, Mr Sinclair, you've been very helpful. I hope our presence here is not too disruptive but we do need to continue with our enquiries.'

'No problem, Chief Inspector, stay as long as you have to.'

The two detectives walked back to the caravan. Siobhan said, 'A nice man, sir. I don't see him as being involved, do you?'

'No, Siobhan, I don't.'

'And he's got a nice butt, pity he's not staying.'

Prior gave her a hard look but said nothing.

The rest of his day proved a disappointment, with no new information coming to light. He knew he must be patient and wait for something to break in the case. He decided to take advantage of the lull. He sent his team home early and set off himself to give his daily report to Owen. Having done that, he spent the evening with his family.

37. Breakthrough.

'A chain is no stronger than its weakest link.'

19th century proverb.

The next morning Prior checked that there were no new developments on the estate and drove to Truro Police Station. Parking his car, he went straight up to his office. All thoughts of Britain's creaking criminal justice system were pushed from his mind when he saw Monk. He was sitting at Prior's desk with a smug expression on his face. He was dressed in a freshly-pressed suit, white shirt and stainless tie. The only sign of his slovenly attitude was his hair, which looked unwashed and untidy. Superintendent Owen had obviously been as good as her word and put a boot up his rear.

The desk was tidy. There were just two official brown envelopes in the in-tray and a few files in the pending one.

Monk greeted him with a smirk, 'Good morning sir.'

Prior nodded, 'Good morning, Bob. I see you have caught up with the correspondence. Nice to see.' He picked up the two envelopes and saw that they were addressed to him and marked private and confidential. He looked around the office and saw that all was reasonably tidy and there were no tell-tale piles of papers that had simply been shuffled around.

Hanging on a hook on the wall was the clip of Force crime bulletins. These were issued daily and contained information on crimes in which neighbouring divisions might have an interest. They also detailed crime in other forces with possible links to the Devon and Cornwall Constabulary. The bulletin was something each divisional DCI kept abreast with, as it was a good indication of crime trends. On occasion it also contained information relevant to an ongoing enquiry.

He unhooked the bulletin from the wall and started to scan through the pages. An item in the previous day's bulletin caught his eye. As he read it, his heart skipped a beat. Adrenalin began coursing through his veins. It was an item from London's Metropolitan Police, West Kensington Station. A man had been arrested trying to sell gold coins, Roman coins. It was the arrested man's name that riveted his attention, Trevor Bolton, the cab driver who had picked up the two prostitutes from the Sinclair Estate on the night of Wright's murder.

He looked up and spoke, trying to keep the excitement from his voice. 'This item from the Met. Bob, Trevor Bolton caught trying to sell gold coins. Did they contact us about it?'

'The blagger? Yes, a DCI from West Kensington nick phoned me.'

'And?'

'Well, they wanted to know what we had on him. I told them he was a local slag and told them about his previous.'

'I'm sure they already had that from CRO. What else did you tell them?'

Monk frowned. 'What else is there?'

'Didn't you check with the collator?'

'Hardly seemed worth the effort, sir, he's the Met's problem now, not ours.'

Prior took a deep breath, trying to control his rising temper. After a moment he said, 'Really? If you had got up off of your fat arse and spoken to the collator or even checked the active enquiries on the computer, you'd have seen that he was interviewed in our murder enquiry. This information could be vital to that enquiry.'

His temper finally frayed. 'You are about as useful as a spare prick at a wedding. In fact you're worse, you're a fucking menace. Get out of here, go and sit in the canteen. I'm taking this to the Superintendent; I want you suspended.'

Monk looked totally taken aback. 'But I've done what you told me, dealt with everything in the tray. Owen's been in this morning and told me how tidy the place is.'

'You're obviously too thick to understand, the object of keeping things tidy, as you put it, is so that urgent things get dealt with and that we spot things that effect our on-going enquiries.' He waved the bulletins at Monk. 'Like this. Now get out of my sight.'

Monk slunk out of the office. If he'd had a tail it would have been between his legs. Prior waited a moment while he regained control of himself. Then he too left the office and climbed the stairs to Owen's office, taking the crime bulletin board with him.

Her door was closed. Looking into the office next door, he spoke to her secretary. 'Alice, I need to see her urgently. Is she busy?'

'She's just doing an AQR. She should only be ten minutes.' Annual qualification reports were done on every officer in the division and culminated in a discussion of the contents with the divisional chief.

'The moment she's finished, tell her I need to see her. I'll be in my office.'

Returning to his desk, he picked up the inter-force directory and found the number for West Kensington Police. Dialling the number, he negotiated the automated switchboard.

Eventually a live voice at the other end of the line said, 'DCI Baird.'

'Hello, DCI Matthew Prior here, Truro Police.'

'Blimey, is that in England?'

Despite his anger Prior chuckled. 'Only just. Thirty miles further on and you're in the North Atlantic, next stop North America.'

'What can I do for you, Matthew?'

'This arrest your lads made two days ago; robber name of Bolton, trying to sell gold coins. Do you remember it?'

'Yep. Spoke to a DI Monk at your office about it. Might just as well not have wasted my time.'

'Yes, I'm sorry about that. He's my deputy but not for much longer. What can you tell me about the arrest?'

'Basically what we put in the bulletin. He went to this coin dealer in the Portobello Road and tried to sell him some coins. But he chose the wrong dealer; this one's honest. The dealer smelled a rat and called us. But he's a shrewd old bugger, didn't let on he was ringing us. Bolton was still there when my boys arrived. We nicked him. Said he'd found the coins in a field in your neck of the woods. That's why I phoned your office.'

'Have you still got him in custody?'

'Nope, without a loser we've nothing to hold him on. The coins are not reported stolen, far as we knew they were legit. Thanks to the prick at your end who gave us nothing, we had to let him out on bail.'

'Shit. Sorry, I know it's our fault at this end, I'm wheeling the DI you spoke to in front of our Super when I get off the phone. You know Bolton is still on probation after his last conviction for blagging?'

'Well your man Monk showed no interest, so we didn't hold Bolton.'

'Sorry, I'm not trying to blame you; the fault is clearly with my deputy. The reason I've called is that I'm dealing with this head on a stake murder and another one that's related. I'm working from our mobile incident room, which is why I wasn't here when you called. Do you still have the coins?'

'Yes, you made the nationals with your enquiry. I loved the way you handled the press conference. Saw it on the box, couldn't have done better myself. The coins? Of course we've still got them; we're not stupid up here in the big smoke you know. We know they have to be bent'

'Good, I didn't think you were stupid. I just wondered if you had enough evidence to keep the coins.'

'Well, if they're not nicked they must be treasure trove. But the fact that the toe-rag was trying to sell them on the open market makes them dodgy, so we're making further enquiries. Is Bolton your killer then?'

'I don't think so; he's got a cast-iron alibi for the time of the first killing. But I think he might be an accomplice. I think the coins might prove to be the motive for the murders.'

'Well they're safe in our hands, they're not going any-where.'

'Great, what can you tell me about them?'

'The dealers proving helpful, he's trying to put a prove-nance on them. He reckons they're worth about five grand.'

'How many coins are there?'

'Twelve. But your toe-rag told the dealer that he had a lot more.'

'Toe-rag? I'll have to remember that one. So, he said there were more coins, that's very interesting. Thanks, you've been a great help. Sorry again for the cock-up at this end.'

'No problem. Yours is not the only force full of wankers, I'm surrounded by them here.'

Prior laughed into the phone, 'It's not much consolation but I suppose it's comforting to hear we're not alone in our suffering. I'll be in touch.'

Prior put the phone down and looked up. Superintendent Owen was sitting in the chair opposite him. She too had a smile on her face. 'Do I gather you've had a breakthrough Matthew?'

'You do indeed, ma'am. No thanks to that idiot Monk.' He spent the next five minutes explaining the events of the last half hour and their implications.

When he'd finished, Owen said, 'Well done with the case, thank god you spotted the bulletin. Now, Monk. We can't leave him in charge of the office whilst you're away, he's obviously totally incompetent. Do you intend to discipline him? It seems like a clear case of neglect of duty.'

'I don't think I've any choice, he's a danger to everyone around him.'

'Hmm. How much service has he got?'

'Twenty-six years give or take.'

'Let me have a word with him. If you do report him for discipline, the least he'll get is a demotion. He may feel it's better to retire on a DI's pension than face that. In the meantime, I will suspend him from duty.'

'Brilliant, ma'am, that will get him out of my hair. The only problem is that I don't have another DI. John Pearce is on paternity leave, won't be back for two weeks.'

'I'll have a word with headquarters, they will have to find us one.' She smiled then added, 'At this rate you'll have half the senior officers in the force retired, I'll have to watch my P's and Q's around you.'

Prior laughed, 'Only the dross, ma'am, I think you're safe.'

She gave him a sharp look, but then she smiled and said, 'Well that's a relief.'

After a pause, she added, 'What is your next move with Bolton?'

'I'll have to give that some thought. He's obviously the link to the killer. But if I just arrest him, he's sure to clam up. He won't want to be charged with accessory to murder. I'm thinking that we'll put a 24-hour watch on him and do a quiet check on his phone records. He has to be in touch with the killer.'

'So you're certain this is related to the murders then?'

'Absolutely, my instincts tell me this is the break we've been looking for. It gives us the motive for the murders, greed. It all falls into place. There had to be something buried on the estate; we were looking for the wrong kind of treasure. By the sound of it, the killer is sitting on a lot more coins. If we catch him with them, we'll have him dead to rights.'

'Good, keep me informed and let me know if there's anything else you need.'

He smiled broadly at her. 'Your support is all I need, ma'am, and I'm getting that in spades. Thank you.'

She returned his smile.

As Owen left the office, Prior picked up the phone and dialled DS Quigley. When he answered, Prior said, 'Albert, get two of the team down to the address of Trevor Bolton, the Handycabs driver. If his car's not there find out if he's working. Wherever he is they must find him. I want to know where he goes and who he meets. Tell them not to lose sight of him but make sure he doesn't spot them. Tell them to be careful. He's an old lag and will spot a police tail if they're careless.

I'm on my way to you and I'll explain when I get there. But it's vital that we find Bolton ASAP and not let him out of our sight. Get the rest of the team together if they're not busy, I want to brief them. I think we've had the break we've been waiting for.'

Prior briefed the senior of his remaining DS's at Truro and left him in temporary charge of the office. As he drove to the Sinclair estate he had the radio tuned to Classic FM. He hummed to the music as he drove. He loved light classical music but only played it when he was in a good mood. He worked on the theory that music enhanced the mood he was in at the time. When he was in a bad mood he usually found that music made the mood worse. But that was not the case now, his spirits were soaring.

38. Roman coins.

'If there were no receivers there would be no thieves.'

14th century proverb.

Back at the caravan Quigley had gathered the team together with the exception of Foster and Waring who he had sent to watch Bolton. Prior gave those there the new information. There was a buzz of excitement as he finished.

Siobhan said, 'So you think Wright first discovered these coins down by the stream sir? But where, we searched the whole area and how did Bolton get hold of them? He has an alibi for the time Wright was killed.'

'I think that Wright discovered some coins. The fact that he suddenly had money to buy drugs and a surprise for Jenna suggests that he'd come into some money. I think the where is in the stream, the one place we didn't look. As far as his alibi is concerned, maybe he's an accomplice brought in to help sell the coins.'

'Of course, in the stream!' She frowned. 'But surely the fact that he had money means he must have sold the coins he found, sir.'

Fred Trimble said, 'We know Wright wasn't that bright. Maybe he couldn't keep the find to himself. Perhaps the killer found out and tortured him to find out exactly where he got them from.'

Prior nodded. 'That's what I'm trying to figure out, Fred. Let's put together what we actually know before we speculate. We are only guessing that Wright came into some money. All we actually know is that he was tortured and killed. Then a week later Sinclair was also killed. The one thing that seems to connect these events is the location. Wright was working there the day before he died, and Sinclair was killed there. Everything seems to revolve around the stream. Now we discover that Bolton was caught in London trying to sell Roman coins. This can't be a coincidence.' He paused; there was no interruption.

He continued, 'Now for the speculation. We have been searching for a motive for the two deaths; a hoard of gold coins would certainly provide a motive. If Wright did find some coins, what did he do with them? Let's suppose he sold them. The question then is where?'

Siobhan snorted, 'Well he certainly didn't go to London to sell them. We mapped his movements for the whole week before his death. That would have taken a whole day. He hadn't taken any time off work and Jenna would have said if he'd been away for some time.'

Prior nodded. 'So if he did manage to sell them it could only have been locally. Roman coins are not the sort of thing you could sell in a pub. Anyone know any rare coin dealers around here who are not too fussy about provenance?'

Quigley shook his head. 'No bent ones in Truro, that I do know. We had a case last year where a valuable collection of coins was stolen from a country house. We had the Antique Squad all over town and they gave the two dealers here a clean bill of health. I seem to remember there's a guy in Redruth, a guy who deals in stamps and coins. His name came up not so long ago in another case.'

'What do we know about him?'

'Sails a bit close to the wind. If my memory serves me correctly, he's been interviewed on a couple of occasions about receiving stolen goods but never been charged.'

'Right Albert, check if he's the only one locally, there may be more. Do a collator's checks on him and any others you find. Do that right now.'

Quigley nodded and got on the phone.

Siobhan still had a frown on her face. 'But how did the coins get in the stream?'

'We were using tunnel vision Siobhan. We were looking for burial sites and we assumed nothing had changed in 1800 years. Julie Davies noticed something we hadn't spotted. When she saw how the current had undermined the roots of that yew tree, she said it was very likely that the stream had gradually changed course over the centuries. It's the sort of thing a layman wouldn't think about which is why we didn't spot it. But if the stream had changed course, anything buried nearby centuries ago might be underwater now.'

No one responded. They were all deep in thought.

He continued, 'I gave this some thought on the way here. Suppose the coins were buried somewhere for safekeeping back in Roman times? Maybe by a soldier who was saving them for his retirement? They were probably the spoils of war. It could have been a Roman soldier or even a Celt who'd won them in battle.

Whoever it was, he could hardly take them to a bank, there weren't any. What better place to hide them than in the sacred ground where the locals' ancestors were interred. In those days everyone was superstitious, no one was likely to dig there for fear of upsetting the gods. Then, maybe the guy who buried them got killed in battle or something; the Celts were always fighting with their neighbours as well as the Romans, so the historians tell us.'

Siobhan grinned, 'Not a bad pension plan in those days, sir. No insurance companies then either. As long as you remember where you've buried them, of course.'

Prior nodded and continued, 'Then, over the centuries, the bank of the stream is slowly worn away by the current. You've seen how fast it runs after it's been raining. Eventually the pouch or whatever the coins were buried in is exposed. After all this time it's probably rotted, so coins start to leak out and are carried downstream. Maybe Wright saw one on the streambed farther down and began to work his way upstream looking for more. Then he was killed before he found the main hoard.'

Siobhan smiled, 'That's got to be it, sir. That would explain why Wright was killed. The killer must have seen him searching for the more coins and wanted to know where the source was. That's why he tortured him. And then Sinclair sees him searching upstream so he bites the dust'

'I think we can go further than that, Siobhan. Something Jessica said yesterday, the fact that the killer left the body where it was, tells us he was finished with the spot. I think he's already found the main cache of coins. I think he too was trying to find where he could sell them. Maybe he tried local outlets and no one would take them. So he sent Bolton to London on a trial run to try the market there.'

They fell silent again while each ran the idea through their minds. Then Quigley said, 'I can't see anything wrong with the theory sir, it makes sense.'

'Nevertheless, it is still just a theory. But there's one way to test it. We'll get the underwater search unit down there. If our theory's right, there might still be some signs left, maybe even the odd coin. They have the equipment to find it.'

Jean Wade spoke, 'Not to put a damper on things, sir, but who in their right mind would trust Bolton to sell the coins?'

'I've been thinking about that as well. Bolton must have a connection to the killer. Perhaps the killer didn't want to risk selling them himself; there could be all sorts of reasons.

But this is the last link in the chain. I want to know everything about the man Bolton, friends, family, girlfriends, boyfriends, associates. The lot. I want to know what he has for breakfast and what toilet paper he uses. Do a check on his phone records. See if he's computer literate, does he have an e-mail address? What pubs he uses. Find out how he contacts the killer. If Bolton was trying to sell the coins on the killer's behalf, the killer will want to know how he got on, so he's sure to be in contact with him.'

Siobhan smiled again, 'I would think he probably uses the cheap single-ply stuff sir, yuck! But seriously, doesn't this put Bolton in danger? The killer has already murdered two people, I don't imagine he will stop there.'

Prior nodded. 'If the killer knows Bolton cocked-it-up and got himself arrested, he might well be in danger. I wonder if Bolton realises?'

Quigley, who had rejoined the conversation added, 'He's not very bright sir, probably not. But he must be close to the killer or he wouldn't have been trusted with the coins in the first place. Incidentally, sir, the man in Redruth is the only dodgy rare coin dealer this side of Exeter that we know of. The collator in Redruth confirms what I told you about him.'

Prior nodded his thanks. 'Good, and Wright didn't have a car so he couldn't have travelled far and there's a bus goes to Redruth.'

Siobhan insisted, 'I think Bolton's definitely in danger, sir. As Jessica said, this killer's a ruthless son of a bitch.'

Prior smiled at her. 'I don't remember Jessica using quite those words to describe the killer, Siobhan. Nevertheless you do have a point, Bolton might well be the killer's next intended victim.' He turned to Quigley. 'Have Jane and Alan found him yet?'

Quigley shook his head. 'Not exactly sir. They've checked with Handycabs, he's not at work. His car's parked outside his flat. They think he must be at home. The trouble is they've no way of finding out without letting him know they're there, so they're watching the flat and the car.'

Prior nodded. 'Good, he won't have gone far without his car. Once we've got him under 24-hour surveillance, he should be safe. Bolton might be a toe-rag, as the DCI from the Met. called him, but I suppose we have to protect him if we can.

'Let Jane and Alan know of the danger Albert, we don't want them getting hurt. Now, this puts a different complexion on the surveillance, the killer might just come to us.'

'Shouldn't we warn Bolton that he's in danger, sir?' Siobhan asked.

Prior frowned. He shook his head. 'No, I don't see how we can. All we've got is speculation so far. We've got no evidence of any of this. We aren't even certain this is about the coins. I hate to admit it but coincidences do happen. Let's just keep a close watch on him and do some checks. Let's see what the underwater search unit finds. See that they are here first thing in the morning, Albert.'

Then to Siobhan, 'You and I will go and see this coin dealer in Redruth. Once we have some hard evidence of the connection, we can haul Bolton in. We would then have a lever. We might even get him to turn the killer in to save his own neck.'

Prior turned to the other detectives. 'Right, the rest of you get on with the background checks on Bolton for the time being. DS Quigley will work out a schedule for watching Bolton; you'll watch in pairs on eight-hour shifts. Watch your backs while you are doing it, we're getting close now.'

*

Redruth was one of the less attractive Cornish towns. It was a mismatch of ancient and modern buildings, with little thought apparently given to planning. At the top end of town was a road with the somewhat prosaic name High Street North. In it were several small shops, mostly specializing in goods and services not provided by supermarkets. 'Merriot's Stamp and Rare Coin Dealers' sat uncomfortably between a dry cleaner's and a chippy. All of the shops had narrow fronts and deep interiors.

An old-fashioned bell tinkled as they opened the shop door. There was the sound of shoes descending wooden stairs and a man appeared at the bottom of a staircase at the rear of the shop. He was tall and stooped with a grey, unshaven face. He wore horn-rimmed spectacles with thick lenses that magnified his eyes to those looking in. He was dressed in trousers that hadn't been pressed for years if ever, an open-neck grubby shirt and blue woollen cardigan with a button missing. He looked to be about 60 years of age but could easily have been ten years younger. He squinted at them through myopic eyes; clearly, a lifetime poring over postage stamps looking for watermarks and counting perforations had shortened his sight.

Prior established that the man was indeed Merriot and introduced himself and his partner. 'We'd like to ask you some questions, Mr Merriot.'

The man took the warrant card Prior had produced and held it close to his face. Handing it back, he said, 'What about?'

'You deal in rare coins. Do you get many old ones brought it?'

'Some. Not many though, most are just the last century. Occasionally a few from the nineteenth.'

'What about very old ones, Roman coins for example?'

The man's eyes flickered nervously. 'Very rarely. The Romans didn't have much influence in this part of the country. I've only got one or two.'

'Can we see what you have, please?'

Merriot went behind a counter on the right that ran from the front to the rear of the shop. The counter had a glass top. Beneath the glass were displays of postage stamps arranged individually and in sets and one felt-lined tray of pre-decimal currency British coins. Beneath the displays were rows and rows of shallow drawers. Merriot took a large bunch of keys from a trouser pocket and held them up to his face.

Choosing a key, he opened one of the drawers and pulled out a long narrow tray with rows and rows of what looked like bronze, copper and silver coins. Most were well worn. On some the designs were barely discernible. Those that could be discerned bore the heads of what were obviously Roman emperors.

Prior looked at the coins. 'More than one or two. What about gold coins, Mr Merriot, we're interested in gold Roman coins?'

The man's gaze flicked briefly to Prior, then quickly down again. He licked his lips. 'They are very rare in this part of the country, very rare indeed.'

'But you do have one or two don't you, sir?'

Reluctantly the man said, 'Yes, just one or two.'

'Can we see them please?'

Merriot selected another key and moved further down the counter. He opened a cupboard beneath it to reveal an ancient Chubb safe. He inserted the key and turned it. Then, with a metallic clunk, he turned a large lever and opened the safe door. His head disappeared behind the door and, after a few moments, reappeared. In his hands he held another long narrow tray. The coins in this one were all gold. He turned it to face them and placed it carefully on the counter.

The two detectives leant forward and studied the coins. They were arranged neatly in rows. Beneath each coin was a small card bearing information and a price written in a spidery hand. There were several rows of Krugerrands,

British sovereigns and other European coinage, then a row of gold US 'Golden Eagles'. At the very bottom of the tray were two Roman coins. Prior read the descriptions on the cards beneath. One said, Publius Aelius Hadrianus (Hadrian) 117-138 £495; the other, Honorius 393-423 £295.

Looking up, he said, 'Are you sure these are the only ones you have, Mr Merriot.'

Again he licked his lips before replying, 'Yes, those are all I have.'

Prior pointed to the Roman coins. 'How long have you had these?'

'Just a week or two.'

'Is it one week or two?'

His lips were obviously very dry as he licked them again. 'Probably two weeks now.'

'And where did you get them?'

By now Merriot was showing severe signs of nervousness. 'Er. At an auction I think.'

'Then you will no doubt have an invoice. Can I see it please?'

Merriot was struck dumb. His hands played nervously with the edges of the tray.

After a few moments silence Prior said in a softer voice, 'Listen Mr Merriot, we are not seeking to prosecute you for anything. I've no doubt you bought them in good faith. But I need to know who you bought them from. I could get a warrant if you wish. But that would mean that we would turn the place upside down and who knows what we might find? Now, I don't want to give you a hard time. Let's try again, who did you buy them from?'

Merriot sighed. 'I knew I shouldn't have taken them. I knew they would only bring trouble.'

'Who sold them to you?'

'A young guy. He came into the shop, said he'd found them in a stream.'

Prior and Siobhan exchanged looks. He produced a photograph of Wright and showed it to the coin dealer. 'Is this the man you bought the coins from, Mr Merriot?'

Merriot took the photograph in his hand and held it close to his face. He peered at it closely for a moment. 'It might have been. I'm short sighted, I can't be sure.'

'What did the man actually say to you?'

'He asked me if I bought old coins. When I said yes, he showed me these two. I asked him where he got them from. He said he found them in a stream. He asked me what they were worth and I offered him £250. I asked him if he had any more. He said no but knew where he might find some more. That was it.'

'Did you pay him cash?'

'Yes, he wouldn't take a cheque.'

'Have you seen him since?'

'No.'

Siobhan said, 'What can you tell us about the coins, Mr Merriot?'

'Only what is on the cards. Roman coins vary in value according to their rarity. These two are middle of the range.'

Prior could now see the light at the end of the tunnel and felt a huge sense of relief. They had the connection they needed and he knew the case would come together quickly. He was smiling as he said, 'We'll need a statement from you Mr Merriot and I'm afraid we will have to take the coins. They are evidence. We will give you a receipt.'

'Will I get them back?

'I can't say. I think they are treasure trove, aren't they?'

'Yes, finders keepers.'

'Not quite true. My understanding is that the finder is obliged to hand them in to the authorities, who will probably pay him market value for them. Isn't that right?'

Merriot said nothing. From the look on his face it was clear that he regretted his greed in buying the coins.

As they walked back to Prior's car Siobhan said, 'So you were right, sir, Wright did find some coins. Quite tragic really, he was killed for just two pieces of gold.'

'Yes, it seems so. But what worries me is that we still have no hard evidence. If we have to call Merriot to give evidence of who he bought the coins from, even a half-baked barrister will tear his evidence to shreds. He couldn't positively identify Wright.'

As they reached the car, Prior's mobile phone rang. It was Quigley. 'Bolton is dead, sir, he's been murdered.'

'Shit! Give me the details.'

'Jane and Alan are there now in his flat. He's been clubbed to death. The body was stiff; he's been dead for some time they think.'

Prior sighed deeply. 'OK, give me the address, we'll go straight there.'

39. The Third Death.

'He who lives by the sword dies by the sword.'

17th century proverb.

'Shit! Shit! Shit!' Prior said, slamming his palm on the steering wheel in time with the expletives. 'This is all down to that idiot Monk.'

'How do you mean sir?' Siobhan asked.

He glanced sideways at her as he drove. 'Keep this to yourself, Siobhan. When Bolton was arrested two days ago in London, the local DCI phoned my office at Truro asking for information on Bolton. Instead of doing some checks on his recent activities, Monk fobbed the DCI off with what he knew from memory. He didn't even bother to check with the collator. If he had done, he would have found the connection to our murders. Bolton would still be tucked up safely in a cell in West Kensington and our investigation would have been that much further forward. Monk is too lazy to breathe and he's a danger to everyone around him. Owen has suspended him from duty.'

After a pause, he continued, 'It was pure luck that I called into the office. I'd been chasing Monk to catch up on the paperwork.' He smiled ironically. 'He'd even got the crime bulletins in order but missed the whole point of keeping them tidy, to read them regularly. When I glanced at them, the first thing that caught my eye was an item about Bolton's arrest in London and everything fell into place.'

'I see, sir. I'll keep it to myself of course. But I expect the whole nick will be buzzing with the news by now.'

'Just say nothing anyway, Siobhan. With a bit of luck Owen will persuade him to retire early and we'll be rid of him.'

Siobhan sat quietly for a while. Eventually she said, 'This will add to your reputation, sir.'

'What reputation?'

'They're calling you the hand of god, having got rid of Stapleton. He wasn't very popular, nor is Monk.'

He laughed despite his anger. 'Well if it keeps them on their toes, it won't do any harm.'

'Keeping on my toes now, sir.'

After a few moments she said, 'When is DI Pearce due back, sir?'

'Two weeks. Owen is trying to find us another DI in the meantime.' He glanced sideways at her again. 'Where are you on the promotion list now?'

'Getting closer, there's still a few in front of me.'

'Well if we solve this case that should help push you up the list.'

She laughed. 'Get rid of a few more senior officers and I might have to buy you a beer.'

'I'll keep you to that. But in the meantime we haven't caught this killer yet. Let's hope we get something from this new crime scene.'

Siobhan had a deep frown on her face. 'Something occurred to me while you were talking to Merriot. You're always telling me to concentrate on motive, means and opportunity.'

'Yes?'

'Well, we're pretty sure we now have the motive. Who had the best means and opportunity to have seen Wright when he found the coins?'

He smiled. 'There you go. That's just the way my mind has been working. Go on, Siobhan.'

'Someone who lives on the estate. That means it's a choice between Callaghan, Brighton or the old cowman. We just have to find which one has the connection to Bolton.'

'Exactly, I think we can discount the old cowman, but the other two? Let's find the connection, then we can concentrate our efforts on whichever it is.'

Siobhan smiled. 'I told you it was the butler, sir, when we first met him. He looks like Hannibal Lecter.'

Prior smiled and glanced at her. 'One problem with that theory Siobhan, none of the corpses have been eaten, not even chewed at.'

*

They arrived at Bonneville Crescent, Truro, where Bolton's flat was situated. It was a narrow residential street with parked cars lining both kerbs. Two marked police cars were double-parked outside no.23, blocking the narrow road. Prior pulled up behind them and got out. From the boot he fetched two evidence suits and handed one to Siobhan. All the houses in the row had small front gardens. A uniformed constable stood at the gate of no.23. Recognizing them, he waved them through.

Prior paused. 'Who is keeping the list of visitors to the crime scene, Jones?'

'No idea, sir, no-one's told me.'

'Looks as if it's you then, get yourself a clipboard. Who's inside at the moment?'

'Two of your detectives, and PCs Bradley and Adams.'

'OK, start the list, include them and us. Times of arrivals and departures. Check every ones IDs, no exceptions. No media and no gawkers, understand?'

'Yes sir.'

The two stopped at the front door to the house and put on their evidence suits and gloves. Lurking in the hallway, they found PC Adams.

Prior asked, 'Where are my detectives?'

'Upstairs with the body, sir.'

'Who discovered it?'

'The landlady, Mrs McPherson. She's in the lounge here with PC Bradley. She's taking a statement from her.' He pointed to the closed door beside him.

'Good, has anyone else been up these stairs since the body was discovered?'

'No sir, only the landlady and your two detectives.'

'Good. Make sure everyone puts on evidence suits and shoe covers before they come into the house and tell them not to touch anything. I want a nice clean crime scene.'

'Yes, sir.'

Prior looked around him. The hall led from the front door to a kitchen at the rear. There were two closed doors on his left and a staircase on his right. There was another, smaller door under the staircase.

Prior frowned. 'What's the situation here, Adams, did Bolton just rent a room upstairs?'

'No sir, far as I can gather he rented the whole of the top floor.'

'So why did the landlady go up there, did they have a relationship?'

Adams smiled 'Not unless he was into necrophilia, the old dear's in her eighties. She says there's only one bathroom that they have to share. She saw the body when she went up for a bath.'

'You mean he's in the bathroom?'

'I don't think so, it's in one of the other rooms. I think the old dear saw the body through an open door.'

'OK, keep off the stairs yourself and try not to touch anything.' He led the way up the staircase, being careful himself not to touch the banister or the wall. Four doors opened from the landing. All were wide open. Straight ahead was the bathroom. He looked in. It was an old-fashioned room with just a bath, washbasin and lavatory. The small mirrored cabinet above the washbasin hung open, its contents in the basin; shaving cream, tooth paste, brushes, soap and bottles of pills. Glancing at the labels on the bottles, he saw they were for prescription drugs in the name of Alice McPherson.

They moved on to the second room. The smell of dirty underwear and unwashed bodies hit their nostrils. It was a sparsely-furnished bedroom and contained just a double bed, freestanding wardrobe, chest of drawers and a single upright chair. All the furniture looked old and shabby. The bed hadn't been made and the sheets and pillow were filthy.

Jane Foster, dressed in her white evidence suit and gloves, had been going through the clothes in the wardrobe. She turned as they entered and gave them a wan smile. 'We were too late I'm afraid sir. By the look of the body, a day too late.'

Prior nodded.

'The body's in the front room. Alan's in there.'

'Found anything here, Jane?'

She shook her head. 'Nothing interesting, sir. No way of knowing when the bed was last slept in, I doubt it's been made for weeks. Just a load of dirty clothes and the usual rubbish here, plus of course this awful smell. I don't think there's any doubt he lived alone, I can't imagine any woman putting up with it.'

Siobhan said, 'I wonder what he did for sex then?'

Foster bent down and picked up a magazine from the bottom of the wardrobe.

She held it up. It was hard porn. 'Seems like he preferred the hand, the sheets are a mess.'

Siobhan wrinkled her nose. 'Yes, I can smell what you mean.'

Prior said, 'You know what we're looking for, Jane, anything with addresses or phone numbers on it, anything that gives us a clue to his contacts.'

She nodded. 'Yes, sir. But I think someone has been here before us. Difficult to tell with the mess but it does look as if someone has been through this lot.'

'OK, do your best. We'll leave you to it for the moment.'

The next room they came to was a tiny box room into which had been crammed a small kitchen table, two chairs and a small cabinet with a microwave and kettle on its top. There was no sink and dirty plates and cutlery were piled on the table. A rubbish bin overflowed with empty takeaway packages and beer cans.

The cabinet doors were open. Looking inside, Prior saw two saucepans, a frying pan and little else. The utensils looked cheap but new. 'Not into cooking, was he?'

'Just as well sir, he didn't even have running water; must have filled the kettle from the bathroom.'

Prior turned and took the few steps to the front room. This too was sparsely furnished with an uncomfortable looking three-piece suite, coffee table, sideboard and the inevitable TV. The whole lot wouldn't have brought more than £50 at the nearest second-hand shop. An old, threadbare carpet, probably there from the days the room had been a bedroom, covered the floor.

Trevor Bolton lay on his left side on the carpet in a pool of his own blood. His right leg was thrust forward at the hip as if protecting his genitals. His right hand was resting on his cheek. Beneath his body his left arm extended palm up, as if in supplication. But the killer had shown no mercy.

Two mighty blows had been delivered to his skull. One blow to the back of his head had left his hair was matted with congealed blood. The other had caved in his forehead. Blood spatters were everywhere, one set on the furniture around the body and another on the wall and the back of the door. Clearly he had been struck once from behind when standing up, and again when he lay on the floor. To Prior it appeared that either blow would have been fatal.

DC Alan Waring, clothed in his white evidence suit, was standing beside the settee with his notebook in his hand. Following Prior's gaze, he said, 'Glad I had that course on blood splatter, sir. There are two clear sets that show there were two blows struck. I was just working that out.' He pointed. 'See on the back of the door and the wall here?'

Prior nodded,

'Looks as if the killer hit him from behind just inside the room, which knocked him down.' He turned and pointed to the body. 'Then he struck him again while he was on the floor just to make sure he was dead.'

Prior nodded again, 'Glad you were paying attention on the course, Alan. What else?'

'There's some boot marks in the pool of blood and bloody footprints all over the place. Looks as if the killer searched the place once he'd killed Bolton.'

Siobhan frowned, 'Where was the woman downstairs when all this was going on? There must have been a hell of a racket.'

'Bingo, sarge. She says that she went out at about 6.30 last night, got back at about 10 and went straight to bed. Apparently she's got a downstairs loo, so she didn't come up here until late this afternoon for a bath.'

'Didn't she even come up to clean her teeth last night?'

Waring smiled despite his surroundings, 'She does whistle when she talks sarge. Probably takes them out at night to clean them.'

Prior said, 'Were all these doors wide open when you got here?'

'Yes, sir, just as they are now.'

Prior shook his head. 'That's amazing.' He looked at his watch. 'It's now after 6pm. The body must have lain here all night and all day while the landlady was downstairs. I bet she'll have nightmares when she realises she shared the house with a corpse all that time.'

Waring nodded. 'Wait till you see her, sir, she's almost a corpse herself. She's all of eighty and looks very frail. When she did find the body, she managed to make her way down the stairs and dial 999. We were sitting in the car outside and heard the call for police to respond on the radio. We took the call and came straight in. The poor old dear was standing in the hall in a right old state. Jane stayed with her till the uniform arrived then Sarah Bradley took over. She is taking a statement from her now.'

'Yes, I gather that, Alan. What else have you found in here, any sign of a mobile phone or an address book?'

'No, sir. No sign of the murder weapon either, the killer must have taken it with him. There are several boot imprints on the carpet, but on that surface it's difficult to see any sole patterns. I suppose our best bet is with George and Sally, they might find the odd hair or fibre from the killer.'

Prior sniffed. 'I hope you're right, we'll see when they've done their thing. What we need is something that connects Bolton to someone on the Sinclair Estate, address books, phone numbers, that sort of thing.'

Prior looked around. The doors of the sideboard hung open, their contents all over the carpet. Papers, correspondence, even a few photographs were spread all over the floor. One or two had come to rest in the pool of blood.

He said, 'All of this stuff on the floor, Alan, bag it separately once it's been photographed, the killer might have missed something. His luck has got to change sometime.'

Waring nodded.

Siobhan said, 'I wonder if he was looking for the coins, sir, or even money. Perhaps he thought Bolton was trying to cheat him. Maybe he thought that he had invented the story about being arrested?'

'Yes, that's possible I suppose, I can't see Bolton inspiring much trust in anyone who knew him. But it does appear that the killer did; enough anyway to ask him to sell coins for him.'

'Bolton told the London dealer there were more coins, sir, so the killer must have told him that.'

'Maybe, but people have been known to tell the occasional porkie you know, especially toe-rags like Bolton' He turned back to Waring. 'Is there a land line up here Alan?'

'No, sir.'

'I wonder if the old dear let Bolton use hers, I noticed there's one in the hall.'

Waring nodded. 'We'll check her phone records.'

'OK, don't disturb anything up here until George and Sally have done their thing. We'll let them have a clean run at it.'

40. Mrs. McPherson.

'There are none so blind as those who won't see'

Unknown origin.

Prior and Siobhan went downstairs and found PC Adams still lurking in the hall. Prior ignored him and knocked gently on the door to the front room. A female voice invited him to come in. He opened the door and led the way in.

The room was full of the past. Framed photographs of children, grandchildren and great grandchildren jostled with holiday mementos for places on every flat surface, but pride of place in the centre of the mantelpiece was held by a black and white wedding photo dating from another era. The furniture looked as if it was from a similar time. Old-fashioned doilies adorned the backs of settee and chairs. Everything was covered in a fine layer of dust.

PC Sarah Bradley sat in an occasional chair opposite an old woman. She was small and frail looking, just as Adams had described her. She sat primly with her hands in her lap, nervously twiddling her thumbs. She squinted at them from a distance of ten feet and clearly had difficulty focussing. Her pupils were the palest shade of blue; age and cataracts had turned the blue cloudy and no doubt affected her sight. Prior wondered how she managed to read the numbers on her bingo card.

Introductions were made and Prior and Siobhan sat on the old settee. He said, 'Mrs McPherson, how are you bearing up?'

She gave him a thin smile. 'I'm all right thank you, this young lady made me a nice cup of tea.' Prior noticed that she did indeed whistle her S's and her teeth looked far too perfect to be real.

He nodded. 'Good. Sorry to have to ask you to go over it again but my sergeant and I need to know exactly what happened so we can get after the person that did this. May I ask you some questions?'

She answered cheerfully, 'Yes of course.' Prior realised that in a way she was actually enjoying the company despite the circumstances that had brought them to her home. Clearly, she didn't get many visitors and would make the most of this opportunity.

He smiled sympathetically. 'It must have been quite a shock finding Mr Bolton like that?'

'Oh yes, gave me quite a turn.'

'When you went upstairs what did you actually see?'

'All the doors were open. Mr. Bolton normally kept them all closed.'

'Did you go immediately and look into his rooms?'

'No, I'm not nosy you know, I give him his privacy. I went to the bathroom first. Then I saw someone had tipped all the things from the bathroom cabinet into the sink. I wondered what was going on. Then I looked into his living room and saw him on the floor. I've never seen anything like it, so much blood.'

'I'm sure it was a nasty shock. What did you do next?'

'Well, I came downstairs and called the police.'

'You were very brave, Mrs McPherson. Did you actually go into the room where the body was?'

'No, I've seen a dead body before you know, when my poor Alf died. He had a heart attack and died in his bed. But I've never seen so much blood in my life before.'

'You did the right thing. When did you last see Mr Bolton alive?'

'Yesterday morning, when he went off to work.'

'Did you speak to him?'

'No, I saw him getting into his car through the window here.'

'And before that, when did you see him?'

'Not for a few days, he'd been away.'

'Did he tell you where he was going?'

'No, we don't talk much. Just to pass the time of day, you know.'

'How long has he stayed here, Mrs McPherson?'

'Must be all of three months now. Yes, about three months.'

'Did he get many visitors?'

'No, not many at all.'

'Did you meet any of the visitors?'

'His sister came once or twice.'

'Do you know her name?'

'Alice, Alice something or other. She's married you know.'

'Do you know who to?'

'No, she never said.'

'Do you know anything about her, where she lives for example?'

She shook her head. 'No, we only talked for a moment or two when she knocked at the door, never really had a long chat. That's when she told me she was his sister. Then she went straight up to see her brother. But she was a nice woman, polite you know?'

'When was the last time she called?'

The wrinkles on the old woman's face deepened as she thought about the question. Finally she said, 'Must be two weeks since. Came on a Wednesday she did. I thought it were the postman when she knocked.'

He nodded, 'What about other visitors, did you meet anyone else?'

'No, no-one really.'

'No girl friends?'

'No, he didn't bring anyone home with him. I told him I didn't want any fancy women here.'

'What about phone calls? I notice there's no phone upstairs, did he use your phone?'

'Oh no, he had one of those mobile phones, never used mine.'

'So you didn't receive any calls for him?'

She shook her head, 'No, not that I can remember.'

Siobhan asked, 'Did you and he talk much Mrs McPherson?'

'No. Kept himself to himself you know. He was a taxi driver, works lots of nights, you know?'

'How did you get on with him?'

She frowned again as she framed her answer. 'He wasn't here much and when he was he didn't have much to say for himself. But he paid his rent on time each week. That's why I took him in you see? When my Alf died, I needed the extra money.'

'Do you go to bingo every week, Mrs McPherson?'

'Oh yes, regular as clockwork. Mr Brown from Tetley Street, he picks me up and brings me home afterwards.'

'What time did you leave last night?'

'Half past six. Mr. Brown picks me up sharp at half past six every Thursday.'

'And what time did you get home?'

'Ten thirty, same as usual.'

'Did you not go upstairs last night when you came in?'

She shook her head. 'No, I can't manage those stairs too well, bit of arthritis in my knees. I've got my downstairs toilet you see, so I only go upstairs when I want my bath.'

'Did you hear any noise upstairs during the night?'

'No, I sleep well enough, especially when I'm late to bed like on Thursdays, you know?'

Siobhan smiled and nodded.

Prior heard noises in the hall outside. 'Please excuse me, Mrs McPherson, I must go and talk to my detectives. You've been very helpful, thank you. If you don't mind, I'll leave these two officers with you, they'll take down your statement.' He nodded at Siobhan and left the room, carefully closing the door behind him.

The two CSIs were standing in the entrance doorway putting on their green coveralls.

Bailey looked up. 'Hello, guv. This is getting to be a habit. All these people dying around you, is it something you ate?'

Prior ignored the question. 'George, Sally. For once we've got a nice clean crime scene for you, fill your boots. Find me some evidence then maybe we can catch this toe-rag.'

'Toe-rag, guv? Where'd you pick that up? You been taking a course on Cockney?'

Prior didn't answer. Bailey turned to his companion. 'Right, you go upstairs, Sally, I'll hoover the carpet down here and do the banister for prints, then join you.' She nodded, picked up her metal case and trudged up the stairs. Prior followed her.

He went back to the room where the body lay. Liz Roberts had finished her search of the bedroom and was comparing notes with her partner. They greeted Sally Hinds and stepped out into the hall with Prior to give her room to start her examination of the scene.

The three detectives stood chatting on the landing.

Prior said, 'What did you find, anything new?'

'Not a thing, sir,' Foster said. 'This killer covers his tracks well. He obviously searched this place thoroughly after he killed Bolton but doesn't seem to have left any trace.'

'Let's hope George and Sally prove you wrong, Jane. Let's try to reconstruct how this went down. Bolton obviously let the killer in when he first arrived. There's no sign of forced entry and the old dear was out. And Bolton must have trusted the man to have turned his back on him. Then, as Bolton walked into the room ahead of him, he struck his first blow.'

'Yes, sir. And he must have got some blood on him; it spurted everywhere. His shoes and clothing must have been covered in it.'

'Well maybe the neighbours will have seen something, either when he arrived or left. Parking is a nightmare out there, someone might have spotted a vehicle. The house to house might bring us something.'

He paused. 'I wonder how he knew the old dear downstairs was out? She said the only visitor Bolton ever had was his sister. So, unless it was her, which seems unlikely, the killer could hardly have known the old lady's habits. Did you find any mobile phone invoices?'

Roberts shook her head. 'He had a pay-as-you-go. We found the empty box it came in and the slip with his pin number and the charger. No receipts or anything.'

'So the killer will have taken the phone with him, that and anything that might have had his details on it.' He paused again.

Waring said, 'Perhaps the old dear was lucky she was out when the killer called, he doesn't seem to be too bothered how many people he kills.'

Prior nodded. 'You could be right. Well, let's hope George and Sally do find us something. Maybe that old goat, Penhallon will come up with something useful for a change.'

A voice from the top of the stairs said, 'This old goat is getting fed up with wandering all over the county looking at your dead bodies. You should be more careful what you say, young Matthew, even old goats have ears.'

Prior turned and forced a smile. 'Professor, nice to see you. Sorry about that, a slip of the tongue, we love you really.'

'Hmm! I can only find what's there. Now, where's the body. My wife was just about to serve dinner when you called, I didn't have time to eat.'

Prior smiled. 'Join the club. At least when you've done your bit you can go home. It's in the lounge there.' He pointed to the front room.

*

It was after midnight when Prior got home that night. Jeanette had left him a note in the kitchen. It said, 'You didn't phone! Your dinner's in the bin and I'm in bed.' It was unsigned.

He sighed. Jeanette rarely complained when he was late, unless he forgot to phone. He opened the fridge and made himself a sandwich from the remains of the shoulder of lamb that was there. Then he smiled wanly at the thought that this was not the only cold shoulder he would get tonight.

41. Clarity at Last.

'Minds are like parachutes, they only function when they are open.'
James Dewar 1842-1923

Breakfast in the Prior household began somewhat frostily the next morning. He tried to explain to Jeanette how events had overtaken him the previous evening, she turned a deaf ear. But the children were chatty, and he sat listening to their news. When he kissed them all goodbye, Jeanette offered him only a cheek. He left quickly, his mind already busy with the day ahead.

The underwater search team had already arrived on the estate when Prior got there. They had parked their vehicles on the grass verge beside the drive and were unloading their gear. It was another cold, dank day and he did not envy them their task. But Ben Willis, the sergeant in charge, was cheerful as Prior briefed him on the extent and purpose of their search.

He commented, 'We don't get many treasure hunts, sir, my lads will enjoy this.'

'Good. I'll leave you to organise your gear and join you shortly. I must go up to the van and check my messages.'

DS Quigley was already at his desk, otherwise the van was empty. Quigley greeted his boss and handed him two messages. The first was from Owen telling him that there was a press conference arranged for 5pm that day and he should attend.

He grimaced and handed it back to Quigley. 'Tell her I'll be there.' The second message was also from Owen, telling him that a new DI would arrive on Monday. He frowned and said, 'Albert, this new DI, Marcus Wright-Phillips, do you know him?'

Quigley wrinkled his nose. 'Don't know him, sir, but I understand he's a flier.'

'Shit, that's all we need. We get rid of a dinosaur and get a baby Chief Constable to train.'

Siobhan's voice behind him said, 'Not more of that stuff, sir, I hope it's not too thick, I hate wading through it.'

Prior turned and smiled, 'Good morning, Siobhan. You timed your arrival to a T as usual. You'll know what I mean when you have to start calling a 25-year-old nimby, sir. Anyway we haven't got time for that now. A quick cup of coffee, then it's on with your wellies and we're off on a treasure hunt.'

'Oh goody, sir, should I bring my shovel.'

He ignored her and turned back to Quigley. 'Nothing on the Bolton murder yet I suppose?'

'No, sir, Fred and Jean are trying to trace Bolton's sister, the rest of the team are doing the house-to house of

Bolton's neighbours. George Bailey has taken a whole mass of stuff to the lab and BT are sending us a break-down of the landlady's phone records.'

'Good. We're going down to get the search team started. You've got my mobile number, phone me if anything turns up.' He frowned. 'In the meantime, I think we should start moving the team HQ back to the station in Truro. Without an experienced DI I'm trying to juggle too many balls in the air and I'm a bit remote out here. Please organise that, Albert, and let everyone know.'

There were six members in the underwater search team, plus the sergeant. All were dressed in heated wet-suits. Two would man the rubber dinghies that carried their equipment while four would search the stream. The sergeant would run things from the bank. The men in the water carried powerful torches and wore snorkels as the stream was not deep enough to require the use of un-derwater breathing apparatus. Two of the divers carried metal detectors.

They started the search at the Lamb Lane end and slowly worked their way upstream. The water was murky. Recent rains had washed tons of silt into the stream, so they could not search by sight. The four men in the water operated in two teams. One used the metal detector, the other dug with their hands or a small trowel where the detectors suggested something metallic lay beneath the surface.

Within a few moments of starting one of the detectors pinged. A diver felt around on the streambed and pulled up a length of rusty angle iron. He threw it onto the bank and continued the search.

'Fraid we're likely to get a lot of that, sir,' the sergeant said. 'People use waterways as rubbish dumps.'

The going was slow; it took almost an hour to reach the point opposite the Celtic cross. In that time all they had found were a few pieces of scrap metal. Then they pulled out something more interesting. A detector pinged above one of the deep pools. A diver went down and felt about amongst the muck at the bottom of the pool. A minute later he came up holding something in his raised hand. At first glance it looked like another piece of scrap metal.

But when he handed it to his sergeant on the bank, he said, 'Looks like an old sword sarge.'

Prior and Siobhan crowded around him, their interest aroused. It was heavily corroded but its shape gave it away.

Siobhan grinned. 'I wonder if it's Excalibur?'

Prior also grinned. 'Bit short I think. Unless the historians got it wrong, perhaps King Arthur was a dwarf.'

Sergeant Willis gave the two of them a strange look but said nothing.

Prior added, 'But seriously. At least we've got something for the archaeologists. This should keep them happy for days.'

Willis joined the conversation. 'It actually looks like a Roman sword, judging by the ones they use in films, they were about this size.'

The search resumed. The next find was a spearhead; again, this was heavily corroded but identifiable. This was followed by arrowheads and other small objects that they were unable to identify.

Prior shook his head. 'Amazing! Perhaps this was the scene of some ancient battle.'

Willis nodded. 'Either that or the weapons were thrown into the stream as some kind of sacrificial offerings. There were probably a lot more. These bits have only survived because they ended up in the deep pools and got covered by silt. It's not the first time we've found relics in our underwater searches. There's a lot of history in this part of the country.'

'Whatever, there is obviously something significant about this place. Perhaps the young Mr Sinclair will let the archaeologists explore the place now. But we need to concentrate on what we are looking for.'

Five minutes later the searchers struck gold, literally. A metal detector pinged at a spot where the water ran fast over a shallow bed of large stones. Underneath one of the stones his companion found a small round object. As he stood up with it in his fingers, Prior could see the dull gleam of gold. The man waded to the bank and carefully put it into Prior's outstretched hand. He got out his handkerchief and rubbed mud off the coin. It was the size of a £1 piece but much thinner. On one side it bore the head of a Roman Emperor, on the reverse a symbol that he didn't recognise. 'Bingo,' he exclaimed.

Looking over his shoulder, Siobhan said, 'So you were right, sir, this confirms it.'

'It's you that was right, Siobhan, all along you said this was about buried treasure. We were just looking in the wrong place and for the wrong kind of treasure.'

'Just think sir, three people have been murdered over a few of these.'

He nodded. 'Over the centuries you can make that more like a few thousand; gold fever does strange things to people.'

The team stopped for a break. One of the support team broke out the flasks and handed out mugs of hot coffee. The men relaxed on the bank and Prior explained to them the significance of their find.

As he was talking they heard the excited barking of dogs. Two Labradors came in sight along the path. Moments later they were followed by the stocky figure of Callaghan. In his hand he carried a stout stick.

He smiled as he approached. 'Good morning Chief Inspector, how's your search going?'

'Lots of scrap metal Mr Callaghan. We've left some of it on the bank back that way. Careful your dogs don't cut themselves on it.'

Callaghan nodded. 'What are you actually looking for Chief Inspector?'

'Evidence, sir.'

'I see. Have you found any?'

Prior ignored the question. 'How are you getting on with your new boss?'

'Fine, he doesn't seem to want to make too many changes. In fact, he's left me to it, gone to visit his mother.'

'So your job is secure then?'

'It seems that way, for the time being anyway.'

The team had begun putting away their mugs and flasks ready to carry on with the search.

Prior said, 'Good. If you'll excuse us now, Mr Callaghan, we must get on with our search.'

Callaghan took the hint. 'Yes, and I must get back to my work. Good luck with your search.'

Prior nodded and watched him until he was out of sight.

Siobhan frowned. 'I wonder if that was just natural curiosity, sir?'

'So do I, Siobhan, so do I.'

The searchers resumed their task and within a few moments unearthed another gold coin. Then, at a slight bend in the stream where the current had undermined the bank on the nearside, they found the remains of a clay pot. One of the detectors had pinged at the spot. A diver explored the area with his hands and began to find shards of pottery. Within a few moments there were several pieces lying on the path. Then the base of the pot was found.

Prior tried fitting some of the pieces together; they were indeed a fit. Next the diver unearthed two more gold coins from the silt underneath where the pot had been. It was the coins that had caused the metal detector to ping.

They searched for a further 20 minutes before Prior called a halt. He had the evidence he needed. He had no doubt that a more intensive search might reveal more artefacts but that was a job for archaeologists. They took several photographs of the spot from all angles and the search team began ferrying their gear back to their vehicles. Prior thanked them enthusiastically and left them to it. He and Siobhan made their way up the hill to the van with the evidence.

DS Quigley sat alone at his desk. The rest of the team were still out and about. He said, 'The towing unit will be here later, sir, to tow us back to Truro.'

Prior smiled. 'Good.' He put the evidence bags containing their finds on the desk.

Quigley picked up the bag with the coins in. He held it up to the light. Then he looked at Prior and smiled. 'So you were right, sir, this was all about buried treasure.'

'Yes, Albert, or more correctly, Siobhan was. Now we've proved the why. All we have to do is find the who.'

Quigley nodded. 'Perhaps the other guys will find some answers, sir.'

'I certainly hope so, before anyone else gets killed.'

After a pause he said, 'Right, let's see if we can reconstruct the whole sequence of events. Wright was working down by the stream and spotted something in the water. Obviously, when the rushing water undermined the bank, some coins from the broken pot were washed downstream. Wright found two coins and took them to Redruth and sold them?'

His two companions nodded.

'Good. Then he either told someone of his lucky find or someone saw him searching the stream and cottoned on. They kidnapped him, tortured him to find out what he knew about the source of the coins and, having got what they wanted, killed him.'

Siobhan broke in, 'And put his head on the gate to frighten other people away so he could search for the pot of gold in peace.'

Prior frowned. 'That's the bit that seems strange. It's almost as if he was trying to draw attention to the estate. But let's leave that for the moment. As you were saying, the next thing that happened was that Sinclair happened to walk along the path and found the killer there. So he was killed too.'

Quigley shook his head. 'But why leave the body there, sir, drawing attention to the spot?'

'Jessica covered that, didn't she? He'd finished with the spot. He'd removed all the coins, so there was nothing left for us to find. Except that he didn't reckon with the underwater search team.'

'OK. He's seen us searching the banks of the stream but not the stream itself, so he thinks he's safe. He finds the pot of gold coins and now has to dispose of them. Not so easy, so he turns to a villain he knows for help. But Bolton is not very bright and gets himself arrested in London. Then the killer realises that Bolton might turn him in to save his own skin, so he kills him.'

Siobhan had a frown on her face.

Prior looked at her. 'What are you thinking Siobhan?'

She shook her head. 'Something Gibbons the village constable said sir, Sinclair complained of intruders on the estate weeks before Wright was killed.'

'Yes?'

'Well that means someone was down there before Wright found his coins. Maybe that means someone had been searching for the coins before Wright found the two that he did?'

There was silence for a long moment while they all thought about this. Then Quigley offered, 'Supposing the intruder had already found some coins in the stream before Wright did. Maybe he kept going back to the estate to look for more coins and was spotted?'

Prior shook his head, 'You've just run a truck through my theory, Albert.'

'What theory, sir?'

'Opportunity, Albert. Who had the best opportunity to find what was in the stream? Who lives on the estate and walks his dogs there all the time?'

'Of course, Callaghan,' Quigley said.

The frown had returned to Siobhan's face. 'But why was it Sinclair who complained of intruders. If he saw Callaghan walking his dogs by the stream he wouldn't call him an intruder, would he?'

It was Prior's turn to frown. 'No, he wouldn't. I wonder if there really was an intruder? People tell porkies all the time, especially if they're trying to cover their tracks. What we really need to know is who actually saw him. It was Sinclair who made the complaint. But was he reporting what he saw or what someone told him?' He turned to Quigley. 'Get hold of Inspector Bradley, it was him Sinclair spoke to. Find out what was actually said to him.'

Quigley said, 'He's on nights, sir, I left a message for him to contact us two days ago.'

'Well now its urgent, Albert, get someone to wake him up if he's still sleeping.'

Quigley nodded and made a note on his pad.

Prior said, 'Everything now depends on finding a connection between Bolton and the killer. We'll just have to wait and see what Jean and Fred come up with. Maybe the sister has something to do with this.'

'Or maybe the connection will show up on Bolton's work sheets at Handycabs. I've got Jane and Alan checking those, sir.'

'Good. In the meantime I'm starving. Who's going for the pasties and doughnuts?'

*

Elsewhere things were happening that would throw new light onto the enquiry. Jean Wade and Fred Trimble were busy. In the UK, as in most western societies, our very existence can be traced from the day we are born until the day we die: in theory anyway. The law requires all births, deaths and marriages to be registered. There are registers where these records are kept, both locally and in the capital. In addition, school, medical, employment and unemployment records are kept by government agencies. That is to say nothing of banks, credit agencies, insurance companies and libraries that also keep records.

The two detectives spent two hours searching county records for an Alice Bolton of the right age. They found not a single trace. They extended their search to national records, even extending their search to any woman over twenty with that name. Still they found no fit. There were several Alice Boltons but none with a brother named Trevor. It was as if she had never existed.

Undaunted, they changed tack and started looking into Trevor Bolton's past. If he had a sister it was likely that they had grown up together. They soon discovered that Bolton had been born in a Truro maternity hospital in 1967. His mother was recorded as being Margaret Smith, shop assistant, his father, Alan Bolton, labourer.

From the maternity hospital they found an address for the mother, Rose Cottage in the village of Trewithen. From the 1981 census, they discovered three people registered as living at that address. Margaret Smith aged 32, Trevor Bolton aged 14, and Alice Chesnaye aged 10. 'Bingo', they had found her.

But their troubles were not yet over. There was no record of her marriage; indeed all records of her ceased in 1990. She had simply disappeared.

Wade spoke to the registrar in Truro. She asked, 'How is that possible?'

He replied, 'In theory, if she's still in the UK, it's not. But if she moved abroad or got married elsewhere, we would have no record of that here.'

'But we know she is still in the UK, she was seen visiting her brother recently.'

'That doesn't necessarily mean she got married here, she could have lived abroad for a while. There are all sorts of possibilities. If she got married abroad and came back under a married name, we would have no record of her.'

Wade nodded and said to Trimble, 'We can check with the Passport Office. If she went abroad she must have had a passport.'

They thanked the registrar and left.

Their next stop was the village of Trewithen. Rose Cottage was one of a row of small terraced homes that had once housed the families of the men that worked the local tin mine. But that was history; now the occupants came from all sorts of backgrounds. Their knock was answered by a young woman wearing a quilted dressing gown, despite the time of day. Her hair was a mess and she wore no make-up.

Trimble introduced himself and his partner and asked if she knew of an Alice Chesnaye who had once lived at the cottage.

The woman replied, 'Nope, never heard of her.'

Trimble persisted, 'How long have you lived here, madam?'

'Not long, what's it to you?'

He gave her a hard look. 'I'll tell you what it is to you, madam. If you don't answer my questions, we'll haul you down to the police station and charge you with obstruction. We are conducting a murder enquiry.'

'Keep your shirt on, mister. I don't know nothing about no murder. I've lived here for two years and haven't got a clue who was here before me. Now I've got two babies to feed so if that's all you want, goodbye.'

Trimble sighed and said, 'Good day to you, madam.'

The next avenue to pursue was the neighbours and the hope that someone remembered Alice Chesnaye. It was at the sixth cottage they tried that their luck changed. A woman in her seventies answered their knock.

In reply to their question she said, 'Young Alice, yes, I remember her.' She invited them in and made tea.

When they were all seated in her tiny sitting room, Trimble continued the questioning. 'What can you tell us about the family, Mrs Cox?'

'Family? I'd hardly call them a family. I knew Margaret Smith and her two brats though. Alice were one of them, poor thing.'

'Why was it that the children had different surnames to their mother?'

The old woman smiled. 'Ships that passed in the night, that's why. Margaret couldn't keep a man for long. A few drinks and she were anybody's. She was the village bicycle; half the young men in the village learned to ride on her. She was a bad lot.' The old woman cackled at her own joke.

With a smile on her face, Wade asked, 'And the children, Mrs Cox?'

'What chance did they have? No father and a mother who couldn't keep her knickers on. Young Trevor were always in trouble with the law and Alice were as loose as her mother.'

'Were the children close?'

'Oh yes, Trevor fought many a battle looking after Alice. She was a pretty young thing and the local lads were always sniffing around.'

'Do you know what happened to her?'

'She got married.'

'Do you remember who to?'

This brought a sharp look from the old woman. 'Ain't nothing wrong with my memory young woman. She married that Tom Callaghan, Bill Callaghan's youngest boy.'

The two detectives exchanged glances. Trimble asked, 'How did Trevor get on with Callaghan?'

'When he agreed to marry Alice, they got on fine.'

'When you say agreed to marry her, was there some persuasion?'

'Of course there was, she was pregnant.'

'Was it Callaghan's child?'

Mrs Cox smiled knowingly. 'It might have been; but then there were half a dozen other lads who might have been the father. But as it turned out, it didn't make a lot of difference as she had a miscarriage soon after the marriage. Probably for the best really.'

'Do you know where Alice is now, Mrs Cox?'

She shook her head. 'No, they got married in Ireland you know. Catholics. Then they came back for a while, lived on the Callaghan farm. Then they moved away, he got a job somewhere, I don't remember where. Then the mother, Margaret emmigrated to Australia. She took up with an old widower who had more money than sense. No one hereabouts has heard anything from any of them since. Good riddance if you ask me, they were nothing but trouble.'

The two detectives thanked her and left. The moment they were back in their car, Wade phoned their news through to the caravan.

42. A step Too Far.

'A door must be either shut or open.'

18th century proverb.

The news of the connection between Bolton and Callaghan acted like a trigger. It set off a chain reaction and things began to come together in a rush. Prior and his two sergeants were sitting at Quigley's desk having their lunch. Prior had just taken a bite out of his pasty when the phone rang.

Quigley answered it. He nodded as he listened for a moment. Then he said into the phone, 'Yes, sir, just a moment please, Mr. Prior is here. I think he'll want to speak to you himself.' Holding the mouthpiece to his chest he said, 'It's Inspector Bradley, sir.'

Prior nodded as he gulped down the food in his mouth. He held out his hand for the phone. 'Hello, Kevin, how are you?'

'Weary but well, sir. I'm on nights; I just woke up. How can I help you?'

'Sorry to disturb your sleep, Kevin, but this is urgent. I need to check something. Do you remember a conversation you had some weeks ago with Cedric Sinclair? Something about intruders on the estate?'

'Yes. Two or three weeks ago.'

'What did he actually say to you, the exact words if you can remember?'

'Not sure of the exact words but it was something to the effect that an intruder had been seen on the estate. He wanted extra patrols in the area.'

'Now this is important, Kevin. Did he say who had seen the intruder?'

There was a moment's silence before Bradley spoke. Then, 'He said he'd had a report that someone had been seen wandering about near the Lamb Lane gate. Yes, that's what he said. I remember because he got snotty when I asked him for a description of the intruder.'

'So you're sure it wasn't him who actually saw the intruder?'

'No. He definitely said it had been reported to him.'

'But he didn't say who had made the report?'

'No, I did ask but he snapped my head off. Told me just to do my job properly. Then I got another call from Stapleton.'

'What did he have to say?'

'Asked me what I was doing about the prowler. I told him I'd asked all units to keep their eyes open and told Gibbons, the village constable to pay frequent visits. You know those two were pals, sir? Stapleton made our lives difficult whenever Sinclair complained about anything.'

'Did your patrols find anything?'

'Not a sausage. There's nothing much to steal on the estate except up at the house and that's alarmed. The only intruders we've had in the past were kids fishing in the stream. But that was ages ago. Sinclair seemed to think we had nothing better to do than be at his beck and call.'

'Yes, I know exactly what you mean, Kevin, I had some of that myself. Anyway, thanks for your help, I owe you a pint.'

'I'll hold you to that, sir, see you soon.'

Prior had a wide smile on his face as he put the receiver down. 'Got him! Callaghan was lying when he said Sinclair saw the intruder. Bradley says Sinclair definitely told him it had been reported to him. So it could have been Callaghan who put the idea into his head.'

Quigley said, 'One thing sir, Sinclair made the call some days before Wright found the coins, so Callaghan must have known about the pot of coins then.'

Prior nodded, 'I think you may be right. Maybe he had found coins in the stream himself and was looking for the source. Then Wright made the same discovery and had to be dealt with.'

'A bit drastic though, wasn't it?'

'Yes it was. But that's what gold fever does to some people if the movies are to be believed.'

Siobhan added, 'You can't get much more drastic than cutting the poor kid's head off and sticking it on the gate. But I still can't work out why he'd do that and draw attention to the estate' She turned to Prior. 'It doesn't make sense sir.'

Prior nodded. 'You're right, Siobhan. It doesn't make sense at all. It can't just have been a warning, there's got to be some other reason.' He paused for a moment then said, 'You know Jessica said something that made sense. She said that putting the head on the gate like that showed resentment, either to the landowner himself or all the ruling classes.'

Siobhan still had a frown on her face. 'What reason did Callaghan have to be resentful, Sinclair gave him what sounds like a plumb job?'

No-one answered.

After several moments Prior concluded, 'OK, clearly we haven't got all of the pieces of the jigsaw yet. Maybe we'll never know it all. The important thing is we have our suspect now clearly in our sights. Just one small problem, we haven't actually got any evidence against him. We can't even make a case on what we have.'

This brought the three of them back to earth. They sat munching their pasties in silence.

Quigley eventually broke it, 'I wonder what happened to Bolton's sister, sir. Obviously her marriage to Callaghan didn't last. He lives on the estate on his own and has a woman friend in Truro, so we gather.'

Prior pursed his lips. 'We'll just have to wait and see what the team turns up on her.'

Siobhan was still struggling to put the pieces together in her mind, 'That's another thing I don't understand. Why would Callaghan trust Bolton to sell the coins for him? The man's an out and out villain. Even with the family connection, he's not very trustworthy is he?'

Prior shook his head. 'No but maybe he felt he didn't have a choice. He found the coins on someone else's estate. Strictly speaking they belong to the crown, and the only other person with a claim on them would be Sinclair. So he couldn't go to a reputable dealer. His lack of a criminal record suggests he didn't have any underworld connections except for Bolton. And there's always a risk involved in getting rid of gear that isn't kosher.

The average law-abiding citizen stumbling about in the dark with a hoard of gold coins is asking for trouble. Not just of getting arrested but of getting seriously hurt. I can see how he would have to trust someone. At least he knew Bolton, he was his brother-in-law. Better the devil you know, as the saying goes.'

Quigley added, 'Lucky for us he did choose Bolton, who's not very bright. I looked at his record. He was so thick he made two short planks look like a wafer. But Callaghan obviously didn't trust him with all the coins. He just gave him a few and sent him out to test the market.'

'I wonder how many there are all together?' Siobhan asked.

'Your guess is as good as mine. But three people have now been killed because of them. There could be a lot, the pot was big enough. And if just a dozen sold for five grand, there could be a fortune there.'

They lapsed into silence again.

Then Quigley moved the conversation on, 'Oh yes I forgot, sir. Something else happened while you were down with the search team. Young Mr Sinclair phoned, apparently he's gone to see his mother in Dorset before he goes back to join his unit. He asked how the case was going. Then he said something strange. He said that maybe we would find out who killed his dog while we are investigating his father's death.'

'What? His dog? What did he mean?'

'Apparently his Golden Retriever was poisoned on Friday night.'

Siobhan added, 'That must be the dog Sinclair was walking when I saw him on top of the hill last week. We wondered why he didn't have it with him when he was killed, didn't we, sir?'

Prior nodded. 'Yes, with everything else that was going on I'm not surprised. It didn't seem that important at the time. But why the hell didn't someone tell us about this on Saturday?'

Quigley shook his head. 'I asked him that. He said he didn't know. Of course, he wasn't here. Brighton told him that he found the dog's dead body Saturday morning. Apparently he called the vet who said the dog had got hold of some rat poison somewhere.'

'Get Brighton over here right now, Albert.'

The butler arrived ten minutes later. They interviewed him in the caravan. Prior said, 'Mr Brighton, I understand Mr. Sinclair's dog died last Friday, is that correct?'

'Yes, sir, sometime during the night.'

'How did that happen?'

'Well, Mrs Brighton fed the animal as usual Friday evening. When she went to feed it the next morning it was dead. I called the vet. He examined the dog and said it was probably rat poison.'

'Was the dog kept in the house?'

'No sir not since Mr Reginald went away. It used to sleep in his room but when he left Mr Cedric had a run made behind the house. The dog slept there in a kennel.'

Prior frowned. 'What time did she feed it on Friday?'

'Well, it was fed twice a day, sir, morning and evening. She will have fed it at six Friday evening.'

'You say there's a run for the dog, is it enclosed?'

'Oh yes, sir, otherwise the dog would worry the farm animals.'

'Then you are suggesting that someone poisoned the dog.'

'Oh no, sir. Mrs Brighton found the gate to the run open on Saturday morning. She was most upset, she must have forgotten to secure it properly on Friday and the dog got out during the night.'

'Where would the dog find rat poison on the farm?'

'Around the grain store and the feed stores, sir.'

'Do you mean it's spread in the open where a dog could find it?'

'No, sir, of course not. It's put in small boxes made for the purpose. Only the rats and mice can get at the poison.'

'Well how on earth did the dog get to it?'

'That's a mystery, perhaps some was spilled in the open.'

'Where was the dead dog found?'

'In the run, sir. But the gate was open.'

'So you're saying that the dog escaped, ate the rat poison then went back to its kennel to die? How long does it take for the poison to kill once it's been eaten?'

'I asked the vet that sir, he said its slow acting. It dehydrates the animal. It takes ten or fifteen minutes at least. I assumed that the dog had got thirsty and gone looking for water.'

'Has the dog escaped before?'

'No sir, we are very careful to lock the gate after us.'

'I think you had better show me this dog enclosure, Mr Brighton.'

Brighton led them along the path that led to the rear door of the house that gave access to the kitchen. He led them past the door to a buttress that jutted out where the disused north wing joined the central structure of the building. As they walked, Brighton explained that the dog was kept this side of the yard so that it's barking did not keep the master awake at night.

Behind the buttress was a space some twenty foot by twelve, surrounded by a five-foot high chain link fence. In the enclosure was a large wooden kennel. The gate had a self-locking latch and a deadbolt. Closing and locking the gate, Prior rattled it back and forth. It was solid and would resist the efforts of a dog on the inside leaping at it trying to get out.

He said, 'Surely your wife knows whether she closed the gate or not, Mr Brighton?'

Brighton looked embarrassed. 'She's usually very careful, sir. She says she is sure she closed and locked the gate.'

Prior nodded thoughtfully. 'Show me the grain and feed stores please, where the rat poison is put out.'

Brighton led them to a long brick built structure that stood on its own next to the cowshed. It had a large circular tower at one end. A rainwater-gully ran along the ground beside the wall leading to a drain at the corner. There were four wooden boxes with small holes set at intervals along the foot of the wall. Walking round the building Prior discovered similar traps along the other walls. He said, 'Are these boxes the only place the poison is put Mr. Brighton?'

'On the outside of the buildings, yes, sir.'

'Well, can you explain to me how the dog could have got at the poison. Surely these things are designed to prevent exactly that?'

'I thought perhaps some poison may have been spilled somewhere and the dog found it. Accidents do happen, sir.'

Prior said angrily, 'Isn't it more likely that someone deliberately fed the poison to the dog in its run?'

'Who would do that, sir? I can't believe any of the staff would want to harm the dog.'

'Well, you'd hardly expect someone to kill Mr Sinclair but someone did. Why on earth didn't you report the death of the dog when you were interviewed?'

Brighton looked ruffled. He stood silent for some moments before replying, 'I didn't think the two deaths were related, sir. I understood an intruder killed the master. I thought perhaps Mrs Brighton may have left the gate to the kennel open by mistake.'

Prior nodded. 'So you wanted to protect her?' He sighed. 'If we'd known this earlier Mr Brighton, we might actually have saved a life.'

Brighton looked full of remorse. 'I can only apologise again sir.'

Prior shook his head in annoyance. 'OK, thank you, Mr. Brighton.'

Siobhan had not spoken throughout the whole interview. When they were back in the van she said, 'Why would Callaghan kill the dog, sir?'

'Dogs have an amazing sense of smell, Siobhan, and they are curious. If Sinclair took the dog down by the stream, it could have sniffed out the fact that someone had spent time down there hunting for the damned treasure. It might even have led Sinclair to the coins. I expect Callaghan poisoned the poor thing to protect his secret. What does the life of a dog matter when you're willing to kill people?'

She nodded and remained silent.

He continued, 'If Brighton had not been so keen to save his wife's embarrassment, we'd have solved this case a week ago. After 6pm last Friday, the only person on the estate apart from the Brightons, Tregowan and the old cowman would have been Callaghan. It could only have been him that poisoned the animal.'

Again his two companions remained silent.

Prior looked at his watch. It was almost 2pm and they were late for the Bolton autopsy.

*

Penhallon was in a filthy mood when they arrived 20 minutes late. He said, 'I am not accustomed to being kept waiting, Matthew. Where the hell have you been?'

'Sorry Professor, the case is beginning to break. We've just discovered two vital pieces of information and I couldn't just drop things and leave.'

'Hmm. Does this mean you're going to catch the man who's on this killing spree?'

'It looks very much that way. At least we now know his identity.'

Penhallon looked at him testily. 'Well, let's get on then now you have deigned to attend.'

He started with his usual description of the corpse. Then he moved to the head. 'Two wounds to the head, one above the right ear.' He traced the wound with a gloved finger. 'Hmm. Circular wound perhaps three centimetres deep.' He moved to the other wound. 'Second wound above the right eyebrow.' Again he traced it with his finger. 'Same shape, circular, but deeper, probably five centimetres. Quite a clean fracture of the skull here.'

He turned to Prior. 'I'll tell you what, Matthew, either blow will have given him a nasty headache.' He chuckled. Siobhan rolled her eyes but didn't speak.

Both detectives stood stoically as Penhallon completed his external examination of the corpse. Then they watched as he carved and sawed, going deeper. Only when he'd finished and had torn off his plastic gloves and gone to the stainless-steel sink to wash his hands did he speak directly to Prior again.

Over his shoulder he said, 'You know, Matthew, the dead often bear silent witness to the manner of their own passing. My job is to get them to talk to me.'

'And what does this one tell you?'

'He said, "I didn't see a thing, I was attacked from behind." He chuckled.

'That's useful, is there anything else you can tell us?'

'The murder weapon was almost certainly a hammer.'

'But he didn't tell you who wielded the hammer?'

'No, Matthew, sorry.'

Leaving the mortuary Siobhan said, 'You know, sir, one of these days I'll take a bloody hammer to Penhallon. He's a ghoul and I think he's getting worse.'

'I'm tempted myself sometimes. But there's not much we can do about it. And despite his awful jokes, he'll find whatever there is to find. To be honest I didn't really expect that we'd get much from Penhallon on this occasion. Our best hope is that George comes up with something from the scene. Now, I've got to go to that cursed press conference.'

*

Prior arrived at the police station just in time to brief Owen on their breakthrough before they faced the press. He added, 'But we can't let on that we've had a breakthrough to the press, ma'am, I don't want to warn Callaghan that we're on to him. I just need another twelve hours.'

She nodded. 'OK I'll back you on that. Just tell them what you can and keep control of your temper.'

He did that, for most of the conference anyway. He made a short statement about Bolton's death and appealed for witnesses. Then he spent the next half hour fending off questions. Most speculated about the connection between the three murders. Owen was as good as her word and took some of the pressure off him.

He was fine until the same reporter who had previously upset him said, 'Isn't it about time you admitted your limitations Chief Inspector and handed over to someone who knows what he's doing?'

Prior took a deep breath. 'Having read your column sir, just the once, I might ask you the same thing.'

The place erupted with noise. Prior simply rose from his seat and swept past the swarm of reporters who tried to waylay him with more questions. Owen stomped after him, her face as dark as a storm.

When they were out of earshot she said angrily, 'This time you've gone too far, Matthew. When the Chief Constable hears of this, which he almost certainly will, I'll be surprised if he doesn't take you off the case.'

'Let's just hope I arrest the killer before he hears about it then.'

Owen gave a deep sigh. 'What is your next move?'

'A council of war. Siobhan's getting the team together here in the CID office. I want to see exactly what we have before we move in on Callaghan.'

'I'll attend that. It will save you briefing me separately.'

'Twenty minutes then, ma'am. I've just got a phone call to make.'

43. The big bad wolf.

'Hasty climbers have sudden falls.'

15th century proverb.

6.30pm Friday.

Prior quickly went to his office to phone Jeanette. His daughter, Natalie answered, 'The Prior residence, Natalie speaking.'

'Hello, tiger, how are you?'

'Daddy! When are you coming home?'

'Not for a while I'm afraid, I'm very busy here. But I promise to come in and give you a kiss if you're in bed. Now, let me speak to mummy.'

'Mummy's angry with you daddy, she's been banging things in the kitchen.'

Prior sighed, 'I know, tiger, let me speak to her.'

He heard his daughter put the phone down and shout, 'Mummy, daddy wants to speak to you.' Prior heard the click-clack of her shoes on the kitchen floor.

Then, 'Hello, is that you stranger?' Her tone was not friendly.

'Yes, love, sorry. Things are coming to a head here. I've been rushed off my feet. Is everything all right at home?'

'Apart from there being no man around, yes.' There was a pause, 'When will you be home?'

'I'm hoping to close the case in the next 24 hours, love. Then we can have a weekend to ourselves.'

'So you're going to be late again. Does that mean you've found the killer?'

'I'll tell you everything when I get home. We're closing in. I've got a team meeting now, then I'll decide the next step. Yes, I'm afraid I'll be late again.'

She sighed. 'Be careful, Matthew. I don't want to see your head on a stake.'

'I will. Don't wait up, my love. I'll be home as soon as I can.'

*

The whole team, including the two CSIs, were gathered in the CID office. As Superintendent Owen walked in with Prior they all stood. She smiled to acknowledge the compliment and said, 'Sit down, please.' She herself found a seat at one side of the room. Prior stood facing his team with his head lowered for a few moments as he gathered his thoughts.

Finally he spoke, 'This has been a tough one. I'm grateful for all the hard work you have put in.' He smiled as a thought crossed his mind. 'If this was a film a little birdie would drop the final clinching piece of evidence from the sky and we could arrest and charge the big bad wolf and all take the weekend off. But this is real life and it doesn't happen that way. In real life, if you look up at the wrong time, suddenly you're blind in one eye.' There were a few chuckles from the team.

'No, we need one final push to gather the evidence that will make absolutely certain we screw the killer down tight in front of a jury.'

He looked around the faces in front of him. 'Let's look at the story in the manner a brief might present it to a jury. As we go along we'll see what evidence we have and what we need to get a conviction. You know the form at these sessions, interrupt as things occur to you.' He paused, this time for effect.

It was a full ten seconds before he continued. 'I'll start at the very beginning. Some eighteen hundred years ago a soldier, probably a Roman legionnaire was saving up for his retirement. He turned all the spoils he won in battle into gold coins. And he'd done well, in fact he'd accumulated so much that it was too heavy to carry around with him. Then he had a problem. There weren't any banks in those days, so he had to hide it somewhere, or some toe-rag would make off with it.

He decided to bury it for safekeeping. For some reason he chose the Celtic burial ground beside the stream on what is now the Sinclair Estate.' Prior grinned. 'At least he didn't have to worry about bank robbers, if you will excuse the pun. And as long as he remembered where he had buried it, it should be safe. I'd guess he knew it was a Celtic burial ground and he knew that the locals, being a superstitious lot, weren't likely to dig among the graves of their ancestors.

Whatever his reasons, he chose a good spot. No one found it for all those centuries. His problem was that he didn't live to come back for it; probably killed in a battle like the ones in which he had accumulated the wealth in the first place.'

Prior took a sip of coffee from the Styrofoam cup on the desk beside him. 'So, for 1800 years the pot of gold coins remained in the ground undisturbed. But over the years the nearby stream was slowly changing its course. It was eating away at the bank near where the pot was buried. Eventually the stream reached the pot full of coins. But it was only a clay pot and over the ages, the weight of the earth around it had cracked it, exposing the coins.

Then some of the coins spilled out, probably after a heavy rainstorm when the stream was running high. Coins were washed downstream.' He looked up to see if he still had their attention.

There was not a murmur from anyone.

'Now enters the big bad wolf. He's walking by the stream one day and sees the glint of gold in the water. He fishes the object out and finds it's an old Roman coin. I got an inkling of the excitement he must have felt when our underwater team found a coin. Gold fever, it sends some people mad. So he started to search for more coins. I'd guess that he found a few more as he walked upstream. Then he realised that there was probably a hoard of them somewhere. So he started searching in earnest.

But he had several problems. First, it wasn't his land to begin with, so he had to search in secret if he wanted the gold for himself. Secondly, there were lots of other people who lived and worked on the estate and he didn't want anyone to disturb him before he found the pot. So he told the landowner that he'd seen an intruder on the estate and persuaded him to get the police to keep people away. He also managed the workforce on the estate and could control their movements to some extent.

Fortunately for him, the farmworkers, like their ancestors, were superstitious about the bottomland anyway and weren't likely to go down there unless told to do so. That probably made him feel safe for a while.

Then something happened. This was a working estate and the landowner wanted one of the workers to dig out an old oak whose roots were undermining the boundary wall of the estate. This was too close to the stream for comfort, so the big bad wolf must have begun to worry. He chose a young farmworker, John Wright, who was willing but not too bright, to dig up the tree root.

I'm speculating a little here but we do know two things. First, we know that Wright had been cutting back the brambles that formed the hedge between the bottom field and the stream. He had found an old stone Celtic cross in the brambles and had become curious about it.

He'd asked people about it in the local pub. Old Tom Williamson, the retired gamekeeper on the estate who lived in the village had lent him a book on the Celts. So he was probably more alert to his surroundings than he might otherwise have been.

The next thing we know is that Wright found two coins in the stream. He took them to a dealer in Redruth and sold them for £250. He couldn't believe his luck; that gold fever again. I think it went to his head. There's no evidence to suggest he had previously been a drug user but he went out and bought some amphetamines to celebrate. With the rest of the money he was going to buy a surprise for his pregnant girlfriend.

But the excitement was obviously too much for him. He must have said or done something, and the big bad wolf found out that someone else knew his secret and he wasn't the only one searching for the pot of gold.' Prior paused again and gulped another mouthful of coffee.

'OK, let's look at the evidence we have for this. We have a statement from the coin dealer that Wright sold him the coins. And that he told the dealer he'd found them in a stream and hoped to find some more. From forensics we know he had recently taken amphetamines but had not taken them regularly. We have his girlfriend's statement that he had told her he had a surprise in store for her.

We also have the evidence of our own eyes. Our search team found the remains of the pot and a few coins in the stream. We also found a few coins downstream from the broken pot, so clearly some had been washed away.' He paused again and looked at the faces of his team. 'Is everyone with me on this so far? '

There was a buzz of conversation among the detectives but no one expressed disagreement with his theory.

He let it go on for a few moments then said, 'OK, let's move on. The next thing we know is that the big bad wolf kidnaps Wright, tortures him, and then kills him. He then puts the lad's severed head on the gate of the estate. Now, evidence. What have we got that points to who the killer is?'

There was another buzz of conversation among the detectives.

Above the noise Siobhan said, 'There's the lie that Callaghan told us, sir. He said it was Sinclair who saw the intruder when in fact it was reported to him that there was one.'

'That's a start Siobhan. It gets us thinking although we can't exactly call it evidence. What else?'

Jane Foster said, 'He drives a big diesel Land Rover, sir. If he used it to transport Wright's body, there should still be traces of blood on it.'

'Good, Jane. We never examined his vehicle at the time but the boffins might still find traces as you say.'

George Bailey said, 'Don't forget the wood splinters on the gate guv. Find me the ladder and I'll get you a match.'

'Well done, George'

Sitting and watching all this, Owen smiled to herself. By making this into a story, Prior made it interesting. His team were certainly motivated and drawing the evidence from them gave them ownership of it.

Prior prompted, 'What else people?'

Jane Foster again, 'What about the old dear at Albany Cottage, sir? She heard a vehicle with a noisy engine going up and down the night Wright was kidnapped. I've heard Callaghan's Land Rover; it's got a diesel that makes a lot of noise.'

Prior nodded, 'It's a bit vague in evidence terms but it does help paint the picture and points us in the right direction.'

Albert Quigley asked, 'What about a murder weapon, sir; and the pliers he used to torture Wright?'

Prior nodded. 'Right. When we search Callaghan's place, those are things we should look for.'

He turned to Bailey. 'Anything else from forensics, George?'

'Yes, guv, the gamekeeper's cottage where the wolf did the torturing and killing. Sally and I had a field day there. We found a couple of partial boot prints in bits of mud on the stone floor, with enough of a pattern on to give us a match if you find us the boots that made them. There was lots of debris in the pool of blood, dried skin, hairs and some cloth fibres. Some were the victim's but not all. We might get a few matches there. Oh, and the padlock plate on the door, forced off with some kind of lever. Find us that and we might give you a match.

Prior smiled, 'Thank goodness for forensics, George.'

'There's also the possibility of bloody clothing or things used to wrap the body in. Unless he's disposed of them we might find something. But we'll give the place a proper going over when you move in on him.'

Siobhan added, 'We shouldn't forget the gold coins, sir, it would be useful to find them.'

Prior laughed. 'You're right, of course, but I don't think we're likely to forget them, Siobhan.'

There were no more suggestions.

After another sip of coffee Prior said, 'OK, let's move on with the story. By now the big bad wolf is busy searching the streambed every opportunity he gets. But he can only do this when the farmworkers have gone home or are busy elsewhere. And he can't do it at night. He needs to be able to see what he's doing and can't risk using torches down there, someone at the house might see the light. So it was obviously taking him some time.

One thing we found out today. Someone poisoned Sinclair's dog last Friday night. It was alive at 6pm on the Friday and its dead body was found first thing Saturday morning in its pen. I examined the gate to the pen. It has a latch and a bolt. Unless someone left the gate open, the dog could not possibly have escaped.

Now it makes sense that the killer might feel that the dog could be a danger while he's searching for the gold. I can't think of any other reason someone might have to kill the animal. Now, the timing is significant here; all the farmworkers leave at five and don't arrive before seven in the morning. So the only people on the estate when the dog was poisoned were Sinclair, the Brightons, Callaghan and the old cowman.

Brighton says that he didn't tell us about it at the time as he was embarrassed by the thought that the dog's death was his wife's fault. She thought she had forgotten to lock the gate to its kennel when she fed it Friday evening. He suggested that he thought the dog had probably wandered off and eaten the rat poison thinking it was scraps of food.

But when I investigated, I saw this didn't make sense. With all the farm animals wandering about, farmers have to be very careful with poisons. On the estate the poison is put down in small boxes where the dog couldn't possibly have got to it. So it had to be someone on the estate who killed the dog. This points squarely to Callaghan being the culprit.'

George Bailey asked, 'Who has access to the poison guv? Surely they keep it locked up on the farm?'

'I checked George. It's kept in Callaghan's office, which is locked at night. It's only circumstantial but it's another pointer.'

'The other thing, guv, is the mutt's stomach contents. If it was poisoned there'd probably be meat mixed with the poison.'

Prior shook his head, 'I'm afraid the vet didn't check so we don't have that.'

No-one else had anything to add. Prior continued, 'OK the next murder. Sunday afternoon, Sinclair has his lunch then goes for a walk down by the stream. Someone batters him to death with a stone. Incidentally, I had the underwater team look in the stream for a suitable stone; there were hundreds of them. I don't think we've much chance of finding which stone he used if he threw it in the stream, which seems most likely. So what other evidence is there?'

George Bailey said, 'The coins guv. When we find them, there might be traces of soil or stream debris still on them or whatever he's keeping them in.'

'Good thinking, George, that would put him at the scene. Anything else?'

'Again, bloody clothing, guv. Claret must have spurted all over the place. Unless he's burned everything, we should find traces when we search.'

'Good, that's our best chance. Anything else anyone?'

Siobhan said, 'Just one thing, sir. When does Little Red Riding Hood come on the scene?'

The room exploded in laughter. Prior and Owen joined in. When it had subsided, Prior said, 'Perhaps when you came onto the scene, Siobhan.'

This was greeted with shouts of good natured derision from the rest of the team.

Prior moved on. 'OK, we're probably a bit thin on evidence of that killing but we'll see what turns up. Let's move on with the story. The big bad wolf has now got all these coins and has to convert them into cash. Now, in this country the authorities encourage people to hand in any ancient treasures they find. They will pay market value for anything handed in as treasure trove. In this way valuable items of antiquity are not lost to the nation.

But the big bad wolf's problem is that anything found on the estate is legally the property of the landowner and he hasn't got permission to dig there. In fact, Sinclair specifically forbade people digging on the estate; he wouldn't allow local archaeologists to, so you can be damned sure he wouldn't allow treasure hunters.

So the killer can't hand them in and collect the reward himself. He has to sell them on the black market. But he doesn't have the contacts. He needs someone to sell them for him. Who does he turn to?

It was here that we had the only stroke of luck we've had in the case. Trevor Bolton, a local toe-rag with a record as long as your arm, comes on the scene. He was arrested in London, trying to sell gold coins. For me this was the big break. Before that we had no clear motive for the killings. Sadly, the big bad wolf got to him before we did.

So, the Bolton murder. The first thing we need to prove is the connection between the big bad wolf and Bolton. Thanks to Jean and Fred, we now have that. Jean?'

Wade nodded. 'Yes, sir. We learned from Bolton's land-lady that he had a sister, Alice, who'd visited him. But we had the devil of a job tracing her. In the end we went back to the village where Bolton was born. We learned from the 1981 census that three people lived at a place called Rose Cottage. Margaret Smith, aged 32, Trevor Bolton aged 14, and Alice Chesnaye aged 10.

We wondered why the children had different surnames. It seems that Margaret Smith was a bit loose; in fact she was described by a neighbour as the village bicycle. Half the young men in the village learned to ride on her. Trevor and Alice are her children but have different fathers, therefore different surnames.

The neighbour remembered the family. She said that in 1990 Alice got married to Callaghan, the estate manager. Bingo! There's your connection, sir.'

Prior asked, 'Have you found the sister?'

'Not yet, sir. We know that soon after the wedding Alice had a miscarriage. Obviously she left Callaghan some time but we don't know when that was. We haven't been able to find her under the name of Alice Callaghan or Alice Chesnaye.'

'OK, she could be important, keep looking for her.'

Siobhan frowned. 'Don't you think she might be in danger, sir? If Callaghan thinks she might be able to give evidence against him, he might go after her.'

'Yes, she might well be. And he will no doubt know where she is. That could be why he searched Bolton's flat, looking for her details. We must make finding her a priority.' He turned to Quigley. 'We need to put more people on that Albert.'

For the first time Owen spoke. 'I think the uniform can help with that. Leave that to me. Let your team concentrate on Callaghan.'

Prior smiled. 'Thank you, ma'am.'

Then he turned back to the group. 'OK, now the evidence on Bolton's murder. The pathologist confirms death resulted from two blows to the head with a blunt instrument. From the wounds it would appear that they were probably inflicted by a hammer or something very similar. Nothing much else from pathology, what about forensics, George?'

Bailey smiled and nodded. 'Yes, guv. Good news and bad news. First the bad, there ain't any fingerprints at the scene except those of Bolton and the old dear downstairs, and there's no way she could wield an 'ammer that would make an 'ole in someone's skull.

'We hoovered the carpets, brushed the settee and chairs and just about everything else. Plenty of 'airs and fibres but nothing that didn't belong there.

'He was a right scruff this Bolton, semen on the sheets, as well as all kinds of other stuff too nasty to mention: But no sign of a woman having been there.

In the living room, the blood spurts confirm what old Penhallon said. Bolton was hit once with the hammer on the back of the head when he was standing just inside the door in the lounge, then again when he was lying on the carpet.' He paused.

Prior prompted, 'And the good news?'

'Ah, the good news.' He paused for effect. Then he said, 'One hair, guv, one lovely little hair. I was scratching my head after we did the initial examination.' He paused and smiled, realising what he had said, 'Not literally sir, meta-phorically. I know the killer was careful, but he couldn't be that good that he left no sign of his presence behind him, there had to be something.

'Then Sally and I started scratching away the dried blood on the carpet. Then we found it, in the blood right beside Bolton's head. And it was on the top of the blood, so it could only have got there after the killing. We did the comparison; it's definitely not Bolton's or the old dear's downstairs. So, being as where we found it, it has to be the killer's.'

'Magic, George, will you be able to get DNA from it?'

'It's at the lab now. I've asked them to put it at the top of the list. Should have something the day after tomorrow.'

Prior smiled, 'What colour is the hair?'

'Dark brown, guv, the same as Callaghan's.'

'Let's hope that is the clincher. Anything else, George?'

'Well we might get something from the debris we hoovered up. There's what looks like farmyard muck and cow dung on the carpets. The boffins are doing comparisons with samples from the estate.'

Prior nodded deep in thought. 'OK, let's put it together. We have the connection, Callaghan knew Bolton. We have the motive, Bolton could identify him as the person who gave him the coins to sell. That leaves means and opportunity. Callaghan is certainly big enough and ugly enough.

One thing we can do is revisit Bolton's neighbours, see if anyone spotted Callaghan's vehicle in the street outside. It's certainly distinctive, someone might remember it. We might even find the murder weapon among Callaghan's tools. With the DNA from the hair, we should have him. Anything else before we move on?'

This was met with complete silence. He waited a few moments. 'Right, time we hauled him in. We'll do that at six tomorrow morning. I want the whole team on this. First, safety. He's already killed three people so we take no chances. Authorised shots draw firearms.' He turned to Owen. 'That's if you will authorise it, ma'am?'

'Yes, I think that's justified in the circumstances.'

Prior nodded then turned back to the team. 'Right we'll put together a plan. Go home and get some sleep. Parade here at five in the morning and don't anyone dare be late.'

*

When Prior got home Jeanette was watching TV. She offered her cheek to be kissed without taking her eyes from the screen. He sighed deeply; obviously she was still angry with him.

He said, 'I need a drink, can I get you anything love?'

'I'll have a G and T.' Her tone was not friendly.

He poured the drinks and flopped into an armchair. Taking a large gulp of whisky, he put his head back and closed his eyes. Jeanette looked sideways at him. She saw that he was obviously exhausted.

Her face softened. 'Do you want to tell me about it, Matthew?'

He turned his head towards her. 'Yes love, when your programme is finished.'

She picked up the remote and pressed a switch. The screen went blank. She patted the sofa beside her, 'Come and sit here, you big oaf.'

He looked at her with big eyes, like a dog that had just been let in from the cold. He moved to the sofa and sat down beside her with his arm extended on the backrest. She leant towards him and his arm fell naturally around her.

She said, 'I get so worried when you're late and don't phone. Then I get angry.'

'I know, love. But so much has happened over the last few days, I don't know whether I'm punch bored or countersunk.'

'Tell me what's happened, Matthew?'

'I think we've finally cracked the case. We've zeroed in on the estate manager, everything points to him. We're going to pick him up in the morning.'

'Thank goodness for that, the girls are missing you. They are growing so fast, Matthew, and they need you.'

'I know, love. But this case has really got to me. I can't rest until we have this bastard behind bars.'

She nodded. 'Are you hungry?'

'Famished.'

'Come and keep me company in the kitchen, I'll make you something.'

Half an hour later they lay next to each other in bed. He had set the alarm for four-thirty but was too tired to sleep, his mind busy with plans for the morning. Gradually his breathing slowed and he fell into a restless sleep. But the demons descended as soon as the shackles of his mind were released. When the alarm sounded, he woke with a start feeling tired and washed out.

44. The Raid

'Fools rush in where angels fear to tread.'

Pope – early 18th century.

By 5am the whole team was assembled. Prior wasted no time but went over what each of them was to do. His plan was simple. He would send uniformed officers to seal the Lamb Lane and Penwin Lane gates. The detectives would enter by the Penwin Lane gate and searched both Callaghan's house and the estate office and store simultaneously, while he and Siobhan would question Callaghan.

He allocated tasks accordingly and dealt with questions. When he was sure that each knew what was required of them, he looked at his watch; it told him it was 5.35. He said, 'Right, we travel in convoy so no-one gets lost. Let's go.'

It took several rings to wake Brighton, the butler. Eventually he buzzed them through the main gate. Two detectives and the CSIs went straight to the locked estate office and farm store. They would wait until Prior had obtained the keys then carry out their search. The remainder followed him to the estate manager's home. It was a substantial three-bedroom cottage in its own enclosed garden a hundred yards beyond the farm buildings. As they approached, Callaghan's two Labradors began barking excitedly from inside the garden. There were no lights in the cottage.

The dogs were not vicious and allowed the detectives to pass them to the front door of the cottage. Prior knocked loudly. There was no sound from within. After pounding on the door for several minutes he realised that either Callaghan was not at home or was lying low hoping that they would go away.

Now Prior had a dilemma. He was reluctant to break in as the courts took a dim view of what they saw as unnecessary use of force. He told his team to remain where they were and went to the old cowman's cottage behind the barn. Having heard the noise of their arrival, the old man was standing outside his front door watching all that was happening.

Prior said, 'Good morning. Do you know where Mr Callaghan is?'

'He don't tell me where he goes. But I expect he went to see his lady friend in Truro.'

'Well, suppose you need him in an emergency, how do you contact him?'

'He's got a mobile phone. They got the number up at the big house. I ain't got no phone you see.'

Prior thanked him and walked quickly to the Sinclair house. He saw lights in the kitchen and knocked. Brighton, for once not dressed formally, answered the door in a dressing gown.

Prior said, 'Is the young Mr Sinclair at home?'

'No sir, he is visiting his mother.'

Prior nodded. 'I'm sure you can help me. We're looking for Mr Callaghan, do you know where he is?'

'Yes, sir, he's visiting a friend in Truro.'

'When is he due back?'

'Before dawn. He will have to let the farmhands onto the estate.'

'Do you have his mobile number, Mr Brighton?'

'Yes, of course.'

Prior made a note of the number and said, 'Thank you. No need to call him, we'll wait until he arrives.'

As he was walking back to Callaghan's cottage, his radio crackled and someone stated his call sign. He answered. It was one of the officers at the Lamb Lane gate. He said, 'Mr. Callaghan is here sir, he wants to come in.'

Prior replied, 'OK, let him in and escort him up here.'

He quickened his pace and arrived at the cottage just as Callaghan's Land Rover got there. As Callaghan opened his garden gate, the Labradors greeted him noisily and he stooped to stroke them. Seeing Prior, he said, 'What the hell is going on?'

'We have a warrant to search your house and the farm buildings, Mr Callaghan.' He produced the warrant and handed it to the estate manager.

Callaghan read it in the light of the vehicle's headlamps and quoted aloud, 'To search for weapons and other items that might pertain to the murders of John Wright, Cedric Sinclair and Trevor Bolton.' He looked up and smiled derisively. 'You must be off your head man, I'm not a murderer. Where did you get that idea from?'

Prior ignored the question. 'Would you please unlock your front door?'

Callaghan had a bunch of keys in his hand He found the right one and inserted it into the lock. Opening the door, he made a grand gesture with his hand and said, 'There, anything else?'

'Yes, sir. We also want the keys to your Land Rover, the estate office and the farm stores.'

Callaghan lobbed the whole bunch of keys to Prior. 'They're all there. '

'Thank you, sir.' Prior handed the keys to DS Quigley. He turned back to the man. 'We need to ask you some questions, Mr Callaghan.'

'Well, you'll have to wait until I've fed the dogs, otherwise we'll have no peace.'

Prior nodded and followed him into the kitchen. His other detectives spread out through the cottage to begin the search.

Callaghan filled two bowls with food pellets from a bag and filled the dogs' water bowl and the animals tucked in noisily. Callaghan turned to the detectives and said in a less angry tone, 'I suppose we must be civilised about this, would you like coffee?'

'No, sir, but you go ahead.'

When they were finally seated at the kitchen table Prior said, 'Where were you last night, Mr Callaghan?'

'Why, has something else happened?'

'It is customary for us to ask the questions. If you fail to answer them, we will naturally think that you've something to hide and extend our enquiries. I'll ask you one more time. Where were you last night, sir?'

'You mean that if I answer your questions, you will go away and leave me alone?'

'I mean that we will get at the truth one way or another and it will cause you less inconvenience at this stage if we question you here.'

Callaghan sighed deeply. 'I was seeing a lady friend in Truro.'

'Thank you, sir. We will need her name and address to verify this.'

'I don't want her embarrassed by all this.'

'Nor do I. We simply need confirmation of your where-abouts. Our enquiries will be discreet.'

Reluctantly, Callaghan gave her details, which Siobhan carefully noted.

Prior continued, 'What is your relationship with her, sir?'

'We have a relationship, we are close.'

How long have you known her?'

'About a year.'

'What about your ex-wife, do you still see her?'

Just for a moment there was hesitation in Callaghan's voice. 'Alice? No, I haven't seen her in years.'

'How many years exactly?'

'Goodness, it must be all of ten years. We don't keep in touch.'

'Do you know where she lives?'

'In Falmouth I think; leastways she did the last time I heard.'

'When were you divorced?'

'We're not actually divorced, it's complicated.'

'How is it complicated?'

'We are Catholics and were married in Ireland, we can't divorce.'

Prior frowned, 'How is that sir? Catholics can divorce as far as I know.'

'We were married in Ireland Chief Inspector. It's far more complicated there.'

'Why Ireland, sir?'

'She was pregnant at the time. My mother was Irish, she sent us to my grandmother in Achill to stop the talk in the village. We got married there.'

'And the baby?'

'There was no baby, Alice miscarried.'

'What name does Alice use now, Mr Callaghan?'

'When I last heard she had a new partner. His name is Faulkner. She probably uses his name if not her own.'

'What about her family, do you keep in touch?'

'Hardly. She had no father and her mother moved abroad. I didn't exactly get on with her anyway.'

'And her brother?'

'So that's what this is all about is it? That no-good brother of hers, Trevor. I heard about his murder on the news last night. Good riddance is what I say, he was a nasty brute.'

'When did you last see him?'

'To speak to? Not for many, many years. But I have seen him about in Truro, he's a mini cab driver I think. That is, when he's not in prison.'

'What was your relationship with him?'

'We didn't have a relationship. When I was courting Alice and we found out she was pregnant, he made nasty threats. In fact, on one occasion it came to blows. He and Alice were close. Neither of them had a father, and their mother wasn't the most caring of souls. I couldn't stand the man.'

'Do you know why their mother gave them different surnames?'

'She said it was to get their fathers to pay maintenance but I don't think that worked. The children didn't have the best of upbringings.'

'But you did marry Alice?'

Callaghan nodded sadly. 'Yes, I loved her at the time, or thought I did. Besides, she was pregnant, I had no choice.'

'Where did you live when you were first married?'

'We moved back to my father's farm for a while when we returned from Ireland. Then I got a job in Devon managing a small farm. My father had sent me to agricultural college, but I have an elder brother who got the family farm.'

'And then?'

'And then nothing. Alice and I split up soon after.' His eyes became first sad, then angry. 'Unfortunately she had inherited something from her mother; she was never satisfied with one man. I stayed at that farm for several years. Then, four years ago I applied for this job. It's a much bigger concern and the salary reflects that. I've been here ever since.'

'Did you kill Trevor Bolton, Mr. Callaghan?'

'No, of course not, why on earth should I?'

Prior turned to Siobhan, who said, 'This intruder that was reportedly seen on the estate, who actually saw him?'

Callaghan frowned. 'Intruder, you mean some weeks ago? Mr. Sinclair did as far as I know.'

'Are you certain of that?'

'Well, it was he that told me about it.'

'You're lying, Mr Callaghan. Sinclair told the inspector he spoke to that it was one of his employees that reported the intruder to him.'

'That's nonsense. Why on earth should I lie about that, or anything else for that matter?'

'Why indeed, Mr Callaghan.'

'Look I can prove I'm telling the truth. My secretary was in the office when Sinclair told me about the intruder. Sinclair told me off for not keeping intruders out. He wasn't exactly a reasonable man. I'm sure she will remember; he made quite a scene.'

It was at that moment Prior had a sinking feeling in his stomach; Callaghan was very plausible, too plausible. There was no hesitation in any of his answers and what he said made perfect sense.

His thoughts were interrupted, Callaghan said, 'Look this is crazy. You come here and turn my place upside down and accuse me of murder and lying. What evidence do you have? Now I'm going to call a lawyer. This is intolerable.' He got up and went to the phone.

Prior looked at Siobhan with raised eyebrows. She shrugged her shoulders.

He heard Callaghan say into the phone, 'Mr Peterson? Yes, it's Callaghan up at the estate. I'm sorry to disturb you so early but the police are here. They are searching my house and accusing me of murder. I need your advice.' He stood listening for a moment, and then said, 'Yes, they have a search warrant, they showed that to me.' Another pause then he said, 'Chief Inspector Prior.' Callaghan turned and held out the phone. 'He wants to speak to you.'

Prior got up and took the receiver. 'Prior here.'

The voice of Peterson said, 'Mr Prior, what exactly is going on there?'

'As Mr Callaghan says, sir, we have a search warrant and we are questioning him about the murder of Trevor Bolton.'

'Well you will stop questioning him until I get there. You are aware that I act for the Sinclairs and I will represent Mr Callaghan in this matter. Do I make myself clear?'

Prior paused for a moment as he thought about telling the solicitor he also suspected Callaghan of killing Sinclair who had been Peterson's client. But thought better of it. Instead he said, 'Crystal clear, sir.'

'Good, I'll be there in half an hour. Please let me speak to Mr Callaghan.'

Prior handed the phone back to the estate manager, who listened for a moment, thanked the man and put the phone down. He turned to Prior. 'Now, I want to see what kind of a mess your officers are making.' He turned and walked out of the kitchen. Prior followed him, looking for Quigley who was leading the search. He found him in the lounge. Out of Callaghan's hearing he asked, 'What have you found, Albert?'

'Nothing so far, sir. Nothing incriminating that is. We've been through his wardrobe, no bloody clothing. We've bagged several pairs of shoes for examination. There's a toolbox in the house. It had a claw hammer and some pliers. We've bagged them, but they look clean. And Callaghan seems to collect walking sticks; there are six in the hall. We've bagged them too and will have them examined. But there's nothing that looks like a murder weapon or any gold coins.'

'What about a safe, is there one?'

'No, a couple of locked drawers in his desk but we found the key to them on the ring he gave us. Just papers in them.'

'What about correspondence showing the Bolton connection or his sister's address?'

Quigley shook his head, 'Not so far.'

Prior frowned. 'Well keep looking. Callaghan's called his solicitor. We'll go and see what George has found in the estate office. Get someone to keep their eye on Callaghan, make sure he doesn't do a runner. Tell the team to be careful not to do any damage. I'm just beginning to have my doubts about this.'

Prior and Siobhan walked the hundred yards to the office. Liz Roberts and Alan Waring were there making notes.

Prior said, 'Anything?'

Roberts replied, 'Yes, sir.' George thinks he may have found the ladder used to put the head on the stake, he's in the farm store.'

Prior breathed a sigh of relief. 'Good. Anything else?'

'Rat poison, sir. There were two tins of it on the shelf over there.' She pointed to the top shelf on a wall opposite the desk. 'One's half empty.'

'And tools?'

'George is going through them in the store now.'

'Good, well done you two. When you've finished here, go back to the cottage and wait. I don't think we've finished yet'

He turned and led the way to the store. Bailey and his assistant, Hinds, were there, kneeling and going through one of several toolboxes.

Prior said, 'I hear you've found us the ladder, George?'

'Yes, guv, I think so. There's a few splinters missing and a mark that could well have been made by the cross piece on the gate. It's right where you'd expect to find one if it was leant against the sharp edge of the crosspiece on the gate. We'll take it with us and do a comparison when we've done here.'

'What about the hammer and pliers?'

'So far we've found three hammers that would fit the bill and four pairs of pliers. We've bagged them and will take them with us. What's happening up at the cottage?'

Prior shook his head. 'Nothing there, George, and Callaghan's called his solicitor.' He frowned; 'I wonder if anyone else has keys for this place?' It was clearly a rhetorical question and no one answered. After a pause he said, 'Well done, George, keep looking.' Then to Siobhan, 'Let's get back to Callaghan's cottage.'

His mind was racing ahead as they walked. Apart from anything else, his career was hanging by a thread. When the Chief Constable heard about his performance at the press conference, without a result he was for the high jump.

45. Red Faces

'If a man will begin with certainties he shall end in doubts; but if a man will be content to begin with doubts, he shall end in certainties.'

Francis Bacon 1561-1626.

Prior stopped at the edge of the farmyard where he and Siobhan were alone. He said, 'You know, Siobhan, I think we could have the wrong man. We need to give this some thought.'

Siobhan frowned. 'But we've got the ladder, sir. And maybe the boffins will find something on the tools. And Callaghan had access to the rat poison.'

'I know. Now, we're sure it's someone on the estate but I'm beginning to wonder who else has access to the office and store. There must be a spare set of keys somewhere.'

Siobhan frowned, deep in thought. She said, 'Well, I agree Callaghan was very plausible. But what about the lie he told about who saw the intruder?'

'You heard his reply. His secretary heard the conversation. If she backs his story we have a problem.'

'But that only leaves Brighton or the old cowman, sir.'

Prior nodded. 'Yes it does. And we can discount the cowman; he's far too feeble to attack the likes of Bolton.'

'So that leaves Brighton. But he's got an alibi for Wright's murder; he was visiting his mother-in-law.'

'Yes, he was. Let's have a word with Albert, and whoever took the mother-in-law's statement.'

'That was Liz and Alan, I remember reading it.'

They found Quigley and the rest of the team standing around their parked cars, waiting for further instructions. They had got out the coffee flasks and were chatting. As they approached, Quigley spoke, 'We've finished in the cottage, sir; short of prising up the floorboards and chipping off the plaster that's it. Nothing there I'm afraid.'

'What about the Land Rover?'

'There not a sign of any blood. Nor is there any sign of it having been washed recently. The rear compartment doesn't look as if it's been cleaned for months. There's an old dog blanket and lots of dog hair but nothing else.'

Prior nodded and said, 'Well, George has what he thinks is the ladder used for putting the head on the gate, and there are several hammers and pairs of pliers that need to be examined by the boffins. But there's something else.'

He called Foster and Waring over. 'Jane, tell me,' he said, 'when you took the statement from Brighton's mother-in-law, did she mention what they did after dinner that night?'

She replied, 'Yes, sir, I took her statement. She said she went to bed and they cleaned her place, which they always did when they visited. Then they slept in her spare room.'

'Did she say what time she went to bed?'

Foster nodded. 'About nine she said, but she was a bit vague. She's quite old, sir, and more than a bit senile.'

'So, if Brighton left for a couple of hours after she was in bed and returned in time to bring Mrs Brighton back here early the next morning, she wouldn't know the difference, would she?'

Waring frowned. 'I suppose not sir, no.'

'So, technically, Brighton doesn't have an alibi for the time of Wright's kidnapping and death. Except of course for his wife, and if she's in this with him that means nothing.'

Foster looked worried. 'I'm sorry sir. I suppose I should have asked the old dear whether Brighton had been there the whole time.'

Prior shook his head. 'I'm not looking for someone to blame, Jane, I'm just trying to work things out. Next question, does anyone know what vehicle Brighton drives?'

No one answered.

Prior continued, 'We can find that out from Callaghan. Has his solicitor arrived yet?'

Quigley shook his head. 'No sir, we've been looking out for him.'

'OK, we'll wait till he's here before I talk to Callaghan again. Next question, does Brighton have alibis for the other two killings?' He answered the question himself. 'The answer is no, other than his wife of course. She was the only one on the estate who can say where Brighton was when Sinclair was killed. Even for the time Bolton was killed, there was no one else at the house except his wife as young Reginald had gone to see his mother in Dorset.'

Now Prior was warming to his task. 'Next question. Did Brighton have the opportunity to go searching for gold coins? Did he spend much time out of the house on the estate?' He turned to Quigley. 'Anything in any of the farm-workers statements that said he did?'

Quigley shook his head, 'No sir. But then we didn't ask them anything about Brighton or his movements.'

'Exactly. I think we've ignored Brighton because he doesn't look the type to go wading about in streams. Dressed in his butler's 'uniform' he looks as if butter wouldn't melt in his mouth. One more question. Did Brighton have access to the farm store and estate office?'

Again no one answered.

'OK, let's find out. Jane, Alan, go and talk to the old cow-man, he'll know the answers to some of these questions. Siobhan and I will have another chat with Callaghan once his solicitor arrives. And make a note, Albert, to interview the farm secretary again. We must see if she backs up Callaghan's story about this imaginary intruder.'

Half an hour later, they had the answers to most of these questions. Spare keys for the store and estate office were kept in the key cupboard in Brighton's kitchen. Brighton drove an old Land Rover that had once been an estate vehicle.

The clincher was something the old cowman said. 'Oh yes, Mr Brighton loves his birds. He's always wandering about down in the woods with his binoculars.' He was a twitcher, which corresponded with what the man had told them himself, he and his wife loved to watch the nature programmes on TV. Now Prior was almost convinced.

He called his team together again and briefed them on their new target.

'Fortunately the search warrant we have covers all the buildings on the estate, so we can search Brighton's quarters without breaking any laws. Siobhan and I will question Brighton. Jane, Alan, you two question his wife. The rest of you search their quarters. Do it thoroughly, we've got egg on our faces at the moment, but that won't matter if we're right this time. OK, let's go.'

Brighton was in the kitchen. He had shaved since Prior saw him two hours previously and had dressed in his formal attire; he looked the picture of the family butler again. If he was surprised to see them, he gave no sign.

Prior addressed him, 'Mr Brighton, we have a search warrant and wish to search your quarters. We also wish to ask you and your wife some questions. Where is she?'

Brighton said, 'I thought it was Mr Callaghan you were interested in?'

'The search warrant covers all the buildings on the estate. Where is your wife please?'

For the first time Brighton looked concerned. He said, 'She's somewhere in the house about her duties.' He had even forgotten the 'sir', thought Prior.

Prior turned to Foster and Waring; 'You two go and find her.' Then he signalled to Quigley to start the search. As the detectives trooped through the kitchen, Brighton's eyes followed them closely. But clearly, he saw no way to stop the search and said nothing.

Prior pointed to the chairs around the kitchen table and said, 'Shall we sit down, Mr Brighton?'

Prior had purposely set out to unsettle the man and it was working. When Brighton sank reluctantly into a chair, he was displaying all the signals of the fight or flight syndrome of the guilty man. He sat on the very edge of the chair with his body facing the door to the yard as if ready to run. But he clearly saw there was nowhere to run to.

Prior said in a soft conversational tone, 'Let me take you back to the Tuesday John Wright was killed, Mr Brighton. You took your wife to see her mother. What vehicle did you use?'

Brighton's eyes flickered. He licked his lips. 'My Land Rover, it's the only vehicle I have.'

'What time did you leave the estate?'

'About 5.30.'

'And what time did you arrive at your mother-in-law's?'

'About 6.15.'

'For a twenty-minute journey, why so long?'

'We stopped for fuel on the way.'

'How was your mother-in-law?'

'As well as can be expected, she's very frail.'

Prior noticed the man was beginning to relax again, he felt he was now on safer ground. Prior asked, 'What time did she retire for the night?'

'Your detectives questioned her, don't you have that information?'

'It's usually we that ask the questions, Mr Brighton, and the suspect answers them. In your recollection, what time did she go to bed?'

For the first time Prior had used the word suspect. This clearly shook Brighton. He licked his lips again, 'Sometime after nine, I think.'

'So, she can't possibly account for your movements after that time, can she?'

'But my wife can, I was with her all the time. I never left the house.'

'What did you do for the rest of the evening?'

'I helped my wife clean the cottage. We did it every week for her mother.'

'We have only your word for that, don't we?'

'And my wife's, she will tell you I didn't leave the cottage.'

'But she is your wife, isn't she? So she is bound to back you up. Let me put another scenario to you. Your wife did in fact clean her mother's cottage. But you left as soon as the old lady was in bed, didn't you? In fact, you were in Penwin by 9.30, weren't you?'

Brighton shook his head vigorously. 'No, that's not true. I didn't leave the cottage until 5.30 the next morning to return to the estate. Ask Mrs Brighton, she will tell you.'

'I'm sure she will, Mr Brighton, I'm sure she will. But will she be telling the truth?'

Prior looked at Siobhan. She nodded and took over. 'You enjoy nature, Mr Brighton, don't you?'

'Yes. Mrs Brighton and I watch all the nature programmes on TV.'

'But you like to see nature in real-life, don't you? Aren't you a bird watcher?'

Brighton had begun to sweat. He paused for a long moment, delicately wiping a droplet of sweat from his forehead. 'When I have the time, yes.'

'We know that, Mr Brighton, because the farm workers have seen you about the estate with your binoculars. Where do you go to watch the birds?'

'All over the estate.'

'Does that include the woods down by the stream?'

'Occasionally, yes.'

'Were you doing your twitching last Sunday afternoon, Mr Brighton?'

Brighton shook his head as if parrying the question. 'No, I didn't leave the house on Sunday. Mrs Brighton will tell you, I didn't leave the house.'

Prior intervened, 'The old cowman's cottage has a view down to the bottom, doesn't it?'

Brighton could see the trap that was being set. He wiped his brow, this time with a handkerchief that he took from a trouser pocket.

Prior insisted, 'He can see who comes and goes down there can't he, Mr Brighton? Do you want to reconsider your answer?'

The butler opened his mouth then closed it again. Finally he said, 'I would like to consult a solicitor.'

'I'm sure you would, Mr Brighton; I'm sure you would. And that is your right. But if you've done nothing wrong, why do you need a solicitor?'

'Your questions are confusing me.'

Siobhan took over again. 'Let's talk about something else shall we, Mr Brighton? Where did you meet Trevor Bolton?'

Prior watched the man's eyes as the question was asked. They shot up and to the left, the classic sign of someone seeking to invent an answer. After a long moment Brighton said, 'I have never met the man.'

Prior said, 'Tell me about your expeditions down by the stream, have you ever found anything down there?'

Brighton frowned. 'Like what?'

'Like coins, Mr Brighton, gold ones.'

If Prior had any doubts left as to the man's guilt, his reaction to the question dispelled them. He almost rose from his seat facing the door to the yard.

Prior smiled, 'No, there's nowhere to run Mr Brighton. Where have you hidden the coins?'

As if on cue, the door to the butler's living quarters opened and Jean Wade walked into the room. She was carrying a leather shoulder bag. She held it in two hands; clearly it was heavy. There was a soft clunk as she put it on the kitchen table.

She said, 'We found this under the floorboards in their bedroom sir. There is a loose board and a cavity beneath.'

Prior opened the top of the bag and looked in. Then he raised his eyes to Brighton.

'Well, what have we here, Mr Brighton? Old Roman coins, gold by the look of it. Where did these come from?'

Brighton was looking down at his hands. Clearly he knew he was beaten. He made no reply.

Standing and putting his hand on the butler's right shoulder Prior said formally, 'I am arresting you for the murders of John Wright, Cedric Sinclair and Trevor Bolton.' He then read him the statutory caution.

Brighton said nothing but sat looking down at the floor.

46. Mrs. Brighton.

'Why should a man be in love with his fetters?
Though of gold?'

Francis Bacon 1561-1626.

Jane Foster and her partner had tracked Mrs Brighton down to the comfortable sitting room of Sinclair House, where she was dusting. They interviewed her there in those elegant surroundings. The room was furnished with antique walnut, mahogany and chestnut pieces, all dating back centuries. When invited to sit, she perched herself stiffly on the edge of a delicate looking chaise lounge that had beautiful bowed legs and velvet upholstery.

Foster and Waring were an accomplished team of interrogators. She took a friendly, encouraging approach, while he intervened occasionally with more incisive questions. But on this occasion their skills were hardly needed. It took them less than five minutes to break her down.

Foster started the questioning, 'We're sorry to take up your time, Mrs Brighton but we need to ask you some questions about your husband's movements. I understand he has an interest in ornithology, is that true?'

She nodded nervously, 'Yes, he loves birds and other wild life.'

'I would imagine that here on the estate there are quite a variety of birds, is that so?'

'Oh yes, he keeps records of those that he's seen and their nesting habits.'

'But I imagine that when Mr Cedric was alive, your husband didn't get much time to study the birds, did he?'

'No, Mr Cedric was very demanding.'

Waring took over. 'The day that Mr Cedric was killed, your husband was out bird watching then, wasn't he?'

Her eyes flickered nervously. She replied quickly, too quickly, 'Oh no. He was in the house with me all afternoon.'

Waring's face wore a stern expression when he said, 'Now, we know that's not true Mrs Brighton. It would be better for you to tell us the truth. We know he asked you to lie for him. We know he was out that afternoon.'

A look of fear crossed her face. She shook her head vigorously. 'No he didn't leave the house that afternoon.'

Foster's voice was softer when she intervened, 'Let's go back to Tuesday of last week, the day you went to visit your mother.'

'Yes?' she replied nervously.

'What time did your mother go to bed?'

'I – I can't remember exactly.'

'It was early wasn't it, Mrs Brighton? Didn't she go to bed very early that evening?'

Again she shook her head vigorously. 'No, we spent the evening with her.'

'That's not what she said in her statement. She said she went to bed after dinner.'

Now the woman looked confused. 'I don't know. I can't remember.'

Waring said, 'She went to bed early, then Mr Brighton went for a ride, didn't he? He left you to clean the place and he went off in the Land Rover.'

She licked her lips. Clearly she did not know what to say.

Waring looked at his partner with an expression on his face that said, 'I'm not enjoying this, you take over'.

Foster nodded and said again in a soft voice, 'Your name's Peggy, isn't it Mrs Brighton? Do you mind if I call you Peggy?'

She shook her head, avoiding eye contact.

This time in an almost conspiratorial tone Foster said, 'Listen, Peggy, we know about the gold coins. I'm afraid the game is up. We know what your husband has done to stop other people getting in his way. And he asked you to lie for him. But I'm afraid it's too late now.' She repeated, 'We know what he has done. Now he will be put in prison for a long, long time. There's no need for you get a long sentence too. Why don't you tell us the truth?'

A look of horror crossed the woman's face followed by a series of emotions. Finally, she began to cry.

The two detectives could not believe how easy it was. Peggy Brighton began to pour out the story. She had clearly been swept along by events as they unfolded. The promise of a fortune in gold, together with her loyalty to her husband, had meant she had gone along with his actions without demur and agreed to help him cover them up. As events had unfolded, it was as if she was on a runaway train and had been swept along by them. She had realised there was no going back.

The whole sequence of events had been brought about by a deep resentment, the resentment of a couple who had devoted their lives to the service of the Sinclairs' without proper reward. She, Peggy Brighton, was the daughter of a man who had spent the whole of his working life on the Sinclair Estate. He was one of those forced to take early retirement when Cedric trimmed the workforce on his father's death.

Her parents had spent their married lives in a small cottage in Penwin, paying only a token rent to the estate, as was the case with many of the farm workers. The days of the tied cottage were past but had been replaced by subsidized housing.

Cedric Sinclair had put an end to that and informed them that he was selling the cottage and they would have to buy it or move. There was little prospect of finding work locally. And, on the tiny pension Peggy's father would receive, there was no way they could afford to buy the place. He and his wife found a cheap, tiny cottage to rent in St Agnes. The father died just two years later and the mother's health had declined rapidly.

The Brightons themselves were almost in thrall to the estate. They had quietly sought employment elsewhere when Cedric took over the estate and started his drastic cuts. But the market for butler/housekeeper combinations was in steep decline and neither had the skills that equipped them for other jobs. The cash left them in trust by the old Sinclair would not be paid until they reached retirement age. They had decided to bite their tongues and soldier on.

Then Brighton had discovered a gold coin on the bed of the stream on one of his bird watching forays. Walking back up stream he had discovered several more. He then started searching in earnest for the source. But he had to do so secretly. If Sinclair found out about the coins he would claim ownership, the land was his and he had given no-one else permission to take anything from it.

Then disaster had struck. Brighton had been in the woods on the far side of the stream when he saw Wright uprooting the old oak by the wall. The lad had paused to urinate in the stream and had spotted a coin. It was just after a heavy rainfall and the current was still carrying down the odd coin.

Brighton had watched Wright as he waded into the stream and picked up the coin. Then he watched him start to move upstream searching for more, just as he, himself had some weeks before. He saw Wright pick up another coin. But he could do nothing at the time; he was no match physically for Wright in a frontal attack. Even if he had risked it, he couldn't take the chance. He would have drawn attention to the spot and his opportunity to continue his search for the coins would have gone.

So, he had done nothing at the time. Instead he had worked out a plan. He would attack Wright when he was off the estate. He knew that Jenna, Wright's girlfriend worked in the village pub most evenings. He decided he would kill Wright while she was at work. But he had to wait until his evening off to carry out the plan, as his day's work didn't finish until his master went to bed.

In the meantime, he fretted, thinking that Wright would let everyone know of his discovery or uncover the main hoard of coins or both. But Wright too had been infected by gold fever and had kept his find to himself. His opportunities to search were just as limited as Brighton's and the pot of coins had remained undiscovered

Then on that Tuesday evening, Brighton had taken his wife to her mother's as usual. But they had put the old lady to bed immediately after her evening meal. Mrs Brighton had sat with her until she went to sleep. In the meantime, he'd left the cottage and gone to Penwin village. He'd knocked at Wright's cottage with a large shifting spanner concealed behind his back. In order not to alarm Wright, he'd concocted a story to tell the lad about his being there. But Wright wasn't in.

Then, controlling his growing panic, he'd driven up and down the village street, anxious to grab Wright before Jenna finished her shift. It had been his vehicle going back and forth outside her window that the old Mrs Chivers at Albany Cottage had heard.

When Wright had finally emerged from The Hunters Arms, Brighton had followed him to his cottage and waited for him to go in. Then he'd knocked at the door and when Wright answered, he'd clubbed him with the spanner from his vehicle's toolbox. He'd then taken him away and questioned him to find out whether he'd found any more coins and what he'd done with the two he'd found. The rest of the story, the detectives knew.

Foster interrupted the woman's story only to ask, 'Just one question, Peggy. Why did your husband put Wright's head on the gate?'

She replied bitterly, 'To show his contempt for Cedric Sinclair and what he'd done to us and my parents.'

Waring too had a question but this time his voice was soft when he asked, 'Where did your husband take Wright while he questioned him, Peggy?'

'At the far end of the estate there's an old gamekeeper's cottage that's been derelict for years.'

Waring nodded. 'How do you know this, Peggy?'

The woman's eyes fluttered. After a long moment she said, 'He told me what he'd done.'

Foster looked at her partner, who shrugged his shoulders. Both guessed that she knew about the torture but didn't want to pursue it and interrupt the flow. Foster turned back to Peggy Brighton and said, 'Please go on with the story.'

The housekeeper then told them how twice Sinclair's dog had almost caught Brighton whilst he had been searching for the source of the coins. Sinclair had the habit of walking the dog down by the stream. Brighton had thought that if he killed the dog Sinclair would be less inclined to walk about the estate and he would have more time to find the source of the coins, so he had poisoned the animal.

But he'd been wrong. After Sunday lunch, Sinclair had decided to take a stroll by the stream without the dog. His timing could not have been worse. Brighton had finally discovered the broken pot of coins. He couldn't believe his luck. There were over a hundred and fifty coins in all and he was fishing them out when Sinclair walked up behind him. Brighton had been so engrossed in his task he hadn't noticed Sinclair's approach.

Grabbing a rock from the streambed, Brighton had clubbed the landowner to death. The savagery of the attack was a clear indication of the resentment and frustration Brighton had felt toward the man.

He'd then erased any evidence of his presence at the scene. Then, thinking that he'd recovered all the coins, he left the body where it lay. He'd observed the careful search Prior's team had previously made and was confident they would not look in the stream itself, so they were unlikely to discover his secret. He had reckoned without Julie Davies expertise in spotting the undermining of the stream bank and Prior's determination to uncover the mystery.

Brighton had anxiously watched all the police activity on the estate but had been reassured by their lack of progress. But he still had a problem. He had to get rid of the coins. He couldn't do it legally, so he decided to dispose of them on the black market. But he had no idea how to go about that.

Then he thought of a solution. Some months ago, on the odd evening when Sinclair was away, Brighton had got into the habit of driving into Truro for a drink. The pub he went to happened to be the local used by Trevor Bolton. On several occasions Brighton had heard the man bragging to his cronies of his criminal exploits. Brighton decided to enlist his help in disposing of the coins. But he had not reckoned on the man's stupidity. When Bolton had called Brighton and told him of his arrest in London, he had realized that Bolton could identify him. So he had decided to kill him too. The rest, the detectives knew.

As the woman had been telling her story, Jane Foster had begun to understand how events had escalated and taken over the Brighton's lives. Once he'd found the first coins in the stream, Brighton and his wife had begun to dream of escaping from their life of service and drudgery. They had both been affected by gold fever. Then, as events had unfolded, they had been like people learning to ski who had wandered onto a black slope by mistake. The farther they went, the steeper the slope became and the faster they flew down it. And the faster they went, the more disaster loomed, but by then they were unable to stop.

When she'd finished telling her story, Mrs Brighton actually looked relieved. The two detectives felt sorry for her; they could see and understand her dilemma. Once she'd agreed to lie for Brighton, there was no turning back.

Later when they recounted the interview to Prior, Foster suggested that they might recommend leniency for her to

493

the courts. He'd shaken his head saying, 'I might be inclined to agree with you but for one thing Jane. She knows too many details herself, she must have been complicit in much of this. I think we'll leave it to the judge to make up their own mind.'

47. Tying the Loose Ends.

'As man's knowledge grew and he became more aware of his own powers, he became less afraid of the unknown.'

Of unknown origin.

Prior spent most of the remainder of the day poring over the evidence. Peggy Brighton's statement would go a long way towards proving her husband's guilt. Provided, that is, her evidence could ever be given in court. Prior was only too aware that there are two principles of English law that might prevent it ever seeing the light of day. The first was that a woman could not be forced to give evidence against her spouse. If she rescinded the statement it would be lost. The second was that evidence from an accomplice would not stand alone; it could only be used to corroborate evi-dence from other sources.

And there were no eye-witnesses to any of the murders. All he had at the moment was circumstantial evidence, and some of that was flimsy. Much was dependent on science.

The hair found beside Bolton's body might or might not prove to be that of Brighton; only a DNA match would confirm this. The same applied to evidence found at the gamekeeper's cottage. Blood from any of the victims might or might not be found in Brighton's vehicle, on the tools in his possession or on his clothing. If it were found, the same test would apply. Mud on the coins might or might not tie the coins to the scene of Sinclair's murder and, by inference, put Brighton at the scene.

Prior knew that the battle was not yet won. Knowing that Brighton was guilty was not the same as being able to prove it beyond reasonable doubt. He'd quickly dispelled the team's euphoria; their work was not yet done. On hearing the facts, Peterson had refused to represent Brighton. As the Sinclair solicitor there was clearly a conflict of interests as one of the victims had been his client. He had, however, recommended another solicitor who had quickly arrived. On his advice, Brighton had said nothing at all since his arrest.

However, as the day progressed, more evidence came to light. The cavity beneath the floorboards in the Brightons' bedroom proved to be a treasure chest. Two diamond- and one gold-ring were found plus several other items of jewellery. Enquiries would reveal that these had been pilfered over the years by the butler. Clearly he had started his retirement fund some time earlier.

The jewellery had actually been stolen from guests staying at the house in the days when Cedric's father had entertained lavishly. Two maids had been suspected of the thefts and been dismissed, although nothing was ever proved against them. What made the detectives see Peggy Brighton in a different light was that she had been complicit in the thefts; she was not the innocent she made herself out to be. Resentment towards exploitation by a rich employer might earn a vote of sympathy. But standing by whilst some other poor souls were blamed for their actions was inexcusable.

Importantly, evidence pertinent to the case was also found. Sinclair's missing keys were there, as were the missing mobile phones of Wright and Bolton. Prior had questioned Brighton about these, particularly why he had kept them. But, on the advice of his solicitor Brighton had refused to say anything. Prior concluded that people's behaviour often defied explanation. He smiled at the thought that, if asked, Jessica Bloomfield would no doubt come up with some mumbo-jumbo explaining the odd behaviour. But he would let that one remain a mystery.

The insides of Brighton's Land Rover had been thoroughly cleaned before police seized it. Nevertheless, a mass of potential forensic evidence was found. The initial examinations by experts had revealed traces of blood in the roof fabric and the backs of the seat covers. It had also gathered in tiny spaces between the metal plates of the floor of the vehicle. Tiny fragments of skin had been found in the teeth of one of the pairs of pliers found in the vehicle's toolbox. More blood was found on a shifting spanner in the same toolbox. Yet more blood had been found in the cleft of a claw hammer found in the vehicle. Tiny scrapings of metal found on a crowbar would be matched to the padlock plate prised from the door of the gamekeeper's cottage. The forensic evidence was overwhelming.

Wade and Trimble had visited the Truro pub frequented by Bolton and established a link between Bolton and Brighton. They had been seen talking together on more than one occasion by the pub landlord.

George Bailey had some good news too. He announced, 'Definitely the ladder used to put the head on the gate, guv, the splinters match. And guess what? We found two more splinters in a crack in the floor of the Land Rover. We can screw the bugger down tight.' Prior smiled at the news and the way it had been delivered.

One mystery remained. The discrepancy as to who actually reported an intruder on the estate was never solved. Prior guessed it had been Brighton who had put the idea into Sinclair's head, as he wanted people kept away from the stream while he searched for the gold. But he was not talking. Prior's tidy mind would like to have cleared this up, but he realised it would remain a loose end.

Finally, at 6pm he decided he had enough to hold Brighton for the weekend. He would spend some time with his wife. He phoned the home of a local teenager who often babysat for them and arranged for her to do so that evening. Then he phoned Jeanette's favourite restaurant and booked a table for 7.30. Lastly, he phoned Jeanette, telling her not to cook, as he would bring a take-away for them all. Closing the file on his desk, he put on his coat and left, turning off the lights behind him.

Jeanette was in the kitchen when he arrived home. She greeted him warmly. Then she saw the McDonald's bags he had brought. She said, 'You know I hate that stuff Matthew.'

'So do I love, this is for the girls. The baby-sitter will be here at seven. Get your glad rags on, my lovely one. I'm taking you out for a meal at your favourite restaurant.'

She stood on tiptoe and gave him a lingering kiss. 'You keep this up and you could get lucky later.'

He smiled and tapped her on the bottom. 'I'll take that as a promise. Now, go and get ready, I'll look after the girls.'

They arrived at the restaurant in a taxi Prior had booked from Handycabs; the driver was Norman Mills; one of the three he had interviewed during the investigation.

Once they were seated in the restaurant, Prior ordered a dry white South African wine with the Moules Mariniere starter and a full bodied French Merlot with the lamb that followed. It wasn't long before they both became mellow. He kept the conversation light throughout the meal, although Jeanette was curious to know about the case. Only when the dessert was served did she ask, 'That was wonderful, Matthew, to what do I owe this pleasure?'

He looked down at the tablecloth for a moment before replying. 'It's just to say thank you for putting up with me.'

She smiled warmly and reached across the table to take his hand. 'I don't put up with you, silly man, I love being with you. I'm the lucky one.'

He returned her smile. 'I spend too much time at work. And I bring it home with me. I sometimes wonder if I should find another job.'

She shook her head. 'No. That would destroy you Matthew, you are passionate about your work and you are good at it. Don't you dare change it.'

'Are you sure, love, sometimes I get so wrapped up in it I neglect you and the girls?'

'I'm certain. Now tell me about the case.'

He spent ten minutes going over what the day had brought.

When he'd finished, she said, 'How can anyone that evil lead an otherwise normal life?'

He shook his head. 'That's one for the psychologists. Talking of which, Jessica Bloomfield spent hours and hours bombarding us with psychobabble. But at the end it was just one thing she said that triggered my understanding of the case. When she was comparing the Sinclair and Wright murders she said that the killer had not bothered to move Sinclair's body from where he killed him because he had no more interest with that spot.

There had to have been something there that was the key to the whole case if only we could find it. The killer had been searching for something and he had finally found it and taken it away. That was why he wasn't concerned about us finding the body there. Then, when Bolton was arrested in London trying to sell gold coins, it all fell into place.'

'So, despite your misgivings, she did make a contribution.'

He nodded.

Jeanette sat looking into space for a moment. Then she said, 'Just think, all of this came about because a Roman soldier buried his fortune in a pot all those years ago. I wonder who he was and what happened to him?'

Prior smiled, 'I might be good at my job, my love, but not that good. We showed the shards of the clay pot the coins had been buried in to an expert; he said it was definitely Roman. So, I've no doubt it was a Roman legionnaire. Those who live by the sword, die by the sword. I've no doubt he won the gold in battle. Maybe its poetic justice that he died in battle before he could benefit from it.'

'I wonder if he had a family, Matthew, maybe two little girls like ours?'

Prior said nothing.

'It's romantic in a way, isn't it? I wonder if his family were here with him. If he had one, they probably were. You know, those Romans on garrison duty were here for years and years, many had their families with them.'

He smiled. 'That sounds like the plot to a good book.'

She continued, 'No, I'm serious. Those were terrible times. You know, their hold was never totally secure; the Celts were never completely conquered. Apparently, they believed there was life after death and they were not afraid to die. It meant they were fearless in battle. The Romans were better organised and more sophisticated in their fighting methods, but they didn't find it easy against the Celts.'

Prior nodded. 'We found a sword and, what looked like arrowheads in the stream. Maybe there was a big battle there by the stream. Maybe he was killed at that very spot.'

They sat in silence for a while. Then she said, 'I suppose we'll never know now, will we?'

He shook his head.

After another long silence, she said, 'So the butler will go to prison, what will happen to his wife?'

'It's not that simple, love, we're still waiting on forensics. Provided that comes through, they will both go to prison. She went along with the whole thing, providing him with alibis and covering for him. I felt some sympathy towards her till I found out about the jewellery they stole from guests over the years. She was quite happy to stand by and see two young maids sacked because they were suspected of the thefts'

He looked up to see the waiter hovering with the bill. Looking round, he saw that the restaurant was empty but for them. He paid the bill and they left. A cab was waiting for them outside and they got home to find the babysitter dozing on the couch. The evening finished on a high note and Prior slept soundly that night. The next day they devoted to the girls. There were no phone calls to disturb their weekend.

Epilogue.

'There was a pause – just long enough for an angel to pass, flying slowly.'

Ronald Firbanks 1792-1834

It was several days before all the results of the forensic and DNA tests were through. They confirmed Brighton's guilt in all three murders. He was charged with these offences and several others, ranging from cruelty to animals to thefts.

Alice Callaghan, née Chesnaye, was found alive and well living in Falmouth. She confirmed Callaghan's story about their unfortunate marriage and Callaghan's relationship with Bolton. He would remain as farm manager on the Sinclair Estate. But Reginald Sinclair would not get to return to his regiment. His sense of family duty had returned at the death of his father and he resigned his commission. He returned to the estate and proceeded to undo much of the harm his father had done locally.

The coins were declared treasure trove and confiscated by the crown. After much wrangling in the courts, compensation at market value was paid to the owner of the land. Reginald put the money into a fund for those who had been unfairly dismissed. The first beneficiary was Peggy Brighton's mother, who was moved to a nursing home where she would see out her days in relative comfort.

The archaeology department at the University of West Cornwall was invited to excavate both the hill fort and the burial sites by the stream. The artefacts already found in the stream had been sent to them. They proved to be from the burial chamber of a minor Celtic chieftain. More artefacts were found but there was no gold or other precious metal. The artefacts proved to be of little intrinsic worth but of some historical significance.

As the evidence mounted against Brighton, Prior thanked his lucky stars that he lived in the present day. Forensic science had come a long way in recent years. Without it, he doubted there would have been enough evidence to obtain a conviction for the three murders. He spared a thought for his predecessors who had vainly struggled to catch killers such as Jack the Ripper.

The most important piece of evidence had been the single hair found in the pool of blood beside Bolton's body. That, plus a tiny sliver of Bolton's skin discovered in the cleft of the claw hammer in Brighton's toolbox left no doubt as to the butler's guilt.

On the Friday evening Prior arranged a celebration for his team. It was held in the privacy of the Police Club in

Truro. This enabled the team to let their hair down with their partners. Jessica Bloomfield attended and proceeded to astonish everyone with her capacity for vodka; she drank many of the detectives under the table.

The team's new DI had arrived and had been invited to join the party. As the evening progressed, those that were sober enough noticed that he spent most of his time sitting close to Siobhan. She certainly didn't seem to object.

Jeanette whispered to Prior, 'She says he's got a good butt.'

He grimaced. 'That's all we need, an office romance.'

'Don't be so stuffy, Matthew, let them have their fun.'

He looked at her with a smile in his eyes. 'You won't have to put up with her mooning about the office. Her mind goes blank when she's in love. Anyway, we can forget about that for a week. Pearson's back from leave and with two DI's I can take some time off.'

Owen had paid a brief visit to congratulate the team. Then she had made a diplomatic exit before they got too deep in their cups. George Bailey was his usual gregarious self, but for once Sally Hinds outdid him. The normally taciturn technician positively blossomed after a few drinks and regaled those around her with a stream of outrageous jokes. The evening was a success and a fleet of Handycabs cars saw they all got home safely.

The end.

I hope you have enjoyed this book, If so please take a moment to write a short review and rating.

Thank you, *T. J. Walter*

Printed in Great Britain
by Amazon

57958965R00300